PETER PAPATHANASIOU

THE INVISIBLE

MACLEHOSE PRESS

QUERCUS · LONDON

First published in Great Britain in 2022 by

MacLehose Press
An imprint of Quercus Editions Limited
Carmelite House
50 Victoria Embankment
London EC4Y 0DZ

An Hachette UK company

A CIP catalogue record for this book is available
from the British Library.

ISBN (HB) 978 1 52942 442 3
ISBN (TPB) 978 1 52942 443 0
ISBN (Ebook) 978 1 52942 444 7

10 9 8 7 6 5 4 3 2 1

Typeset by CC Book Production
Printed and bound in Great Britain by Clays Ltd, Elcograf S.p.A.

Papers used by MacLehose Press are from well-managed forests and other responsible sources.

For my brothers, Vasilios and Georgios,
who helped inspire this story

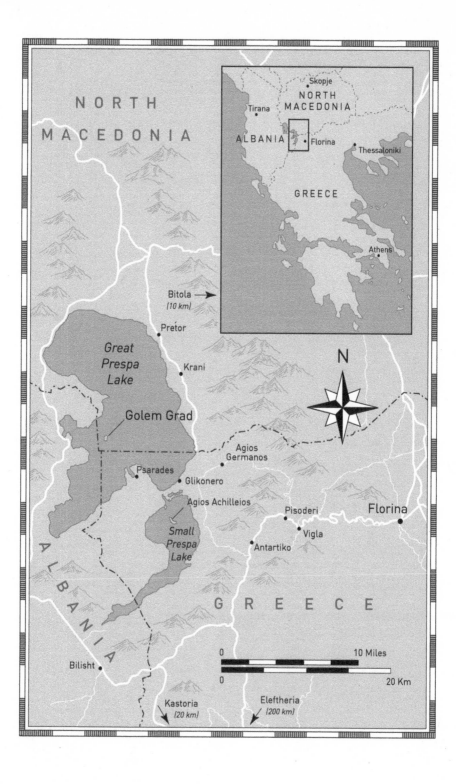

NORTH

MACEDONIA

Great
Prespa
Lake

Golem Grad

Bitola
[10 km]

Pretor

Krani

Psarades

Glikonero

Agios
Germanos

Agios Achilleios

Small
Prespa
Lake

Pisoderi

Vigla

Florina

Antartiko

ALBANIA

GREECE

N

Bilisht

Kastoria
[20 km]

Eleftheria
[200 km]

0

10 Miles

0

20 Km

Skopje

NORTH
MACEDONIA

Tirana

ALBANIA

Florina

Thessaloniki

GREECE

Athens

The men gathered around to inspect the contents of the hefty duffel bag, their Balkan accents almost as thick as their necks. They spoke in low voices, their heavy brows creased as they plotted and schemed. The silver-white sun beat down on their broad, sweaty backs.

"So, as we agreed, yes?" Lefty said. "We have a deal, right?"

The first thug continued to rifle through the bag, holding up individual items, rotating and inspecting them in his grubby hands before moving on to the next. He suddenly stopped his examination and looked up at Lefty with dark, suspicious eyes.

"What's the hurry?" he said, voice light. "Have a drink on us, stay, relax. It's a beautiful afternoon."

A second bald bruiser produced an unlabelled bottle of alcohol from a back pocket and thrust it squarely under Lefty's bulbous nose. The innocuous appearance of the clear liquid belied its potency – the smell alone came close to melting Lefty's eyebrows clean off his face.

"No thanks," he replied. "I can't hang around, I need to get back to Glikonero."

"For . . . ?"

"Work."

The four men laughed uncontrollably, their stomachs quivering, their grill-plated teeth like tiny daggers that jutted at all angles from their protruding lower jaws. A few caught the afternoon sun, glinting and golden.

"You? Work?"

"At a taverna," Lefty said. "They're expecting me. If I don't get back, they'll know something is wrong and call the police." It was an insurance policy in as much as it was a complete fabrication.

"Perhaps," came the reply. "But do they know you're here and doing this?"

Lefty swallowed, his throat suddenly dry. Maybe he should take a hit of booze.

The bottle was passed between meaty grips, swigs taken, chests puffed out and shoulders squared. More grumbles followed. An offer was being prepared. Standing on the shore, Lefty watched the nearby lake water with trepidation. It appeared especially choppy that day and, for some reason, distinctly colder and deeper.

"So, here's what we can offer. How about we give you half as much today, and say that you can marry my sister instead?"

It was a proposition that was followed by more laughter, even louder this time. And all at helpless Lefty's expense.

"Or his mother," said another voice.

"Careful," said a third. "I've seen his mum, she's gorgeous. That's offering way too much."

Lefty had dealt with these reprobates before. They were a motley crew of opportunists and ex-cons and parasites with quick scores and no tomorrow in mind. Lefty fully expected them to negotiate and more often than not try to rob him blind. But they were good customers, loyal and quick to refer new business, so he wanted to keep them onside. At the end of the day, he needed them as much as they needed him. But Lefty still had to be prepared for whatever underhand tricks they came up with. And he was.

"Sorry, no deal," Lefty said. "You know the amount we agreed to, there's no way I can accept half. And this is top-quality gear. See again for yourselves."

The foursome dived into the bag again. Their analysis continued, deeper and more intensive this time, along with some argument and infighting. It didn't take much for the criminal classes to turn on each other when something was at stake and eat their own. Lefty took a step back, brushing some fluff from his black T-shirt, not wanting to get involved. He eyed his small wooden boat with longing, but he couldn't leave without either his booty or appropriate remuneration.

The biggest Balkan brute stood to his full height, in excess of two metres, towering over Lefty and blocking out the sun. Lefty thought he could have been a basketballer in another life, a defensive beast, and his crooked nose suggested he might have been, elbowed in the face going for rebounds. But the truth behind his disfigurement was likely more sinister. His crew cut sat low on his flat forehead, in perfect alignment with the horizon. The others formed a tight semicircle, cutting off Lefty's routes of escape. Their collection of crude tattoos was menacing, dancing across their skin as their taut gym muscles trembled and flexed. The bag was a couple of metres away and well out of reach.

"Look," Lefty said, "if you're not interested in doing business, that's fine. I have plenty of other customers who are. Maybe another day. But for now I won't waste any more of your time and I'll be on my way . . ."

"Stop," barked the leader. "We never said we weren't interested."

"So then, what's the issue?"

"What is always the issue, what men go to war over."

His words hung in the air, but Lefty already knew the answer.

"Price?"

"Yes."

"But half as much is insulting. I simply can't accept an offer that low. If you only want to pay half, then only buy half."

"No. We want it all." He ground out the words like rock-hard kernels.

"As I said, I can't accept such a low offer," Lefty said.

The thug curled his lip into a tight sneer. His colleagues took a step forward.

"Oh, we think you will," he said. "Or maybe, just maybe, we don't actually care either way what you say or do, because out here the outcome will be exactly the same."

Lefty's eyes darted and his fingers twitched.

"Oh yeah?" he said. "And what outcome is that?"

1

The inner-city housing commission towers loomed ahead like decaying tributes to the sky, a frigate-grey smear of winter. Manolis eyed them with unease. He'd got to know the claustrophobic structures disturbingly well over many years and many investigations. It was the same for anyone working in Homicide: the overcrowded high-rises almost single-handedly doubled the city's weekly body count. A combination of weaponry, violence, drugs, grog, poverty and desperation was to blame.

In the passenger seat beside the detective sergeant, Senior Constable Andrew "Sparrow" Smith concentrated on the raindrops sluicing down the windscreen of the unmarked police car. Newly promoted and freshly healed after the case of the stoning in Cobb, the unassuming country cop had accepted a reassignment to the city after Manolis had introduced him to his boss. Detective Inspector Paul Bloody Porter had eyed the young Aboriginal man up and down with a steel-blue glare and asked Manolis if the kid was "up for it".

"Definitely," Manolis said.

"Good. Cos he's your responsibility."

Manolis stood by his assessment, but even he had some reservations about Sparrow and the towers. They were known to test the mettle of the most seasoned lawman, and had even driven a few into early retirement.

Bringing the car to a stop, Manolis applied the handbrake and killed the ignition, which switched off the blaring heater. The cabin took on an immediate chill.

Manolis turned to Sparrow. "Hey," he said. "Relax, mate. You'll do fine."

Manolis had taken the Indigenous cop under his wing and took pleasure and pride in showing him how a real, professional police operation went about its business. Sparrow was still raw but was keen to learn. He swallowed hard, his Adam's apple bulging in his throat. It was his first raid.

"I never really felt like a country mouse until now," he said meekly. The concrete edifices were reflected in his nut-brown eyes.

The stoning investigation had eaten away at Manolis too, both professionally and personally. The death in custody, the inhumanity of the immigration regime, the decrepit and desperate state of his home town. Manolis still wasn't sure he was over it, despite many rigorous psychological examinations and treatments. His sleep was disturbed, he neglected to exercise, and his world became ever smaller as he sought to withdraw. Only his innocent young son brought a bittersweet smile to his lips and helped him temporarily to forget. But Manolis saw Christos growing up way too quickly for his liking and knew he needed to be present in body, at least, even if he wasn't fully in mind.

The grey-white buildings were a defining feature of the city's gaunt skyline. Soulless and brutal, they were built using precast concrete panel technology from another era. Porter often referred to the individual flats as "battery cages in the sky". Manolis loathed the comparison to confined laying hens.

They were headed to the South Tower, a thirty-storey, I-shaped obelisk. Mercifully, they needed only to ascend halfway, to the fourteenth floor. Manolis's lack of fitness and conditioning showed; he needed to stop twice to catch his breath. It didn't help that he was wearing a hefty bulletproof vest and protective equipment. The lithe and more youthful Sparrow sprang on ahead, extra PPE kilos and all, along with the small team of police officers assembled for the raid and arrest. Their target was a known methamphetamine dealer. The gear he was peddling at street level was of questionable quality, but what had attracted the attention of

Homicide was the death of a rival dealer in a business transaction turned sour. Normally, the self-cleansing of the criminal classes had a way of doing the police's work on their behalf and bringing an end to unlawful activity one way or another. But in this instance, Manolis and his men felt compelled to intervene before a full-scale urban war erupted and many more people died, guilty and innocent.

Manolis had triple-checked that the address on file was correct before they set out. In such a monolith, where all the rooms, stairwells and corridors looked the same, the chances of an error were high, and the consequences potentially catastrophic. He checked it again as they approached the door, then gave the signal to proceed. He glanced at his watch: six-thirty; a sluggish, purple-blue dawn melting into day as the city began to thaw. All was proceeding by the book.

The forcing open of the door was always the most stomach-churning moment of a raid for Manolis. It was like stepping into another universe where he could be greeted by any manner of threat or emergency: weapons, ammunition, innocents, hostages, children, babies, overdoses. Intelligence and surveillance helped but were far from foolproof. On this occasion, Manolis expected to find only the dealer, who lived alone with an irregular procession of addict girlfriends. He would likely be armed in some capacity, but the hope was to get to him before he reached for his weapon. Manolis and Sparrow brought up the group's rear, both with pistols drawn and ready. Aside from a stray cat hissing and a hungry newborn screaming, the dark towers lay silent, their sleeping and unconscious addicts not making a sound.

That all changed as the door splintered on impact, its extra locks and latches sent flying like mortar fire from the rotten wood. They'd been installed against building regulations to repel would-be home invaders or other undesirables such as police. Manolis watched his fellow officers disperse, their moves decisive and choreographed as they swarmed through the cramped and darkened rooms. A noxious odour – clear indicator of a makeshift drug lab – assaulted Manolis's nose before his eyes had even adapted to the darkness. Manolis was familiar with them in backyards and garages but had never before seen one in an apartment complex. If it exploded, the consequences would be cataclysmic for occupants and neighbours alike.

"Armed police! Surrender!"

The search was over in a few seconds, such were the confines of the tiny two-bedroom flat.

"All clear, Sarge," came the report. "It's empty."

Manolis rubbed his chin, felt the rough stubble. How could the surveillance team have been wrong? He was told they'd watched the place for two weeks.

"Search it," Manolis said, voice strained. "Top to bottom. Gather everything you can. I want enough evidence to send the bastard away for a very long time. Shouldn't be hard."

He left the boys to do their work. Sparrow joined Manolis on the narrow walkway outside, a blank look on his face.

"So what now, eh, boss?" he asked.

Manolis felt the mugging cold prickle against his unslept face. The city was waking, the first aggressive snarl of traffic building up fourteen storeys below.

"I don't know," he said. "What are your tracking skills like?"

Sparrow flashed a glittering smile that illuminated the morning.

"Not bad actually. My uncles taught me."

"On concrete?"

"Anywhere. They could track a hopping mouse in a dust storm. See, the secret is—"

Sparrow was interrupted by the sound of breaking glass. A young man had rounded the corner, seen Manolis and Sparrow, dropped his plastic shopping bag, and sprinted back down the stairs.

"Jesus," said Manolis. "Was that . . . ?"

But Sparrow didn't reply. He had already identified the individual as their quarry, back from an early-morning visit to the local convenience store, and was in hot pursuit. Manolis followed, his bulky vest bouncing as he ran.

He nearly twisted an ankle going down the steep stairs, three, four at a time, descending with a crash on every landing before going again. Manolis quickly lost sight of Sparrow and was instead following with his ears. He didn't imagine that the chase would detour to a different floor of the high-rise; that would only corner the dealer and lead to his downfall. Unless, of course, he had an accomplice in whose flat he could seek refuge. With so many doors to choose from, Manolis wasn't confident he could locate the fugitive without a positive identification from Sparrow. His hope was that he would turn a corner and find Sparrow reading the felon his rights, having pinned him to the concrete.

But no such luck. Finally reaching ground level, Manolis saw Sparrow standing by a doorway, pointing.

"In here, Sarge," the young man panted.

The basement was murky and oppressive, the air stagnant, and a bank of industrial machines hummed in the background. The overhead strip lights were either not working or strobed erratically. It created an eerie environment where anything could happen.

"Which way?" Sparrow asked.

"You go left, I'll go right," Manolis said.

"We split up?" The constable sounded disappointed and a little anxious.

"No choice," said Manolis. "You'll be fine."

A labyrinth of hallways and passages formed the narrow guts of the building. Manolis's ears pricked as he pressed his back hard against the nearest wall and moved slowly forward, firearm cocked and ready. His breathing was ragged, his heartbeat staccato, the blood pounding in his wrists. All the while, Manolis listened for faint sounds of life amid the mechanical clamour.

Suddenly he heard the unmistakable sound of rapid gunfire. In such a restricted space, it was deafening, to the point of being physically painful. A spasm ran through Manolis so hard that it shook the room. Without thinking, he bolted for the source of the shooting, his body lit with terror.

In a few seconds, he was there. The flashing lights overhead made it hard to discern the size of the room, and the events unfolding were like photographic stills of an action sequence.

"Sparrow? Are you here?"

"Yes, boss! But my weapon's jammed!"

Manolis thrust his pistol forward as the lights died once and for all. Had an unseen hand flicked a switch? The sudden darkness was remarkable, disorientating, and thick enough to touch.

"Police! Drop your weapon! Now!"

Manolis's order was ignored as the shooting continued, bullets ricocheting off the walls like pinballs. Dropping to the floor, he tensed his muscles and squeezed the trigger around which his fingers were clasped. He had only one choice, there was no other. A few ear-splitting moments later, he landed the shot that mattered.

Manolis heard an agonised groan. The metallic hail stopped. Within seconds, the sound of fast-running footsteps disappeared down an unseen corridor.

Manolis had discharged his weapon in the line of duty before, but had never shot a man. The high tide of adrenaline coursing through his veins made him light-headed, his world blurring at the edges.

"Sparrow?" Manolis asked desperately. "Jesus, son, are you OK?"

There was no response.

"Andrew!"

"Yeah, boss," came a slow reply. "I think so. My ears are ringing, but that tells me I'm still alive."

Manolis couldn't work it out. What had happened?

It took some time for his still-twitching fingers to find a light switch, and then the gruesome reality was revealed. The dealer was nowhere to be seen, he'd escaped on foot. Sparrow was unharmed, and so was Manolis. But bleeding from his abdomen – a major artery – and with his back shot up was a street kid who had made the basement his winter home.

Jesus, thought Manolis. The kid was even wearing a replica football shirt like the one little Christos had, the exact same European team. Only it was soaked with dark, copious blood, and the metallic smell of it filled the air. Manolis felt even dizzier now.

All the kid had wanted was to escape the bitter cold. He never imagined getting caught in a shoot-out between good and evil.

And now the good were left to bear the consequences.

2

The problem with air turbulence is that it's invisible. A violent movement caused when chaotic eddies of air are disturbed from calmer states. Unseen by the human eye, yet capable of a fierce and sudden impact. And just as quickly as it can materialise, it can disappear. That is the nature of the invisible – you can never tell when it's there and what it might do. That is its power.

Manolis was no fan of air turbulence. The last leg of his journey from Australia had been the worst of all. He sat deep in his economy airline seat, clutching its economy airline arms, his knuckles and face turning a deathly white as the plane was buffeted up and down. A paperback novel lay in his lap, bookmarked, half-read. Around him, children cried and lights flashed. Passengers stared silently into their glowing blue screens, dehydrated, swollen, sleep-deprived and mesmerised.

It wasn't quite how Manolis had pictured his European summer break, his well-earned respite from traumatic police work. Paul Bloody Porter had looked at Manolis with his tired, bloodshot eyes.

"You have excess leave and need to take it now or else HR will stop sending me e-mails and pay a personal visit," he told his senior detective. "Get the hell out of here and go somewhere far away, purge your system. The investigation cleared you of all wrongdoing. I know it was exhausting to have to relive what happened, and I know you're still hurting. But I have a duty of care to look after you. Your family's originally from Greece, right? Christ, a Greek summer holiday away from the crims and scum and winter and death. Take me with you. Just what the doctor ordered . . ."

Going in search of an isolated rural cottage also wasn't how Manolis had pictured his rehab. And yet, having swapped one form of air turbulence for another, there he sat, clinging to the passenger seat of Stavros's speeding Bulgarian jalopy, winding through tight mountain roads and again fighting down nausea.

"You've got to see the house with your own eyes," Stavros said.

"Uh-huh," Manolis said numbly. Everything at the cottage was supposedly normal, which meant that everything was somehow abnormal.

"I'm telling you, Lefty wouldn't just up and leave like that," Stavros went on. "He'd at least tell me where he was going."

"And the police in Florina?"

"Useless. You'll see that soon enough."

The road to the Prespes region was like a video game that Manolis used to play with Stavros when they were teenagers in Australia. They'd grown up as mates, young men who lived for the weekend, for beaches and discotheques and girls, before Stavros's family returned to Greece. Stavros still drove like a rambunctious teenager, impulsively and offensively. They had so far swerved past a herd of wild donkeys, nearly cleaned up a tribe of goats, narrowly avoided freshly flattened roadkill, and spotted a big brown bear plodding by the roadside.

"You wouldn't want to see one up close," Stavros said, re-pocketing his phone. It had rung a minute earlier – his Albanian electrician with, apparently, more excuses. Blood boiling, Stavros had a harassed look. He spoke in between answering his mobile, playing with the radio and taking deep drags on his full-tar cigarette. He wasn't wearing a seat belt but Manolis was, and it could not have been secured more tightly.

As the car lurched and swayed, coughed and sputtered, Manolis tried to keep down his lunchtime *pita*. So far on his trip, his two chauffeurs had driven with identical recklessness. Aggression and distraction seemed to be traits of all Greek drivers, along with a lack of self-preservation and an adherence to the principles of chaos theory. At least Manolis's cab from the outdated airport of exhaust-blackened Thessaloniki to its crumbling train station had been along a smooth motorway. Positioned in a gorge, the small mountain town of Florina was at the end of the line.

Stavros came on strong with a smell of nicotine and cologne. As usual, he was over-groomed, with gelled hair and designer stubble. He wore a thick dress ring on each index finger set with a prominent slab of glistening stone. Having collected Manolis from the empty, forlorn station in Florina, Stavros was anxious to show him the state of Lefty's house and ask his professional opinion as an investigator. It smacked of desperation. But that was Greece all over; at least, as Manolis saw it.

Lefty was well known to Manolis from previous visits to the region. Manolis's parents, Maria and Con, had immigrated to Australia from Florina in northern Greece after the Second World War. Lefty had always treated Manolis as his special guest, picking up the tab for food and drinks and offering endless cigarettes.

"And a body hasn't been found?" Manolis asked.

"No. Of course, there are many ways that Lefty could have died naturally. But a body would have been found after a week, don't you think?"

Manolis nodded. "Sounds about right," he said. In his experience, most dead bodies were found within the first seventy-two hours or not at all.

"Lefty vanishing like that without any explanation is completely out of character. I'm telling you, despite his past, his life is now incredibly routine. If he ever plans on going somewhere other than Florina, he always lets others know, especially me, and often weeks in advance so that we won't worry about him. But this time he said nothing."

Stavros spoke quickly, his words running into each other.

"He could have left in a hurry," Manolis said, "if something urgent came up."

"Maybe, but he would have somehow called me later to say where he'd gone. Nope, I'm not convinced. I'm telling you, his disappearance is suspicious. It's no accident."

Just as Stavros said "accident", he was forced to slam on the brakes.

There were five wild boar blocking the right half of his lane. He beeped angrily as he swerved past them and pointed out the ski resort of Vigla to his left, telling Manolis that it had a lodge from which the lakes were visible.

"Sorry, I'm in no mood today," he admitted.

Manolis felt the same. After he'd travelled a day in the air and was feeling utterly depleted, his old friend had greeted him with bad news. It reminded him of every recent visit to Maria. Before even saying hello, his elderly mother would bombard Manolis with an endless list of new problems and old grievances. Her bathroom tap was dripping, her phone wasn't working, the doctors misdiagnosed her diabetes thirty years earlier, her brother still owed her money. Every complaint was another tiny weight on Manolis's slumping shoulders, and his soul.

"I haven't been able to sleep much, I've been so worried about Lefty," Stavros added.

"Worried?"

"I'm scared he's been abducted. Or worse."

They were driving in a westerly direction away from Florina and towards the tiny village of Glikonero. The name translated as "fresh water" in Greek because it was perched on the shores of Great Prespa Lake, one of two high-altitude freshwater lakes in the Prespes region. The lakes were distinctive because they straddled three national borders: Great Prespa Lake was shared by Greece, Albania and the Republic of North Macedonia, while Small Prespa Lake was shared by Greece and Albania. Manolis had visited the region only once before. He remembered lonely roads and forbidding ranges. But its seclusion meant that it was also pristine and beautiful with abundant wildlife.

"Lefty's been abducted?" Manolis asked.

"Or worse."

Manolis exhaled and shook his head lightly. "That's a pretty big call, mate. It makes it something else altogether, something criminal. What makes you think there's foul play involved?"

Stavros tossed the burnt remains of his smoke out the window and promptly lit another.

"I know Lefty too well, he's like a brother, he wouldn't just leave without telling me," Stavros said. "Even though his past was unsettled, he's a creature of habit now. Perhaps that's come with age, with slowing down. But I'm convinced that something's happened to him and that he's not simply left because he wanted to."

Stavros let Lefty live rent-free in his rural cottage on condition that he helped work on it from time to time, painting and repairs and the like. Having grown up as an orphan, Lefty had been introduced to Stavros's family by a friend of Stavros's father. Stavros now looked after Lefty like a little brother as a way of honouring his late dad. It was a close and enduring friendship that Manolis's late father, Con, had always respected.

"There's one other thing about Lefty," Stavros added. "I had kind of suspected it, but it was confirmed when I visited the police."

Manolis looked across at his driver with wide eyes, his face slack. "What's that?"

Stavros went on to describe how Lefty was what Greeks called "an invisible" – someone who lived without a scrap of official paperwork. The Florina police didn't have a single record of him in their system, even though he was someone with whom they often spoke, socialised and did business. No-one had any record. Not a government office or a hospital or a private corporation or a charity or even the local public library.

"People like Lefty can only exist in countries like Greece," Stavros said. "So much that happens here happens off the books, off the grid."

Stavros described Lefty as a walking embodiment of the *fakelaki*, which was a financial practice that Manolis knew well. The cornerstone of Greece's invisible economy, the *fakelaki* was the little envelope stuffed with cash that greased palms and secured expedited services from public officials and private companies. The concept of a nod and a wink pervaded every level of Greek society, from politicians to plumbers,

25

from surgeons to shopkeepers; nowhere was free of behind-the-scenes bribery, corruption, backslapping and back-stabbing.

Manolis struggled to conceive of a life without paperwork and how anyone could function that way in the modern world, even in Greece.

"Surely Lefty has a bank account or a driving licence?" he asked.

"He has nothing," Stavros said. "Absolutely nothing. No bank accounts or credit cards, no driving licence or social media accounts. He has no lease with me and is sent no bills. In all my time as his friend, I've never seen anything official with his name on it."

Stavros veered to avoid an oncoming logging truck laden with cargo. The knotted mountain roads had forced the heaving truck to barrel into the other lane. Stavros didn't care who was in the wrong and neither did the truck driver. Both smashed their fists into their horns for a full half-minute as they came within centimetres. Manolis held on to his seat and clenched his teeth.

Every time Manolis had seen Lefty in Florina, he was dressed like an ageing rock star in black leather and cowboy boots. He may have been short, but he was big in personality and presence.

"How does Lefty get around? Does he have a car?" Manolis said. He didn't imagine that Lefty's lack of a driving licence was any real impediment to him getting behind the wheel.

"To get from home to Florina, Lefty usually bums lifts from friends and acquaintances. And when he can't do that, he hitch-hikes or walks. If he walks, it takes him most of a day and blisters his feet."

Manolis looked at the litter-strewn roadside and tried to picture someone standing there with an upturned thumb or handwritten sign. It seemed unlikely.

"Hitch-hiking's pretty dangerous," he said. "That's why people have stopped doing it. Maybe that's why he disappeared."

"Possibly," Stavros said slowly, thoughtfully. "But Lefty knows almost everyone on the road between here and Glikonero."

"That can't be right," Manolis said. "What about tourists and truck drivers, especially those crossing the border? The road's full of trucks."

"He probably wouldn't accept a ride from those people. Lefty's invisible, not stupid."

Manolis made a mental note of the word "probably".

Lefty claimed he'd never worked a day in his life. Manolis had never taken him seriously, but now reconsidered. Stavros had said that Lefty had no pension or superannuation. "All he has to see him through life are his mind and his mouth." It had made him a polyglot who spoke Greek, Turkish, Macedonian, Albanian, Bulgarian and several other assorted Balkan languages. He even spoke a little English that he'd picked up watching TV in the *kafenion*.

"He especially loves those terrible American soap operas," Stavros said. "I find that bloody hilarious."

Stavros still spoke with an Australian twang. Manolis liked that. And although he couldn't quite place it, he had the impression that his old friend was distracted, distant, on edge. He paused for a long time between speaking, and when he spoke, his words came out slippery.

"Do you know what else has been happening in Lefty's life recently?" Manolis asked. "The people he's been seeing, the places he's been going? What's his house like?"

Stavros flicked his smoke, letting the ash evaporate in the hell-hot summer air.

"My cottage is fairly, um . . . basic," he said. "You'll see."

Manolis stroked his chin. The thick facial growth sprouting from his jet-lagged face was spiky. He needed a long shower and sleep. His eyelids were pulling, but it was still only early afternoon.

"What's Lefty's surname?" Manolis said. It was such an obvious question, one that felt strange to ask.

Stavros laughed heartily. He tossed his smouldering cigarette out of the window with purpose and with no regard for fire; another action from a previous era. He immediately lit a third and blew out a burst of smoke. It was a lot of smoking, even for Stavros.

"Lefty uses four different surnames depending on who he's dealing with," Stavros said. "He claims to be originally from Crete and although he's never married, he says he's fathered four children by four different women from four different countries. Four! It's so unbelievable that it's probably true. But frankly I don't know what's truth and what's a lie anymore."

"And he's obviously not answering his phone . . ."

"What phone? Lefty has no mobile, only a landline and an old answering machine. And the landline is dead, ruined in an electrical storm last year and never repaired."

They drove for a while without speaking, just the agonised whirring of the engine in Manolis's ears. It was a brand of car that Manolis had never heard of before. The region was rife with them.

"How's your kid?" Stavros asked suddenly.

For a moment, Manolis didn't know how to respond. He nearly blurted out "dead" before he realised who Stavros was referring to. Too many of Manolis's thoughts were stuck in that infernal basement. His mind wandered there by default. The psychologist's lament, a post-traumatic stress disorder in full effect. Manolis had refused all offers of antidepressants. He wondered if that had been the right decision. He'd even felt guilt about leaving the country, about daring to follow his boss's well-intentioned instructions. It meant he couldn't be there for his son, and young Christos hadn't been able to grasp why Daddy needed to go away so far and for so long.

Bloody hell, thought Manolis. As a cop, he was incompetent; as a mentor, he was inadequate; as a father, he was absent; and as a son, he was poor. As a mess, he was world-class, though.

"Christos is good," Manolis finally replied, his tone subdued. "Cheeky, but good. I can't wait to bring him to Greece one day. But I'll need to negotiate a time with Emily and her new partner. Unfortunately, he reminds me of some of the blokes I've put behind bars."

Stavros laughed. "Lefty always said he couldn't wait to meet your boy," he said. "He adored little kids and doted on them around town."

Manolis's first thought was that that sounded a little sinister, but then he remembered that Greece was a country where the concept of family extended beyond the immediate household. He had often seen children playing in the Florina streets until late at night, safe and sound in their village embrace. It was in stark contrast to life in Australia.

The cabin went quiet again. Stavros returned to his combative, preoccupied driving, and Manolis to his thoughts.

Lefty was certainly a unique character. He came across as a loveable, harmless hustler who boasted an inexplicable ability to live without a single scrap of official paperwork. It was an attribute that Manolis found strangely compelling. A man whose name didn't appear on any official documentation didn't come across as someone who wanted to be tied down, or could be trusted.

Lefty's disappearance was a worry in itself, but it also affected Manolis. In addition to recharging his batteries, Manolis had made the trip to Greece for another purpose, one that involved Lefty intimately. He wasn't going to tell anyone, but Con had left something for Lefty in his will – a set of *komboloi* that had deep sentimental value. They were worry beads that Lefty had once gifted to Con, beads that he claimed had belonged to his own father and that Con wanted returned home after his death. Manolis had stored them safely in his suitcase, which was sitting in the back of Stavros's jalopy. So although Lefty was a relatively quick transaction, he was an absolutely crucial feature of Manolis's visit.

The dashboard clock showed that they'd been winding along the mountain road for nearly an hour. Manolis hoped they were close now, if only for the sake of his stomach. He was tired of feeling queasy. He'd already seen glimpses of slate-blue water through the trees.

"Somebody out there knows what happened to Lefty," Stavros said without warning. He nodded his head lightly as he spoke, as if to underscore his statement. "Either whoever is responsible, or someone close to them. It's hard for people to keep secrets, they often want to tell someone."

Taking a bend, the vast, ominous expanse of Great Prespa Lake spread out before them.

3

They drove in the direction of the lakeside village of Glikonero, past rows of grapevines and silent fields of fava beans and wild thyme. Manolis rolled down his window with its stiff manual handle to let in a noisy crack of air. The smell of fresh herbs and clean air on the tussocky meadows calmed his senses and cleared his mind. The air tasted medicinal, an antidote to the polluted world beyond the protective halo of the mountains. Its warmth, after months of the rime of winter, was like a welcome caress. With the steep hairpin roads behind them, Manolis breathed deeply and gradually felt himself return to his body. Increasingly stunning views of the lakes unfolded at every bend and viewpoint.

Having finally stopped gunning the accelerator, Stavros had started the gentle cruise towards the village centre, and was describing the Prespes region to Manolis, a coffee-coloured forearm gesticulating out the window. Separated by a narrow isthmus, the two lakes were shaped like jagged teardrops and were the highest bodies of water in the Balkans.

"They were once one big lake before thousands of years of sediment carried by the nearby river accumulated and cut it in two," Stavros said.

A channel now connected the two lakes, while a sluice gate controlled the flow of the smaller lake to its larger counterpart. They were linked by subterranean channels to Lake Ohrid to the north. Early cartographers had left the lakes off their maps, which had preserved their mystery.

"They're Europe's oldest lakes, more than three million years old," Stavros went on. "There are stories of massive monsters living in the water."

"Of course there are," Manolis said with a smile.

Stavros chuckled. "If you've got a big lake, you've got to have a monster or giant serpent in it. People claim to have seen enormous shapes and shadows in the water, and even heard voices. It's funny stuff."

The lake region was where dark, brooding granite met pale and porous limestone, where dolomite clashed with marble, and where the Mediterranean pushed northwards into the Balkans. As the place where the boundaries of three countries met, Great Prespa Lake was defined as a geographical tripoint.

"There's another one in Europe: Lake Constance, where Austria, Germany and Switzerland meet," Stavros said.

"How do you cross into Albania and North Macedonia from Greece?" Manolis asked.

"You can't. At least, not legally. There are no paved roads here to link one country to another. To cross to North Macedonia, you need to head back to Florina. There's a road that takes you through industrial zones to Bitola, and there's a customs station at the border. To cross to Albania, there's a road west to Bilisht from Kastoria, and more border control."

Manolis pointed at the lake ahead. "What about crossing the water?"

Stavros shook his head. "Illegal," he said. "It's very different at Constance, crossings are easy, big commercial ferries, millions of tourists each year. Here at Prespa it's like the Dark Ages."

A potholed road edged with plastic rubbish curved anticlockwise around the smaller of the two lakes. The island of Agios Achilleios sat in the middle, reachable by a floating pontoon bridge, and was, according to Stavros, home to just one family. He now drove with a single lazy finger on the steering wheel, his seat reclined back a notch for increased comfort. He picked at his off-centre nose with his other hand. They passed loaded mules on the roadside and villagers toiling in the fields. Manolis's nostrils filled with the ripe smell of mud.

"There were once many villages dotted around the lakes here. The area was home to five thousand or so peasants," Stavros said.

"How many are there now?"

"Two hundred Greek Prespians at most. And in Glikonero, there's only about twenty permanent residents. The donkeys outnumber the people."

Lefty's village was minuscule. Manolis wondered how many suspects there could possibly be in such a small hamlet.

"The Prespes is the most depopulated region in all of Greece, if not all of Europe," Stavros said. "No-one wants to be here. It's the only Greek region without a sea coast. Unsurprisingly, it's also one of the most destitute. Empty and poor and landlocked."

The demographics were attributable to the Greek civil war, which from 1946 to 1949 tore the country apart and saw fierce fighting in the north where guerrilla fighters were known to hide.

"Most of the locals left the area to escape the poverty and political strife," Stavros went on. "The region went from many thousands of people to only a few hundred, and all of them starving and traumatised."

Manolis furrowed his brow with the effort of memory. Had his parents left this part of Greece for those reasons? They had never talked about it; at least, not to him.

"The region flanks two international borders with unstable neighbours," Stavros said. "One group are paranoid oddballs, the other are drunken barbarians. Their men continue to kill each other in blood feuds. We may be bone poor here in the north of Greece but it's still relative glamour compared to that lot."

Stavros laughed contentedly. Manolis joined in, if a little uncertain.

"All that bloodshed meant that the Prespes region became a sensitive military area for many years," Stavros said.

"So people couldn't visit here? It was off limits?" Manolis asked.

"Correct," said Stavros, fumbling with his cigarette lighter. "Outsiders who wanted to visit needed special permission, a licence granted by the Ministry of Defence, and were escorted by soldiers, which meant that no-one bothered to come."

During the 1950s and 1960s, the Prespes region was largely abandoned. It remained restricted for entry and little developed until the

1970s, when it began to be promoted as a tourist destination. In the decades since, the lakes had been dying. Warmer temperatures had impacted snowmelt, reduced their depth and depleted the native fish population. The beaches were getting longer every year. There was more toxic algae. And despite stricter environmental regulations, the locals continued to dump their rubbish in the lake water.

"The Greek Prespians are quick to pin the blame on their neighbours across the border," Stavros said. "But in truth, the Greeks littered, the Albanians fished with dynamite, and the North Macedonians used the lake as a septic tank. Everyone's to blame. And to think, all this is happening in a national park."

"Our national parks in Australia are highly protected," Manolis said.

"You would think this common natural environment would bring the three countries together, not drive them apart. Conservation and protection efforts are now under way, but it may be too little, too late. Still, the Greek military dictatorship once had plans for major road construction, drainage and mechanised farming here, which would have destroyed the natural environment altogether. Luckily the park outlived the dictators."

"Why such disregard for nature?" Manolis asked. He didn't expect a well-reasoned answer.

"We're only one generation past the threat of starvation. It's probably also a form of rebellion against the state – we Greeks love anarchy."

They were now driving past the smaller Prespa lake on the way to its bigger watery cousin. Glikonero was situated on its southern shore. Manolis felt momentarily dazzled by the lake's unexpected intensity, lozenges of light reflecting off the water and burning bright like phosphorus. Everything was so vivid that it was mildly unnerving, the entire world wrapped in a cellophane gloss.

"I always feel a chill in my bones when I come here," Stavros said. He scratched his chin pensively.

"Oh really? Why's that? Because of Lefty?"

"No, it started long before he went missing. The landscape is magnificent but there's something melancholic about it too, the borders are so close by. This region wasn't even a part of Greece a hundred years ago and in the short time since, there's been so much conflict and death."

He described how the Nazis had entered Greece through the Prespes region during the Second World War, with Florina being the first major town they occupied. Some Glikonero residents still had Nazi paraphernalia in their homes as souvenirs.

"The far north has an untamed frontier feel about it, it's a land of shysters and cowboys," Stavros said. "The place breeds these characters because it's a border region that has changed hands so many times. And because of its instability, opportunities have opened up. It's got just the right climate for swindlers and fast-talkers. When you stop and think about it, the Prespes region was the obvious choice for someone like Lefty to disappear into and call home. Hand in glove."

Stavros was talking a lot of sense. Lefty was in his element up here, away from the attention of the rest of the country. Historically, the Prespa region was a hinterland, with uncharted lands too rugged for tax collectors to traverse. If Lefty was going to live under the radar as an invisible, this was by far the best place to do it.

Two stands of ancient juniper trees lined the road and ushered their arrival in the desolate village of Glikonero. A large gold-rimmed cross hung crookedly from a sagging skein of wire stretched across the main road. The village had preserved some of its original houses, a watermill and a medieval church that were a thousand years old. It was the grandeur of stone and its synchrony with the natural world.

Stavros pointed. "There are lots of abandoned hermitages on the cliffs up there," he said. "They have these incredible frescoes painted on the rock walls."

The lake was a crescent-shaped pane of quaking summer-blue. It was crowded with birdlife drawn to the waters by a multitude of fish. A pod of grand white pelicans floated by on the choppy currents. Circling above the opaque water were colonies of squawking seagulls, hungry, their flight arcs spiralling and rising with the thermals. Manolis's ears rang with the constant hum of migratory birds, their wings chirring. A collection of small towers on the road to town had been specifically designed for birdwatching. The Prespes region was at the crossroads of bird migration routes between Europe, Africa and Asia, a non-stop traffic of rich avian activity.

"Pelicans come every spring, thousands of the exact same birds," Stavros said. "They're an endangered species."

"Speaking of endangered, why are the roads here so deserted?" Manolis asked, looking around. "Where is everyone?" It was now late afternoon and well past the time for siesta.

"Most of the people who live here are elderly," Stavros said. "Seventy or above. They don't leave their homes very much. Lefty was a carer to some of them."

Checking his phone for the time, Manolis noticed it lacked reception.

"Is there no mobile coverage here?"

"Afraid not," Stavros said. "It stops outside Florina, blotted out by the thick mountains, which just adds to the feeling of isolation. There are no CCTV cameras here either, in case you were wondering, so people's movements in and out of Glikonero can't be monitored."

On either side of the road were enormous overgrown gardens with vegetables and fruit trees. Rows of grapevines interspersed with beehives ran north to south, waiting to be hand harvested. There were broken-down old cars recycled as greenhouses for growing vege-tables and herbs, and backyards with chickens and goats and pigs. Men stacked logs while hunched-over women wearing floral kerchiefs gathered rosehips in cloth sacks. Somebody was burning garbage; a vinegary smoke hung in the air, the scent of hard living. Strings of peppers, fire-engine red and shaped like a cow's horn, hung from balconies like bloody curtains. Thick, knotted strands of garlic were strung alongside, ostensibly to ward off evil. It sounded like Lefty had needed more garlic.

They finally pulled up in front of Lefty's cottage, the brakes of Stavros's jalopy letting out a pained squeak. The house appeared derelict and abandoned, like so many others they'd driven past. The stonework needed repair, several roof tiles were missing, and raggedy weeds were swarming the foundations. The paint was peeling or wildly scarred and the wooden framework was rotting. Some of the windows had shutters that hung loose from single hinges, and some had lost their shutters entirely.

"It's not much to look at, outside or in," the landlord said sheepishly. "But I think Lefty preferred the house this way – in plain sight, and yet never seen. Like himself."

"No wonder he never did any repairs," Manolis said. The steady lowing of an unseen herd sounded in the near distance.

Fighting his way through the tangled undergrowth, Stavros jimmied open the front door with a lift and a shove. There was no doorbell to press or iron knocker to clatter.

"And no lock?" asked Manolis.

"It's never locked," Stavros said. "No-one locks their doors around here, or in Florina."

It gave the impression of a united community where people trusted one another, even after a man had gone missing. But if it was indeed a crime scene, thought Manolis, it had not been secured.

Inside, the house appeared undisturbed, neat and tidy. It smelled of dried herbs and spices; there were bouquets of oregano and thyme nailed to the wall. The ceiling was decorated with intricate patterns of mould like fine embroidery. Manolis noticed the room lacked all furniture and appliances.

"Doesn't the house have electricity?" he asked.

"No," Stavros said.

"What about gas?"

"No."

"Heating?

"No."

"Is there running water?"

"Again, no."

Stavros looked away. He seemed vaguely embarrassed to have let Lefty stay in such conditions.

"I couldn't have let anyone other than Lefty live here, they wouldn't have paid a euro, or stayed for free, even. But Lefty loved it, he felt like a king in his castle."

In the far corner of the room, a pile of blankets on the floor had been slept on, but not in.

"The winters were the worst for Lefty," Stavros said. "He rubbed his body with olive oil to stay warm. And when it snowed, he stayed out all night in Florina clubs and *kafenia*. It was the only way he could keep warm. He often stayed till dawn, talking to whoever he could find."

"Did he ever spend the night at your house?" Manolis asked. He had in mind Stavros's spare room, which Stavros had said Manolis was welcome to stay in for as long as he wanted.

"He did. Usually whenever he was kicked out of venues at closing time. I told him my house was always available, but Lefty preferred his independence."

"Obviously a proud man," Manolis said.

"To the point of stubbornness."

Stavros said that Lefty had been known to try and pick up women just so he could go home and use their showers. He otherwise washed in Great Prespa Lake, which was also where he cleaned his clothes, beating them on the rocky shores.

"They used to baptise babies in the lake," Stavros added. "We would joke that Lefty got baptised whenever he washed."

A collection of old plastic bottles filled with water sat by the door.

"Is that lake water?" Manolis asked.

"No. There's a foamy spring nearby. Lefty usually filled his bottles there. It's pure drinking water that flows straight off the mountains."

Led by Stavros, Manolis walked around, carefully inspecting the room.

"See, this is the strangest thing that tells me that something's not right," Stavros said.

"What's that?" Manolis asked. He stepped over a pile of clothes, lake-washed, folded and stacked.

"That there's nothing strange at all. It all looks perfectly normal."

"Have you touched anything in here?"

"Not even a pencil."

Manolis's eyes whipped around the room. There was a foil wrapper with leftover food that was ready to eat. Lefty's cowboy boots were there. So was his black leather motorcycle cap with chain detail and rivet-studded brim, hanging on a nail hammered crookedly into the wall. Stavros said that Lefty wore the cap to make him look bad. Same with his boots. Lefty's sunglasses and owlish reading glasses were placed neatly on a newspaper. The paper's date coincided with the day Lefty had disappeared, and so did the calendar on the wall. The days had been meticulously crossed off, with the last date being the day before he was last seen. His medications were also in place.

"He even left this behind with a few euros tucked inside," Stavros said, holding up Lefty's battered leather wallet.

Manolis took the wallet, inspected it. There was only money inside; there wasn't a single piece of identification or a shop receipt or business card, not even a photograph of Lefty or anyone else.

Manolis paced around the room for a second look. He re-examined small details and took in the overall scene. Eventually, he scratched the back of his head and said:

"The fact that there's no sign of a struggle is something that wouldn't interest the police. They'd want to see evidence of a fight or forced entry. Frankly, this room would bore them to death."

"I know," Stavros said. He pointed out that a forced entry would be hard to prove since, as he'd said, no-one in the area ever locked their doors.

Still, Manolis could see why Stavros was concerned for his old friend. The sight of something so normal felt strangely abnormal. And while, on the one hand, it was clear why the Florina police were unconcerned about Lefty's welfare, such behaviour still seemed out of character even for someone as unorthodox and invisible as Lefty.

A sudden and hefty knock on the door interrupted Manolis's ruminations.

4

"Stavros? Hey, are you there?"

"Come in, Kostas."

A dark face with deep-set eyes appeared from around the door. A crooked smile followed seconds later showing nicotine-stained teeth.

"I thought I saw your car parked outside. How are you? I came to see if there was any news on Lefty."

Stavros sighed. "Nothing yet. No word from him, and nothing from our always hard-working police force. I'll go see them again later. How are you?"

"Our police are good for nothing except drinking coffee. As for me, I can't complain. My knee hurts. Rain must be on the way."

Seeing the unfamiliar face, Kostas introduced himself with arm extended. His white singlet showed off a thick forest of chest hair the colour of tarnished silver on a sun-kissed chest.

"I'm a good friend of Lefty's," Kostas said, his voice slow and harsh from a lifetime of tobacco.

"This is Georgios," Stavros said quickly. "He's a labourer friend who has come to help work on the house in Lefty's absence."

Manolis fired him a long, unblinking stare. Stavros could only smile guiltily; he knew he'd gone too far. But he also knew that this was the perfect opportunity to provide cover for Manolis, since the local residents were unaware of his true profession.

"I knew Lefty a little as well," Manolis said, shaking hands. "Sorry to hear he's missing."

Kostas let out a long exhalation, a deep release of tension and disappointment that came from the reminder of Lefty's absence. His gaze settled on the patch of floor where Lefty had made his bed.

"It was a complete shock," he said. "I knew something was wrong when he didn't turn up for work on Sunday."

Manolis paused. "Sorry?" he said. "Work? What work?"

Stavros stepped forward, offered Kostas a smoke. He put it behind his ear for later.

"He means his taverna," Stavros said. "Kostas is the owner, and Lefty works there on a casual basis."

"Doing what?" Manolis asked. "Is he a waiter or chef or . . . ?"

Both Greek men laughed wholeheartedly, their gold chains tinkling against their oversized crucifixes.

"Not quite," said Kostas. "He mainly cleans out the toilets and washes dishes and mops floors. He's also the unofficial greeter of guests and source of live entertainment."

"His job, basically, is to just be himself," Stavros chuckled.

"He can't be anything else."

"I can't remember ever seeing Lefty cook anything more than a tin of beans," Stavros added.

Kostas said he paid Lefty in bottomless coffees and the odd meal, which he sometimes took home in foil. Manolis shot a cursory glance at the silver wrapper that Lefty had left behind.

"I sometimes pay him a little money when I can spare it," Kostas said. "Business has been terrible." He let out a sad laugh.

"Did Lefty go to the taverna before he went missing?" Manolis asked directly.

Kostas glared at Manolis, then looked him up and down. Manolis felt self-conscious; his line of inquiry had gone too far, too soon. Kostas's eyes darted to Stavros before returning to Manolis.

"Well actually, yes, he did," Kostas said calmly.

He fumbled with thick fingers for the smoke behind his ear, then popped it in his mouth. Stavros promptly leaned in and lit it. Manolis relaxed his forehead. He needed to be more careful if he didn't want to alarm the locals.

In between determined drags, Kostas explained that the last place Lefty was seen was at his taverna on Saturday night.

"He'd had a few whiskies but no more than usual. There was nothing in his behaviour to suggest it was anything other than an ordinary night."

"And was anyone else in the taverna that night?" Manolis asked. He scratched his aquiline Greek nose.

"A few tourists, but nothing memorable happened," Kostas said. "It was just another night. I only got suspicious the next day when Lefty didn't show up for work as scheduled. To me, this meant he went missing somewhere between Saturday night and Sunday lunchtime."

Manolis regarded Kostas sceptically. It was a bit of a leap to be suspicious of someone who didn't turn up for an unpaid job, particularly when that person was Lefty. People also fell ill overnight or had minor accidents that left them incapacitated. Manolis thought to say something but in the end stayed quiet.

"Fair enough," he said.

"How's Petros?" asked Stavros. "Back on his feet?"

The road outside echoed with the sudden quarrel of roosters and half-wild cats. The men paused their conversation to hear the outcome.

"He's using a stick," Kostas replied. "But at least he's walking again."

He turned to Manolis. "Our local priest," he said. "Father Petros rolled his ankle while he was out hunting. Until he went missing, Lefty was looking after him."

He said that Lefty acted as carer to several of the village's elderly residents.

"He's that kind of person," Kostas said. "Always putting others ahead of himself."

Kostas fondly recounted some of the late-night conversations he'd shared with Lefty. It was often over a bottle of aged whisky or fiery local *tsipouro* and a pack of cigarettes as they looked at the moonlight reflected in Great Prespa Lake. He said that Lefty cherished his invisibility; it was a protective cloak to hide him from corrupt public officials and politicians.

"He feels that to do otherwise, to pay taxes and create work for bureaucrats, is to help criminals," Kostas said.

"Surely he must have been on the books at some point in his life?" asked Manolis. There would at least have been a birth certificate, even if he was an orphan.

"He was," Stavros said. "I remember. But he apparently paid a policeman to wipe him from all official records."

"See," said Kostas. "Corruption. It sabotages all attempts at progress in this country."

"Pay the price and you can buy anything," Stavros added.

Manolis made a face. "But how is that even possible?" He was referring more to the intertwined nature of official record-keeping, the complexities of computer systems and documents, not amoral public officialdom, which he'd seen first-hand.

"It's very much possible," Stavros said. "Especially here in Greece. We're held together with rubber bands and sticky tape."

"Part of our charm." Kostas smiled.

In a world where so much was interconnected, and where one major disaster could bring about system collapse, it was people like Lefty who flourished.

"But Lefty still gets lonely," Kostas said. "He's told me so. He also knows that loneliness is a feeling that only gets stronger with age. That's why he cares so much for the villagers here. He looked after me last year when I was sick with flu. It took me a full month to recover."

Stavros could only nod. His experiences with Lefty were similar.

"I haven't met anyone else in Glikonero yet," Manolis said. "Stavros tells me the people don't go out a lot."

Kostas agreed. "We're an old little village," he said, voice sad. "Old in history and old in age. There are people like me who have been here for a long, long time, and with age comes sicknesses and injuries. We hoped to grow and renew as a village, but that hasn't happened. We're only getting older and smaller. If something doesn't change, we'll soon be gone altogether."

In contrast to its current population, the village had once been home to many people, including children. Kostas said he felt saddest at Christmas, when there used to be a big party at the taverna. He would dress up as Santa and give presents to all the kids.

"But there are no children now," he said. "They've grown up and left and none have taken their place. Christmas was once a happy time of the year. Now it's tragic, just a reminder of what we've lost." He wiped his eyes.

Much of Kostas's trade now came from tourists and mountain bikers passing through the area, especially during the summer months. He closed the taverna during the coldest months of winter. People came to ski at Vigla, but very few ventured further west to the Prespes region, where the roads became treacherous, impassable sometimes, on account of the heavy snow.

"Please come to my taverna soon so I can host you for dinner as my guest and welcome you properly to our village," Kostas told Manolis. "I promise you the tastiest local produce imaginable."

*   *   *

"Labourer friend? Come to help work on the house? Really . . . ?"

Manolis was incredulous. Stavros couldn't help but smirk.

They were back in Florina and walking from Stavros's house to the police station. It was a short distance along a series of tight streets and steep, tessellated pavements. They stepped carefully around open bags of concrete mix and ducked under dangling electrical wires. Manolis cringed at such obvious hazards but knew they were a mainstay of Greek organisation, or lack thereof.

"*Ela reh*, Georgios," Stavros said playfully. "I'm sorry I said that to Kostas. The opportunity was there to provide you with the best cover, so I took it. But wait, let me buy some cigarettes. Be right back."

He disappeared into a tiny shop in the *plateia*, the central square around which the town had been built. Manolis knew he would strike up a gossipy exchange with the proprietor, another old friend, and be longer than expected. He leaned against a nearby wall and got comfortable.

Manolis had recently kicked the habit, but realised his resolve would be tested in a country where smoking was a national pastime, as were long, circular conversations. He had considered giving in to the irresistible pull of the past and smoking while he was in Greece, but in the end decided to stay firm. Instead, he chose to occupy his fingers with his own set of *komboloi*. The turquoise worry beads had also once been his father's, and were one of the few possessions Manolis had kept of Con's after he died. Carrying them in his pocket was one way of ensuring that his father was always with him.

Looking around the square, Manolis saw women on balconies beating rugs with absurdly large paddles and young children kicking battered footballs. Stray dogs lazed in the sun, their bloated white bellies exposed, while skinny cats rummaged in overflowing rubbish bins. Among the young women showing plenty of bra strap and swarthy men chain-smoking, a man suffering from cerebral palsy stood awkwardly on crutches. He held an upturned baseball cap outstretched and spoke to passers-by with slow, slurred speech. Most ignored him; a few tossed him their spare change. But Manolis stood transfixed. The man was wearing the same replica European football shirt as the teen he'd tragically shot and killed in the basement in another hemisphere. It was a global sporting brand – it made sense they'd be all over Greece too, where football was king.

Manolis bit his lip. The haunting wasn't merely when he closed his eyes. It seemed to be following him now.

He bought a coffee and some sesame bread for the man from a nearby street vendor and also gave him a fistful of euro bills.

"Thank . . . you," the man mouthed crookedly.

Stavros suddenly appeared. "Andreas, my boy, how are you?" he asked, smiling at the young man. He tossed an unlit cigarette into his cap. A second smoke went into Stavros's mouth.

"C'mon, let's go," he muttered to Manolis. He cupped his shoulders against the wind and sparked the cigarette to life before drawing on it hungrily.

As they walked, Manolis asked Stavros how he knew the young man.

"He's a town feature," Stavros said, his voice coated in nicotine. "A good kid."

"Is he homeless?"

"No, just poor. Unfortunately, his mum is unwell so he's trying to help her out."

The station was deserted when they arrived. Stavros whacked a stainless-steel desk bell in an attempt to summon a soul from a back room. It made only the faintest of sounds; no-one came.

'It sounds broken,' Manolis said.

Stavros sighed and took the initiative, striding confidently behind the counter and down a hallway. Manolis tried to stop him but Stavros assured him that he was a known quantity and that this was business as usual. A smell of insecticide and sour tobacco filled every nook and cranny.

As they walked, a memory came to Manolis. Lefty sweet-talking the local police was the reason he'd been able to secure his Greek identity card – the *taftotita*. Within Greece, the plasticky *taftotita* was as good as a passport for proof of identity, and was a valid international travel document in Europe. Manolis still carried the ill-gotten identification in the depths of his wallet. Lefty had secured the laminate with what Manolis suspected were prohibited goods he'd smuggled across the border from North Macedonia: American cigarettes and Japanese electronics, French clothes and Italian shoes, Scottish whisky and Russian vodka. The Florina police were every bit the nouveau riche that particular summer.

They finally came across a young constable in a stuffy office with no air conditioning. He was sitting at his chipped desk absently scrolling through his phone, an indifferent expression on his illuminated face. His tie was tossed to one side, his interest seemingly in the same place. A half-drunk frappé coffee in a tall, icy glass, the top smeared with murky brown streaks, sat on the desk, while a half-smoked cigarette drooped from the side of his mouth.

"*Ela*, Yiannis," said Stavros. "How are you?"

"*Kalimera*, Stavros, what's happening?"

"The same. How's the family?"

"The same."

He introduced Manolis as a friend from Australia and they shook hands firmly for a few seconds. Constable Yiannis immediately regaled Manolis with his admiration for Australia and his desire to visit. He went on to describe his extended family who lived there, seeming genuinely surprised that Manolis did not personally know them. Meanwhile, Manolis scanned the station, his eyes settling on several of its antiquated features. Not only were the equipment and vehicles from a bygone era, but the police still used handwritten catalogue cards instead of computer records. The desks all had heavy glass ashtrays. Ceiling tiles were missing, the parquetry was dirty, and the decor outdated. A yellowing calendar with a topless female model hung on the wall, the month incorrect. A large decorative *mati* – evil-eye talisman – hung alongside to ward off malevolent forces.

Yiannis graciously offered cigarettes. Stavros accepted, lit up; Manolis declined. Yiannis leaned back in his office chair and let the Mediterranean sunlight strike his impeccable face. His colour was unfathomably healthy, his skin cinnamon-brown, his veins smooth and blue. To his surprise, Manolis was envious.

After a few minutes of small talk, Stavros asked: "Is there any news on our little friend?"

Yiannis shook his head in the negative. Stavros shook his in frustration.

"Um, if you don't mind me asking . . ."

Manolis asked what the police had found so far. He knew they were limited in what they could reveal, but he represented a concerned friend, not some nosy journalist on the sniff for a story.

Confirming what Stavros had told him, Yiannis said they had

conducted a cursory investigation but felt there was no case to look into. Lefty was familiar to them, his personality and habits were known, and they figured he would probably be back soon, wherever the hell he had gone to do whatever the hell he was doing. On hearing that, Stavros turned to Manolis with a cold gleam in his eyes.

"Someone from Glikonero told us that he went away," the constable added. "So he's not missing, he's just not here."

Apparently, thought Manolis, just as a person who doesn't exist can't be murdered, neither can they go missing.

Manolis coughed into his hand. "Who told you that? And where did they say Lefty had gone?"

Yiannis dismissed Manolis with a gesture and looked back down at his phone. "Sorry, I can't disclose that information to members of the public."

Stavros fixed Manolis with a gimlet eye, his annoyance growing by the minute. Manolis looked around in case any other officers were in earshot. His attention was momentarily captured by an old oil painting on the wall, a wooden fishing boat in the harbour of an idyllic Greek island.

"I understand that," he said. "In that case may I speak to your supervising officer? Preferably a sergeant or higher."

Still staring at his digital distraction, Yiannis said: "Of course you may. But he's not here."

Stavros snorted. "And when is Nikos ever here these days?" he said. "He's forty-two years old and retired before all of us."

Yiannis chuckled. "That is not untrue," he said. "The boss is a shining inspiration to us all."

Stubbing out his smoke in an ashtray, Stavros hiked up his trousers and arched his back. He was unhappy with what he was hearing, tired of the platitudes, and had had enough.

"A local man is missing," Stavros said. "You know who he is. He's no stranger – he's a friend, even if he's not in your official records. He could very well have been killed, there could be *a murderer* on the loose, other people in danger, local residents, *your mother*, and all you lot do is carry on like nothing's happened. And the most galling thing is that it's not like you have anything better to do."

Maybe it was Manolis's presence that bolstered Stavros; he was no longer a lone wolf fighting a solo battle. Whatever it was, Yiannis wasn't flustered by his anger, staring calmly at Stavros with his fresh face and lustrous eyes. Manolis sensed the officer was merely following orders. And if he wasn't, there was a limit to what the police could do even if they did happen to think that Lefty was missing, because there were no official records of him being alive. Deep down, Manolis wasn't sure what to feel. He would need to see things for himself.

Eventually, when Stavros had run out of arguments and angles, the young constable said: "I'll have another word with the chief when he arrives." He spoke with a glassy clarity.

Manolis touched Stavros lightly on the shoulder. "Come on," he said. "Let's go."

Stavros twisted the rings on his fingers in annoyance and took a cigarette for the road to calm his jangled nerves.

Meeting the youthful Greek cop made Manolis think of Sparrow. It wasn't his fault his handgun had jammed in that housing commission basement – an examination revealed it was faulty. And the internal police investigation had cleared him of all wrongdoing in the teenager's death. The dealer was later caught and charged with murder, attempted murder, drug manufacture and trafficking. He was going away for a very long time. At least that inquiry had been swift and conclusive. The more complex investigation into the political tendrils at the Cobb immigration detention centre was protracted and exhausting.

But the accidental shooting in the basement had rocked Sparrow's world too. The teen turned out to be a runaway from an abusive, drug-riddled home. Unlike Manolis, Sparrow had decided to throw himself at his new job as therapy. Manolis thought it was probably a good thing for the emerging cop; idle hands, et cetera. His young system could handle the stress. Manolis's couldn't. Porter's orders. PTSD and all that.

"Keep in touch, mate," Manolis had told Sparrow. "Write me an e-mail. Or maybe even a letter."

Sparrow had smiled. "Old school. I like it."

As they left the station, Stavros was still bristling with anger and muttering to himself despite sucking on his smoke as if it was an inhaler.

"Lazy bureaucratic bastards," he said. "More interested in cashing a pay cheque. Without a body, they won't lift a finger."

Manolis had originally felt defensive of his fellow law enforcement officers. It was a professional solidarity, a brotherhood unconstrained by geographical borders. He didn't want to overstep any jurisdictional boundaries. But given the police's laissez-faire attitude, he knew he had to act. And especially when the station's blue *mati* seemed to represent the extent of the local police's peacekeeping activities.

Manolis also had his father's *komboloi* and the family honour to uphold. Part of him just wanted to hand the worry beads to Stavros to give to Lefty if he was ever found, and utter a silent apology to Con's memory. But he knew he couldn't. And this was despite what he'd learned about his father in Cobb. Manolis had never told his mother about the knife he'd dug up from the hard outback dirt. And he never would. The guilt would be his alone.

It would also be his task alone to close the loop and locate Con's sister. Aunt Poppy had gone to Australia to find a husband, and it was her accidental, shameful pregnancy many years ago in Cobb that had kicked things off. Con had wreaked violent, village-style retribution on the young Aboriginal man, Jimmy Dingo, who had sullied the family's name. Aunt Poppy was promptly sent back to Greece, and Manolis never heard from her again, not even on visits to Europe. But he was determined this time. Manolis didn't know if Poppy had become a mother, or even whether she was alive or dead. But he planned to find out.

The realisation had rocked Manolis, the thought of having lived with a dark secret in his household for almost his entire life, an unspoken horror that his parents had kept hidden. And not only that – he and Maria had shared their lives with a killer. Maria had slept in the same bed as a murderer each night, although Con never saw himself in that way – he had merely upheld the family's honour according to his Greek village traditions. Manolis struggled to comprehend how his father had walked away from such a shocking act and got on with normal family life.

"OK," Manolis said suddenly.

"OK, what?" Stavros replied.

"OK. You can count on your labourer friend. I'm in."

5

In his investigative mind, Manolis's strategy was straightforward. During his first few days in the Prespes region, he would live up to his new vocation as a labourer by doing a little light maintenance work on Stavros's cottage in the mornings. He would then down tools for a packed lunch and a few chapters of his latest book. The afternoons would be set aside to scope out the village and region, somehow making himself known to the reclusive locals and asking about Lefty. With so few residents, it wouldn't take long to introduce himself. And surely, in such a small village, where word spread freely among the gossipy Greeks, everyone would already have heard of his arrival from Kostas, the taverna owner.

Manolis had searched for missing people before, when he worked in Homicide and other departments. He knew the major reasons why people went missing and ways to track them down; these included checking phone records, bank account activity, hospital admissions, border crossings and use of e-mail addresses. But every case still needed a degree of local knowledge, which always took time to establish. And in the case of Lefty, no such records existed, so it promised to be even more challenging.

Stavros lent him a small sedan so he had his own transport.

"This is my friend's car," he said. "She's old and retired and prefers not to drive anymore."

The sedan had no side mirrors and only one working wiper blade. It refused to steer straight, belched smoke like a brewing volcano, and would not go over eighty kilometres per hour. It was another make and model that Manolis failed to recognise from some nondescript Eastern bloc country. He didn't relish the prospect of driving to the Prespes each day in such a deathtrap, let alone encountering an assortment of wildlife on the winding mountain road. Manolis was fortunate to be versed in manual transmission madness, he didn't need power-assisted automatic everything. But driving on the right side of the road didn't come naturally to a motorist so used to the left; he kept turning on the sole wiper blade when trying to use the indicators and accidentally crossing the road's central line. Unnerved by sightings of bears and donkeys, packs of grey wolves, herds of chamois and flocks of sheep and goats, he drove with extreme caution, both hands on the skinny steering wheel. There was never any danger of approaching the jalopy's maximum speed, nor of Manolis arriving at Glikonero with his full complement of nerves intact.

Stavros's only word of warning had concerned the animals that roamed the area.

"Be careful," he said over strong coal-black coffee. "They've been known to attack humans." His cadence was measured.

"You mean deadly attacks?" Manolis asked.

Stavros nodded solemnly. "It's rare, but it's happened. Tragic."

Manolis came from a country with some of the deadliest creatures in the world, whether it was venomous box jellyfish at the beach, brown snakes in the park or funnel-web spiders in your shoes. Still, there was now an improbable but nonetheless possible theory that Lefty had been killed, and potentially even eaten, by a wild animal.

Stavros had provided Manolis with some basic tools and work overalls from his cellar. Manolis now looked the part, while Stavros had essentially appropriated free labour to work on his cottage. It was something that Manolis was initially reluctant to embrace – the idea of spending part of his holiday doing hard manual activity. But the inner-city apartment dweller found working away on the cottage for a few hours each morning surprisingly therapeutic. In many respects, it was similar to restoring cars, with which he was more familiar. The process of working with his hands grounded him. It dragged him away from the slabbed concrete jungle and rooted him in the soft mountain soil. Being in such a quiet location was meditative, a powerful antidote to the breakneck pace of the modern world.

In between stripping away old paint and pulling up strangling weeds, Manolis searched through Lefty's house and belongings in the hope of finding a clue. He knew he should wear protective gloves to preserve the scene, but in view of its already insecure nature it was pointless. Manolis hoped to find an item specific to Lefty, be it a document or photograph or, best of all, a handwritten letter. But although he turned over the cottage's entire contents several times, there was nothing to indicate Lefty's whereabouts. What was even more staggering was the lack of anything personal. The few articles in the cottage – the clothes and shoes and household items – could have belonged to anyone. Manolis had never seen anything like it. Homeless people who squatted beneath overpasses and in public parks had something distinctive in their belongings that identified them. Even that poor kid in the basement did. But Lefty's invisibility was on a scale that Manolis hadn't appreciated until that moment. Lefty was formidable in both his presence and his absence.

After he had read a chapter of his book and eaten his lunchtime *pita* stuffed with spinach, cheese or leek, Manolis would spend the afternoons exploring the region. In Glikonero, he walked the village's roads and offered tins of food to hungry stray cats. They were reluctant to approach at first, but Manolis was patient and persistent. Finding a flattened cat on the road one day, Manolis went back later with a shovel, delicately scraped its scrawny body off the tarmac and buried it by the roadside. He couldn't stand to watch its gradual decay and the thought of its carcass being feasted upon by talon-clawed birds. Further afield, birdwatching towers revealed hundreds of pelicans, egrets and greylag geese bobbing lazily along the surface of Great Prespa Lake. The nearby fruit orchards were replete with spotted woodpeckers, the chortling of red-rumped swallows, and the fizz of black redstarts. Surrounded by rocks and sand,

Great Prespa Lake was substantially deeper and more treacherous than its lesser cousin, which was encircled by dense reeds. Both lakes were eerie. Irregularly shaped, they held the turbulent memories of the region's past. Clean, crisp shards of light made everything appear vibrant; the air pulsed with colour. Manolis felt strangely anchored, here in the centre of Europe, in a place that was so rich in nature and history. It was a sensation he'd never experienced before.

Feeding the strays had offered a distinct challenge for Manolis in the form of the tin opener in Lefty's house, which reminded him of a connection he had with the missing man. The tin opener was left-handed and so was Lefty. Lefty by name, lefty by nature. Manolis had also been left-handed before his mum had forced him to convert to his right.

Seeing her young son colouring in and holding his fork with his left hand, Maria was aghast; in the Greek Orthodox church, as in many other religions and cultures, left-handedness had always been seen as a sign of evil and a symptom of neurological problems. Every time she saw young Manolis using his left hand to draw or wave or eat, she would whack it with a wooden ruler and tell him to switch to his right. When that didn't work, Maria took Manolis to the local church in Cobb and asked the priest for an exorcism. The priest didn't know what to make of it, and in the end placated her by offering a blessing. She also took Manolis to their family doctor and asked if he could fix the problem, only to be met with an even blanker expression. In the end, Manolis's teacher rang his home, similarly horrified that he was writing left-handed, and asked what Maria planned to do about it. Eventually, many red welts later, Manolis switched and became right-handed.

Lefty had once told Manolis that the same thing had happened to him, but that he later relearned how to use his left hand. Manolis had marvelled at Lefty's discipline and intelligence in reprogramming his brain and relearning such a fundamental motor skill; he knew he could never do it. He also felt that having endured the same traumatic childhood experience brought them closer together. To Maria's immense relief, her only grandson had turned out to be right-handed.

Observing the local flora and fauna, Manolis soon encountered the local residents. His first was the priest, Father Petros, out on a walk through Glikonero with his elegant stick.

"So you're the new arrival," the priest said, arm outstretched. "Welcome, it's good to have a fresh face in town."

"Nice to meet you too," Manolis said, shaking hands. Clearly, the local gossip mill was working as anticipated. The priest's fingers were large and his grip firm. Another right-hander, thought Manolis.

They exchanged small talk, pleasantries. Father Petros's voice had a hypnotic quality. Tall and intimidating, the priest wore mirror sunglasses, black robes and a traditional stovepipe hat, his long and luxuriant bushranger beard only adding to his mystique. As a child, Manolis had been dragged to church by Maria every Sunday, made to stand when she stood, sit when she sat, and cross himself at all the relevant moments in the mass. At the front of the church, the Orthodox priests chanted and swung their censers, the smoke from the burning incense billowing towards the parishioners like flying dragons. With their elongated robes that touched the floor, the priests moved about the church like ethereal creatures, their feet unseen. It was a weekly ritual that had left an impression on the young Manolis, who regarded the Orthodox priests as mysterious figures with an otherworldly quality.

"How's your foot?" Manolis asked suddenly, looking down. "I heard you had an accident, but you appear to be walking OK now."

Father Petros tapped his right foot with his walking stick. "It was pretty weak for a while there, the ligaments in my ankle, but the strapping has helped. Lefty applied it. He knew what to do, how to wrap it tight."

Leaning against a crumbling rock wall for support, taking the weight off his injured foot, Father Petros detailed some of the ways in which Lefty had regularly helped him, both at home and at church. This included hanging laundry out to dry, bringing him hot meals from the taverna, sweeping the floors, and disposing of burnt-down candles.

"Lefty doesn't have much to offer by way of schooling or intellect or grooming," Father Petros said, "but he's streetwise with a heart of gold. And he's excellent company."

"I know," Manolis said. "I've always enjoyed being around him too. He's charming and makes me laugh."

"Charming! That's the word. A definite charmer."

Father Petros spoke of his deep affection for Lefty, saying that a lot of people found him friendly and would agree that he didn't have an enemy in the world, but others felt differently.

"Really . . . ?" Manolis tried not to sound too interested.

"Funnily enough, that's actually a side effect of his honesty," Father Petros said, shooing a blowfly from his sunglasses. "As you know, Lefty speaks his mind, and if he doesn't like a person, he lets them know as much."

"Hmm," Manolis murmured.

"Don't you think? I like this attitude, I think it's refreshing, a lost art. People are too scared to be themselves anymore, to say anything, so I like that Lefty is true to himself. He's a tonic. But unfortunately, not everyone feels the same. Perhaps they're jealous of his freedom, his carefree nature. I mean, even his name – Lefteris – means freedom and liberty! Frankly, I can't think of a more appropriate name for such an unrestrainable, independent character."

Manolis digested the priest's words for a moment. This was his first indication that Lefty was not universally loved, and that he had foes who might want to do him harm. A pair of rubbery skinks appeared in the gaps of the rock wall before disappearing just as quickly.

"Of course, the English word 'character' comes from the Greek *kharax* – the chisel, or the mark left by a chisel," Father Petros said. "I firmly believe you chisel out your character from your own raw material, like a sculptor creating a statue. It's an uncovering process, not a building one. If Lefty were an artist, he would polarise the critics, like all the greatest sculptors and painters and writers. Loved by some, loathed by others."

"I must admit, I haven't yet met any of those people," Manolis said, hoping to extract some names.

The priest grinned, revealing a set of unnervingly white teeth from within his charcoal-grey beard. "I think you'd need to be around for longer," he chuckled, "to truly know Lefty."

Father Petros added that, even for him, there was still a great deal that was unknown.

"Lefty isn't very religious, but I've still tried to earn his trust and get to know him in my role as village priest," Father Petros said.

His cheerful expression suddenly disappeared, his cheeks deflating as he gave a soul-wrenching sigh.

"I've failed entirely," he said gloomily. "Lefty may be the most honest person you'll ever meet, except when it comes to himself and his own history, which I know is littered with sin."

Lefty's many stories were often exaggerated. Manolis had always found this entertaining, but now that he stepped back, he saw how it might have annoyed some people who had to deal with it on a daily basis. Lefty's unfettered nature would have been frustrating to someone boxed in by responsibilities. As a charismatic rascal who ignored the norms of society, Lefty clearly had the potential to polarise. To some people, happiness was a burning car.

"So, what do you usually hunt?" Manolis asked directly.

Father Petros narrowed his eyes.

"Why do you ask?" he said slowly.

"Just curious. I've seen many animals here."

"Are you a hunter?"

"Me? No."

Father Petros tugged at his beard thoughtfully, regarded Manolis again.

"Well, it's mainly just rabbits," he eventually said. "And occasionally, the odd pheasant or pig. Nothing that is protected, though."

"Of course not."

"No brown bears or anything like that."

"No."

The two men went silent a moment, the frantic quacks of wild ducks filling the air.

"Of course, my favourite animal from around here is the lynx," Father Petros said.

"Lynxes? Really, you have those here?" Manolis said.

The priest nodded wisely. "I've only seen one once, in the late afternoon light. A chamois ran out into the open with a lynx in hot pursuit. It was like watching a nature documentary on TV. Lynxes are the ghosts of the forest – they're exceptionally rare. People have lived here for decades and never seen one, although experienced hunters can always tell a lynx kill from a fox or wolf."

"How's that?"

Father Petros stood back from the wall and stretched his leg. He rotated his ankle, winced lightly. Transferring the weight back to his walking stick, he relaxed again.

"Lynxes are clever. Whether it's an antelope or roe deer, a lynx will eat its kill over a number of days, covering up the carcass and returning to it twice a day. A lynx is methodical; it suffocates its prey or breaks its neck before it goes for the body's vulnerable parts. And then it's a gourmet, eating only the meat, never the skin, organs, bones or head."

"That's pretty clever," Manolis said. "And how long have you lived here?"

"Years," was all Father Petros said. He checked his watch. "And I'd love to stay and chat but I'm late for an appointment in Florina. I don't like to drive fast, especially with my foot the way it is."

As he hobbled away, he turned to Manolis, proposing dinner at Kostas's taverna the following night.

"I can tell you more then," Father Petros said. "Looking forward to it. See you."

6

At Kostas's taverna overlooking Great Prespa Lake, Father Petros and Manolis shared a meal as they watched the purpling sunset. By that hour, Manolis would normally have left for the day, wanting to avoid driving the sinuous mountain roads at dusk or in the dark. But this time, he made an exception.

It was a long, slow dinner of never-ending courses and plates that gradually overwhelmed the table. The night was warm and agreeable under a canopy of bright stars – a billion points of light – and the cooking was simple and uncomplicated. Manolis breathed deeply, filling his ragged lungs with summer air. The Greek oxygen seemed to agree with him, especially in the evenings, which had a velvety feel. The windows and doors were open and the ceiling fans were whirring. Father Petros was suitably late, which Kostas explained was normal for the priest. He ran on Greek time, and then some.

The evening began with gold-rimmed crystal glasses of grape-distilled raki as an aperitif. Manolis diluted his with water, causing it to turn milky-white like the louche of absinthe. It still set his mouth on fire. The men raised toasts to each other's health. Father Petros then blessed the meal and everyone crossed themselves multiple times from right to left in the Eastern Orthodox manner. Wearing a cloth hand-kerchief on his head as a makeshift chef's hat, Kostas also sat and ate, playing gracious host to the village's new arrival and the respected local clergyman. The depth of flavour in the food owed a debt to the quality of the produce, which was organically grown and locally sourced. As much as he had tried, Manolis had never been able to master Greek cuisine at home, even though it always seemed so simple: olive oil this, lemon juice that. But it wasn't he who was at fault; as Kostas said, it was the ingredients, the soil.

The taverna's decor played on the lakeside theme with delicate azure colours, faux fishing nets on the walls, and glossy plastic fish. There were foxed photographs in tarnished frames of armed men with thick, heroic moustaches wearing white fustanellas. A few disco balls twirled mournfully in the breeze. Soft *rebetiko* music – the woeful music of Greece's refugee and working class, of the displaced – emanated from a wall-mounted speaker. It was the soundtrack of the region.

Father Petros ate voraciously, piling more and more oily food onto his plate, letting the flavours meld and combine, and mopping it all up with dense white bread. Manolis thought he had the appetite of a man half his age. The priest explained that he was "stocking up" and probably wouldn't eat the next day. Manolis watched him slurp down half a dozen oysters in swift succession, relishing the warm burning in his throat from the brine.

Together, the three men talked about their lives, their backgrounds. Trying not to appear nervous, Manolis drank sparingly and watched his companions closely. There was sympathy and laughter, disagreement and argument in the typical Greek way. Kostas and his humble taverna were an obvious focus of conversation.

"It was a business that I inherited from my father," he said.

"And he always claims that his dad was a much better cook," added Father Petros, liquid fat glossing his lips and beard.

"Oh, stop it," Kostas said. "That's because he was. I've tried to recreate some of his recipes but I never get them right because he didn't write anything down."

Kostas's lamentations were met with a chorus of support and praise from his patrons for the delicious food, which elicited a small reflective smile. It made Manolis think again of his own dad, who once ran a restaurant in the city. Before that, soon after immigrating to Australia, he'd operated a milk bar in the country. Like the taverna in the village, the milk bar in Cobb was the focal point of the small outback town, where people gathered to eat, drink and gossip. But unlike the taverna, the milk bar was intended to be a temporary enterprise that would lead to something grander and more upmarket. Con had hoped that his only son would one day take over and run his restaurant, but all Manolis could manage was to wait tables for a few summers. He soon headed off to the local police academy for a career he considered more enthralling than roasted aubergine and vine leaves. It was a decision he'd never regretted, but he did ruminate on it from time to time, especially when he remembered all the unique recipes that were now buried in the ground with his dad.

Father Petros said that his father had taught him how to shoot and hunt. Unlike Kostas, he had been born on a tiny, overlooked island in the Aegean with more goats than people. Because of its similar lack of tourists, the Prespes always reminded the priest of his home.

"I'm especially drawn to the area by the water and the fishing, something I did throughout my youth and still love to this day," Father Petros said. He swallowed a spoonful of gooey fava bean dip.

The priest admitted that he still yearned for the salty tang of the Aegean in his nostrils, but said that his heart now belonged to the mountains.

"The islands and mountains couldn't be more different, though. The first is matriarchal and by the sea, the other patriarchal and in the clouds. But in both, people and nature are bound together."

The fishing in the Prespa Lakes was also bountiful, which pleased Father Petros immensely.

"There's trout, giant carp, bream, gudgeon, tench and more dirty eels than your heart could desire," he said.

"Aren't some of those protected species?" Manolis asked.

"Yes, and I toss those back. The carp are still regenerating. Many years ago, they used the wrong mosquito pesticide and poisoned large numbers of fish."

While he found fishing calming and meditative, he still preferred to go hunting for game.

"Both have the thrill of the chase, but hunting a wild animal is so much more exhilarating than just sitting on the shore and lazily dropping a line in the water," Father Petros said. "With a land animal, you're stalking, analysing, anticipating, adjusting and readjusting. With fish, it's all unseen, invisible, beneath the surface of the water."

He turned to Manolis. "One day soon I'll take you hunting," he said, baring his food-encrusted teeth. "We'll shoot wild rabbits and pigs and Kostas will cook them for us to eat here the very same night."

Manolis chewed his mouthful of bread carefully and swallowed. After a while, he said:

"I actually don't eat meat. And I'm rather fond of animals."

Father Petros frowned. But as the thought settled, his expression grew into a smile before it finally became a hearty laugh.

"I thought so," he said. "I noticed you avoiding all those delicious meats that Kostas prepared."

"The *mezethes* are vegetarian, and there are so many that there's no risk I'll go hungry," Manolis said.

He smiled gratefully at Kostas, who gave a gentle nod.

Manolis turned back to Father Petros. "As for hunting, as you may have guessed, I'm not a huge fan," he said. "But I'm aware that animals like rabbits carry disease and are destructive to crops. So maybe, just this once, I'll tag along and watch you in action."

For Manolis it was a chance to observe a man with bloodlust in his eyes up close. It was a mental image that was difficult to reconcile with a man of God who traditionally espoused a message of peace and goodwill to all living creatures.

"That's fine," said the priest. "Each to his own." He chomped down hard on a grilled octopus tentacle, savouring its fat-suckered saltiness.

Both hosts confirmed Manolis's impressions of his parents' homeland as a country blessed with immense natural beauty and warm, generous people, but with poor prospects for growth and prosperity.

It was the main reason why so many Greeks had emigrated over the previous century, including Manolis's parents. Not because they didn't love the old country; they simply didn't see a future there.

"I just love this wretched country too much, future or no future," Father Petros said.

Throughout the meal, Manolis couldn't help but notice the young waitress, who seemed to wear a permanent scowl. Kostas introduced her as Roze. Manolis smiled and offered his hand in greeting, and Roze shook it nonchalantly before rushing back to the kitchen, her jet-black ponytail swinging as she walked. It brushed against the nape of her neck, which bore a small tattoo of a cherry-red rose. She had a second tattoo around her wrist with lettering Manolis couldn't quite make out. She wore classical Grecian sandals with open toes and leather straps that spidered up her pale legs. Her ankles were slender, her toenails painted pomegranate pink.

"She's from Albania," Kostas said.

"How long has she worked with you?" Manolis asked.

By now, Kostas was alternating swigs from a bottle of retsina with bites from a cold, raw cucumber. One served as fire, the other as extinguisher.

"Only a few months. She came in the spring with the warmer weather. There's an endless stream of ethnic Albanian migrants who seek a better life in Greece, with many crossing the border and looking for work."

Watching her deliver and clear plates of food, Manolis noticed that Roze was eavesdropping attentively on the conversation. Taking a sip of his after-dinner coffee, Manolis complimented its flavour, which was intense and balanced. Kostas quickly credited Roze for being such an excellent barista. She fired Manolis a rare smile of appreciation and silently cleared the remaining plates. He thought her eyes held a degree of mystery and misfortune.

The villagers came across as self-reliant and a little eccentric. With such a collection of strong personalities, there was also a noticeable tension in the air. In the course of the conversation, Manolis was careful to conceal his true profession and instead recounted a fake history of his life that he'd prepared. He'd grown up in Thessaloniki before moving to Australia with his parents, where he'd met Stavros. Both families then returned to live in Greece around the same time, and he and Stavros had stayed in close contact ever since. Manolis was divorced, a father of one, both of which were true, although his son was younger than he claimed. He'd learned his trade in Australia and worked for many years on sunburnt building sites, but he was now semi-retired and was his own boss doing small jobs when he pleased. He was helping Stavros out as a favour.

Unfortunately, neither Stavros nor Father Petros was familiar with anyone named Poppy who matched the description of Manolis's aunt. This was dispiriting: by virtue of his position, Father Petros would have known almost everyone in the region, while Stavros was familiar with the residents of Florina. Perhaps Manolis should have asked his mother.

"I guess she could have married," Manolis said. "Changed her surname."

Fortunately, discussion of Lefty came easily, since his disappearance represented a significant event in such a small village. Manolis still hadn't seen many residents. His hosts described some of the villagers that Lefty regularly looked after in their own homes, how they all loved him and now missed both his care and his company.

"Since Lefty disappeared, we've found it hard to sleep at night," Kostas said, rubbing his red-rimmed eyes.

"Because you're scared?" Manolis asked. "You're worried that something similar may happen to you?"

Father Petros laughed, his big round belly bouncing against his thighs.

"Not really, no," he said. "What do we possibly have here that people would want to harm us for?"

"It's more because we think of Lefty, some of the last things he said, what he did," said Kostas. "We toss them about in our minds in the hope of working out what may have happened to him." He helped himself to a toothpick and began to pick away at his molars.

"We may be old but we Prespians are built tough," Father Petros said, puffing out his chest. "Our lives haven't been easy so there's very little that scares us now. Not disease or death, let alone attack and abduction."

Manolis contemplated his black coffee, the delicate *kaimaki* foam on the surface that was still holding its form, thick and even across the surface of the cup. It was the sign of a quality brew and an experienced coffee-maker. His *komboloi* sat comfortably in his hand, and he flicked them back and forth every so often with a light clickety-clack. The worry beads added to his cover, his credibility as a native of Greece. Both Father Petros and Kostas had already complimented him on the set, admiring their shape and distinctive colour. Manolis was interested to notice that he preferred to play with the *komboloi* using his non-dominant left hand.

"So, what were some of the last things Lefty said and did before he disappeared?" Manolis asked carefully. It was frustrating to be working undercover; it limited his investigative capacity.

Father Petros and Kostas looked at each other dubiously for a few tense seconds before averting their eyes and shaking their heads.

"He had a few whiskies like usual, told a few stories, maybe even a dirty joke, and went home at his regular hour," Kostas said.

"I wasn't at the taverna that night but I'd seen him earlier in the day," said Father Petros. "He told me he'd gone fishing that morning with Elias but they hadn't caught anything. And he complained of having a stiff back, but that was nothing unusual."

Given Lefty's sleeping arrangements, it was unsurprising that his back hurt.

"Wait, who's Elias?" Manolis asked.

Kostas rolled the toothpick from one side of his mouth to the other. Father Petros helped himself to a second *kourabies* shortbread biscuit, his fingertips stained snowy white with powdered sugar like cocaine.

"He and Lefty are, how do you say, business associates," Father Petros said.

Kostas fired a stern look his way. "Should we really talk about this?"

"Why not? It's common knowledge."

Kostas muttered something under his breath and took another sharp swig of retsina.

"What is?" Manolis repeated. "Who's Elias?"

Manolis's village hosts nodded conspiratorially. Elias was the local border guard with whom Lefty often went fishing in the lake. They were friends, but their relationship went further.

"Lefty would use the lake to smuggle black-market goods across the Albanian and North Macedonian borders and sell them for a profit," Kostas said. "He was blasé about the borders and often cut across them in a small motorboat late at night. It was fairly harmless. If he was seen from one of the watchtowers on the lake's shores, he would bribe the border police by giving them a cut of the profits. The good old *fakelaki*. And the Greek guard he did the most business with was Elias."

"I've never liked this arrangement," Father Petros said, licking his sticky fingers clean.

"It was harmless," said Kostas.

"No, it wasn't. They were companions in sin."

"You're no saint . . ."

Manolis felt the need to interject, his tone placatory. "So Elias helped facilitate Lefty's sojourns into Albania and North Macedonia by letting him pass freely?" he asked.

"Yes," Kostas said. "Police boats normally intercept anyone seen crossing the lake's international borders. But when Elias is distracted, disinterested, or out having a smoke, many boats still get through."

The news only confirmed what Manolis largely suspected, although the extent of Lefty's smuggling suggested something more complex than a one-man operation. It explained how Lefty was able to live, even as an invisible: he had a source of income, albeit irregular and ill-gotten. The enterprise opened up a whole new world of secret underground dealings that might explain what had happened to him. And while Manolis had some experience of organised crime in Australia, the prospect of navigating a murky Balkan underworld did not greatly appeal. Manolis wondered why Stavros hadn't shared such a significant detail before.

"Useless Greek police," Manolis scoffed, trying to fit in. "Always so corrupt. I can't tell you how many times I've paid off traffic cops in Thessaloniki to avoid speeding fines, and parking inspectors to avoid tickets."

The villagers laughed and clinked their glasses in mock celebration. "The *fakelaki* is alive and well in Greece!" beamed Kostas. Manolis shook his head lightly in dismay.

"What kind of goods was Lefty smuggling?" he asked innocently.

Manolis expected to hear about alcohol or cigarettes or designer clothes. They all sounded relatively harmless, but Manolis suddenly imagined the clothes as mafia fakes, and the alcohol and cigarettes as dangerous counterfeits, spiked with additives and poison. He prayed it wasn't guns or drugs or trafficked sex workers. Manolis's face was numb with horror. It was possible that he was among accessories to major crimes.

"You name it, Lefty could get it," Father Petros said. He twirled his long moustache, then quickly added: "Apparently so, anyway."

Manolis let the words hang between them. He sat absorbed in his own thoughts, gently rubbing his worry beads. The lake now appeared calm and reflective under the radiant full moon, like polished glass. At other times it appeared turbulent, simmering with a bubbling energy, roiling with a schizophrenia that seemed to stem from its secretive depths. There were tiny villages across the water, and every single one of them most likely harboured its own set of secrets. Manolis could make out a few muted lights on the far shore and wondered whether Lefty was perhaps staring back at him from his own resplendent dinner table with friends.

Could Elias and Lefty have fallen out over a smuggling deal? Such disagreements were possible – probable, even – in the criminal world. Perhaps Lefty had had a run-in with another guard who was unfamiliar with his operation and somehow had a conscience? Or maybe a villager had grown tired of Lefty's activities and paid him back for being unpatriotic?

"There were stories of black-market goods dumped at the bottom of the lake for scuba divers to retrieve," Kostas said. "That was one way of smuggling things across the border without being seen. At times, even the government did it."

"Sounds sophisticated," said Manolis.

"Too sophisticated for Lefty, though," Kostas said. "The lake is deep, it would take an expert diver with oxygen tanks to go down there."

"But then, I wouldn't put anything past Lefty," Father Petros said. "He'd find a way to do it, and if he couldn't, he'd know of someone who could."

"He wouldn't need to do anything like that if he had Elias working with him," Manolis said. He needed somehow to track down this shady character.

"If there's one industry in which Greece has always been strong, it's shipping and trade," Father Petros said. "Lefty saw himself as merely living up to a rich tradition."

Kostas offered cigarettes; only Father Petros accepted. Roze had disappeared.

"Father, you mentioned that some residents don't like Lefty," Manolis said. "Who did you mean?"

The priest and taverna owner again exchanged furtive glances, then replied, almost in unison:

"Sofia."

She was Lefty's cantankerous old neighbour who had attracted particular attention from locals given her history of animosity with Lefty.

"Sofia and Lefty have argued for years," Kostas said. "It's usually been over minor issues, trivial matters, things that the rest of us dismiss as Lefty's mischievous streak and love of practical jokes."

"The problem is that Sofia's always taken them more seriously," Father Petros said. "She feels tormented by Lefty."

Manolis wondered what Lefty could have done. Had he thrown eggs at her door, left dog faeces on her doorstep, or toilet papered her trees? It sounded like the way unruly children behaved towards a neighbour who complained of excessive noise. Did kids even do that stuff anymore?

Kostas described how Sofia sold home-made meals to tourists who visited Glikonero and even minced her own meat.

"Out of loyalty to me, Lefty tried to turn customers away from Sofia's food by describing it as disgusting and poisonous and directing them to my taverna instead."

Kostas was grateful for the extra business and never tried to stop Lefty.

"You should have," Father Petros said.

Kostas retorted that Sofia's mince was of questionable quality and had never been forensically tested.

"But it wasn't just that," Father Petros said. "It was worse."

Stained vultures, blowflies and the stench of rotting flesh were not uncommon in the mountains. But to Lefty, these were signs of opportunity: one man's roadkill is another man's practical joke. Lefty had often taken dead animals that he'd found on the road and left them in Sofia's yard for a laugh. On one occasion, he'd even cut off the tail of a dead wild donkey and tossed it on Sofia's doorstep. On hearing that, Manolis felt a familiar kick in his bloodstream, a quickening he couldn't help. It was the thought of an animal being eviscerated, disrespected, even after it was dead; it registered like a deep internal pain. Lefty's behaviour must have made Sofia feel victimised and humiliated.

"Cruelty to animals is shocking," Manolis said, swallowing his rage.

"I agree," said Kostas. "It crossed a line."

Father Petros stayed quiet and drew forcefully on his cigarette, making it glow lava-orange.

Above all others, Sofia was the resident the villagers believed was involved in Lefty's disappearance. The recent arrival in Glikonero of Zain, a Syrian refugee who worked as Sofia's live-in handyman and gardener, only added to the likelihood.

"Wait until you see Zain," Kostas said. "He's young and strong and muscular. Rumour has it that he was once an amateur boxing champion in Syria."

Father Petros stubbed out his cigarette with a satisfied smile and vicious twist.

"Rumour also has it that Sofia paid Zain to kill Lefty."

"You definitely can't trust Zain," Kostas said.

"How can you have any faith in someone who broke the law to get here?" asked Father Petros.

"And who steals from peasants," Kostas added. "We've lost clothes from clothes lines, fruit and vegetables from gardens, even chickens and pigs from backyards."

Manolis crossed his arms and tilted his head slightly. The evening had been enlightening, but it was getting late and he was dreading the drive back to Florina with weak headlights and impotent brakes. Just then, the bouzouki music stopped abruptly, the CD having ended. Cicadas chirruped like castanets from the nearby shore. Marsh frogs croaked, and a Eurasian eagle owl hooted in a nearby tree.

Manolis couldn't put his finger on it, but he was starting to feel decidedly suspicious and uncomfortable around these people.

"Rumours, eh?" he said, forcing a tired smile. "That's good to know. It'll give me something to think about as I settle in."

7

Manolis returned to Glikonero the next day. He still hadn't seen Lefty's neighbours. Sofia lived in the next block, separated from Lefty by about twenty metres and an impenetrable stone wall. There was no noise from inside her house, which might have been down to its solid construction. Was she even home? There was also no sign of young Zain.

Manolis approached the house with an excuse at the ready. Coming over to say hello seemed trite and might have attracted suspicion from a stranger not used to visitors. But asking to borrow some coffee was believable and invited conversation.

To get his bearings, Manolis circled the outside of the house. The garden was sparse and boasted many dry or dead trees and plants. For a gardener, Zain didn't appear to have much of a green thumb. There was a shed and a cosy sitting area with outdoor furniture faded by the sun and mottled by the rain. An axe was embedded in a chopping block outside the shed, a healthy woodpile next to it. Manolis tried to peek in through the house's small and grubby porthole windows but could see nothing. In the end, he climbed the six well-worn steps that led up to the back entrance. Having observed his mum struggling to get around, Manolis knew the elderly weren't very fond of steps. He stopped when he saw that Sofia's wooden door was splattered in thick ribbons of bright-red paint. Taking a step back, he examined it. It looked like blood.

Manolis knocked firmly on the hefty door and waited. No response. He tried again, waited . . . Still nothing. Eventually, noticing that the door was in its natural state of being unlocked, Manolis entered. As he walked through the neat galley kitchen, he called out. He didn't want to startle a senior citizen with a weak heart, and nor did he want to be mistaken for an intruder and be met with a shotgun to the face.

"Hello? Is anyone here . . . ?"

Moving carefully through the rooms, Manolis kept calling out so as not to frighten Sofia. When he finally found her, she looked quite calm and unsurprised to see him. It was a reaction that Manolis found disconcerting.

Sofia was sitting in a shabby armchair in the far corner of the living room, a boxy old TV blizzarding with the volume down. Her legs were hidden by a crocheted blanket, and a lambswool shawl was tossed over her shoulders. It seemed excessive for early summer, but Manolis recognised it as a feature of old age: feeling cold, even during the hottest months. In Con's final days, he had taken to running the electric heater on full bore throughout the day despite the mild autumn weather.

"Who are you? Have you come to make me disappear as well?" Sofia asked Manolis plainly. She spoke with a faint rasp.

Manolis took a moment to scan his surroundings and take in the room. It was unlike any he'd ever seen before, and it disturbed him. As Stavros had warned him, it was full of artefacts – flags, brooches, insignia, badges, armbands – emblazoned with a swastika or Nazi eagle or both. Manolis felt a hot flash of tension in his forehead, momentary vertigo, as if the walls were closing in. He tried to look away but his eye only caught more blood-soaked items. It was like walking into a grotesque museum exhibition. All the while, small, grey-haired Sofia sat motionless, awaiting an answer to her gentle enquiry.

Leaning against a wooden chest of drawers, Manolis tried to speak but found only dust in his throat. Eventually, his voice croaky, he intro-duced himself as the labourer working next door and asked if he could borrow some coffee.

Sofia harrumphed and said: "You mean, next door, at the devil's house?"

A tirade of vitriol followed, as if the old woman took Manolis for Lefty. She spat through a mouth devoid of teeth save for two gold incisors that caught the pale light as she spoke.

"I swear, that man is Lucifer himself. What sinful business have you with him? What vile and disgusting act has he sent you to inflict on me now? Don't you people realise I'm just a helpless old lady?"

Holding up his hands in mock surrender, Manolis tried to calm Sofia before pretending not to know of the history between her and Lefty. All he was guilty of doing was agreeing to help his friend Stavros work on his house, and he barely knew Lefty.

"May I?" Manolis gestured at a spare armchair, asking if he could sit. When Sofia nodded, he moved aside a pile of yellow newspapers. The chair squeaked under his weight. It was lumpy and bore strange stains.

"What are you talking about?" Manolis asked. "What kinds of things has Lefty done? Did he throw the paint at your door?"

"I don't know. Probably," Sofia snapped. "But that was different from what he usually did to me. The paint was because of Zain, not me."

Her gaze drifted to the wall, her eyes seeming to settle on a large grey imperial eagle. It was as if she were communicating telepathically with the bird, which looked over its right shoulder in Manolis's direction as if it were somehow scrutinising him and relaying messages back to its owner.

"Why Zain?" Manolis asked.

Sofia looked back at him with cold blue eyes.

"You really have no idea what Lefty has done to me?" she asked, her tone acerbic.

Manolis shook his head. "I don't know a thing," he said in his sincerest voice. "All I know is that he's missing and that's why I'm here, to do the work that he was supposed to have done on the house next door. That's it. I have no allegiance to him or anyone else in Glikonero."

Sofia didn't take her eyes off her visitor.

"The fact that that man did nothing to maintain the house that he was squatting in speaks volumes about his poor character," she said.

Manolis leaned forward. "I'm sorry to hear that you and Lefty have had a troubled past. I've always found him to be friendly and agreeable, but I can't say I know him well. Can I ask what he's done to you, or to Zain? I may be able to help . . ."

Sofia kept staring at Manolis intently, her pupils darting, looking for signs of honesty, of trustworthiness, or an absence of treachery at least. Manolis lowered his eyelids and softened his cocoa-brown eyes. Sofia finally blinked and looked away. With a long sigh, she summoned the energy to dredge her memory and recount some of the horrors that Lefty had inflicted. She spoke rapidly, as if ripping off a sticky bandage, trying to minimise the pain. She blinked incessantly, as if something was irritating her eyes, and repeatedly cleared her throat.

Sofia confirmed the stories told to Manolis at the taverna, about Lefty telling people that her food was poisonous, and the roadkill left to rot in the sun at her door. There was more, though.

"Lefty's behaviour got so bad that I once had to summon the police in Florina and complain. He had sabotaged my business, abused my customers, put crushed glass under their tyres, poisoned my plants, stolen clothes from my clothes line, run off with my outdoor umbrella and destroyed my garden furniture."

She had asked that a restraining order or similar be placed on Lefty to keep him away from her, even though he was still her neighbour.

"That's a serious move," Manolis said.

Sofia scoffed. "No regrets," she said haughtily.

"And what did the police do?"

She cackled, her voice sounding weathered and ancient, her blue eyes glittering.

"Nothing. They came all the way from Florina, asked some questions, ate some food, drank some coffee, smoked some cigarettes, and eventually gave Lefty a warning. They told me they could do no more without proof that he was responsible. You want proof? Go outside and look at my yard, or ask anyone in town."

The police hadn't mentioned their visit to Manolis. But then again, they were of the opinion that Lefty wasn't missing, and weren't interested in questioning anyone.

"And what about the paint on your door?" Manolis asked.

"Meant to be blood," Sofia said. "Thrown to make a point. Because I've taken in Zain, I'm seen as siding with the enemy."

A tabby cat covered in patches of matted and filthy fur appeared from behind the wood stove in the corner. It picked its way through the room, mewing. Sofia ignored it. Manolis gave it a friendly pat, which left his hand covered in a greasy residue.

"But I must apologise for my rudeness," Sofia suddenly said. "I haven't offered you anything. Would you like a drink, a coffee, or something to eat? I have some fresh-baked *paximathia*, made with oranges grown nearby . . ."

Manolis noted the rapid change in her demeanour, which again sent a shiver through him. He wondered if Sofia had her full mental faculties.

Manolis loved the hard, dry bread that Maria had once baked, their house filling with its spicy aroma. In Greece, it was a food traditionally eaten by farmers in the fields or the military in warfare. It was also served at wakes, regarded as the most appropriate sweet for sombre occasions.

Sofia went to stand, only to promptly sit back down again with a light whump. She looked momentarily startled and clutched her forehead.

"Are you alright?" Manolis said, standing out of concern.

"My blood pressure," Sofia said slowly. "It drops when I get up too fast after sitting for a long time, so I feel dizzy."

"Then please sit. I'm fine, I don't need anything to eat or drink, though thank you for the offer. Do you need some water?"

"That would help."

Manolis fetched a tumbler from the kitchen and filled it from the tap. The pipes hammered with the pressure. Sofia's arthritic fingers trembled as she took the glass in both liver-spotted hands and downed it in three swift gulps. Manolis saw the bone through her papery skin. Her wrists were a grey estuary of veins.

"Thank you," she said. "I feel better now."

She described how she had felt tormented by Lefty, and that she merely wanted peace and quiet.

"It's why we live up here in the Prespes. We are Greece's misfits, the descendants of war and exile. We are used to being left alone to fight for ourselves. If I wanted to sit in my house and be annoyed all day, I would move to Athens or Thessaloniki."

A framed photograph on the wall behind Sofia showed a dashing young couple standing by the lake. The moustachioed man was in uniform, the woman in a net-covered hat and elegant summer dress. Neither was smiling for the camera.

"Is that you?" Manolis asked.

She glanced at the photograph. "With my husband, when we were younger."

Sofia had been married for forty-five years, and widowed for about a decade. She'd not had any children.

"Not a day goes by when I don't miss my Dimitrios," she said wistfully. "He used to say that the dead must go to a good place because no-one ever comes back. But I can't help but feel lonely without him."

Manolis paused. Judging Sofia to be around the same age as his mum, he imagined she might have known his aunt. Perhaps they were even friends, shared cups of coffee and gossip. But just like Father Petros and Stavros, Sofia didn't remember an older lady named Poppy. Manolis sighed. Between his aunt and Lefty, he felt like he was trying to find a pair of ghosts. Given what his aunt had endured in Australia, Manolis wouldn't be surprised if she hadn't wanted to be found. And given what his family had gone through, he wondered whether the past was better left alone. After all, Con seemed to have lived a virtuous life after making his one big mistake.

Aware that the entire village blamed her for Lefty's disappearance because of their ongoing feud, Sofia had withdrawn into the safety of her home. She now had only Zain to keep her company, with the Sunday church service as her sole weekly excursion. The accusations that she'd somehow harmed Lefty ignored the fact that she was riddled with arthritis.

"I couldn't hurt a small dog, let alone a grown man," she said.

Manolis turned in his chair to face Sofia more directly. "So why do you think Lefty targeted you? He never mentioned you to me."

Sofia shrugged her bony shoulders beneath her shawl.

"Boredom, I suspect," she said. "Because he thought he was being funny. Either that or because I called him out."

"Called him out? On what?"

"On whatever foul rubbish he was smuggling across the border with that other dishonest bastard, Elias."

Manolis paused. Sofia looked at him with unblinking eyes.

"Which was . . . ?" he asked.

"Drugs," she said sharply. "If you want a reason for why Lefty's gone, I would bet it's because he was mixed up in that business, and something's finally caught up with him. Nothing good ever comes from drugs. All they do is bad. They attract bad people and bring bad outcomes."

Nodding gently, the policeman in Manolis could only agree. Drugs were, after all, the reason he found himself in the Prespes in the first place.

"Do you know what kind of drugs?" he asked.

Sofia shook her head. "No, but I could smell them from here, and they were nasty."

Even with his highly tuned nose for the illicit, Manolis hadn't noticed any suspicious odours at Lefty's house. And the smell of drugs like cannabis and cocaine often hung around for sustained periods.

Sofia pulled her shawl more snugly around her neck and shoulders. She looked like she was ready for an afternoon nap. Manolis watched her carefully. Could this frail old woman really have been responsible for Lefty's disappearance? To that end, there was still one factor he needed to explore.

"I haven't seen Zain at all," Manolis said. "I'd like to say hello. Which is his room?"

"He's staying out the back in my woodshed," she said.

Manolis arched his eyebrows with interest. "Oh really? He's not here in the house with you?"

"Certainly not." Sofia looked offended, her eyes narrowing, her mouth curving down on one side. "I couldn't have him staying here in the house with me. *People would talk*. And anyway, it's quite cosy out in the shed."

Manolis smiled. "Of course." He was familiar with the Greek sense of shame. It was especially strong in elderly women, including his mother. Public perception was paramount, it mattered more than anything, even at the expense of personal happiness. It was a mentality that had shaped Manolis's childhood.

"Could I meet Zain sometime? Where is he now?"

"Out collecting firewood, I'm afraid," Sofia said. "We need to start stockpiling for winter."

Manolis recalled the healthy woodpile in the yard. "When will he be back?"

"I don't know, he's usually gone all day."

She was adamant that Zain had nothing to do with Lefty's disappearance.

"He's just a boy, an innocent," she said. "He couldn't possibly do anything like that."

Manolis considered Lefty's neighbour and long-standing nemesis. Sofia came across as unflustered and honest and open. She made no effort to hide her dislike for Lefty, admitting that they argued constantly, which everyone in Glikonero knew. In a small mountain village where sound tended to carry, shouts followed by a sudden quietness would have been noticed.

"If something had happened to Lefty, someone would have heard it," said Sofia. "But no-one has reported hearing anything the night he disappeared. Don't you find that strange?"

"It's certainly unexpected," Manolis said.

Sofia flashed her gold incisors.

"Like I've always said, I don't know where he is. But I'm also not sad that he's gone."

8

Manolis was now walking further each day, heading deeper into the rugged countryside and steep hills on the southern and eastern sides of Great Prespa Lake. Stavros had lent him a pair of thick-soled hiking boots and sturdy aluminium walking poles, which helped Manolis wander further and longer into the afternoons. He was feeling fitter and stronger, sleeping more soundly during the star-studded night and waking with renewed vigour and vitality. He had expected to gain a few kilos, as always, from the country's luscious food and pastries. But that was no longer a risk, one positive that came from his holiday being sidetracked.

Manolis had yet to come across the elusive Zain. He'd even banged on his shed door twice and found no-one at home. Zain seemed to be out all day, only returning to Glikonero at dusk when Manolis drove away. Manolis had begun to wonder whether the timings might not be coincidental.

Walking along one of the many hiking trails that criss-crossed the region, Manolis became acquainted with the goats and dwarf cattle that roamed freely across old, fallow fields. All were wary of him, just as Manolis was of the region, whose isolation was more apparent still when he was out in the open. At times, he felt the high cornflower sky could crush him. A red deer, a stag with branched antlers, stood in a clearing. The grand herbivore exuded an air of elegance and authority as it assessed the unfamiliar visitor. The air was rich with the tart-spicy smell of citrus, of oranges and lemons that had fallen from trees and started to decompose. Traditional cairns marked some of the wending trails, their stones delicately balanced without the help of mortar. According to a Greek myth, the first cairn marked the burial site of Hermes, the god of overland travel.

Deeper into the lonely hills, there were beech forests, quiet and immense and foreboding. Sunlight pinpricked through the trees, green and sweet. In the luminous shade, the leaves appeared as transparent as membranes. It was there that Manolis identified something more sinister – fresh bear tracks, huge paw imprints in the earth, each individual claw cutting into the soft soil like a knife. Nearby, there were large blood-red danger signs warning the public of natural threats: brown bears, wild boar, European wildcats, grey wolves, water buffalo. The signs were riddled with bullet holes. Manolis didn't know what he might do should he ever come across such an animal. Avoid eye contact, make a lot of noise to scare the animal, try to appear big, play dead . . . ?

Stumbling over the remains of churches and abandoned ghost villages, Manolis examined the vestiges of former societies and tried to picture the daily routines, the harsh but simple lives. He could very well have had kin there. Over the lake, panoramic views swept across to North Macedonia and Albania. Back home in Australia, Manolis's city apartment had extensive views of a six-lane highway from a balcony as wide as a bathroom towel.

From time to time he saw groups of people walking in the distant hills. Manolis couldn't tell if they were fellow hikers, backpackers or tourists, or the latest migrants sneaking into Greece across its insecure borders. They walked slowly and with purpose.

Looking out over the lake and its illusory gleam, Manolis contemplated the water – its depth, its temperature – and how many people might have drowned there over the years. Manolis had dredged decomposing bodies from waterways that were much less chaotic than Great Prespa Lake. From the water's edge, the currents appeared capricious and mercurial, a place of mysterious vortexes, monster carp and coiled eels. Kostas claimed that he used to swim in the lake when he was younger but always had an ominous feeling of something lurking underneath, with eddies that dragged you under. Would the lake hold dangerous animals such as freshwater crocodiles, bull sharks and stingrays? Manolis racked his brain. The waterways he knew back home came with death rolls, razor teeth and stinger venom. Here, a straightforward drowning in such treacherous waters was more likely, particularly if someone had had too much to drink. And Lefty liked a drink.

The western shore of the lake was bordered by cliffs, while the eastern side had flat, desolate beaches. Manolis could see what looked like abandoned hermitages on the cliffs; he wanted to have a closer look, but that would take time and probably need a local guide. Maybe Lefty was hiding out up there for whatever reason, perhaps simply for a change of scenery, a more grandiose view, a place to meditate. Manolis didn't put it past him.

Manolis continued to explore the countryside, often stopping to eat a handful of walnuts or cherries from his backpack or read a chapter of his novel or play with his father's *komboloi*. Con's absence had been felt acutely by Manolis, who hoped that reconnecting with his dad's homeland would bring him closer to his memory, despite its lingering taint. It was an overwhelming attachment, a need for Manolis to return to his family's origins and feel the resonance of place. Now in her eighties and too frail to travel, Maria had stayed at home in Australia, which suited her adult son just fine since he needed a break from her too. This return to Greece was also an attempt by Manolis to understand his background in the hope that he might avoid repeating mistakes and becoming a prisoner of his past. His marriage was one mistake. His dad's wretched memory was another. The street kid he shot was a third. He didn't want his own fatherhood to go down the same gurgler.

Sitting on a smooth rock, Manolis was forced to close his book when a flock of sheep came bounding by, their jaunty meadow bells jangling gently, their cotton-white fleeces dazzling in the afternoon sun. Manolis savoured the sight and only wished he had young Christos by his side so he could tousle his hair and share the purity of the moment. But that thought quickly evaporated when he was confronted by the menacing sight of a large snarling dog.

It wasn't quite a brown bear, but the animal appeared just as ferocious. And to the dog, Manolis also posed a threat – or, at least, to its defenceless, vulnerable flock. The presence of big, deadly predators such as bears and wolves had changed such dogs. They had evolved to be more muscular than ordinary sheepdogs, and vastly more aggressive. The breed was unrecognisable to Manolis. It appeared to be some kind of mongrel.

The dog closed in. It bared sharp white fangs to tear into his flesh, saliva dripped from its jaw, and a growl seemed to come from deep within its belly. Manolis was rooted to the spot. Moving a muscle in any direction would only cause the beast to react, and react instinctively. It was like having a gun pointed at his head, the trigger being squeezed by an unstable, impulsive assailant. Whenever he'd previously encountered an attack dog, it had been in an urban environment. Manolis had either had police backup and been able to extricate himself, or he'd had a tranquilliser gun. Out alone in the open, neither of those were options.

After a few tense moments, Manolis forced himself to relax his vocal cords and let his words fall like treacle, slow and reassuring.

"Easy, mate. Whoa, boy. Just relax. I'm not your foe. I'm a friend."

He drew on his police training in how to deal with people having panic attacks or mental episodes. They could often only hear the tone of someone's voice, not the actual words said. A calm, soothing voice was vital.

The creature kept snarling, took a determined step forward. A cold trickle of sweat snaked down Manolis's spine. With his eyes fixed on the dog, he placed his walking poles gently to one side and raised his hands above his head, his fingers unclenched, palms exposed in an open and obvious surrender. The gesture was involuntary, impulsive, a reaction to the threat. But the dog wasn't convinced and took another step forward. It barked forcefully as if Manolis wasn't obeying its orders, and continued to growl with a savage air. Around them, the lambs continued to graze on the lush green slope, oblivious to the tense stand-off that was taking place.

Since the dog was ignoring his white flag, Manolis needed to try something else. With great care, he took a small step backwards, paused, then took another, and another. The only option was to finesse his way to safety. He couldn't outrun the mongrel.

"Easy, mate. Take it easy, boy. I'm not gonna hurt you. I'll just be leaving now."

But the dog had seen enough. It broke into a swift stride with Manolis in its cross hairs. Regretting the decision to abandon his walking poles, which had at least offered an ounce of protection, Manolis had time only to turn, crouch and brace himself for a vicious attack.

A piercing wolf whistle cut through the air like a guillotine. Manolis opened his eyes, stood up and saw a faithful canine sitting to attention, its owner walking towards Manolis with a leisurely gait.

It was an elderly shepherd supported by a long crook. The man was clean-shaven, his alabaster hair thick and woolly, as if to match his healthy flock; it fluffed out from beneath the brim of his mariner's cap. His lips were thin, surrounded by soft creases that disappeared when he smiled. Tipping his cap with old-fashioned, gentlemanly elegance, he introduced himself as Angelo.

"And this is my loyal companion Apollo. He accompanies me wherever I go. I'm sorry if he scared you, he's trained to protect the sheep. I've had too many taken over the years by wolves and foxes, and even by bears."

Standing to his full height of just over six feet, Manolis felt the adrenaline drilling through his body. He steadied himself to return the man's handshake, noticing how small his hands were and that his grip was a little weak. Angelo had a faraway look in his eyes as if he were more connected to the past than to the present.

"That's OK," Manolis said. "He was just doing his job. Good boy." He resisted the urge to pet the animal who now was sitting by his owner's side, panting lightly and dutifully awaiting further instructions. Manolis took a sip of water from his canteen to remoisten his mouth and calm his Morse code heartbeats.

Angelo lived on the shores of Great Prespa Lake on the outskirts of Glikonero. Manolis must have walked past his house a few times but couldn't picture it.

"It's somewhat hidden, tucked away behind our overgrown garden, which seems only to get bigger each year," Angelo said.

"And you live there by yourself?" Manolis asked. He was more comfortable about asking direct questions now he'd seen how willing the locals were to talk. He attributed it to the quieter rural surroundings; in a metropolis, people were more guarded and less friendly. But it may have been due to the more welcoming nature of Greeks.

"I live with my sister Anna," Angelo replied. "Just the two of us, like an old married couple, bickering and driving the other crazy. But the truth is, after all this time, we probably couldn't live without each other."

Failing to recognise Manolis as a familiar face, Angelo went on to describe the region as being more dangerous than most outsiders realised, and expressed concern as to whether Manolis should be out there by himself.

"There are wild donkeys and boar, bears and wolves and foxes, deer with sharp antlers, and even snakes."

"And sheepdogs," Manolis said.

He glanced at Apollo as he did so. Apollo wagged his tail at a friendly, contented pace. Angelo laughed, which came out more as a high-pitched cackle.

"But it's not just the dangers and peculiarities of the wildlife," he warned. "It's also the landscape. There are deep caves and mineshafts, and even a few sinkholes. Easy enough to fall into, and it could take years before anyone found you. And if you're really, really unlucky, there are some unexploded mines buried in the ground, left over from the war. People come here to enjoy themselves, to experience nature and explore the area, which is welcomed. But they still need to be careful. This isn't a holiday resort, it's a wild area."

"Thank you, I will be. What's that you're carrying?" Manolis gestured at Angelo's other hand, the non-crook one, which held some kind of shiny wand. "Is that a metal detector?"

Angelo nodded. "Well spotted," he said.

"For landmines?"

"No."

"No . . . ?"

Angelo studied Manolis's face a while, as if assessing his trustworthiness. After a few seconds, he relaxed his own features and said:

"Well, don't tell anyone, but I'm searching for buried treasure . . ."

There were long-held rumours of stolen British gold coins buried in the ground in the vicinity of the great lake, and perhaps even in the lake itself.

"It could just be a myth, people have looked before, they've come from all over Greece, from all over Europe, but never found any," Angelo went on. "But no-one knows the area around here like me." He smiled craftily, his wrinkles bunching up, which took years off his age.

"You must know it very well . . ."

"Like my own hand. I used to look in the lake. I have a boat and would go out trawling with my net."

"Is that right?" Manolis said. "When did all this happen? How old are the stories about the treasure?"

"It supposedly all happened during the civil war. They were bloody years that divided time in two: before the war, after the war. Like when Christ came. This area hasn't been the same since."

The German occupation of Greece during the Second World War was thought to be the country's darkest military hour. But whereas that brought the country together to fight a common foe, the civil war tore it apart.

"That's why I now carry a metal detector," Angelo said. "I often just find rubbish, there's a lot of it in the ground. But one day, you never know. Finding a landmine would be a good outcome if it means a hazard gets removed. But people still come here to search for coins and claim even to have maps that show where they're buried. I wish I had a map."

Manolis let his mind wander. Lefty probably had similar interests, given his breezy nature. Perhaps a lucky strike had played a part in his disappearance. Lefty's story may have had a happy ending, with him now on a beach somewhere, as opposed to a sinister one, with him now in a ditch.

Manolis said he was working as the labourer in Lefty's role. Angelo smiled and said that Lefty helped Anna and him around the house and in the garden especially.

"So what do you think happened to Lefty?" Manolis asked. "Some people say he may have been abducted."

Angelo leaned reflectively against his crook, let it absorb his weight. Apollo barked at some pygmy cormorants thronging noisily overhead, croaking asynchronously.

"He left," Angelo said.

"Sorry? He left?"

"Correct. Lefteris isn't missing. He just left the area."

Angelo claimed that Lefty had told him as much and bid him a fond farewell. Angelo was obviously the man the Florina police had spoken to.

Manolis crossed his arms. "OK," he said. "I didn't know that. Do you know where Lefty went? People are still looking for him . . ."

"He said he was going to Lesbos," Angelo replied. When Lefty had told him, he hadn't been sure whether or not to believe him.

"Lesbos? You mean, the island?"

"That's the only one I know. Have you been there?"

"Um, no . . ."

Considering the new information, Manolis pulled a face. Was what Angelo was saying a true statement, or was it a carefully formulated lie that he was now spreading to conceal the truth behind Lefty's disappearance? Or was it a lie that Lefty himself had told Angelo to conceal where he was actually going?

Manolis uncrossed his arms. "Lesbos, eh. Did he say why he was going there? And when he planned on coming back?"

Angelo patted Apollo affectionately, which made the dog spring to life with enthusiasm and gambol by his side. After a moment, Angelo said:

"No, Lefty didn't say why he was going or when he'd be back, and I didn't press him. At the time, I didn't think it was all that important; I mean, it wasn't the first time he'd said he was going away. And even if I had asked, Lefty would only have lied about it anyway."

9

There were numerous daily rituals that Manolis had established since arriving in the wild north, and that he now looked forward to. Every day began with a short walk to the nearby bakery in Florina for a selection of freshly baked *pita*, which he sometimes bought for both breakfast and lunch. He would also buy a few tins of pet food to feed the strays that he encountered on his walk home; there were always more animals than tins. The drive from Florina to Glikonero was the least enjoyable part of the day because of the potholed road and the danger posed by the wildlife. But then, at the other end, Manolis's reward came in the form of his morning coffee, which he bought at the taverna, expertly prepared by Roze.

Kostas often joined Manolis to solve the world's problems with the help of some caffeine. They sat outside in the bright sun, looking out at the lake and the two complicated neighbour states. Although the three peoples shared traditions, culture, history, ethnicity and landscape, relations remained bitter and tense, like three siblings constantly getting on each other's nerves. The three countries had even refused to share time zones, with Greece always a stubborn hour ahead of Albania and North Macedonia. Kostas could never decide which country he liked more, and in the end usually opted for the one he disliked less.

"It's Albania at the moment," he told Manolis. "Mainly because of Roze. She's an excellent worker."

With Kostas not there one morning, and the taverna empty as usual, Manolis struck up a conversation with the young Albanian. She looked tired, with dark rings under her teal-blue eyes. Manolis bought two coffees and pulled out a chair for her. Roze seemed reluctant at first, smiling shyly, and admitted that she was embarrassed by the attention.

"In Greece, Albanians are viewed like garbage," she said, her voice harsh. "No-one cares about us, we are invisible. We are the toilet cleaners and slaughterhouse workers; we are the soldier ants of Greece."

It was a familiar immigration dynamic, although Manolis noted her use of the word "invisible".

"Every country has that," he said. "In Australia, it was once the Greeks who did those jobs, back when there was a massive wave of immigration after the war. My parents were those people. There's no shame in that."

Roze offered a fragile smile. Her eyes sparkled at the mention of Australia. It was a wild, untamed country that fascinated her, she said. Manolis told her a little about his former life there, describing the country's many natural wonders, animals and weather.

"I miss it a lot," he lied.

The truth was that Manolis was enjoying the change of scenery, the chance to nourish his soul. The only thing he missed about Australia, the only thing that tugged on his heart, was his son, and Sparrow to some degree too.

"I'd love to go one day," Roze said.

"Then you should."

"But it's so far away." She admitted she'd only ever been to three countries: Albania, Greece and Italy. "And North Macedonia, if you count the other side of the lake."

"It's just a day on a plane," Manolis said. "But in the same way you've never been to Australia, I've never been to Albania."

She looked at him with wide eyes. "If you ever want to go to Albania, you only have to walk a few minutes in that direction," she said.

Manolis laughed. Roze's Balkan accent was smooth and smoky, her grammar almost perfect. Her intonation was unlike any Manolis had ever heard. He'd not met many Albanians before.

"What's your family like?" he asked. He wanted to understand this stranger to the village, to understand what motivated her.

Roze blew on her coffee. Manolis noticed her flawless eyelids and their slow droop every time she paused to think.

She spoke in broad terms about what she called her uninteresting family, her even more boring life, and the entrenched poverty that had consumed them both. But she was nonetheless proud of her homeland and said she was sending money home to help her mother. More interested in alcohol and affairs, her father had left to pursue both some years ago. She didn't miss him.

Roze then revealed what Manolis had already suspected – that she had crossed the border into Greece illegally.

"I just walked across the mountains," she said with a light laugh. "The border there is not secure."

She obviously didn't realise she was talking to a policeman.

Roze talked about a time in recent history when Albania was run by a ruthless dictator, the country rife with tyranny, nepotism, kleptocracy and propaganda.

"We were sealed off from the world, locked in. If you tried to get out, the secret police rounded you up and took you straight to a firing squad. There was no trial or jury. Listening to foreign music, to rock 'n' roll or rap, could get you thrown in jail, and so could chewing gum. My mother said there was once an electrified fence that ran around all of Albania, for thousands of kilometres. I never saw that but I have seen the bunkers."

"What bunkers?" Manolis asked.

"Our great leader was a supremely paranoid emperor who built all these solid bunker fortifications across Albania to protect us from foreign invaders who never came. Why would anyone attack us? Albania has nothing anyone could possibly want. We don't have oil or weapons or political power or even much territory. So these empty concrete domes now haunt the treeless land, they are indestructible and the country is too poor to remove them."

"How many bunkers are there?"

"Hundreds of thousands."

Roze described Kostas as lazy but was thankful he paid her in cash. It wasn't much, but it was still more than she could earn in Albania where both jobs and money were scarce. She admitted that if she'd stayed in Albania, a life in crime would have been inevitable, which Manolis noted. She talked about her dreams and aspirations for "a better life", which one day included having many children.

"I want a big family," she said. "But to do that, I need money to support them. Love won't be enough. But I can't decide what to do, and I don't know very much, I barely finished school . . ."

Roze's humility endeared her to Manolis. Her dream was admirable, and was the same dream that his own parents had had when they emigrated to Australia. It determined her course. But he knew he needed to block out the shared history and view her as impartially as any other suspect in Lefty's disappearance. She was an outsider who'd been exposed to a criminal underworld and was now living in Greece illegally, both of which she freely admitted to.

Manolis sipped his coffee and complimented her on its rich, smooth flavour before switching the conversation to Lefty by mentioning the latest minor repair he'd avoided doing at the house and that he was going to work on later that day. It was a rather strange feeling to be fixing things when Lefty was missing, almost as if he could still feel his warmth on the door handle or smell his musk in the air.

Roze played with her teaspoon, twiddling it nervously between her fingers. She said her relatively short time in Glikonero meant she didn't know Lefty well.

"But he's always been very kind to me at the taverna," she added. "He always tips me well even though he gets free coffees."

It was a remark that made Manolis pause. From the way he lived, it seemed that Lefty was dirt poor but kind-hearted, giving away what little money he had. No-one really knew about his finances, though, including the sums he was apparently making from the black market. Perhaps he had a secret hiding place somewhere for all his ill-gotten savings.

"You see Lefty often?" Manolis said.

"Almost every day. He has a fixed routine, you could set your watch by it."

"I find that hard to believe from someone as unrestrained and unpredictable as Lefty . . ."

Roze described how she would see Lefty following the same route every morning, perambulating through the surrounding grassland and hills at the same time. She claimed it was a safe route: there was little likelihood of encountering wildlife, landmines and other such hazards.

"At the taverna, he always had the same number of drinks, then would walk home at the same time."

"How do you know he had the same number of drinks?"

"Because I served him. Kostas sometimes did as well, if he wasn't having a drink himself. But it was usually me."

For Lefty to vanish without any explanation made Roze believe that his disappearance was deliberate, not accidental, and involved foul play. "It's to do with the people around here."

Roze drained her coffee. "Another?"

"I'm good, thanks." Manolis never usually said no to a second cup, but he felt he'd suddenly hit on something and didn't want to lose the momentum.

"When you say 'the people around here', what do you mean?"

He expected her to talk about the feud between Lefty and Sofia, which for obvious reasons had attracted the most attention. And Roze did mention it. But she also talked more broadly about the social dynamic at play within the village.

"Everyone knows the civil war shaped the north of Greece, even we Albanians across the border. But there's been another civil war going on right here in Glikonero. The village has been fighting with itself for years. The grudges run deep and feuds die hard."

Manolis scratched his chin, felt its emerging roughness from a recent shave. "How do you know something like that?" he asked. "You haven't been here all that long."

Roze removed the elastic band from her inky-black hair, gathered together the loose strands, and retied her ponytail.

"I once asked Kostas why I never saw many residents at the taverna. I thought it was a lost business opportunity – I wanted to bring in more customers beyond the occasional tourist. Kostas didn't give me much of an answer, but it turns out that most residents have either been banned or have had a run-in with him. The only place you'll see everyone together is at church on a Sunday. They put their personal arguments aside for God."

Sitting back in her chair, Roze recounted some of the village's history, which she'd been told by Father Petros and Lefty one evening after too much retsina.

"Glikonero functioned quite normally when it had more people," she said. "The taverna was at the heart of the village. They used to hold regular council meetings here. But disagreements soon crept in over the allocation of funds, and no-one could decide what to name the village's two roads. There were problems with the mail service; letters began to go missing or were being steamed open. And someone told the Florina police that firearms and opium were being hidden at the taverna."

It had all the hallmarks of an intricate black-market operation. Lefty and Kostas and Elias working together and using the taverna as a front to sell their illicit booty to passing tourists in search of excitement and adventure on their holiday. Lefty would draw them in with his charm, Kostas would make the transaction, and Elias would look the other way, the whole thing driven by drink and drugs and profit.

Roze described how the police had been called to deal with cases of harassment, vandalism, slander, theft and even assault. Someone's pet donkey had apparently been shot and eaten. Manolis winced at the notion.

"The police don't come here anymore, they've grown tired of us," Roze said. "We've been blacklisted, left to fend for ourselves." She sounded almost embarrassed.

Manolis now understood the police's apathetic attitude to Lefty's disappearance. He knew of instances where his own police colleagues had avoided certain parts of town. The inner-city housing commission towers had once been on the list of no-go zones.

Everyone claimed they had the village's interests at heart, Roze told him, but the trivial disagreements had gradually eaten away at Glikonero like termites. Battle lines were drawn and factions formed.

"Many people who came to the area with high hopes have since cut their losses and left," Roze said. "And others who are young enough to leave are weighing up their options."

"What about you?" Manolis asked.

Roze paused, then said: "I must admit, I didn't expect this amount of trouble when I arrived. I feel like I've walked in on an argument, and now I just want to back quietly out of the room."

Some neighbours had managed to studiously ignore one another for more than a decade, which was quite a feat in such a small village. Others, meanwhile, yelled abuse at each other. No villager – let alone the polarising Lefty – was universally liked by all the other residents, not even the righteous Father Petros.

"Lefty is the bane of Sofia's life, but she isn't the only villager who might wish him gone," Roze said. "They won't admit to it. Why would they? It's much easier to point the finger at Sofia and Zain."

Manolis nodded and silently wondered what Roze's reason might have been.

"Do you and Sofia get along?" he asked. "What about Zain?"

Roze said she tried to avoid the small-town politics; Zain did too. It helped that they were the only two young people in the village.

"It's a plus for Zain that he speaks Arabic and only understands a little Greek and English," she said. "And from what I've seen, Sofia is just a nice old lady. I don't really listen to Lefty when he calls her names. I know his cheeky nature and believe all the stories about him tormenting her for his amusement."

Drumming two fingers on the lip of his coffee cup, Manolis digested what she'd said. Young Roze was a valuable source of information. As an outsider who heard conversations in the taverna, she was a wealth of local knowledge and secrets. But Manolis still had his doubts. Everyone in the village remained a suspect.

"Of course, there are things that could have happened to Lefty that have nothing to do with the villagers," Roze said. She examined her nails, which were painted a dark and moody shade of aubergine.

Manolis cocked a curious eyebrow. "Like what?"

"Well, he's known to hitch-hike, so something could have happened to him out on the road. It would explain why a body has never been found. His body wouldn't have been disposed of near the village where it would have been easy to find. It would've been tossed into a car and driven some distance away, or dumped in the lake with rocks to weigh it down, don't you think?"

As she spoke, Manolis felt his skin tingle. Why had someone in Roze's position given this so much thought?

"Sorry," she said. "That sounded pretty morbid. I'm just speaking from personal experience. I've had some pretty close shaves with motorists offering me lifts when I've been out walking alone. I used to accept the odd ride depending on the driver and car and weather. But not anymore. I'd rather walk all day through the snow."

"Did something happen to you?" Manolis asked.

Roze gave her wristwatch a desultory glance. "I better get back to work," she said, standing. "Kostas will be here soon."

She picked up her coffee-stained cup. Manolis passed her his, and thanked her.

"I know it must be strange coming into a situation like this," she said. "To keep hearing about Lefty, whose disappearance is the reason you're here. If you'd like, I'd be happy to help you search for him."

Manolis looked at her, unblinking. Had he made it obvious that he was actively looking for Lefty? But Lefty was such a prominent topic of conversation that, in a sense, everyone in Glikonero was searching for him. Perhaps Manolis came across as less of a threat because he was an outsider, like Roze herself; he had no allegiances within the village.

Or maybe Roze had taken a shine to Manolis because his Australian connection made him exotic. Should he invite her into his world? There were obvious advantages, but he could be putting himself in unnecessary danger. Where was Sparrow when Manolis needed him?

"Sure," Manolis eventually said. "Thanks again for the coffee."

Roze smiled. She began to walk away, then turned back. She held up her wrist, showed the tattooed lettering to Manolis.

"This is my older brother's name," she said. "He disappeared in Albania a few years ago. He's been coming to me in my dreams every night since Lefty vanished. It's why I can't sleep."

10

Sitting in the nacre of morning light on Stavros's sun-streaked, red-tiled balcony, Manolis and his host savoured their coffees and *pita* pies, slurping the velvety brew and crunching the crackling filo pastry. The streets below echoed with the sound of children on holiday for the summer, of shrieking and laughing and basketballs being bounced. The ringing of church bells and carolling of young birds – common nightingales, golden orioles and subalpine warblers – filled the air like canon music.

Manolis was filling Stavros in on all he'd learned so far, trying to get a sense of what was legitimate and what was embellished or altogether fabricated. Stavros was listening somewhat absently. He was grateful for the day off from his security job at the nearby lignite mine, the combustion of dirty brown coal still supplying much of Greece's electricity. But he had a long list of errands to run and delinquent labourers to chase down. Now his parents were dead, Stavros often thought about returning to Australia, but it made financial sense to stay in the comfort of Greece. There he could live rent-free, work hassle-free, and retire early to take care of the family's properties as the world's smallest real estate baron. Manolis envied Stavros and his simpler, slower life in rural Greece compared with his of inner-city policework. And Stavros wouldn't be working until he was seventy. He just needed to make it to retirement and hope that his persistent, phlegmy cough was due to nothing more than his persistent, lifelong smoking. Many of Stavros's workmates had already retired and promptly died of cancer or a stroke.

Now well and truly immersed in the region, Manolis wanted to hear Stavros's perspective on the multitude of theories for Lefty's disappearance. They were mounting by the day and hard to keep track of. Being undercover every time he stepped into Glikonero was tiring, so Manolis also appreciated the chance to relax, be himself, and talk freely to Stavros using his full investigative mind.

Stavros fortified himself with a fresh cigarette. He confirmed Roze's description of Glikonero as having been at civil war for some time. Naturally, it wasn't something that people were proud of and wanted to advertise.

"Being so isolated, the villagers once had to fight for each other, it was them versus Greece," Stavros said. "But now that Greece has all but forgotten them, they've turned on each other. That's Greeks all over, really. We argue, we fight. The opponent is irrelevant. Better to argue than be bored."

"I find that surprising," Manolis said. He'd always seen Greek villages as serene and tranquil, and his experience of Glikonero hadn't suggested otherwise; there was no discernible undercurrent. But perhaps that's what was unsettling: what he was seeing was fabricated.

Stavros brushed away some fluff from his crisp open-collar shirt with the sleeves rolled to the elbows and adjusted his oversized Italian sunglasses. His stylish stubble was even thicker today, his white teeth were worthy of a dentist's brochure, and his chino shorts were too tight over his thighs and crotch. Manolis liked that his friend looked like he was on a perpetual European holiday.

"Personality clashes are part and parcel of small-town life, like siblings arguing," Stavros said. "When you live so close to one another and you're such a stubborn people, it's bound to happen."

Thinking back, Manolis remembered his dad arguing with his many siblings over trivial matters that fast became massive issues and resulted in them not speaking for years. To this day, Manolis had cousins around his age whom he barely knew as a result, all because of his bloody dad.

Stavros felt the old feuds were harmless. "Grudges are healthy, they keep people alive, get them out of bed in the morning."

That was certainly one way to look at it.

Seeing two young women walking by, Stavros leaned over the railings of his balcony and flirted with them at high volume. Manolis was astounded; such behaviour felt like a throwback to another time. Stavros, who'd never married, described the women as old friends. Manolis couldn't see how; the women looked like they were barely in their twenties. They were dressed immaculately in haute couture, their make-up flawless, and wouldn't have looked out of place in a glossy magazine. They fanned themselves theatrically at Stavros's advances and walked on.

"What about the motorists that drive through the area?" Manolis asked. "Could Lefty have been killed or abducted while hitch-hiking, or been the victim of a hit-and-run accident, with his body dumped far away?"

Negotiating the tight mountain roads each day, Manolis had dodged a multitude of logging trucks and transport vehicles and oil tankers that saw cars as mere speed bumps. Lanes were optional.

"I think a hit-and-run is unlikely," Stavros said. "Despite the poor state of the roads and the recklessness of the drivers, there haven't been many such accidents here over the years. The other thing to remember is that loud noises carry in such an isolated location, and no-one said they heard anything the night Lefty disappeared. If there had been a car accident, especially in Glikonero, there would surely have been the sound of squealing brakes or a loud thud."

There would also have been a bloodstain on the road, along with remnants of vehicular damage – glass and metal – and Manolis had not seen either.

"But what if a cyclist had hit him, some daredevil going too fast?" Manolis asked. "That wouldn't have made much noise at all, and I hear the area is popular with mountain bikers due to all the hills and trails."

Stavros shot him a sceptical look. Manolis admitted it was improbable, but he knew of elderly pedestrians in the city who had been run down and killed by careless cyclists, often speeding couriers.

Manolis proposed the simpler idea of Lefty drowning in the lake. Stavros considered it with a long, smoky exhalation. He finally shook his head and said that Lefty liked a drink but that he never got drunk. He was a strong swimmer from his time in Crete, so it was doubtful he would have drowned, and the body would have washed up by now anyway.

"Unless it was dumped and weighed down," Manolis said.

He recalled previous murder cases where badly decomposed bodies had taken several weeks to wash up, and in waterways much shallower than the vast Prespa Lakes. But he was not a specially trained police diver, and the Florina police seemed to have neither the equipment nor desire to scour two dark and deep freshwater lakes for a body they didn't believe was there. It sounded like the police needed an assailant standing over a dead body holding a bloody knife or smoking gun before they would set foot in Glikonero. Manolis raised the possibility of an accident, of a wild animal attack or an unexpected fall. Stavros dismissed these scenarios as unlikely.

From the street below the balcony, a flat-capped rabbitoh called out to Stavros. He had a full cart of freshly caught bunnies that he was hawking door to door and didn't expect them to last in the heat. Stavros waved back and said he wasn't interested. The elderly man walked on with his shopping cart of furry carcasses, all stretched out. Further up the street, he made a sale to an old lady in black. Manolis watched the man sling a rabbit from his shoulder and skin it on the spot.

Could the customer be his Aunt Poppy? Manolis had started seeing her everywhere. He felt like he'd been haunted by old Greek ladies draped in black his entire life. These mysterious individuals were at every Greek gathering he'd ever been to. They moved slowly and silently, spoke in low murmurs, and seemed to be from another place and time. When Manolis was young, he'd been scared by them and wondered whether they possessed some form of mystical power. Now he was older, he wasn't sure he felt any differently.

"How was Lefty's health?" Manolis asked suddenly.

Lefty had several medications stored in his cottage, but there was nothing that looked serious – only non-prescription painkillers, anti-inflammatories and reflux treatments, along with some empty glass phials from another era.

"Could Lefty have had a sudden heart attack while he was out walking?" he said.

Stavros held his coffee in his mouth a moment as he thought, then swallowed.

"Like with a drowning, wouldn't a body have been found somewhere by now?"

"Not if it was eaten by a wild animal," Manolis replied. "If he'd somehow collapsed and died, raptors would have been circling his body – hawks, eagles, falcons and vultures. And if a bear or wolf or dog or pig had got to him, scavenged him, there'd be nothing left of Lefty at all."

Stavros shook his head in a rhythmic motion. "From what I saw, Lefty was in excellent health and spirits. He got regular exercise and fresh air during his mountain walks, and I don't think he had any history of heart problems or blood pressure. Those could have been old medications that you saw."

"What if he was taking illicit drugs? They can do funny things to your heart."

During his career as an investigator, Manolis had seen many otherwise fit and spritely individuals drop dead from secret substance abuse. What were initially thought to be suspicious circumstances were turned on their head by a toxicology report.

Stavros again shook his head. "Lefty was firmly against drugs," he said. "I mean, he didn't even smoke cigarettes, which is unheard of for a Greek. There's also no way he would have been smuggling drugs."

"But if the price was right? For money?"

"You mean blood money. I don't think it's possible."

It was clear that Stavros didn't want to believe that his old friend was involved in such a dark practice. Manolis remained open to the possibility.

"What about Lefty's mental health?" he asked.

Stavros looked at him for some time. He finally blinked and said:

"You mean suicide? Again, I doubt it. Also, the Church doesn't approve and would have denied him an Orthodox funeral."

"Would that matter to Lefty? I hear he isn't very religious . . ."

"He isn't. And most Greeks aren't anymore. But they still identify as Orthodox Christians and respect the traditions."

In view of Lefty's slippery nature, Manolis wondered whether Lefty might have faked his own death for some unknown reason. Perhaps to avoid a debt, or secure a windfall. Such an outcome would have suited him – alive but dead, real but invisible. But Manolis didn't raise the prospect with Stavros. He also didn't mention the possibility of Lefty being a spy or even a double agent, given the tension with their international neighbours. Manolis had known a few spooks in his time and Lefty fitted the profile perfectly.

The two men sat for a while listening to the sounds of Florina, a thin air of tension between them. It was another clear summer's day with the temperature hot but tolerable. Working outdoors for so many hours each day had turned Manolis's skin a deep, glossy caramel.

Stavros extinguished his smoke in a thick glass ashtray shaped like a seashell. Manolis helped himself to another delicate slice of *tiropita*. He savoured the mouthful, chewing and swallowing slowly with eyes closed.

"I swear," he said, "if I was a condemned prisoner, that could very easily be my last meal."

Every time Manolis visited Greece, it felt as comfortable as a well-worn sweater. He heard every vowel of his name pronounced correctly, mellifluously, bouncing like a song lyric. Everyone looked like his favourite cousin. He saw aspects of his own personality mirrored: passion, generosity, chaos, illogicality. And everything he ate seemed to agree with him, as if the food were inherently in tune with his gut bacteria. The feta and yogurt were smooth on his tongue, not bitter like the Australian versions.

Stavros smiled proudly. "That bakery has been making these pies for half a century. It's a family-run business and an integral part of Florina life. We fairly raise our babies on its bread and pies."

There were no small businesses near where Manolis lived that had such incredible longevity and support from the local community. Places that he remembered from his childhood had now been turned into supermarket conglomerates or multistorey car parks.

"Out of interest, have there been stories of any other people disappearing in the region?" Manolis asked.

Stavros looked at him. "What are you saying?"

"Nothing. I'm just entertaining the remote possibility that there may be a serial killer operating in the area."

It was always in the back of every homicide detective's mind when they were presented with a new case. Who else had gone missing or been murdered? In every country on earth, there were still hundreds of unsolved murders and disappearances. Could they be linked in some way?

Staring into the middle distance, Stavros went on to describe a cold-case killing.

"I can't remember when it was exactly, but it wasn't far from Glikonero. A man was found dead one morning, shot square between the eyes. He'd been walking through grassland in the Prespes region."

"Did they find the weapon?" Manolis asked.

"No."

"Was he shot from up close or from a distance?"

Stavros narrowed his eyes as if trying to visualise it. "I'm not sure," he said slowly.

"You can tell from the wound. Was there major head trauma, or just an entry hole?"

"Does it matter? The man was still dead."

"It absolutely matters. People shot from close range aren't usually killed by accident. Think about it."

Manolis's words hung in the air a moment. Eventually, Stavros replied:

"I don't know. I didn't see the incident. I didn't know the man. This was just what I heard on the *kafenion* grapevine. It was a long time ago." His voice was tight, his tone testy.

"Look, sorry," Manolis said. "This is just what I do: interrogate, question. I'm looking for traction, a way in."

"I understand," Stavros said in his normal voice. "But I can't tell you what I don't know. What I do know is that there have definitely been some disappearances in the Prespa over the years. That's probably more due to the land's steep and rocky terrain, though, rather than a newsworthy serial killer. Sorry to burst your police bubble."

Stavros drained his coffee and replaced the cup in the saucer just as his phone trilled. Almost immediately, he began to argue loudly with whoever was on the other end. Manolis looked away as if he was interrupting something private.

He thought about the chalky amphitheatre of mountains around the Prespa lakes. They loomed sublime and imposing, as if carved by the very hand of God. Shrouded in white mist, the lakes contained a vast quantity of water within galleries of stone, and had shaped the culture of those who lived near them, from ancient hermits and holy men who'd chosen spiritual seclusion to more recent settlers in search of rural life. But the landscape was also treacherous and inaccessible. It did not welcome people.

Stavros continued his phone call unabated, the Greek obscenities flying. By now, Manolis had deduced that it was with one of the many slippery tradesmen who were giving him the runaround. Stavros came across as tough and uncompromising. It was a caustic side of his friend that Manolis had never seen before.

While Stavros continued to argue, Manolis's thoughts turned to Lefty. At times, Manolis had wanted to touch Lefty to check he was real and not a trick of the ever-changing Greek light. Someone like Lefty couldn't survive in Australia, or in most countries for that matter; he could only exist in a place such as Greece, where official paperwork went missing like foreign tourists. In a modern world, where digital traces of human activity – credit card purchases, internet searches, locations, likes, dislikes, fears – were collected and attached to a person's identity and emotional pulse for commercial gain, Lefty was the ultimate throwback in a throwback society. He had successfully turned his back on the twenty-first century and lived the life he wanted. Arguably, it made Lefty the last person in the world who should ever go missing. His very nature meant he might never be found again. The world was failing, anyway. More losers than winners, more poverty than wealth, more tragedy than joy. Perhaps Lefty had it all worked out perfectly; the rest of humanity was naive, trying to win at a game that was rigged from the outset.

Stavros ended his call with a blasphemous expletive. He extinguished his smoke in disgust.

"Sorry," he said, composing himself. "It's this electrician, this Albanian cowboy. I swear he's descended from hyenas. He's cheap, but you get what you pay for."

"What's the issue?"

"The same old. I better visit the bank and stuff another *fakelaki*. If he finishes the job by Christmas, then I'm a monkey's uncle."

Stavros extracted his wallet and began to rifle through a sheaf of receipts. Manolis looked up at the mountain that loomed over Florina. It was steep, wooded and daunting. On its meridian was an enormous white cross that was illuminated at night, floating in the darkness like a holy spirit. The cruciform was thirty-three metres tall, one metre for every year that Christ was alive. It protected the town's residents from evil and misfortune. Had it failed in its duty to Lefty?

"I guess he could have slipped and fallen," Manolis said suddenly. "Broken a leg, shattered his pelvis, or worse."

Stavros gave a perfunctory nod. "Compared to everything else we've

111

discussed, that's the most likely," he said. "But to find his body, we'd need tracker dogs and choppers and a search party. And there's no chance of those coming our way."

"Really? If a man goes missing in a remote location, I think that's precisely when you might get those resources."

"But it depends on the man," Stavros said. "If it was a lost tourist in a rich country like yours, different story. But not for an invisible like Lefty. He's inconsequential."

Manolis recalled Sparrow, thousands of kilometres away, and the tracking skills he claimed he'd learned from his uncles. "They could track a hopping mouse in a dust storm," the young cop had bragged. If that was true, surely a grown man – even a man like Lefty – would pose little challenge.

And while the landscape was the most logical reason for disappearances, including Lefty's, there was a factor that Manolis had not previously considered.

"This is a region steeped in myths and folklore," Stavros added.

"You mean, Greek gods and such?" Manolis said.

"Mm, not really."

"I only know about Aboriginal mythology. I studied it at school a long time ago, and don't remember the stories very well."

At that moment, Manolis needed Sparrow to magically appear and laconically explain the major tenets of Aboriginal spirituality. The deities and gods, the songlines, and how they were altogether older and superior to anything else the world could offer, even the ancient Greeks. They were, after all, the world's oldest civilisation.

"But explain to me," Manolis said, "how any of this is relevant to the investigation?"

Stavros smiled sheepishly. "You're right to be a bit cynical. And I'm not suggesting Lefty was abducted by a god or ghost or spirit. But the power of legends and myths is strong in this part of Greece. It makes many people believe and do strange things. It also makes us suspect the local Romani population when things go wrong, because they claim to possess mystical qualities and healing powers."

Manolis was immediately intrigued, even though he didn't understand where Stavros was going with this. Reaching for his cigarettes, Stavros lit a fresh one. He inhaled deeply.

"When I was a young boy in Australia, my mum would tell me stories about Romani people, though she called them gypsies. She said they would come and take me away and eat me. She would say it when I was being naughty, an empty threat to scare me. It took me time to realise that she was recounting stories told to her by her own parents in Florina when she was a little girl. Of course, there were no such people in suburban Australia, but there are in Florina and its surrounds – they wander the streets, forests and mountains. And to this day, there are still stories of nomadic ethnic Romani who have abducted local people, including small children."

Abductions? Cannibalism? But why? Surely, thought Manolis, this was a myth in every sense of the word.

"Romani claim to have a deep spiritual connection with the land," Stavros continued. "They refuse to live in Glikonero or even to visit because they feel the land is poisoned and the village haunted by ghosts."

Manolis thought those sounded like stories of the bogeyman. They were common to the folklore of many countries, and often used by adults to frighten children into behaving.

"And the Romani people are definitely real," Stavros said emphatically. "I've seen them with my own eyes."

"That may be true, but it's a bit of a stretch to say they abduct children," Manolis said. "That's just attributing the bogeyman myth to a defined group, which is pretty unfair."

Stavros's dark eyebrows drew together. "You get bad people everywhere. And if you talk to people around here, they'll tell you that there was once a child in Glikonero who was abducted by Romani. Everyone remembers it, so it's not just a rumour or something told to scare other children into being good. It really happened. So anyone walking out there in the hills is fair game, I guess."

It was then that Manolis realised the identity of the group of people he'd seen walking across the countryside. They weren't tourists or backpackers.

"Do the police believe any of this?" Manolis asked.

Stavros put out his second cigarette butt on top of the first, extinguishing it with a sharp sizzle. He checked the time on his phone and cursed.

"I better get moving," he said, avoiding Manolis's question. "I've got to go find this bloody house painter who still owes me two days' work. What an idiot I was for paying him up front. Thanks again for helping to look for Lefty."

"No problem," said Manolis, wrapping the remaining *pita* in foil to take to the Prespes. "Lefty isn't like anyone else I know."

"But that's the problem," Stavros said. "People say that if you took Lefty up into the mountains, deep into the woods, and killed him with an axe, there would be no crime. After all, how could you murder someone who doesn't exist? For all intents and purposes, Lefty does not exist. He is there, but he is not there. And yet, he's larger than life."

Manolis let Stavros's words settle in his mind.

"But if you ask me, I think you should be more watchful of Roze than of any other villager, maybe even more than Sofia," Stavros said.

"Roze? Why's that?"

Stavros fumbled for his keys.

"It's just a feeling I get, her energy," he said. "She's young, self-absorbed, likes melodrama and being the centre of attention. She's untrustworthy and unpredictable."

"Because she's new?"

"In a word, yes."

"That sounds overly simplistic. I think you're being influenced by your history."

"I can't help but be influenced by history," Stavros replied. "History is everything to Greeks. Kostas told me that her family are actually Romani. That's why he's able to get away with paying her so little. How else do you think she was able to cross the border so easily?"

11

With some trepidation, Manolis decided to move into a small cottage in Glikonero. It was on a plot of land a short distance from Lefty's place and also owned by local property mogul Stavros. From the start, he'd offered it as a base but Manolis had resisted, preferring instead to stay in Florina and drive to the Prespes each day. But he'd grown tired of dodging wildlife, rock debris, logging trucks and freight vehicles, especially in the evenings when he was tired. The new house was basic but it had electricity and plumbing, and needed less repair work.

The morning view from Manolis's window in the east was a bucolic scene of fruit orchards, vegetable plots and a cow pasture. He slept well and awoke refreshed. The orchards were heavy with summer stone fruit: cherries, plums and apricots. The world around him had regained its vibrancy, the air thick with the scent of woodsmoke and humming with birdsong – quails, turtle doves and shrikes. In his inner-city apartment complex, Manolis's alarm clock was usually a blaring emergency siren, honking traffic, or his phone ringing with bad news.

But it wasn't all agreeable and harmonious. The water heater worked sporadically, which made for some bracing cold showers. And Manolis continued to marvel at the Greek practice of tossing used toilet paper into a bin instead of down the toilet. The country's ancient plumbing and pipes needed a complete overhaul.

Manolis was also unnerved by some of the myths he'd heard, of the Romani and their mysterious powers, and by being in an isolated location where a man had recently gone missing. But he found himself becoming absorbed in the strange world of the Prespes, a world of black-market smugglers and illegal immigrants and Romani who claimed the land was cursed. For peace of mind, Manolis fastened a thick padlock to his front door.

Now that he was spending more time in Glikonero, Manolis started interacting more regularly with the residents. On any given day, he saw villagers tilling the soil in their gardens and collecting basketfuls of summer vegetables. He fed more local strays with the help of Lefty's left-handed tin opener, and continued to work on Lefty's house. He was also finally able to track down the elusive Zain.

Manolis first saw him in a vacant lot, shirtless and working out. He was boxing a hefty lamb carcass that hung from an old olive tree. Gnarled and twisted, the tree looked as if it might be thousands of years old. Manolis stood there, covertly watching the energetic young Syrian, observing how gracefully he moved and glided as he worked on his technique, ducking an invisible combatant, his feet dancing. Zain's body was coltish, lean and tight, with strong muscles playing underneath his dark skin and an impressive six-pack. It was a physique built for action, not talk. He exploded into violence with every powerful strike. Zain was clearly an athlete working towards a bright future with greater life goals in mind than a sleepy existence in a remote mountain village. This was just a stop on his long journey.

Manolis considered his approach. His was an unfamiliar face, while Zain was a man who had fled a war zone and probably entered the country illegally like Roze, so would be wary of strangers.

Stepping forward, Manolis smiled and waved hello. Zain stopped boxing and spun around, eyes wild, jaw set, his chest heaving with exertion and fear. As Manolis walked over to him, smiling reassuringly, Zain jumped a nearby fence and sprinted away. Although he was in better shape than he had been thanks to his daily walks, Manolis was never going to catch the younger, fitter man.

When Manolis next came across Zain, he found him chasing a panicked, squealing pig around a muddy pen, slipping and sliding and changing direction every few seconds. It was an aerobic exercise designed to improve agility and sharpen reflexes. Again, Manolis watched him silently, pondering his approach. But he was seen by Zain before he made his move, and with the same outcome. Manolis called out this time, but to no avail. The pig oinked.

Drawn to the shores of Great Prespa Lake, Manolis had begun to explore its vast expanse. The lake had brackish waters and was full of bulbous weeds that pulled at his feet. He often walked around its banks, over sharp rocks and grainy sand, but he had never seen another soul, not even a fisherman taking advantage of the rich bounty on offer. It was almost as if the locals avoided the lake. He wondered if Father Petros had a secluded spot where the bites were more plentiful. The silence was so absolute that Manolis could hear the flapping of birds' wings overhead.

In the near distance, the tall watchtower also appeared empty. It looked out over the entire lake, with a wide field of vision that would allow whoever was in it to spot any incursions across international borders. A frayed Greek flag flew on a tall pole. Eyeing the shores across the lake to the north and west, the countries of North Macedonia and Albania, Manolis estimated them to be only a few kilometres away. It wouldn't take long to reach those shores, perhaps only ten minutes by motorboat. For a seasoned athlete with good lung capacity, it would be swimmable.

On the southern shores of the lake, there was a rickety wooden jetty constructed from several misshapen planks of old timber. The jetty swayed and creaked with the currents, the structure looking as though it would crumble into the seething water with the slightest weight. Manolis set a tentative foot on the jetty, walking carefully towards the slender motorboat moored at the other end. He'd decided to "borrow" it in order to conduct a rudimentary reconnaissance of the lake.

"Come on . . . come on . . . ugh . . ."

It took Manolis several arm-wrenching attempts to pull-start the small outboard motor. It spluttered and spewed intermittent puffs of greasy black smoke. The currents rocked the boat sideways as it puttered across the lake. Manolis was not a particularly strong swimmer but was capable enough and imagined he could make it to shore in the event of a catastrophe. He'd already checked the boat for leaks and it appeared watertight despite its battered appearance. There was no flotation vest, but there was at least a faded painting of a swimming mermaid on the boat's side.

To Manolis's left, a cramped, uninhabited island loomed in the middle of the lake. Its name was Golem Grad, which meant Big City. The isolated island was encircled by stark white cliffs and was officially North Macedonian territory. It was home to many seabirds, which Manolis could see circling the tiny rock like planes above a busy airport. Their singing was even more pronounced than on the mainland; it sounded like a noisy rave was in full swing. A flock of nesting passerines sat at the end of the thinnest, frailest branches, their cylindrical nests bobbing up and down.

Manolis eyed the solitary rock with curiosity and apprehension. The cliffs were impressively high, about thirty metres. The island had been formed after being torn from the nearby glacial massifs during an earthquake. It was solidly protected and reminded him of a fortress in both its size and shape. Could Lefty be holed up there somehow, a king safe in his castle? It was not out of the realm of possibility. Manolis hadn't considered it before, and now reasoned that it rather suited Lefty's personality – the island was a constant presence, but went unnoticed.

Looking down at the water, consulting the muffled landscape, Manolis wondered at what point he had crossed an international border into another country. Technically, he would also have travelled back in time, if only by one dogged hour. He'd expected there to be buoys marking the border, or even a series of naval mines. There wasn't even anything on the shore that made it clear where one country, and mindset, ended and another began.

Forging on, steering towards the opposite shore that was North Macedonia, Manolis felt certain he'd crossed into foreign waters by now. He was closer to the land ahead than the land behind. His suspicions were confirmed on hearing a loud and sudden siren blaring in his wake. It made him jump in surprise, which caused his knife-slashed boat to teeter. Looking back, Manolis saw it was a police border patrol dinghy with a large air horn that was closing in at speed, blue lights flashing asynchronously.

It was Elias, the border guard. Here at last was Manolis's chance to meet Lefty's supposed black-market business partner.

Manolis switched off his outboard motor and let his boat come to a natural stop. Having overshot the mermaid boat, Elias circled back around with his two supercharged outboards and pulled up alongside with an unamused, sweat-slicked face.

"Identification, please," he said in a gruff voice that bounced off Manolis's chest.

Elias was burly and completely bald, or had shaved his head using a rough razor. He wore wrap-around sunglasses with polarised yellow lenses, a graphite-grey uniform, and thick-soled safety boots. A tightly trimmed military moustache completed the aura of someone in authority. Manolis thought he looked like a weightlifter gone to seed.

"Sorry, I don't have any ID on me," Manolis said. "It's all back at the house."

"What are you doing out here? Where do you live?"

"Glikonero."

Elias peered at Manolis from over the top of his sunglasses. "Really?"

"Yes."

"I haven't seen you before."

"I've only just moved in."

Elias eyed Manolis from top to toe, his eyes as keen as a bird of prey's.

"And this is your boat?"

Manolis thought of lying, then decided against it. In such a small region, it was likely that Elias knew the boat's owner.

"No, I'm just borrowing it."

"From . . . ?"

"The owner."

"Borrowing it for what purpose? Why the hell are you crossing the lake? On a blustery day like this, no-one should be out here. You could drown."

Manolis was crossing the lake to assess how easy it was to pass through international borders, but he wasn't going to admit that to the very man charged with protecting them.

"I wanted to go and sit on that beach over there," Manolis said. He pointed innocently towards North Macedonia.

Elias paused, scrutinising Manolis for a second time.

"I think I'd better escort you back," he said. "Follow me."

Returning to Greek territory, the two men moored their respective watercraft and stood on the shore opposite each other, the water lapping on the sand. Some ravens flew overhead, gronking like frogs, a dark smudge in the sky.

Manolis said he was new to the area. That he was aware of the borders but unsure of the rules. Elias puffed out his barrel chest and gave him a stern lecture on the movement of people and goods across the lake and international border. The speech featured much gesticulation and pointing in the Mediterranean way. Manolis played along, acting naive, sincere and ultimately apologetic for any trouble he might have caused.

"Sorry, but I'm just a labourer in town, here for a short time while I work on Lefty's house . . ."

On hearing Lefty's name, the sardonic lines in Elias's face hardened and a darkness washed across his eyes.

"Lefty, eh? Hmm . . ."

"Yes," Manolis said. "Do you know who I mean?"

"Yeah, I know him. I know Lefty very well. There's only one Lefty."

Elias said that he was saddened by Lefty's disappearance and that Lefty owed him a considerable sum of money.

"Which is why I'm upset and annoyed," he said. "Frankly, I don't know if and how I might get any of it back."

Manolis didn't ask how the debt had come about. Since Elias was volunteering information, he let him have the floor.

"I was home the night Lefty went missing. Honestly, if you ask what I think happened, I suspect his past finally caught up with him . . ."

Elias described how Lefty had come to northern Greece on the run from something. He wasn't sure what – the law, the government, a woman, other disgruntled creditors.

"Why else would anyone come up here? Look around you. It's a dead end. The young have left, only the old and useless have stayed. I think we're forgotten by everybody up here, even God himself."

Elias's resentful tone made Manolis wonder if he was in the Prespes region as some kind of punishment posting. Given his corrupt nature, past transgressions were distinctly possible.

"You obviously know a bit about Lefty's background," Manolis said. "I don't know him well but he sounds like he's lived an exciting life. What makes you think he's been hiding out here from something?"

Elias coughed into his hand and wiped it on his work shirt.

"Lefty lived in Turkey for a while and there are some pretty wild and dangerous men there who aren't fond of us Greeks," he said in a bitter voice. "And in Eleftheria, the previous village where he lived, Lefty was barred from local businesses and hated by the residents, who didn't appreciate his mischievous nature."

A leopard can't change its spots, thought Manolis.

"I don't know Eleftheria," he said. "Where is it, and when was this?"

"About a hundred kilometres from here and ten years ago. Lefty was basically run out of town."

"And he told you all this, that he was banished? It's not something I would want to admit."

Nervously stroking his moustache and looking down at his feet, Elias seemed suddenly tight-lipped, as if he'd said too much. Could he actually be afraid of Lefty?

"I wouldn't imagine those are the kinds of things that anyone would readily advertise," Manolis added.

"You're right, they're not," Elias finally said. "But let's just say this is a small part of the world and if you've done something or someone wrong, your reputation precedes you. Lefty was pretty stupid to think that it wouldn't."

Elias's remark made Manolis wonder why he would ever enter into business with someone so untrustworthy. But experience had taught him that the criminal classes considered such characteristics assets, not liabilities. The two parties would inevitably turn on one another, and the lowlife who reached for their gun the fastest would be declared the winner.

"I heard of a famous French poet who said that the greatest trick the devil ever pulled was convincing the world he didn't exist," Elias said. "He could have been talking about Lefty."

Just then, the wind blew and a wedge of mute swans shot up from the lake. They flew overhead in a wide, sweeping arc before disappearing into the solar haze like tracer fire.

"Is Lefty going to pay you for fixing his house?" Elias asked.

"No, the owner is," Manolis said.

"Just as well. You mightn't see a euro otherwise."

With every conversation, Manolis was gradually piecing together a profile of his ultimate goal. It helped that the local residents were so candid, and yet the details of Lefty's own story remained slippery. Were the villagers' stories all fabricated as well? That seemed unlikely. But in the case of someone who lived a life so undocumented, hearsay was all Manolis had to go on. And hearsay evidence was, essentially, no evidence.

But at least Elias had now provided Manolis with a geographic lead, which he quietly noted and planned to investigate.

12

Manolis embarked on a more comprehensive search of Lefty's run-down cottage. He'd heard so many contradictory stories and differing recollections of events that he felt no closer to getting a read on the disappearance of the living ghost that was Lefty. Finding some personal documents or photographs or handwritten notes was key to uncovering his current whereabouts. Without such an item, Manolis would never gain traction. But his hopes were dashed by Stavros, who said that Lefty's personal documents had been destroyed in a fire, and that his past was a series of dead ends. There were no discernible links to living family members, not even a distant cousin or uncle. And there was no evidence of siblings or children, despite Lefty's assertion that he had, at some point, fathered four children. Manolis wondered if he was wasting his time and energy.

In need of a fresh pair of eyes, Manolis took Roze up on her offer, enlisting her help in the house search.

"In case I miss anything," he told her. "It's already a mess, so don't hold back in turning things over. I'm sure Lefty wouldn't mind anyway."

Beginning at different ends of the house, they sorted through its contents. Manolis thought that Roze was more likely to find something significant on her first search of the house than he was on his fifth. Unlike Manolis, Roze searched rapidly, tossing items left and right. That stemmed perhaps from her youth and impatience, or may simply have reflected a lack of experience and precision. A comprehensive search of premises required specialist training.

"Nothing," grumbled Manolis after a fruitless hour. He ran a hand through his thick ash-grey hair. "Still nothing."

"I'm not surprised," Roze said. She was sweaty. "Being Lefty, he was never going to make it easy."

"Then we need to take things up a notch . . ."

"How?" Roze looked around at the flotsam and jetsam strewn across the floor. "We've ransacked the place."

"Internally, yes. But there's more we can do."

He pointed up at the mould-riddled ceiling, then down. Manolis was suggesting they search under the cottage's floor and inside its roof, locations not typically searched by law enforcement unless they suspected something illicit had been hidden – a distinct possibility in Lefty's case.

Manolis said he would search under the floor; it would be the dirtier and more precarious of the two jobs. First, he fetched a splintered but strong wooden ladder for Roze and helped her climb up into the roof cavity. She had stripped down to her shorts and sports bra in anticipation of the heat. Manolis passed her a flashlight and a bottle of water.

"Hopefully the structure's stable and there are no hazards," Manolis said. "No protruding nails or animal droppings or dust to make you choke."

Roze huffed. "I'll be fine," she said and scooted up the ladder. Manolis went outside to access the underfloor area via a wooden hatch on rusted hinges.

Manolis needed a moment to compose himself before he entered the dark space. It was as dark as a basement, but, he reminded himself, it wasn't one, and the chances of there being anyone down there were basically zero. Manolis knew he was being irrational, but his nerves and his PTSD were still too raw.

The space was tight, cool and damp, as he'd expected. Manolis's flashlight cut through the darkness like an ivory blade, illuminating every floating speck of dust, spider's web and scurrying rodent. It hurt to breathe; Manolis coughed and hacked and struggled to heave oxygen into his lungs. Crawling around on his chest and stomach, his shirt accumulated filth and his knees burned with pressure. Manolis regretted not wrapping a shirt around his face as a makeshift mask. He had never been comfortable in confined spaces, and felt his heart rate rising by the second, his pulse growing evermore prominent in his throat, and his breathing increasingly restricted.

"Well, hello there," Manolis said to himself. "What's this then?"

Buried away deep in the furthest corner, a dull metal box caught the flashlight's flare and shone like a dirty mirror. It might only have been a piece of old rubbish, but still it was something.

With the flashlight in his left hand and the metal tin in his right, Manolis commando crawled back to the access hatch as fast as he could. Returning to the warm sunshine, calming his breathing, Manolis studied the box. The faded Greek lettering was indecipherable. It was probably someone's once-beloved cigarette box. It would have been passed from hand to hand in the local *kafenia* as swarthy men with dispiriting moustaches helped themselves to a five-minute respite. Manolis's father might have been one of those men as he discussed a new opportunity that had presented itself in Australia.

"I think I've got something," Manolis called out to Roze in the roof. There was no reply.

Shaking the tin, Manolis heard it rattle. It wasn't just a discarded item of garbage – there was something inside, and it clearly wasn't rolling paper and tobacco. Wiping the tin with a dirty sleeve and blowing the dust away, Manolis tried to clean the box. It appeared not to have been opened in a long time, and he expected it to put up a fight before it revealed its contents. But instead, the lid came open easily with a gentle snap. As he lifted the lid, Manolis's eyes widened.

The sunlight made the metallic contents gleam. It was a key ring with two large keys. Manolis held it up, studied it, rotating it on the tip of his index finger. The keys appeared old-fashioned, almost like antique skeleton keys. Manolis wondered if that was all they were – antiques – or if there was a matching lock somewhere.

Slipping the keys into his pocket, Manolis examined what was underneath them in the box. Uppermost was a thin stack of faded and torn photos of young children. Manolis regarded the photos with a frown, scrutinising each one closely. The photographs were in no way suggestive or incriminating. The children appeared clothed and happy, often posing with beloved toys or plates of food. Given the age of the photos, the children were probably now adults. The photos were cherished mementos of Lefty's children, perhaps, treasured keepsakes of a more innocent time. Although it seemed that Lefty's name didn't appear on a birth certificate as the father of a Greek child, that could have been due to the wishes of the mother.

Beneath the photographs were three Greek passports. Manolis didn't recognise any of the names on the passports and failed to recognise two of the photos, a middle-aged man and a young woman. But he did recognise the third photo. It was of another young woman, and she looked identical to Roze.

"Fakes," Manolis said to himself. "They must be . . ."

His gaze settled on Roze's passport. Was Roze her real name? Was she using a fake name to travel across borders? Where was she going next? What other illegal activities was she involved in? In his experience, criminals often flouted multiple laws; once they broke one, it was easier to break another.

Manolis couldn't be certain of anything but was immediately suspicious of both Lefty and Roze. The search revealed that Lefty's illicit activities extended even further than he'd appreciated. Lefty was clearly smuggling a number of black-market goods across the border, with an operation that extended to fake passports. Such items would fetch high prices from people who wanted to secure their passage to Greece, and Europe more generally. And for a man who was known for not having any paperwork bearing his real name, he could just as easily have had several fake passports of his own that bore a number of aliases. The discovery might also explain why Stavros had warned Manolis to be wary of Roze; the passport might be the tip of a criminal iceberg. Or was it that Lefty had discovered her true identity and was now blackmailing her in some way? At that moment, anything felt possible.

For a brief moment, Manolis thought to confront Roze and ask her about the passport. But he imagined she would only lie; after all, anyone with a fake passport had something to hide. Instead, he pocketed the document for safekeeping and studied the other items a while longer, looking for clues. The keys were especially strange since Lefty never locked his house, and they did not appear to be car keys. And who were the other two people in the passports? They did not seem to be Glikonero villagers; at least, none that Manolis had seen.

Roze appeared, much of her ponytail having shaken itself loose, her dark hair partially obscuring her face. Her shoulders, elbows and knees were grimy.

"I think I've got something too," she said in a satisfied tone. "Come and see."

Manolis held up the cigarette box. "Recognise anything in here?"

Roze considered the keys, photos and passports for a few minutes and said that nothing looked familiar. Manolis watched her closely to gauge her reaction to the passports, and swore she hid a degree of disappointment when she realised hers was not there.

"Do you know who the two passports belong to?" Manolis asked. "I've not seen these people in the village."

She shook her head slightly, as if trying to loosen a thought. "Nor have I."

"What about the children in the photos?"

Roze looked again. "No," she said. "Sorry, I don't know them either. I know Lefty was very fond of kids, though. Every time a family came to the taverna, Lefty would play silly games with the children, make them laugh and give them ice creams and lollies."

"Hmm. Stavros said much the same, how Lefty doted on young kids. But not in a sinister way."

"I'd tend to agree. But come and see this . . ."

With a turn on her sneakered heels, Roze led Manolis back into the house and up the ladder into the roof. The space was several degrees warmer than the rest of the house, having accumulated the heat of the day as it rose and pooled. Manolis's shirt quickly stuck to his back with fresh sweat. Roze crawled on ahead like an agile feline while Manolis plodded like an old bear, all the while hopeful that the timber joists and beams would hold his weight.

"Over here," Roze whispered. She had lowered her voice. It was unnecessary, but it felt natural given what they were doing.

Her flashlight illuminated what appeared to be a metal toolbox and large black duffel bag. It was a bounty that made Manolis's find look like chicken feed.

"Whoa," he said.

"I tried to move the bag but it weighs a ton," Roze said. "I need your help."

The bag was both heavy and cumbersome and took some moving, but they managed it between them, then brought down the toolbox.

They stood silently for a moment, panting and taking in the sight before them. Whatever these two large receptacles contained, Lefty hadn't wanted anyone to know about them.

"There's a padlock on the toolbox," said Roze. "Would one of the keys you found open it?"

It was a good idea but it was clearly a modern padlock with a thin keyhole alongside a thick antique one. Manolis crouched, studying it a moment, before returning to his feet.

"I doubt it," he replied. "But wait . . ."

Manolis returned with his labourer's hammer and crowbar. It took three swift blows like shotgun fire for the padlock to crack like a soft-boiled egg.

"Padlocks like this are just for show," he said, proffering the now dented and broken bolt in his palm. Realising he sounded like a criminal, he quickly added: "In my job, I sometimes have to break locks to access yards when residents forget to leave them open for me."

Together, they gathered around the toolbox as if it were a pirate's chest. Wiping his mouth with the back of his hand, Manolis lifted the lid in a single movement to reveal the treasure inside. A second later, wads of creased cash almost sprang from the box with the release of pressure. They had been crammed in tight.

"Oh wow," Roze said, a little breathless.

"You're not wrong," said Manolis. "There must be tens of thousands here." It was a rough estimation based on previous hauls of cash that he'd found with search warrants or in the back of stolen cars, although euros were an unfamiliar currency.

"Shall we count it?"

Her eyes were bright and eager; she'd never seen so much money. Normally, such a cache would have been sealed and taken to headquarters where it would have been counted electronically, fingerprinted and stored.

"Sure," Manolis said.

It took them a few minutes of careful accounting. Roze licked her thumb as she counted the notes and Manolis wanted to tell her not to. He could smell his fingers by the time they had finished. The final sum was close to a hundred thousand grubby euros.

"How the hell did Lefty gather so much money?" Roze said.

"Clearly an incredible businessman and skilled entrepreneur," replied Manolis. "Astute with investments and portfolios, stocks and bonds. Now, the bag. I have a sneaking suspicion I know what's inside . . ."

"Really? What?"

"Open it and see."

Manolis's assessment was based on his police experience. The items he had in mind had a certain weight and feel that were distinctive.

Clasping the slider, Roze unzipped the bag slowly. As it lost its shape around its contents, Manolis smiled contentedly.

"Oh my God," stammered Roze. She instinctively snatched her hands away as if they were too close to a hot fire.

It was a stockpile of assorted firearms and ammunition. As Manolis picked up each item and examined it, he was impressed by the range of hardware. Some of them were high-powered assault weapons made in Russia. Clearly, they and the cash were the fruits of Lefty's smuggling enterprise. There were no illicit drugs.

"Looking at all this, I think we can safely say that Lefty's sudden departure was not something he'd planned," Manolis said.

"He wouldn't have left all this behind," said Roze. "He'd be crazy."

Manolis nodded. "But when I see all this, it's pretty clear he had weapons that he could have used for his protection if something had happened."

Roze pinched her chin in thought. "But the weapons were all in the roof. How would he have accessed them in the case of a sudden confrontation?"

It was an insightful observation. Manolis had assumed that someone who stockpiled so much weaponry would have carried a piece on his person as well. That was even more conceivable given Lefty's chequered history. If it caught up with him, he would have been adequately prepared. It may have reflected the nature of his illegal operation – that prohibited firearms were part and parcel of being a smuggler – or of his troubled relations with the other villagers, which had led to his needing guns for his personal protection.

But what if someone else also had a gun, and that person – or people – had got the drop on Lefty?

13

Having conducted a fruitful search of Lefty's house, Manolis was inspired. Over a lakeside breakfast one overcast morning, he contemplated his next move: to search the other houses in the village. He needed to find something that connected Lefty to a resident, a personal item that would not otherwise be expected, although it remained a problem that Lefty had few such items. Manolis planned to take extra time at Sofia's house, as unsettling as that was with her decor. That residence warranted a more extensive search, including of her well-stocked meat freezer. And these searches would need to be conducted alone and without the assistance of Roze. She remained under as much suspicion as any villager, if not more, given the fake passport Manolis had found. This was despite, or perhaps because of, her seemingly genuine efforts to help him. Manolis wasn't sure how he felt about Roze. She came across as young at heart but with an old soul. Her offers of support and cooperation might have been genuine, or they might have been the perfect cover for her own felonious background.

Because he wasn't working in an official police capacity that came with a search warrant, Manolis needed to scour the residences surreptitiously. Fortunately, the stubborn old villagers refused to lock their doors, even after Lefty's unexplained disappearance. They did as they had for decades; it was consistent with their assertions that they had nothing to hide.

From his time spent in Glikonero, and despite its many fractions, Manolis had sensed there was still some kind of consilience within the town. It was rooted in the hardship experienced by all the villagers, no matter their allegiances. The burden wasn't that Lefty was missing or that he might not come back alive – it was the thought that one of their own neighbours might have done something terrible and slipped seamlessly back into their ordinary routine without skipping a beat. That said, even knowing that a killer might be living in the village, the stoic villagers remained fearless, believing that they were in no danger themselves. There had been a target on Lefty's back thanks to his colourful past. The lives of the villagers had been tame in comparison, which meant they had nothing to fear.

For Manolis, stake outs were the most boring side of investigative work. There was nothing entertaining about an indeterminate number of hours of sitting and watching and waiting; even desk work was preferable. Manolis was fortunate now to be able to delegate surveillance to junior officers who reported back to him. But not in Glikonero. He found himself taking up strategic positions around the village where he could sit and watch without arousing suspicion. To pass the time, he read his book and played with his turquoise *komboloi* in his left hand. It was then just a matter of waiting until each resident left their home. Unfortunately, elderly people did not like to go out a great deal. It was something Manolis had seen in his housebound mother.

Eventually, it was the same weekly ritual that had extracted his mother from her home that drew out the aged residents of Glikonero: Sunday morning church service. Having grown up at a time when the church's influence on society was strong, the villagers retained a devotion to God that extended to fasting on certain significant religious days, celebrating saints' days as name days, and attending Sunday services. Maria also used the Sunday service as a way to catch up on all the gossip in her community, and she knew that if she didn't go, then she herself would be the subject of their gossip.

With the Sunday morning church bells still ringing, Manolis seized his opportunity. Entering the unassuming cottages, he was shocked by what he found. There was a huge amount of Nazi paraphernalia on walls and shelves; no effort had been made to hide the items from view. As he delicately went about his work, Manolis felt as if the imperial eagles and crooked swastikas were watching him, and these reminders of pure, blinding evil unsettled him. He could not make as thorough a search as would be possible with a warrant – Manolis's rummaging needed to be swift and undetectable – but his investigative experience meant he could move like a ghost through the rooms.

If the Third Reich memorabilia was not sufficiently shocking, Manolis found even more alarming items inside kitchen drawers and bedroom cupboards: rifles, shotguns, handguns and large hunting knives, all readily accessible. With so many weapons within arm's reach, Manolis began to question whether the Nazi items were souvenirs of a former time or if they reflected a current-day mindset.

"What the . . . ?"

As he examined floors and walls and surfaces, Manolis came across numerous curious marks. There was a bloodstain on the kitchen floor of one resident's house, and a stain on another's back steps. It was definitely not red paint. The stains were large and circular: gravity's effect on an injured body. It was possible that a human had bled so extensively, but the stains may also have been from animals, hunted or shot in self-defence. With so many wild animals in the area, the residents of Glikonero might conceivably keep weapons in their homes for their own personal protection should they ever find a hungry bear rummaging through their pantry.

Manolis spent the most time at Sofia's house. Zain was nowhere to be seen, as usual. Sofia may have dragged him to church, as Maria once did with a young Manolis, although Zain would not have been Greek Orthodox. The hardware that Manolis found at Sofia's house could not be described as weaponry, but it was no less disconcerting. There was a large meat grinder made of heavy-duty stainless steel that had a distinctly clinical air. Clamped to a bench in the kitchen, the grinder had serrated plates, a razor-sharp spinning blade, and a powerful crank handle. Manolis turned the handle once; it felt effortless and well-maintained. Its size and sharpness suggested that the grinder might be able to process bones as well as meat. The contraption was spotless, meticulously cleaned and oiled.

Hanging on a wall outside the house was a collection of buzz-toothed hacksaws. These were equally sharp; Manolis touched one of the blades and felt it puncture the skin on his fingertip like a vampire bite. The tools appeared well used and far from new, but they'd been cared for and were clearly effective at their job. Manolis wondered who used them since the arthritic Sofia, with her stiff and painful joints, couldn't possibly have operated such saws.

The contents of Sofia's multiple chest freezers were equally unsettling. They were stocked to the brim with unlabelled plastic bags of minced meat in different shades of pink, grey and brown. There were also some thick slabs of unminced meat. Turning them over in his hands, examining them, Manolis couldn't identify their origin through the many tight layers of opaque plastic wrapping. He lifted them to his face but his vegetarian nose could detect no smell. In the end, when he heard a noise nearby, Manolis pocketed a random bag and raced out the door. The disturbance turned out to be a stray cat knocking over a flowerpot.

At Angelo and Anna's house, there were fewer overtly disturbing items on the premises, including, noticeably, no Nazi paraphernalia. But there was one curio: Angelo's Greek passport with its burgundy cover. Manolis found it in a bedroom drawer.

"Female?" Manolis muttered to himself.

The gender in the passport was noted as "female". At first, Manolis thought it was an error, another example of incompetence in the slovenly Greek bureaucracy, some bored administrative clerk who had typed incorrectly while distracted by his phone or cigarette or coffee. Then Manolis wondered if it might have been Anna's passport, though the photograph inside was clearly Angelo. Why would Angelo need a passport? The humble shepherd didn't come across as an international man of travel, as someone with wanderlust. But then Manolis realised that most of the villagers would have passports so they could cross into nearby Albania and North Macedonia when required. For the residents of Glikonero, it was like travelling to the next suburb. Manolis took the passport as well, considering it to be another fake like the ones found at Lefty's house, and potentially an item of significance.

Roze's residence was a one-room cabin tucked away within a copse of juniper trees on the eastern edge of town. It was a former wood-shed that had been converted into a summer dwelling and wasn't fit for human habitation in winter. Kostas had said she could stay there for free since it wasn't being used. Its size meant that Manolis was able to search it in a matter of minutes, and he found little other than Roze's few personal items, which would have fit snugly into a backpack. She did not have another passport, Albanian or otherwise. There was also no ID or other identifying paperwork; she either carried her wallet around with her, or had none and was residing in Greece in the spirit of Lefty. Stuck to the wall of the cabin was a photograph of what appeared to be a teenage Roze standing with her arm around a taller, older boy. They were in front of a gushing fountain on a cloudy day. Roze was wearing a denim jacket and had longer hair. The boy was in a vintage-style base-ball jacket and ripped jeans. Both were smiling broadly, a mixture of awkwardness and rebellion. The boy could very well have been a friend or boyfriend, but since the photo was so prominently displayed, it was probably her brother who had disappeared. Roze hadn't elaborated and Manolis hadn't pressed her. Was his case just gathering dust in a dented filing cabinet in an Albanian police station?

The last house that Manolis searched proved the most intriguing of all. Unnerved by the number of stuffed animal heads mounted on the walls, he was about to exit through the back door when he stopped. He couldn't believe it when he saw it, thought his eyes were playing tricks. It was sitting in plain sight, hanging limply on a coat rack just beside a collection of colourful icons of Christ.

"Oh my God . . ."

It was a black leather motorcycle cap.

Picking it up, feeling it, studying it, Manolis realised the headwear was identical to the cap at Lefty's house that he always wore to underscore his healthy disregard for authority. The cap had a distinctive chain detail and a thick, rivet-studded brim. The design suited Lefty's personality: it was both stylish and anarchistic. It also made him look more intimidating, to counter his slight stature. The cap smelled musky, of dry sweat. Its pungency made Manolis screw up his nose.

Glancing up at the religious icons, Manolis crossed himself, according to custom, then looked back down at the cap in his hands. Surely this was no coincidence, particularly since the owner of the house was Father Petros. Why would a priest wear a leather biker cap?

Suddenly, Manolis heard a noise outside and the sound of heavy footfall on the back stairs leading up to the house.

14

The footsteps were getting louder. Manolis barely had time to think. He could stand there, be detected, and offer an excuse. Or he could seek to avoid detection; in other words, hide.

Tossing the motorcycle cap back onto the coat rack, Manolis took off into the house, heading down the hall with light but swift footsteps. Behind him, he heard the rattle of the door handle and the squeak of its hinges as it swung open. Ducking into the first room he found, Manolis concealed himself behind the door and hoped the cap he'd replaced on the rack had stopped swinging.

Why had church finished so early? Something must be wrong . . .

His breathing ragged, his pulse racing, Manolis closed his eyes and took a series of deep breaths through his nose. All his senses were concentrated on his hearing.

A dwarf cow suddenly mooed outside, making Manolis jump.

Within the house, the noises and rustling seemed to be confined to the kitchen. There was movement and muttering, words he couldn't make out. He focused, trying to block out the birdsong. There was no longer any sound of footsteps, which made Manolis think he was safe, but he remained pinned to the wall, chest heaving, palms sweating.

As the voice grew louder, Manolis realised that the language was unfamiliar and incomprehensible. The intonation, the pronunciation, the accent, the sound, the pace. What language was it? It wasn't English or Greek. And it didn't sound like Father Petros's deep baritone either.

Was it . . . Arabic?

Who spoke that?

Just as the voice disappeared, the back door slammed shut and Manolis exhaled a sigh of relief. The answer came to him: the voice belonged to Zain. But what in the world was he doing in someone else's house, inside Father Petros's house? Local residents refused to lock their doors in a show of community and stoicism. It was a mindset born of fortitude and a vein of obstinacy that was generations deep. But that was hardly an open invitation for people to walk in at any time, especially when the homeowner wasn't there.

Manolis waited for at least two silent minutes before he moved, and then he emerged gradually, peering around corners one eye and limb at a time. In the kitchen, Zain had left a large aluminium tray of food on the mahogany table. The tray felt warm and smelled of something rich and meaty. Outside, the shed door had been left open. The coast was clear. Manolis decided to follow Zain and see where he was going.

The fleet-footed Syrian made his way to the shores of Great Prespa Lake. Manolis struggled to keep up and watched carefully from a safe distance. Zain wore a backpack and appeared to be carrying some garden tools and rubber boots that he'd collected from Father Petros's darkened shed. Zain loaded the items into a tiny wooden boat that he freed from a dense tangle of reeds. Rotating his arms like helicopter blades, loosening his muscles, he warmed up for the long crossing ahead. He then sat down, removed his shirt, took a deep breath and started rowing across the lake.

The church bells pierced the mountain air like thunderclaps, drowning out the trilling of the lake birds. They went momentarily quiet as if spooked, before returning to their harmonies one peep at a time. Manolis eyed the lake intensely, watching as the black dot that was Zain grew ever smaller within its vast blue expanse. Zain seemed to be rowing in a north-westerly direction across the lake, the same course he had taken from the start. But his destination shore and country – Albania or North Macedonia – remained indiscernible. In the end, it was neither.

He berthed his boat on the small island of Golem Grad in the middle of Great Prespa Lake.

"What's he doing there?" Manolis asked himself.

He scratched his chin, intrigued. Why would the young man possibly be going to this tiny, empty island? And why was he carrying garden implements and wearing safety boots? Was he working on something, building something, tearing up something? Was it some kind of new training exercise? Or was he, conceivably, taking supplies to Lefty, or to someone else? Manolis was suspicious, stubborn and determined. One way or another, he needed to keep following.

The last time Manolis had attempted to cross the lake, he'd been in a motorboat that made an excessive amount of noise and soon attracted interest. He would not make the same mistake this time, even if the journey took longer and shredded his arms and back. Locating a small wooden boat, he began the long and tiring row to Golem Grad. His triceps and deltoids were soon screaming in pain, becoming more and more fatigued the further he rowed. Lacking the power and momentum of a motorboat, the rowing boat yawed in the strong current and Manolis struggled to hold it in a straight line. He kept having to turn around to see where he was relative to the solitary island ahead, then adjust his technique. The process was back-breaking and turned Manolis's down-hill ski run into an arduous slalom course.

Manolis knew very little about Golem Grad other than what Stavros had told him: that it was deserted, couldn't be visited without permission owing to its sensitive environment, and was home only to a few ancient ruins and churches. Since the island was officially part of North Macedonia, there were tour operators on the northern shore, he'd been told, but those were not options for Manolis. On this day, Elias did not appear inclined to intercept the two boats crossing international waters. Perhaps he didn't care about activity on the island – the mainland was different, it was a gateway, while the island was self-contained, isolated and led nowhere. Then again, it was Sunday morning and Elias might still be in church.

As the island's grim white crags loomed ahead, Manolis considered his entry point. Thanks to the island's rocky cliffs and high stone walls, he could see neither where Zain had docked his boat nor an accessible opening. Above, giant birds circled threateningly, as if there was something of great interest below. A swarm of dark eels swam in the water beside Manolis's boat, their long bodies squirming and slime-skinned. The island was tiny, only a kilometre long and half a kilometre wide, with a coastline draped with summer blooms. The crumbling walls looked as if they might once have been military fortifications to protect the island from aggressors. The island was especially rich in aquatic birds, long-billed pelicans and thin-necked cormorants in particular. They made their nests on the branches of thousand-year-old juniper trees and peeled off soul-rending cries into the sky.

Manolis was forced to stop just off the island's shore to take a deep, tired breath and rest his aching muscles. There was an intense burning between his shoulder blades, and the pain had now transferred to his lower body, his quadriceps and hamstrings and gluteals. Fresh calluses had sprouted on his palms from the sustained friction with hard wooden oars. His forehead and cheeks glowed deep red from the blood avalanching through his veins. He would need a moment to get his breath back before attempting to traverse up through the rocky terrain.

Seeing Zain's boat in what appeared to be an access point, Manolis landed on the rocky shore, dragging his boat high up the beach to make it secure. If it were washed away, he could be there for a very long time. There was no guarantee that the villagers on the mainland would realise he was missing and come looking, especially after Lefty's disappearance. What were Manolis's chances of survival? Was there drinkable water or food or shelter on the island? Manolis had never foraged for food in his life and had only ever camped out at a caravan park. He did not want to think about it. He started walking.

Finding a gap in the island's natural rocky barrier, Manolis strained to lift himself up and through, grazing his fingers in the process. As a destination, the island was not hospitable. Manolis felt like an interloper, one who was trespassing on foreign soil; officially, he was. He finally reached a plateau where he could walk without hazard or fear of falling. The island's petrified trees were white and austere. Their pallor suggested they were dead or dying, but, on closer inspection, Manolis saw that they were bleached with guano, the droppings of hundreds of roosting cormorants. He soon spotted more wildlife: slow-moving tortoises on patches of earth and fast-hopping rabbits bounding across the spongy grass. The air was dense with the fragrance of blossom, sweet and heady. Alpine swifts swirled and screamed overhead, while nightingale song swelled from deep within a dense shroud of emerald trees. The music of it brought a strange but eerie calm to Manolis as he stepped carefully across the ground. He had no idea what he might see once he caught up with Zain and wanted to stay out of sight.

The island felt distinctly warmer than the mainland, as if it had its own microclimate. Manolis's shirt clung like a garish second skin, his throat oily with humidity, his open-toed sandals cumbersome but cooling. The lush setting felt almost tropical, with its mats of stone-fastened lichen and mosses and sprouting fungi.

Ruins were dotted across the island, old churches and monasteries. Manolis pictured monks kneeling at morning prayer, peering out at the mainland as if it were an orbiting planet. There were also overgrown foundations and the remaining stumps of what appeared to be ancient houses. Boasting an other-worldly beauty, the island was probably home to a few apparitions too. From the outside the island appeared dry and rocky and tumultuous, but inside it was fertile, flat and serene. No wonder it had been home to kings and rulers over many centuries and was able to support such a wide variety of flora and fauna. It would be an appealing location into which to disappear.

A momentary break in the swirling birdsong and rustling of elm trees alerted Manolis to an unnatural sound in the near distance. It sounded as though someone was digging, grunting with exertion. Keeping low, he ran in the direction of the commotion and concealed himself behind a bushy fir. He could hear only one working shovel and one voice, which probably meant just one person. Moving swiftly between the shrubs and trees, following the noise, trying to stay camouflaged, Manolis found a better viewpoint.

A shirtless, hard-working Zain stood in a grassy clearing. He was ankle-deep in a large hole, wearing a grubby baseball cap and industrial rubber boots that stopped just below his knees. There was a dirty shovel in his hands. A long woodcutter's axe lay on the ground beside the hole, its steel blade glinting in the summer sun. After a few moments to regain his breath and wipe his brow, Zain plunged the blade of his shovel into the earth with a hiss and tossed the clod of extracted soil to one side. Was he digging up something or planning to bury something, or perhaps someone? Manolis moved to try to see inside the hole.

As he changed position, stepping sideways, Manolis kept his eyes fixed on Zain, who continued to dig. Stepping on what he thought was a fallen branch, Manolis tripped on another, and fell over. As he gathered his senses, he realised the gravity of his situation.

He'd landed in a nest of venomous horned vipers, their tongues midnight black, their irises a copper colour. Manolis had never seen that number of reptiles at once; it felt unreal. His experience with snakes was limited to watching them from behind thick protective glass at zoos and encountering the odd backyard visitor that slithered away seconds later. Having been disturbed, the vipers were agitated and swarming, engaged in a combat dance, while Manolis was frozen with fear and confusion. He loved animals, but he'd never imagined his life being threatened by one, or that a killer could be so beautiful.

15

When Manolis was a child and couldn't sleep, and his dad wasn't out all night drinking and gambling at the *kafenion*, Con would sit at the end of his bed and tell him stories from Greek mythology. As an adult, Manolis couldn't remember much about them other than that they featured gods and goddesses and demons and other creatures. In those stories, snakes were always sinister, never good and virtuous. No matter what was happening in the story, Con always spoke calmly and softly. Young Manolis would fall asleep to the cadences of his deep voice, which resonated like a finely tuned bass guitar.

Today, Manolis did not dislike snakes in the same way he didn't dislike any animal. He couldn't blame the snakes for doing what came naturally. But he didn't have a fondness for them either. Having lived in Australia, he knew they were poisonous, and their venom could kill quickly.

The horned island vipers continued to mass, as if mobilising as one united force against the trespasser in their territory. The serpents weren't especially long, only about a metre in length. Their skin was thick and scaly, as if reinforced for conflict, and their level of toxicity looked high. What distinguished them from other snakes was the single horn on their snouts; it pointed diagonally forward in a menacing manner. It was almost as if a snake had cross-bred with a heavily armoured rhinoceros. Their camouflage was equally effective, with Manolis soon realising that there were more vipers than he had originally thought, at least a dozen. His sandalled feet and bare ankles looked exposed and succulent. The rippling snakes expressed their displeasure by hissing loudly and darting their forked tongues.

"Gah!"

It was a primal sound that emerged from Manolis's throat as one of the vipers shot forward. It was still some distance from Manolis's legs but it was unequivocally coming closer. He didn't know whether to flee or stay. To move might make them see him as even more of a threat, while not moving made him an easy target.

Hearing a disturbance nearby, Zain dropped his shovel, picked up his axe, and came to investigate. Seeing Manolis in danger, he swung into immediate and decisive action. Wielding his axe like a samurai warrior would his sword, he lunged forward and chopped the heads off some vipers and slashed others in half. Manolis curled his legs into his chest, making himself small, and trying to stay out of the way. It was all over in a few seconds. Those snakes who hadn't been decapitated or left in multiple pieces desperately slithered away to safety.

Manolis looked up at Zain, breathing heavily. There were tiny spatters of snake blood on his thick rubber boots. It was now clear why he was wearing them.

"Thank you," stammered Manolis. "Thank you for saving me. Those snakes looked poisonous."

Zain looked down at the stranger for a long, ponderous time. He didn't make eye contact at first, hiding beneath the shadow of his cap. But when it eventually came off, his irises were an arresting green. Underfed angles jutted out from his face.

"They are full of poison," he said. "They have eyes like cats, shaped like slits. But they are protected too, they are a threatened species."

"Oh," Manolis said. "I'm sorry you had to kill them. I hope you don't get in any trouble."

"I do that sometimes. I act first and think later. But the snakes thought you were a threat, they were trying to protect themselves."

Manolis nodded numbly, his energy sapped.

"Snakes do not usually start fights but they do end them," Zain added. "Still, human life is more important."

Manolis felt sheepish for causing the law to be broken. Zain smiled through crooked teeth and thickened lips, telltale scars of years in the ring.

"What are you doing here?" he asked. His voice had a sudden threatening tone.

Manolis stood to his full height, dusted himself off, straightened his shirt.

"I'm new to the area and was exploring," he said calmly. "I've never been out here before."

"It is not safe here on the island. As you can see, there are many snakes. And they have much poison that can kill. You should not be here."

Manolis looked down at Zain's safety boots, grubby from all the soil he'd dug.

"If it's so unsafe, then what are you doing here?"

"Nothing," he said.

"You look like you're digging."

"Yes."

"Digging for what? For treasure?"

Zain's eyes darted, his breathing quickened. Eventually, he relaxed and he reached behind his sun-smacked back. From his rear trouser pocket he pulled out a piece of heavily creased paper the colour of weak tea. He unfolded it to reveal a hand-drawn map of the island complete with several marked locations. Manolis's ability to read Greek was rudimentary but even he could tell the map's purpose.

"Gold," Zain said. "Coins."

Manolis smiled. Combined with Angelo and his metal detector, Zain's activities showed that the prospecting spirit was alive and well in the Prespes.

"Father Petros lets me borrow his tools and boots to search," Zain said.

147

Manolis nodded his understanding. "And where did you get this map?"

Zain thought a while before responding, his eyes shifty. "From Sofia. She had it at home."

Manolis scrutinised the map, turning it around in his hands. It looked old and genuine enough.

"Uh-huh," he said. "And where did she get it?"

"I do not know."

Zain walked Manolis over to where he'd been digging, showed him the excavation site, how it aligned with the map. He'd dug in a few different locations over the summer but with no luck. That said, he was in no hurry because he felt he had a distinct advantage over all the other prospectors who'd ever come to the region: they'd never searched on the island.

"Because of the snakes," he added.

"Of course," said Manolis.

And the snakes were also the reason why Zain was so certain of his strategy.

"The snakes are here because they are protecting the treasure," he said.

Out of the corner of his eye, Manolis saw a pair of reptilian security guards unwind. He reeled back until Zain reassured him they weren't venomous. Manolis watched the snakes slither between some rocks, their zigzagged tails disappearing like retracted vacuum cords. Unlike the horned vipers, which were thick and grey, these serpents were long, thin and black. It was only then that Manolis realised that what he'd seen in the water beside his boat weren't eels.

Zain said that the snakes' only real threat were golden eagles, who fed almost exclusively on them. The elegant raptors flew across from the mainland for a feed, snatching the coiled reptiles with their spiked talons as if they were cinnamon rolls. They then returned to their nests in the rocky mountain crests, often to divide their kill among their hungry fledglings.

"The island is like their pantry," Zain said.

"What about you?" Manolis asked. "You're not scared of snakes?"

Zain laughed. "No. I used to practise my boxing in Syria with desert cobras."

The two men went and sat under the shade of a thick oak tree. Manolis eased himself warily onto the grass, scrutinising the immediate area like a forensic pathologist. He was still on edge. Zain proudly brandished his razor-sharp axe, which still bore the dried reptile blood of its earlier victims.

"We are safe here," Zain said, a cockeyed grin on his face.

"I can't help but think of the myth of Medusa," Manolis said.

"Snakes instead of hair, yes," said Zain. "What are you doing here?"

Manolis delivered his usual labourer story, which Zain admitted to having already heard.

"I know who you are," he said. "Sofia told me."

"OK then. So, who are you?"

Zain deflected the question with a dismissive gesture. "I am nobody," he said.

"What about your family, are they still in Syria?"

Zain seemed reluctant to talk about himself, as if he had something to hide, and said only that he'd reached Greece by fishing boat, landing on an island whose name he didn't remember, before boarding a commercial ferry to the mainland. Like Roze, he was an illegal immigrant. Just as Ahmed Omari had been in Australia, before he was sent to the purgatory of mandatory immigration detention in Cobb. Zain hoped to settle in a more prosperous country in northern Europe such as Germany or Denmark, where he could continue boxing and compete professionally. It was the reason why he pursued a fitness and training regime as best he could in rural Greece, and often needed to improvise.

"I have a trainer but he is in Syria," Zain said.

"Do you have any family?" Manolis asked.

"My parents and brothers and sisters."

"How many?"

"Five. I am the oldest."

"Where are they?"

"In Aleppo. They wanted to leave but not yet. I left because I am the oldest."

"And you are unmarried? Have you any children?"

"Not married. No wife and children."

Zain offered Manolis a bottle of water from his backpack. Manolis thanked him and slaked his thirst. Zain sipped from his canteen. The two men sat listening to the breeze and insect hum, to the aquatic birds that spread across the sky like astral spray. They were somewhere in the middle of the island in a relatively sheltered location with lush foliage and mossy rocks that were a vivid green.

"It's pretty beautiful here," Manolis said.

"Here is like no other," Zain replied.

"Have you ever seen anyone else here?"

Father Petros was the most likely visitor. As the local clergyman, he would visit all the old churches in the region, if only to check on their upkeep and light a pencil-thin candle. But Zain began to describe someone even more familiar before eventually saying the name:

"Lefteris."

It was a surprising answer, yet completely predictable.

Lefty may have used Golem Grad as a place to do business. With its lack of visitors and strategic position between three countries, it was a perfect rendezvous for smugglers of black-market goods across inter-national borders, especially if the island was left unpatrolled by Elias. Lefty may even have had an illicit stash of booty somewhere on the island, like he did at home. Golem Grad was big enough and isolated enough to allow for storage and transactions, yet small enough and insignificant enough to slip under the radar. In fact, an island like Golem Grad suited Lefty's invisible personality perfectly. Just as he was larger than life in person, yet invisible on paper, so, in the same way, the island was in plain view in the middle of the great lake, yet never visited.

"I know that man," Manolis said.

"I know," said Zain. "Sofia told me."

Manolis glared at him a while.

"Have you ever seen Father Petros here visiting the churches?" he asked.

"No. Never."

"And what was Lefty doing here when you saw him?"

"Sitting in the sun. Walking around. I only saw him twice."

"Did you talk?"

"Yes, but only a little."

"How did he get here?"

"Boat."

"But it was definitely him?"

"Oh yes, it was him. I know Sofia and he were not very good friends."

That was an understatement. Sofia would have told Zain in great detail about her history with Lefty and maybe even embellished certain stories. It was possible that Zain's cool veneer hid a good deal of anger. He might come across as a diffident young man but his loyalties needed no explanation.

Another liquorice snake slid past. Manolis was unperturbed this time, emboldened by Zain's confident presence and hefty hatchet. As an iridescent yellow butterfly landed on Manolis's arm, a thought occurred.

"Could Lefty have been bitten by a snake and died here on the island?"

Zain scratched a taut pectoral muscle in thought.

"It is possible. There are some very poisonous snakes here. As you saw."

"Have you ever been bitten by a snake?"

"Yes. Mainly dry bites."

"What are dry bites?"

"No venom. Only fang and teeth marks. Just a bite. Most snakes do not want to kill people, they just want us to go away."

Horned vipers had long fangs and highly toxic venom but didn't usually bite without provocation. That was why Manolis had ended up in their cross hairs – he had disturbed their territory. But what if Lefty had done the same?

"I would have found his body," said Zain. "The island is small."

"Have you ever properly looked?"

Zain stared at the ground and scuffed his solid boot into the grass. "No."

Manolis stood. "Shall we . . . ?"

Together, the two-man search party spent the rest of the afternoon combing Golem Grad, searching every square inch, with Zain and his watchful axe leading the way. They walked east to west, and south to north. They spoke about the village to pass the time; it was, after all, one of the few things they had in common. Manolis tried to press the young man for information, especially about Sofia. Zain was guarded, describing Sofia simply as "a nice lady" whose mood turned oil-slick black whenever Lefty's name came up in conversation.

"And what did you think of Lefty?" Manolis asked.

Zain shrugged his broad shoulders. "He was friendly to me. But I did not speak to him a lot because of Sofia."

As they walked, Manolis saw thin snakes slithering across the ground and hanging like vines from the dry branches of trees. Zain assured him they were not dangerous. He said the pelicans that lived on Golem Grad were all old, some as old as forty.

"This is their retirement village."

Zain added that Manolis needed to watch above his head, not just beneath his feet.

"The waterbirds bring up the fish parts they cannot digest. The pelicans can hold three kilos of fish in their gullets so be careful you are not hit with a flying fish head."

As they walked, they saw remnants of ossified snake cartilage and shells of dead turtles. Zain picked up an empty shell and showed it to Manolis.

"The climate is changing," he said.

He talked about a time when the lake had frozen; a bad winter, Sofia had called it. The Prespians had moved their cattle to the warmer island in the hope they might survive. But the wolves followed and a massacre ensued.

"The villagers then shot all the wolves," Zain said. "And mongooses were brought in to eat the snakes but did not survive the winter. So the island is a graveyard for hundreds of dead animals and their ghosts."

With no roads on the island, the two walkers blazed their own trail across uneven ground. The few churches they encountered were modest buildings, their interiors boasting faded frescoes and heavy cobweb curtains. They were home to even more slithering reptiles, mainly dice snakes, so-called because of the black spots on their coloured bodies. Zain said they reminded him of the Snakes and Ladders board game he played as a child with dice. Manolis said he used to play that too, and had started to play it with Christos.

By the time they reached the northern shore of Golem Grad, Manolis had seen more snakes than he'd ever wanted to encounter in his lifetime. Some were quite beautiful and graceful in their undulating movements. But they were still snakes. And there was no sign of humanity anywhere, alive or dead, no sign of Lefty.

"I'm sorry," said Zain. "He is not here."

He said he had dug up the odd human femur or skull during his excavations. That made Manolis stop.

"Human bones? Here, on the island? Dead bodies?"

"They are relics, the bones of ancient monks," Zain said. "But they are very big. The monks who once lived here were giants. One of them chose the island as a test of faith and lived here alone for two years. He lived in a tree house built above the reach of the snakes and would only go down on the ground at night."

On the return leg of the journey they walked around the western edge of the island with the sun on their backs. It was the shore that faced Albania, which Zain pointed out as Roze's home. The lake sparkled brightly, mirroring the petrol-blue sky, as miniature waves curled over its surface.

"I will stay a while longer today," Zain said, looking over his shoulder.

"It'll be dark soon," said Manolis, pointing at the low sun.

"I know, but I want to keep digging. I will be fine. Snake blood is cold so they hide when the sun goes down."

Shaking Manolis's hand, Zain returned to his prospecting. As Manolis began the slow row back to Greek soil, he considered the young Syrian pugilist. Why would he abandon his search for buried treasure to help Manolis scour the island for Lefty? It struck him as odd. Perhaps Zain was genuinely concerned about Lefty's disappearance, despite his being Sofia's adversary. Or maybe he had other reasons . . .

But Manolis couldn't dwell on it for long. As he left behind the island, the fetid kingdom of cormorants, his thoughts quickly turned from its black leathery snakes to the black leather motorcycle cap he'd seen at Father Petros's house.

16

The view through the chipped windscreen of Stavros's battered Bulgarian clunker was of a potholed mess of a road that lacked markings and was littered with huge piles of donkey droppings. Manolis bobbled about like a dashboard figurine while Stavros ashed a cigarette out of a half-open window and smashed the accelerator to the floor. Unbroken cloud clotted up the sky like a great grey brain. Gentle rain was falling, sounding a light toccata on the car roof and making the narrow road greasy. The sedan slid like a hockey puck, fishtailing slightly as the rear wheels lost traction. Manolis felt a low-grade nausea burrowing in his stomach.

"The road to Eleftheria is atrocious," grumbled Stavros. "But we're making excellent time today."

"Uh-huh . . ."

Manolis forced a grin through clenched teeth. Every kilometre or so, an ornate shrine appeared by the rock-strewn roadside. Translated as "little candles", these *kandylakia* were erected in memory of those who had lost their lives in car crashes.

"Lots of *kandylakia* on this road," Manolis said.

Stavros rubbed the wooden crucifix dangling from the rear-view mirror for luck. He repeated this with every sighting.

"They're not all bad omens," he said. "Some are for those who survived road accidents and they're dedicated to their patron saint."

"But they still had accidents . . ."

"Ha. Yes. But I prefer to see the *kandylakia* as regular reminders to appreciate every moment we're alive."

The two friends were travelling in a south-westerly direction to the village from which Lefty had been expelled for being a serial pest – or at least, that's what Elias had said. Manolis was curious to hear first-hand if the border guard's account of Lefty's chequered past was true, and see what else he might learn about Lefty's unwritten history. Stavros said he knew Lefty had lived in Eleftheria for some years but he never spoke of what took him there or made him leave.

"I thought it might have been a woman in both cases," Stavros said.

The countryside was changing, becoming less hardscrabble and more fertile as they approached the warm Ionian Sea. Dollops of green shot past the windows in the form of rich, verdant olive groves. Eleftheria nestled in a lost valley that was unreachable by straight roads; so far, they had canted around lethal hairpin bends and driven up steep switchbacks and down dirt tracks. The town's name was a feminine version of Lefty's own name, so it was perhaps no wonder that he'd once chosen to live here.

Manolis had decided to be selective in revealing what he'd found during his house searches in Glikonero. He'd grown increasingly suspicious of everyone, including Stavros, and although it might be illogical, he'd decided to trust nothing and no-one other than his own gut. Instead, he talked about the number of weapons that he'd found in the village.

"I have two revolvers at home myself," Stavros admitted.

Manolis glared at his driver. A sly whip of a smile broke across Stavros's lips.

"Both were my father's," he said. "And I think it may be the same for other residents: they're more likely old keepsakes than active weapons."

Manolis was less certain. Most of the weapons he had seen did not appear to be antiques.

The rain was getting heavier. So was the weight of Stavros's foot on the accelerator. Manolis gripped the roof handle above his seat.

"You may be right about the firearms," Manolis said. "But I found something else that I thought was really odd . . ."

He went on to describe Angelo's passport, which noted his gender as female, and posited the theory that Lefty had been smuggling lucrative black-market passports across international borders. He decided not to mention the three additional passports he'd found at Lefty's house. On hearing the description of Angelo's passport, Stavros looked across at Manolis and chuckled.

"Lefty may very well have been smuggling passports," he said. "But not in this case . . ."

Manolis waited for an elaboration that never came.

"So, what does that mean?" he finally asked.

Stavros adjusted his sunglasses on the top of his head. On the horizon, flint-grey clouds still cast a dull, leaden pall over the sky. Stavros gunned the engine until he almost rammed the car in front, an old hatchback with no rear window, then jammed on the brake. Their heads whiplashed in unison. Stavros abused his horn mercilessly.

"Sorry, I should explain," Stavros said. "To be honest, we don't even think about it anymore, it's such old news . . ."

He went on to describe how Angelo was actually Angela, and one of the region's last sworn virgins.

"These are women who opted to live as men to escape the domination of the Greek patriarchal system. The price was a vow of virginity and chastity."

"So, wait . . ." Manolis said. "Angelo, er, I mean, Angela, is really a woman and chose to become a man because it's better to be a man than a woman in this part of the world?"

"Basically. But there's more to it than that."

The motives for such a choice were exclusively a social construct and not prompted by sexuality or physical changes.

"There were personal circumstances at play here," Stavros said. "In Angela and Anna's family, the only male heir, their brother, died in a blood feud, stabbed to death in a vengeance killing. That meant that property could no longer be passed on in patrilineal fashion. Because Angela was a virgin daughter, she was able to assume the role of patriarch by swearing a pledge of lifelong celibacy in front of the village elders. By means of this declaration, Angela secured the family estate and honour within Glikonero. But she was forced to become Angelo, which meant dressing like a man, working like a man, and assuming both the liberties and burdens of a man."

Manolis tried to picture Angelo and whether he had noticeably feminine features. He couldn't remember. Was there a softness in Angelo's eyes and hands? Did he have an Adam's apple?

"You can't tell by looking at Angelo," Stavros said. "Not that it matters. He's always spat and smoked and cursed, and moving and dressing like a man has become second nature now."

An oncoming logging truck swerved to avoid a pothole and crossed onto Stavros's side of the road. He blasted his horn again until the truck jerked back out of the way, missing the jalopy by centimetres. Seconds later, the car was overtaken by two helmetless motorbike riders travelling at breakneck speed.

"When exactly did all this happen?" Manolis asked, breath returning to his body.

"Years ago," Stavros said, flicking his cigarette butt out the car window. "My parents might remember it, but not me. To me, Angelo has always been a man. People who didn't understand the practice used to tease Angelo and call him a lesbian in disguise."

"That's pretty narrow-minded."

"Women who became sworn virgins did so to protect the family. It's a choice of practicality, not happiness. By declaring himself to be a man, Angelo wasn't striking out at gender norms – he was submitting to them."

Manolis found the practice fascinating, and deemed Angelo's sacrifice worthy of the utmost respect.

"These days, it's dying out. There's only a handful of sworn virgins left here and in Albania – maybe a hundred," Stavros said. "They're like a lost tribe. In the modern world, women have more freedom. Did you hear about the newest *kafenion* to open in Florina?"

"No. What about it?"

Stavros smiled cheekily. "It's for *women only*. Men are only allowed entry if escorted by a woman. It's the only one of its kind in Greece and apparently really hip. There's lace draped across a red couch, colourful crystal decanters on the counter, women's hats hanging from the ceiling. They host book readings and live music."

"That's really great," Manolis said. "We have similar things in Australia, but I understand the significance of that here."

"It flips the script completely."

"How's the coffee?"

"Meant to be excellent. Anyway, the point is that women no longer need to become sworn virgins to escape their condition."

"What about Anna, the other daughter?"

"She tried to have children of her own but couldn't," Stavros replied. "That's why the two sisters now live together like an old married couple."

"And what happened with the blood feud?"

"Angelo was safe. A woman who became a sworn virgin wasn't seen as entirely male, so was spared the blood feuds and being murdered by a rival clan."

They arrived in the village of Eleftheria just as the rain began to clear. They saw litter-strewn streets, broken or boarded-up windows, many stray animals and only a few cars from the current century. Some of the buildings hinted at a former glory that was now concealed in a melancholy stain. The scattering of faces that Manolis saw through his lightly fogged window looked tired and raddled, slightly wild even. People were quick to glare rather than smile. Everything had a look of scouring hunger.

The two men headed straight for the first *kafenion* they saw. The air was thicker and warmer than in the mountains, but felt decidedly precarious.

"See that?" Stavros said, gesturing to the other side of the wet road.

Manolis turned. "What, you mean that funny-looking red car?"

"Pretty cool, don't you think?"

He was pointing at a paint-chipped vehicle that he called "an original Styl Kar". It was a three-wheeled truck first made after the Second World War. Manolis wandered over to inspect it. As a car enthusiast who'd recently rebuilt a 1970s Valiant sedan that fast became kindling in Cobb, he was enthralled by the truck's quirky design and colourful history. It looked like it only held two passengers, and was unlike any other vehicle he'd seen. The tray was laden with deformed watermelons, the truck's suspension sitting low.

"These vehicles were once all over rural Greece," Stavros said. "Ex-military motorcycles leftover from the war were transformed into light trucks."

He described them as Frankenstein cars, engineered from parts of different vehicles that were welded together to form strange new contraptions. Manolis loved the idea, the ingenuity. He kicked a tyre with a degree of satisfaction. He'd still not quite got over his Val being torched in Cobb.

"The trucks proved very popular in Greece because they were surprisingly efficient," Stavros said. "But the most important feature for the Greeks was that they didn't fall into the same tax category as four-wheeled automobiles, so were much cheaper to run."

The inside of the *kafenion* was dark, the air in the room sepulchral. Patrons sat with heads hung low, a room full of jobless, downtrodden men anaesthetised by the warm fug. There were old photos on the walls of armed men with imperial moustaches in white fustanellas looking strong and triumphant. The atmosphere was quiet and menacing. It was in stark contrast to the women's *kafenion* in Florina that Stavros had just described.

Stavros ordered two coffees and made small talk with the bearded barista as he helped himself to a complimentary bowl of pistachios. Lukas said that business was appalling and that the economy was even worse. His forearms and hands were covered in dark tattoos. He wore ripped cargo shorts and an old replica football shirt. Manolis was relieved it wasn't the same club as the kid he'd shot and killed, but he relived the memory nevertheless. At times, he felt it like a ghost limb, something missing from his body.

"It's nice to see some new faces around here," Lukas said. "Are you just passing through? I assume you're not here for any purpose . . ."

"Actually, we are."

Stavros reached into his wallet and produced a crumpled photo of Lefty that he slid across the table to Lukas. The photo was a print of an image taken with Stavros's phone and one of the few photos of Lefty in existence. For obvious reasons, Lefty didn't like to be photographed and often demanded that people delete photos of him on their phones and not share them around. A photo was a digital representation, and Lefty was determined to leave no such fingerprints in the world.

Seeing the image, recognising the face, Lukas's eyes grew large and he bristled with anger, claiming to be owed a considerable sum of money by the man in the photo. Snatching the print, he showed it to the aproned proprietor, Vangelis, a bald man with scurfy features. Manolis noticed a look pass between them that seemed to boil the air in the room.

"This worthless bastard owes me hundreds in unpaid bills and outstanding debts," Vangelis seethed. "I loaned him some money and he never paid it back, he disappeared."

Manolis looked across at Stavros. Stavros rolled his eyes as if what he was hearing was completely unexpected and nonchalantly tossed the meat of a pistachio into his mouth.

Word swiftly spread through the *kafenion* like a contagion, the photo being exchanged between cigarette-stained fingers, examined, squeezed, rumpled and handed on. Patrons reported similar debts and grew enraged. One man claimed that Lefty had borrowed money from his teenage son, and another from his elderly mother on a pension. A small crowd soon formed, baying for Lefty's blood and demanding to know his current whereabouts. Manolis watched a man open a beer bottle with his teeth. Two others bashed their fists on tables. Manolis felt a flash of panic as he wondered how far this might escalate.

"This is getting out of hand," Stavros said to Manolis.

"Agreed," Manolis replied. "But let me try something . . ."

Having finished his muddy coffee, Manolis tapped the ceramic demitasse loudly with a teaspoon, like a guest at a wedding seeking attention for a toast. As a hush settled, he tried to restore order.

"Look, I'm sorry everyone, but we don't know where Lefty is either. He's missing and we're looking for him. But I think we can help you provided you're willing to help us."

From behind the bar, Vangelis let out a loud, derisive laugh.

"Help you? How the hell can we do that?" he boomed. "What more can we give? Look around you, we have nothing."

Manolis had to write down everyone's names and the money they were owed and Stavros had to pay the bill and leave a sizeable tip before they could safely exit the *kafenion*. Noting everyone's names played into Manolis's plan – it added to his list of potential suspects with a motive to harm Lefty. Altogether, the sum of money owed by Lefty totalled about ten thousand euros, which was not insignificant. Stavros provided his phone number and promised that he would be in touch as soon as they found Lefty.

As final details were exchanged, an old man who had been sitting alone quietly approached Manolis. He had a thick rush of white hair and an antique walking stick with an ivory handle. Introducing himself gently as Odysseas, he said that Lefty didn't owe him any money but having heard that Manolis was from Glikonero, he wanted to talk about the history of the Prespes, since he'd grown up there. Manolis thought that Odysseas might have known his father or aunt, and he asked him about both, but he didn't. Odysseas did, however, claim that the region was once full of sick children during the time when entry was restricted. Manolis was intrigued – could this be why there were no children in Glikonero today? Had some illness once swept through the region that meant it needed to be quarantined from the rest of Greece? Or had there been some contaminant in the water or soil that poisoned the most vulnerable? Manolis pressed Odysseas for details but he said he couldn't remember, he was too young at the time, and was now too old to recall.

Back behind the wheel, Stavros floored his jalopy even harder now, anxious to escape from Eleftheria.

"Well, so much for that," Stavros breathed. "But at least we got out alive."

"Yep," Manolis said, tone tight.

Stavros flicked on the radio, found some modern Greek music, and turned up the volume. As the village grew smaller in his side mirror, Manolis exhaled his tension. The adrenaline seeped from his body as the sharp metallic bouzouki music assaulted his ears.

After a couple of minutes' driving, Manolis's forehead began to throb like a second heart. He couldn't tell if it was from the experience in the *kafenion* or the loud music echoing through the car, or something else. For the first time since he had accepted the case of the missing Lefty, Manolis was experiencing mixed emotions. He'd always thought of the man as shady, but in a loveable, endearing way that didn't cause major harm. But he now realised he'd underestimated Lefty; he was beginning to sound like a professional con man. It made complete sense given his undocumented status and the large stash of money at his house. What else could it be? And surely Stavros, now coolly smoking a soothing cigarette, would have known all about it? Things just didn't add up.

It was also clear that Lefty had not been run out of town, as Elias had described. Lefty had left voluntarily, leaving behind a trail of financial destruction and some very angry creditors. He had pauperised the entire village and left it in modern Greek ruin. And maybe other villages too, before he'd disappeared into the night.

Stavros lowered his window a crack, letting the cabin fill with fresh air and fresher smoke, and made the music louder still.

The search for Lefty had changed. Manolis was hunting a shape-shifter, a chameleon with no moral compass. If anyone was going to light the wick of anarchy, it would be Lefty. And given the reception in Eleftheria, Manolis wondered if Elias had intentionally sent him walking head first into the jaws of an ambush.

17

The recent rain had amplified the sweet, almost intoxicating smell of pine needles. The scent filled Manolis's nostrils, making them twitch and flare ecstatically.

In a sun-dappled forest to the east of Great Prespa Lake, the tall slender trees swayed gently overhead, barely making a sound. Manolis wore sturdy, snake-thwarting hiking boots and was carrying a backpack. With a view to getting to know Father Petros, he'd finally accepted his invitation to go rabbit hunting. In the back of Manolis's mind was the black leather motorcycle cap he'd seen at the priest's house, which he thought was Lefty's. It was a crucial clue – his only clue, in fact.

His ankle healed, Father Petros now walked unaided, albeit gingerly. His rifle was slung casually over his shoulder and he even wore combat fatigues. Manolis was perplexed by the sight of an elderly, bearded priest brandishing a firearm at small, defenceless animals; it ran counter to the clergy's message of love between all creatures. But Manolis knew that rabbits had overrun the region, where they wreaked havoc on crops and gardens. He'd therefore agreed to accompany the holy man while he went hunting, although had refused the priest's offer of a loaded gun.

Father Petros would regularly stop and fill his lungs, inhaling the clear forest air.

"Every morning and every night, when I wake and before I sleep, I stand on my doorstep, say a prayer, stretch my arms out wide and take ten deep breaths," he told Manolis. "I sleep better, and I credit my staying fit and healthy to the clean air up here. The lake is like a balm."

Manolis forced a smile. He often thought about young Christos on either side of sleep, thoughts that were bittersweet. And deep within Manolis's sleep, the teenager he'd shot and killed left his lungs feeling tense. The kid's prospects may have been grim, but he still had his whole life ahead until Manolis took it away. The street kid, the dead unnameable street kid, and the unspeakable sin at Manolis's hand. The bitter realisation was starting to consume him, one intrusive recollection and flashback at a time.

"Do you have any children?" Manolis asked.

"A daughter," said Father Petros. "She works as a nurse in Crete."

"Does she have children?"

"Afraid not. I would love to become a *papou* before I die. My wife missed out."

"I'm sorry to hear that. I didn't realise you were a widower."

"Thank you. My beloved Zoe. She lived a long life and didn't suffer in the end, the cancer took her quickly. It doesn't get much better than that, though it would have been nice if she could have held a grandchild in her arms."

Away from the rest of the village, the two men could talk freely and without censorship. Father Petros came across as a typical alpha male, more of an outdoorsman than a theologian. He was confident in leading the conversation and spoke proudly about his hunting conquests and how much he loved to shoot and fish. He even did his own taxidermy, a skill he had painstakingly perfected over many years. The mounting of an animal was an art form that involved months of meticulous work, with every single project a labour of love. Manolis nodded without enthusiasm. He'd already seen the gruesome products of that hobby.

"Zoe hated it," the priest added. "The practice, she found it distasteful. But I love it."

"Can you perform taxidermy on a human?" Manolis asked suddenly.

Father Petros stared at him. "That's a pretty dark question."

"Just curious," Manolis said with a smile.

"I mean, there are animals and then there are humans . . ."

"But we're all animals, no?"

Father Petros chuckled. "Well, yes," he said. "But the idea of preparing a human body in such a way has a disturbing and shameful history. I won't go into it, other than to say that theoretically it's feasible, but technically it's not possible."

"Why's that?"

The priest composed himself and gathered his thoughts. "Human skin discolours significantly after the preservation process and stretches a lot more than animal skin and fur. It's nowhere near as sturdy. So any maker would have to be very skilled at creating a replica of a body and touching up the skin tone. The handling of human remains is not something a taxidermist does. That's for a mortician."

"But what about that old communist leader whose body has been on display in Russia for years and years?"

"You mean Lenin's mausoleum. He's embalmed, which is different. Even then, the body needs to be retouched every year to keep him looking healthy."

The men walked on. Father Petros seemed to know a lot about human taxidermy. Through the river willows, the sharp clacking of mistle thrushes pelted the air.

"Everything my father did, I do," the priest said proudly. "He was a priest as well. And yes, I enjoy my pastimes, including hunting and taxidermy. But nothing compares to priesthood. I love all my parishioners like a shepherd loves their flock."

It was at that moment that Father Petros asked why he hadn't yet seen Manolis at church.

"You should come sometime," he said. "It'll do you good, fill your soul."

Manolis looked away into the thick forest. He was still searching for wildlife, something exotic like a soft-eyed deer or bushy-tailed fox. Overhead, the thrumming of woodpeckers could be heard.

"I used to go to church as a child with my mother but I'm not religious now," he said sheepishly. "In that respect, I'm like my father."

Father Petros smiled warmly. "That's fine," he said. "You don't need to be religious to come to church, I would still welcome you. With the exception of Zain, the whole village comes on Sundays, even Roze, and I know that not all of them are religious. It's a way to come together as a community. I would also welcome Zain if he chose to come."

The mention of Zain's name allowed Manolis to raise his prospecting on Golem Grad. Father Petros said that he'd gladly lent the young man some tools to aid him in his quest.

"They were sitting in my shed doing very little," he said. "It was the least I could do to help a new arrival. He's young and fit and eager. Imagine if he finds something when no-one else has all these years. It would make me very happy, to think I'd had a hand in that. He'd be set for life and could bring his whole family to the safety of Europe."

Father Petros admitted that there were some churches on the island that could have used his attention but said that the snakes were too much for him. "I don't like snakes and I've come close to being bitten twice when hunting. I like to hunt, but not for snakes. You don't shoot snakes. They're not pests like rabbits. And despite being deadly, they're actually vulnerable."

Manolis chose not to mention his trip to Golem Grad and that it had claimed several members of a protected species.

"There's one of the pests now . . ."

A fast-running rabbit had snagged the priest's attention. It was darting through the trees, its fluffy white tail flicking like a beacon. Drawing his weapon, tracking its movements for a few seconds, taking aim and squeezing the trigger, he was able to bring it down with a single, clean shot to the head from some distance. Seeing the rabbit drop, the priest flashed a neon smile from beneath his long beard and stroked it contentedly. He was a skilled marksman, which Manolis found both surprising and disconcerting.

"Single-shot kills are deeply satisfying," the priest said. "It is the most humane way for the animal, and it saves on bullets."

Manolis gave a lopsided smile as they walked to retrieve the body.

"I credit my military training," Father Petros said. "All young Greek men have to do two years of compulsory service in the Hellenic Army. Did you still have to do your service even though you moved to Australia?"

Manolis didn't know whether to lie. To say yes would have invited further questions and given him away. To say no required explanation.

"I got a special exemption," he lied. Then added: "Because of my age."

Father Petros laughed. "Shame," he said. "My army years were some of the best of my life. I was young, full of energy, I made many friends and had a great time. And now I'm a crack shot and expert hunter."

"Do you know if Lefty ever did his compulsory service?" Manolis said. Had he done so, it would have left a permanent record and old contacts – army buddies, sergeants.

"If he did, he never spoke of it," Father Petros replied. "Knowing Lefty, he probably talked his way out of it, as with everything else in life he wants to avoid."

They arrived at the bunny. Father Petros bent down to inspect its limp, still-warm body. There was a perfectly circular bullet hole in the side of its head and a thick crimson trail of blood starting to gum up around the wound, black clumps clinging to the animal's fur.

"A good size," the priest said. "A healthy adult. I think I'll take it to Kostas, he can make a delicious stew with some carrots, onions and celery." He wrapped it in a dark plastic bag and handed it to Manolis, who placed it gently in his backpack.

They kept walking through the pines, their amputated needles blanketing parts of the forest like a lush carpet. The trees swayed and whispered prayers into the stillness as if summoning the long-forgotten voices of seasons past.

Father Petros said that he had actually been the very first person to raise the alarm with the police about Lefty's disappearance.

Manolis stiffened. "When was that?" he asked.

"Um, let's see . . ." The priest counted with his broad fingers. "Sunday, Monday, Tuesday . . . that's three. Three days after he was last seen."

That wasn't encouraging. It was a desperately long time when so much could have happened.

"Lefty was a creature of habit, but it was still some time before we realised he was missing," Father Petros said. "When he didn't show up for church on Sunday, I went to check on him. He wasn't home, but nothing appeared awry, it looked like he'd just gone out. I thought he'd maybe gone to Florina for the day."

"Speaking of Florina, do you think the police have done enough since then?" Manolis said.

Father Petros's reply was curt and direct. "No."

He added:

"But I can see where they're coming from . . ."

When Lefty went missing, the police had little with which to build a profile – no mobile phone, computer, e-mail, social media, bank accounts or paperwork to speak of.

"Lefty was just a single man with a dead landline and answering machine who told tall tales about his life to anyone who would listen – friends and visitors at the taverna," the priest said. "That's all the police had to go on. It's practically nothing. Lefty was so hard to reach, so unreal, that he was effectively a myth."

Manolis thought Father Petros's description made Lefty sound profoundly lonely and isolated, which was perhaps a natural conse-quence of being an invisible. It was a hard way to live, both practically and emotionally.

Manolis let his mind wander. In cases of missing people, proof-of-life checks would be the first step. But Lefty was no typical case. Without either a mobile or landline, a record of calls could not be retrieved. With leaky international borders and corrupt border police, there would be no reliable record of travel or border crossings. Hospital reports might have been useful if a body had been found, but only if it could be identified, and Lefty had no official identification; he would be John Doe. And in Lefty's case, it wasn't possible to check whether he'd accessed any bank accounts or social services, because he had none.

"So, you can hardly blame the police," Father Petros said. "They're lazy, that's without question. But they can only do so much, and this case falls beneath their threshold for caring."

"From what I've seen, the police have done absolutely nothing," Manolis said.

"You're not wrong," said Father Petros. A shadow fell across the priest's face. Rifle in hand, he eyed Manolis and said:

"If you took Lefty deep into the woods and shot him in the head like this . . . like he was a rabbit . . . as far as the law is concerned, there would be no crime. After all, how can you murder someone who doesn't exist? There is no record of his life, which means there can be no record of his death and no trial for his murder. It's as if he never existed, he was never here on earth, there's no written record. The only possible record of such a killing is a mental one between the killer, their conscience and almighty God."

His measured, dispassionate words echoed something that Stavros had once said. It made Manolis feel distinctly uneasy in such an isolated location, the vast enclosure of pines suddenly appearing dark and mysterious. Could this priest, this devout man of God, have conceivably shot and killed Lefty on a rabbit-hunting expedition, disposed of the body, yet saved his black leather cap as some kind of sick souvenir? Could a religious man really commit such a crime? Manolis pushed the thoughts away and kept walking, careful not to trip on the thick roots that lay in wait and not to ask about the cap.

Moments later, without warning, Manolis felt a pair of strong hands grip his shoulders like a vice. Instinctively, he swung around, his stance defensive. He now regretted not accepting the offer of a loaded weapon.

Father Petros's eyes were wild. He waved his rifle squarely in Manolis's face.

"Look," he said. "There."

Manolis scanned the pine forest but there was no movement to catch his eye. Just the trees, standing and fallen, and rocks, large and small. A dark silence engulfed the mottled forest as if it was in a vacuum. Manolis looked harder, narrowing his eyes. What was this evasive priest playing at?

"Where?" Manolis said. "I can't see anything. Oh . . . whoa . . ."

He didn't see it until it moved. Slow and lolloping, the camouflaged rear end of a large brown bear wobbled from side to side between a tight thicket of trees. Having never seen one close up in the wild, Manolis marvelled at the glorious creature. It was clumsy yet balanced, vicious yet gentle, sniffing the air in search of food. An alarm suddenly went off in Manolis's head: he had a dead rabbit in his backpack, and bears had an exceptional sense of smell.

"The scent-detecting area of a bear's nose is ten times larger than any dog's and a hundred times larger than a human's," Father Petros whispered. "They have very small brains but incredibly large olfactory bulbs. Bears are generally solitary creatures, and I wrapped that bunny up nice and tight so I think we're safe. But still, I'm not going to risk it . . ."

Manolis looked at him. "What do you mean?"

The priest didn't answer. Before Manolis knew what was happening, Father Petros's fingers had crept onto the trigger of his weapon. Manolis thought the priest was preparing to claim the ultimate hunting trophy as he pointed his rifle squarely at the endangered bear. A target so large and so slow posed no challenge whatsoever. Manolis wanted to rush Father Petros, knock his rifle off target and save the bear's life. But before he could move, the priest extended his arms to the failing sky and fired two shots into the air like whips cracking. Without looking back, the bear broke into a fast scamper and rumbled through the trees like a small earthquake, disappearing into the thick forest.

"Like snakes, bears are protected," Father Petros said coolly. "But that hasn't stopped people around here laying illegal poisoned bait in retaliation for attacks on their livestock. A bear's behaviour can be unpredictable, but it's guaranteed to want to eat if it senses food is near. Someone recently found a bear's body floating in the lake. It was probably trying to quench the thirst caused by a poisoning."

Manolis swallowed hard. Father Petros brought down his weapon, comfortably easing it by his side, and said:

"Some people just have no sense of compassion or empathy for other living creatures . . ."

18

Deep inside every seasoned coffee drinker is a barista just waiting to break out. And Manolis was no different.

At the empty taverna, Manolis was showing off his coffee-making skills to Roze by preparing her a morning cup. And because she was a good soul, kind and patient, she was humouring him. Manolis could tell she would one day make a great mother. He knew she would say the brew was delicious, no matter what. And he didn't at all mind.

As he made an unholy mess in the kitchen, scattering coffee beans, spilling milk and clanking implements, Manolis updated her on recent developments. Roze appeared to be listening absently, absorbed in her morning newspaper.

"This is interesting . . ."

"What's that?" Manolis asked.

She read out an article about a British tourist, a teacher on holiday with her husband, who had gone missing on a Greek island after going out walking alone one morning.

"After several weeks, her body was eventually found at the bottom of a deep ravine, crushed by a large boulder that had been dislodged. Search and rescue teams were hampered by the fact that the teacher's mobile phone had been switched off. An extensive land and air search involved military helicopters equipped with infrared cameras, drones, emergency rescue officers, sniffer dogs and local volunteers with intimate knowledge of the rocky terrain. The body could not be recovered until specialist rescuers arrived from Spain."

"That's tragic," Manolis said, wiping up a puddle of milk.

Roze continued. "Although investigators said that it appeared the teacher had slipped and fallen in an accident, the authorities were not ruling out the possibility that she had been pushed."

"Well, that makes it something else altogether," Manolis said.

"So they're wondering whether the woman's death was actually a murder and not an unfortunate accident?"

"Correct."

Roze sat back in her chair and folded her arms across her chest. She was wearing an ocean-blue tank top that showed her muscles.

"Greece is the most mountainous country in all of Europe," she said. "Tourists and hikers are found dead in steep gorges and isolated ravines every summer, or never found at all. To say those could all be murders is a bit of a stretch."

"I don't think they're saying that. But I imagine the police always consider it a possibility. It just takes some time before they can unequivocally rule it out."

Manolis handed Roze her coffee and sat down with his own cup. "Hope you like it."

She examined the brew the way a wine merchant might inspect an antique bottle. She sniffed it, blew on the milky froth, and sipped.

"Mmm, delicious," she said with a smile.

Manolis grinned as he tasted his own. It wasn't bad at all.

Roze took her oversized sunglasses off her head and laid them on the table. "I think we should go out and search the land for Lefty," she said. "No-one's done that yet."

"You mean, like a search party?"

"Give it a name if you want. I'm familiar with the land having walked across the border. That counts for something."

Manolis wasn't convinced. It seemed like a case of diminishing returns given the remote chances of success.

"I'm not much of a hiker," he admitted.

"Nor am I."

"The land is huge, we can only cover so much."

"I know, but it'd be something." Her tone was assured, almost wheedling. "At least we'll know we tried."

Manolis pulled at his earlobe. "Yeah, OK," he said. "No harm in trying."

Remembering what he'd been told by old Odysseas in Eleftheria, he asked if there had ever been a virus which had swept through the region. "Do you know if something like that ever happened here, something that especially impacted the children?"

Roze shook her head. "I don't, but the older residents might. We had sicknesses in Albania when I was little, I remember my mum being scared for us kids. But you should probably ask Kostas. He'd know more."

"OK."

"I probably shouldn't say this, but he and Lefty had a big argument the night Lefty disappeared."

"An argument? And you're only mentioning this now?"

Roze became defensive, her tone lowered.

"I didn't say anything before out of loyalty to Kostas. I don't want to lose my job and have to go back to Albania."

She described how she'd overheard them yelling at each other in the taverna's kitchen. She didn't know why they'd argued.

"It could have been anything because they fought all the time. That's also why I didn't think it was important at the time and just went back to what I was doing. They argued for sport, like most Greeks do. Albanians too."

Roze added that there had been two groups of tourists at the taverna the night Lefty disappeared. Manolis wondered if the passports he'd found hidden at Lefty's house might have belonged to the tourists.

"Lefty entertained them with conversation and stories, jokes and flirting, while they bought him drinks in appreciation. When they left, one of them, a young woman, gave him a fridge magnet from their homeland as a gift."

"Where were they from?" Manolis asked. "Do you remember?"

He didn't recall seeing any such souvenirs at Lefty's house, although he could easily have missed a small item like a fridge magnet, especially if he wasn't aware of its significance. Something distinctive like a country magnet could be a good lead.

"I can't remember," Roze said. "Some Eastern bloc country or former Soviet republic, I think. Their Greek was poor. The other group were pale-haired, from a Scandinavian country. Their vowels were clipped; they spoke fast."

Just then, Kostas arrived, shirt untucked, eyes watery and bloodshot, in desperate need of both caffeine and nicotine. He announced as much and Roze made herself scarce to fetch them. Kostas slumped in his chair with all the grace of a dying buffalo.

"I didn't sleep well," he groaned. "Bad dreams."

"Good morning," Manolis said cheerily. "That's no good. What kind of dreams?"

"I don't really want to relive the experience a second time . . ."

"It might help you process what you saw."

"I've never been a big believer in that kind of thing. How'd you sleep?"

"Soundly, no nightmares at all," he lied.

The day was overcast, a ceiling of pewter-coloured clouds blanketing the sky, reflecting silver in the clear mountain lake. The lack of wind meant there was barely a ripple on its surface, the water was as still as tinted glass. Even the birdlife had fallen silent for some reason. Manolis wondered if rain was on its way.

"To be honest with you, and without going into too many details, I had a dream about Lefty," Kostas said suddenly.

Manolis looked at him with a calm, steady gaze. He half closed his eyelids.

"Oh, right. You didn't happen to see where he was, did you?"

Kostas chuckled. "Unfortunately, no. I've been unsettled since he disappeared, and it's to do with this argument we had."

Why had Kostas mentioned this so soon after Roze? Was it a

coincidence or something more? Manolis sensed he was missing something. He wondered if Kostas and Roze were more than just co-workers at the taverna and had choreographed their approach. Manolis decided to play it cool and console Kostas as a friend, but also to try to find out as many details as possible.

Roze returned with a perfect cup of coffee and a half-full cigarette packet.

"Thank you, darling," breathed Kostas.

She smiled at him warmly. Kostas lit and inhaled, sipped and swallowed, and was again at peace with the world.

"Thanks again for the coffee," Roze said to Manolis. She took the empty cups back to the kitchen.

"You're a barista now?" Kostas asked.

"Just living out a fantasy," Manolis said. "Look, I'm sorry to hear that you and Lefty argued. But you shouldn't be blaming yourself for his disappearance. It's just bad timing."

"I know," Kostas said. "But I can't help but feel guilty."

"What happened when you argued?"

Kostas tapped his yolk-yellow lighter nervously on the table. Manolis pulled out his *komboloi* and started a slow, hypnotic play with his fingers.

"Maybe I can help put things into perspective," he said.

Kostas exhaled extravagantly. "There's not much to say," he said. "It was all so trivial . . ."

He described how he'd accused Lefty of stealing money from the till and chocolates from the pantry.

"It sounds so pointless now. A few euros and some empty calories. But how were we to know he would vanish?"

"Was it the first time that had happened?" Manolis said. "Had you accused him before of theft?"

"That's the thing: it wasn't the first time. Maybe the third. I'd noticed little things going missing in the past few weeks. And I said it half in jest, as if Lefty would steal such trifles. He's too big a player. And now that I think about it, it was probably just my poor bookkeeping. I can't say it's a strength of mine, I was never very good at maths at school. Roze has been helping since she arrived, but she's not much better than me."

Kostas reiterated that he was convinced that Sofia and Zain were responsible for Lefty's disappearance, and that it was just a matter of time before their complicity was discovered.

"She's probably turned him into gourmet pies," he grinned. "Cooked him with herbs and spices and been feeding him to tourists. What an absolutely genius way of disposing of the evidence."

Manolis listened and said nothing. The only sound was the gentle clack of his worry beads passing through his fingers.

"Good morning," said a voice from behind Manolis.

It was a bright-faced Angelo with loyal Apollo at his side. Manolis greeted him warmly, as if meeting him for the very first time. He had to stop himself staring too intently at Angelo's face and features.

"I've brought some fresh meat and produce," Angelo said, pointing at his shopping trolley.

Kostas gratefully helped him unload it until the table was completely covered. There were two magenta-pink lamb carcasses and an assortment of vegetables of a size and colour that Manolis hadn't seen before. Apollo barked with delight at the sight of the lamb.

"Those vegetables look incredible," Manolis said. "Are they from your garden?"

"Yes," Angelo said proudly. "Anna and I produce more than we can possibly eat ourselves."

"For which I am very grateful," joked Kostas.

Manolis picked up an aubergine. It was a deep indigo colour and as heavy as a gym weight. A single cucumber was as long and thick as a baseball bat. These were not items that were available in your average city supermarket or even in a farmer's market. They seemed almost mutant in their appearance, exaggerated, as if they'd been injected with some radical growth serum.

"Anna is a marvellous cook," Angelo told Manolis. "You must come eat dinner with us one night."

180

"Thank you." Manolis smiled. "I'll do that." He pictured the aubergine being transformed into a dense and oily tray of moussaka.

Angelo and Apollo continued on their way while Manolis helped Kostas carry the food to his storage room. It was somewhere that Manolis had not seen before: in a far corner of the taverna, beside the kitchen, a hidden trapdoor led down a wooden staircase to a long, dark corridor. Manolis had an acute moment of anxiety before he went down the stairs, his heart and breathing racing. He was not yet at peace with underground spaces.

"I would never have known this was here," Manolis said carefully.

"It used to be an air-raid shelter," Kostas replied. "Just be careful walking down the stairs. One of the steps is rotten and needs replacing. I've tripped before and twisted my knee."

The single light bulb, naked and of low wattage, also needed upgrading. It was activated with a pull-string and hung precariously above the staircase, swinging back and forth like a skinny pendulum.

The corridor smelled dank and musty, as if there was a deep-rooted water leak. Kostas described the smell as normal. As they walked along the corridor, all external sounds seemed to melt away, leaving only echoey footsteps. It was so hard to see that Manolis was forced to follow the sound of Kostas's voice and shoes. The further they walked, the more he felt a rush of dread and disorientation. He was not sure where Roze had gone.

The sound of a heavy lock being undone and a door creaking open returned him to his body. A second pull-string light bulb illuminated the world again and calmed Manolis's breathing. He blinked until his eyes could focus on the large white room before him. There were tins of food, jars of preserves, bags and packets of pasta and rice, and unopened bottles of alcohol. The sound of dripping water and the humming of fridges and freezers filled the tightly packed air.

"Several of these shelters were built in key locations throughout the village during the Second World War," Kostas said. "They protected us from German bombing raids. Now they protect our food from bears."

Manolis stepped into the room and placed Angelo's glorious home-grown produce inside a refrigerator, although the room was so cold that it didn't feel necessary.

"How many people would have sheltered in here?" Manolis asked.

Kostas shrugged wearily. "As many sardines as you could fit. It all depended on the level of threat and where people found themselves in the town when the siren sounded."

"It must have been terrifying. Did people sleep here?"

"If they had to," Kostas said.

"Do you remember hiding in these shelters?"

"A little. I was still young, my mum and dad protected us. The shelters were also used during the civil war. I was a bit older then, and that was an even worse war for us, if you can believe it. The Greek air force conducted bombing raids on many villages in the Prespes, strafing the land from above and even dropping napalm on their own people."

Manolis had never fully appreciated the devastation wrought by the civil war. No wonder his parents and aunt had fled to Australia – it was partly, he imagined, to escape some horrible memories. At that moment, he could very much relate to that desire, albeit in reverse.

"That's awful," Manolis said. "Do you know the locations of the other shelters?"

Kostas scratched the back of his head. "I'm not entirely sure," he said, storing the lamb in a sturdy chest freezer. "I'm pretty sure the church had one – Father Petros would know – and there was one at a private residence somewhere. But these days I think mine is the only one that's used for anything practical."

19

A friendly Apollo greeted Manolis when he arrived at Angelo and Anna's house for dinner. He wagged his tail and yipped and yapped as Manolis stepped through the rusty gate and into the lush garden at the back of the house. Plump chickens pecked the dirt and fluffed their feathers and zigzagged madly. A network of peavines tendrilled along a wire trellis. It was late afternoon, the shadows starting to lengthen as the heat of summer retreated for another day. The steady white-noise drone of hovering bumblebees filled the garden.

Manolis found Angelo bent double, tilling the soil by hand using an old hoe. Anna waved to him; she was in another part of the garden in rubber boots, collecting wild greens. Manolis walked over to help.

"Am I doing this right?" he asked after a few minutes of yanking. "Some of these look like nasty weeds."

Anna laughed. "Those are the most tasty and nutritious of all," she said.

"I've never seen leaf vegetables like these before . . ."

"Some are native to this area. They are medicinal, our secret weapon against sickness and disease. Can you help chop some wood?"

"Sure."

Angelo appeared with a razor-sharp axe.

"Thanks," he said, handing it to Manolis. "Just be careful."

He brandished his index finger, which was missing its tip. Manolis froze.

"Only joking," Angelo said. "I lost this when my hand got caught in a rope that was attached to a runaway calf. But still, be careful."

Manolis chopped firewood for the stove from a stack in the corner of the insect-filled garden. He was startled by a massive armour-plated beetle that ended up on his sandalled foot, its carapace black and glossy.

"That's a *Carabus gigas*," Angelo said. "They look dangerous, eh? But they're harmless, they only eat snails."

"Giant by name and giant by nature," Manolis said, examining its rugged beauty.

"It's supposedly the largest ground beetle in all of Europe. They tend only to come out at night, so you're lucky to see one up close like that."

Manolis was impressed by the size of the garden and the vast quantity of fruit and vegetables it produced – too much, he thought, for two people. But he realised that it would see them through the winter, which would soon be felt in the vagrant shadows and at nightfall. Food would be frozen, pickled or preserved, and firewood stacked. When the snow started falling in November, it could last until April or even May, the nights white with ice and crackling like broken glass. Despite the obvious lack of convenience, Manolis liked how life moved with the seasons. He could buy apples throughout the year from his local supermarket in Australia, but they only sometimes tasted of apple.

With the food collected and wood chopped, Manolis joined his hosts inside their cottage to prepare the evening meal. He peeled and sliced vegetables and added them to an earthenware pot that was nearly a century old. Everything took time, which Manolis rather enjoyed; the new pace of doing things, meditative and slow, allowed one to appreciate the minutiae of life. Food cooked in the old style.

The end result was worth the effort. The vegetarian meal was the most delicious Manolis had tasted in Greece. It contained peppers and aubergines and *gigantes* and potatoes and rice, and was garlicky and oily and salty. It probably added years to Manolis's life.

"The magic is in the soil," Anna said. "The peppers contain a natural relaxant that helps reduce anxiety and cure insomnia."

"It's true that I give Kostas food for the taverna," Angelo said. "But it's also true that I keep the very best produce for us." He winked and smiled cheekily.

"That seems fair." Manolis smiled back. He helped himself to another mouthful of sweet giant beans.

Apollo was fed a selection of raw beef offal, bloody and plump, and given a long bone to gnaw on. He eventually fell asleep like a drunk on the living room rug.

As the evening passed, Manolis was distracted by the sound of a miniature grandfather clock hanging on a nearby wall. It was squat and ugly but had a reassuring pendulum and resonant chime that rang out every half-hour. It was the sound of a bygone era.

"I like your clock," Manolis said. "My parents had one just like it when I was young, in the hallway of our house. I hear the chime and am transported back to when I was a schoolkid."

"We're fond of it too," Anna said. "We've had it for decades. I would swear my heart beats in time with that clock."

The chime was what Manolis had once listened for in the middle of the night. Waking from a bad dream, distressed and overtired, he would be unable to go back to sleep until he heard the clock's resonant chime and could work out the time and how many hours remained before dawn.

It was the first time that Manolis had spent any extended time with Anna. She was a handsome woman with a striking countenance, her face wrinkled and elegant like old parchment. She wore a triangular headscarf that struggled to retain her lank grey curls, and came across as comfortable in her own skin, a calming presence.

Manolis tried to talk about the villagers but noticed that his hosts preferred to avoid gossip. It was almost as if the subject was beneath them. But Lefty was different. When his name came up, Anna confirmed what Angelo had already reported – that he'd said he was going to Lesbos.

"I assumed he had told the rest of the village too, so was shocked when I heard that he was considered missing and people were worried," she said.

185

"When did he say this?" Manolis asked.

"Only a few days before he disappeared. He was here collecting some garden produce for Kostas's taverna, a wooden box we had prepared, right here in the kitchen." She pointed to the doorway where Lefty had once stood.

"And did he say why he was going to Lesbos? For a holiday, or to see a friend, or for business?"

"He didn't say," Anna replied. "But that's Lefty. And I didn't ask either."

Manolis played with his cloth napkin. His presence at dinner had brought out the fine china.

"How would you even get to Lesbos from here?" he asked. It was potentially the longest internal journey possible within Greece, from one of its most western points to one of its most eastern, and from the north all the way to the south.

Angelo moistened his throat with a sip of cold water. "Probably either a plane or ferry from Thessaloniki would be the fastest way."

There was always the possibility of travel records, thought Manolis. But Lefty could have been travelling under any name, or might have stowed away in the hold of a large Aegean ferry.

"Although you could also go overland to Lesbos and not need to buy a ticket," Angelo said. "After you left Thessaloniki, you would continue driving east through Thrace and into Turkey, then head due south. Lesbos is only a few kilometres off the Turkish coast, which is a very easy journey. Asylum seekers are crossing all the time in small inflatable boats, trying to reach Europe."

Would Lefty have chanced two international crossings, into Turkey and then out again, just to reach Lesbos? It seemed risky. But he was already doing business with Elias, who could have referred him to other corrupt border guards who would wipe the record clean. In a country as large as Turkey, the demand for black-market booty would be enormous, and Lefty already had history there with what sounded like some similarly colourful and crooked characters. Manolis had forgotten about the popularity of Lesbos for migrant crossings, with the island housing a large refugee detention centre. Was that in any way relevant, and could Zain have once landed there?

"But going overland into Turkey from Greece isn't so easy," Angelo said. "It's not like crossing into Albania or North Macedonia; the border is more heavily patrolled."

He went on to describe a phalanx of modern security measures that included steel walls at crossing points, humming robot drones and observation towers with long-range night-vision cameras and banks of searchlights.

"Because it's Turkey," Manolis said.

"Correct."

"But I'm sure Lefty could find a way, even past all that . . ."

"Oh, I have absolutely no doubt about that," Angelo said without hesitation.

Out of respect for his hosts, Manolis decided to change the subject and ask about their own history with the village and the Prespes region.

"You have nearly two hundred years of life between you and are still very healthy," he said. "I've got to ask – what's your secret? Is it the pure food, the clean mountain air, the manual labour and exercise?"

Angelo and Anna looked at each other and laughed. Manolis felt like a news reporter conducting an interview, but he was genuinely curious.

"I think it's all those things combined," said Angelo. "They benefit both the body and mind."

"And soul," Anna added. "Coffee?"

"Please," said Manolis. "One sugar."

She crossed herself in thanks for the meal and left to find the *briki* pot.

"But it's also resilience," Angelo said, pointing at his chest. "It's in here, it's your heart, your fight. As you said, there's nearly two hundred years of life between us, which is a hundred years of history. We've seen a great deal of pain and joy in that time. Thanatos is not going to take us out of this world easily."

His words had an almost threatening tone about them, cautionary words meant for the Greek god of non-violent deaths, warning that this soul was battle-hardened and would not be harvested without a bitter fight.

"Since being here in Glikonero, I've learned that the civil war was especially horrific for this region," Manolis said. "I mean, I knew it was bad in Greece, I read about it at school. But I never realised the extent of what happened here."

Angelo's eyes grew large, his face turning pale. "Those years were by far the hardest of all," he said.

With a long exhalation, he described how much of the local population had emigrated during the war to escape the endemic poverty, famine, sickness and political strife that soon engulfed the region. The fighting was especially fierce in the isolated and inaccessible northern mountains.

"This area around the Prespa Lakes was controlled by the *andartiko* who roamed the mountains," Angelo said. "Our guerrilla fighters are considered folk heroes as one of the strongest European resistance movements during the Nazi occupation. Having lost control of the countryside during the Second World War, the Greek army tried to push the partisans back into the mountains during the civil war. The Greek air force even conducted daily bombing raids on our villages, in the worst cases dropping American-made napalm. And all this after we survived the scourge of Hitler and Nazi Germany."

"I heard about the napalm," Manolis said.

"We were lucky that we still had the underground shelters from the earlier war," said Angelo. "But can you imagine? Almost overnight, those young men who had fought in the resistance to protect Greece were suddenly marked for elimination by Greece. That happened in no other European country. The army exacted revenge on the men who had joined the *andartiko* by burning their children alive and forcing their mothers to watch."

Manolis was speechless, shocked into silence.

"The police then came from Florina and took away dozens of young women who were the wives and sisters of *andartiko* fighters. They imprisoned them for years and routinely tortured them."

Angelo took another sip of water. Manolis listened.

"And then there were the thousands of children who became political refugees and were evacuated to neighbouring countries and the Eastern bloc. These were all organised campaigns. More than anything, it was that which changed the face of northern Greece forever."

Anna returned with a silver tray that carried three Greek coffees in delicate ceramic cups and a plate of *koulourakia* pastries. She placed them on the table with a gentle clink. Manolis noticed that the golden-coloured pastries were twisted in the shape of snakes. He wondered if that was just a coincidence, but still helped himself to one, biting off the head with a snap and savouring its sweet vanilla flavour.

"What changed the face of northern Greece?" Anna asked, having caught the tail end of the conversation.

"The child evacuations," said Angelo.

"You shouldn't be talking about those," she said, tone hushed. "They are old news and best forgotten."

"Our guest was asking. The worst thing we can do is forget they happened. That would be to dishonour the memory of all the children that were lost."

Angelo reached for his coffee with a shaky hand, sipped a toothful and closed his eyes. He sat motionless for a while, as if steadying himself with his thoughts and memories. Thick lines formed across his forehead. Reopening his eyes, he relaxed his brow and looked across at Manolis.

"As you may know, the civil war was fought between the Greek government army and the Democratic Army, which was the military branch of the Communist Party," he said. "The government army was backed by the United Kingdom and United States, while the Democratic Army had the support of Yugoslavia, Albania and Bulgaria. The removal of children by both sides was very emotional and highly contentious. Over three years, about thirty thousand children between the ages of five and fifteen were taken against their will and made to walk hundreds of kilometres across international borders. The older children had to sometimes carry their younger siblings. Together, they trudged along the shores of our two great lakes in order to cross the borders to the north and west."

"Why were the children removed?" Manolis asked.

"For their own good," said Anna. "To save them from the fighting, from injuries, malnutrition and disease. Many were already sick and impoverished from the Second World War. Another war was too much for them."

"Where did they go?"

"The official Greek position was that the children were taken by the Democratic Army to Eastern bloc countries to be brought up under a socialist regime," Angelo said. "They travelled at night and hid in forests to avoid being bombed."

"Meanwhile, the Greek government took their children to homes in other parts of Greece," Anna added. "Many in the south."

"They were hardly homes, though," said Angelo. "They were more like camps."

"The children slept in stables and were sent to work in tobacco or textile factories," Anna said. "They had to beg for food and were fed lettuce leaves and orange peel, or they ate snails. They were also made to pledge loyalty to the Greek monarchy and Church and reject communism. They were separated from their parents and some were even illegally adopted by American families having been sold to the highest bidder."

"It fast became very political and very complicated," said Angelo. "There were no winners, only losers."

He described how the geography of northern Greece had an important influence on the events of the civil war.

"The Democratic Army controlled the Prespes. The area's isolation and inaccessible mountains were well suited to the partisans' guerrilla tactics. Meanwhile, the Greek army controlled the plains and valleys because of its superior motorised transport, armoured vehicles and air power. The Democratic Army mounted occasional attacks on cities and towns in government-controlled territory, while the Greek army regularly attempted to push into the mountains to drive out the partisan forces."

"We were caught in the middle," Anna said. "Glikonero was occupied by the Greek army by day and partisans by night. The partisans stole food, animals and supplies. They forcibly recruited villagers to join their cause, and executed those they thought were collaborating with the Greek army."

"Meanwhile, the Greek army burned villages and evacuated residents in order to eliminate the Democratic Army's support base," said Angelo.

"Caught in the middle," Anna repeated, tasting her coffee. The backs of her hands were tanned and dirty from manual labour, her dry skin cracking.

"The Greek army portrayed themselves as 'protecting' or 'saving' children at the request of parents and welfare organisations," Angelo said. "Meanwhile, they claimed the Democratic Army were 'kidnapping' or 'abducting' these children, marching them across the northern border in order to 'denationalise' a whole generation."

"The reason doesn't matter," sighed Anna. "Either way, the children left the area and never returned when the war was over, or since."

"Look around you," Angelo said. "Only old people."

Manolis listened quietly, occasionally slurping at his cup but barely able to taste the coffee. His focus was on his hosts, who were visibly upset – Anna's cheeks were crimson while Angelo was wiping his eyes. It was the reckless dispensability of children, brought into the world in an instant, and discarded just as swiftly, as if they were lesser humans.

"I'm sorry to hear all this," Manolis said. "I had no idea the village had been so affected."

"We lost an entire generation of children, and have never been the same since," said Angelo, a profound sadness in his voice.

191

"At least the local forests have thrived," Anna said. "Fewer people has meant less demand for firewood."

She said that Albanians often sneaked across the border with donkeys to steal Greek firewood following the widespread deforestation of their own country by their government. For the same reason, the region's brown bears were now largely confined to Greek territory, where the population was flourishing.

Manolis was quietly intrigued by such events and wondered about the impact on his own family. His parents had never once mentioned the harrowing exodus of children. How close had Con and Maria come to being involved? Their ages at the time of the Greek civil war were about right. Had they been involved and chosen never to speak about what had happened? Did it guide their decision to emigrate from Greece, knowing they one day hoped to have their own children and couldn't risk them being taken?

Manolis suddenly realised that this forgettable time in Greek history was the reason why the old man Odysseas had described the Prespes region as being full of sick children. The children who remained would have been malnourished and ill, while the memory of those who departed left the area spiritually bereft. The Prespes region was almost completely depopulated in the decades following the evacuation, which Angelo described as "sombre years, claustrophobic and empty, as if the land was still grieving the loss of its children and somehow trying to heal". When entry restrictions were lifted in the 1970s, tourists arrived, and new life was breathed in.

"We were lucky, Anna and I," Angelo said. "We escaped. We avoided evacuation because our parents lied about our ages. Meanwhile, other parents lied about their children's ages in order to *include* them in the evacuations."

"Why would they do that?" Manolis asked.

"Because they had been brainwashed into thinking that it was best for their children."

"Our older brother was less fortunate during the war," Anna said, wiping her eyes with a napkin. "Theodoros wasn't taken, but he was killed in cold blood. To this day, we've not forgotten him."

She pointed to a black-and-white photograph on the wall in a silver frame. It was of a young man with dark hair wearing a crisp white shirt and raven-black trousers with the lake in the background. He stood unsmiling.

"I'm sorry for your loss," Manolis said.

"Thank you," said Angelo. "It was a long time ago, but I often still think about Theo."

Now that their deceased brother had been raised in conversation, and the absence of a male heir, Manolis decided to delicately broach the topic of sworn virgins. Angelo appeared embarrassed, his face reddening as he rubbed the back of his neck. He stared at his coffee cup as he downplayed his transformation, saying that it was so long ago that he'd almost forgotten, and was an oath he took gladly in the name of family. As he spoke, Anna gazed at him lovingly.

"What I did was governed by strict rules that were five centuries old," he said. "But with it came freedom."

"Women now have more freedom," said Manolis. "That isn't meant to trivialise what you did, but how do you feel about it today?"

Angelo gave a small shrug of indifference. "How should I feel? My life and decisions are behind me. I'm glad to see that times have changed, but it wasn't always like this. Women were once seen as burdens on families and meant for someone else's household. On your wedding day, you stood with your eyes down, you were like a well-trained animal. On your wedding night, your father would slip a bullet into your suitcase; the bullet wasn't for you, it was for your husband in case he discovered you weren't a virgin. You then lived with your husband's family as a slave, taking all your orders from them. You never talked back. You never looked your husband in the eye. You made no decisions, even when it came to your own children. You didn't smoke or drink or shoot a gun. From dawn to dusk, your life was hard labour."

"Would you ever consider becoming a woman again?" Manolis asked.

Angelo fired him a dark look. Manolis wondered if he'd crossed a line.

"Not at all," Angelo said calmly, eyes softening. "I can't resign from this role. It's true that I dress like a man and now prefer the company of men over women. But I think that's more out of habit than anything else. I was never a tomboy, and physically I know I'm a woman. But mentally, I'm neither a man nor a woman. I've always fought for women to have the same rights as men and believe that genders are just labels that humans have created to divide us into two arbitrary categories. In the modern world, they don't matter."

"Have you ever regretted your decision?" asked Manolis.

"Not even once," Angelo replied. "I haven't lived this way because I wanted to be a man in any physical way. I did so to take on the role played by men and get the respect of a man. I am a man in my spirit, but having male genitals is not what makes you a man. Bodies are not simply made up of blood and bone and organs."

The more Angelo talked, the more Manolis realised that being a sworn virgin was less about becoming a man in a paternalistic society and more about attaining purity. It was about absolving and dissolving, about becoming clean and virtuous until a new physicality was achieved that was almost without gender. It was powerful and commanding.

"I took the oath to find a place and purpose in my family," Angelo said. "But I also took it to find a place in my country that otherwise offered no place for me."

He sipped his water thoughtfully, moistening his lips and throat.

"But, truthfully, now that you ask, the oath did leave me with one small regret – that I never dandled my own baby on my knee. I am blessed to have enjoyed a long life, but to have become a parent and shared my life with my own children, to have seen them grow and taught them about nature and the world, that would have only made my time sweeter."

Anna admitted she felt the same, but didn't go into the reasons why she'd been unable to have children, and Manolis didn't press. Instead, he reached for his wallet, pulled out a photo, and mentioned that he had a young son.

"He's beautiful," Angelo said. "You must be very proud."

"Christos is a good boy, inquisitive and full of energy," Manolis replied. "He can also be naughty at times, but that's just kids. I still love him to pieces."

Anna took the photo, held it up to her rheumy eyes.

"To have a boy is good," she beamed. "Around here, having a boy is still seen as a blessing. Daughters are a misfortune. Women have more rights now, that's true. But a girl is still not worth as much as a boy. And never will be."

Anna's words settled in the room. Apollo snuffled in his sleep; he was dreaming. The grandfather clock ticked.

"On another topic, I don't suppose you happen to know anyone named Poppy?" Manolis asked suddenly. "I believe she's an older lady but I don't know if she is married or has children."

Angelo and Anna stared at each other blankly. It seemed like Manolis had hit another dead end.

"Poppy? Are you sure that's her name?" Angelo asked.

"Poppy is short for Calliope," Anna said. "Like my friend."

Could this have been the case with Manolis's aunt? He suddenly realised he'd had her name wrong all along, that he'd been using the moniker he'd called her as a small child, as she'd been introduced by his parents. Theia Poppy was so much more playful and easier to say than Theia Calliope. No wonder he'd failed to gain traction with any of his earlier enquiries.

"My friend, she lived here once," Anna went on. "Calliope was a spinster with a small cottage in the hills nearby. A lovely lady, she lived alone, and died during a very bitter winter some years ago."

Manolis struggled to retain his composure. He felt pinned to his seat, unable to speak. The room seemed to recede. Anna's tone was pragmatic and reflective of place. People lived, people died, the seasons changed.

"Who is she?" Angelo asked. "A friend of your family?"

Manolis sat forward and let out a stale, sour breath. "Well, I can't be sure, but she may have been my dad's sister, my aunt."

"I see," said Anna. "Well, I remember Calliope once saying she had an older brother, but he wasn't in Greece, he lived far away in Australia. So she probably wasn't your aunt."

"Oh, right," Manolis said, remembering his Greek cover. "Yes, of course." His stomach cramped at the realisation.

Manolis stood, excused himself from the table, asking for the bathroom.

"It's down the hall, second door on your right," Angelo said. "Are you OK?"

"I'm fine." He folded his napkin and left it on his plate. "But thank you."

Manolis already knew where the bathroom was from having been in the house before. His true reason for leaving the table was to discreetly return Angelo's passport to its rightful home; it had been sitting in his pocket all evening. Ducking into the bedroom, he slipped it back into the drawer. But as he turned to leave, he was startled by the sight of Angelo blocking the doorway. He had followed Manolis.

"Are you lost?" Angelo asked. "The bathroom is the next room along."

"Oh sorry, yes . . . I was confused. It's this one, right?"

Stepping past Angelo, Manolis felt the weight of his gaze. His pulse tripping, Manolis opened the bathroom door, stepped inside, and locked the door behind him.

20

"In the Name of the Father and of the Son and of the Holy Spirit . . ."

Father Petros's deep and sonorous voice resonated through Glik-onero's small church. Finally heeding the advice from the good father, Manolis had agreed to attend Holy Liturgy on Sunday morning. Ordinarily, he wasn't much of a churchgoer, but on this day he went to witness the villagers gather together under one roof for the only thing that transcended their grudges with each other: their devotion to God. In a village plagued with social dysfunction, Manolis was curious to see the group dynamic. True to form, Father Petros was late, with the service beginning a full half-hour after the scheduled time.

The church was cosy and ornate, with only three rows of pews, warm shades of wood and colourful images of saints. It smelled of those long departed; Manolis pictured them circling in the air above the congregation. Meanwhile, all the living residents were in their Sunday best: Kostas and Roze, Angelo and Anna, Elias and Sofia. Stavros had come from Florina for the day, and wore a taupe suit. Only Zain was absent; Manolis pictured him with a shovel in one hand and axe in the other while panicked snakes slithered for cover. As Manolis had expected, the parishioners largely ignored each other; there was little eye contact. In her role as village outcast, Sofia had her own pew.

Manolis couldn't remember the last time he'd attended a Greek Orthodox Church service and felt strangely overwhelmed by a wave of sentimentality. It was the combination of saturated colours, calming sounds and fragrant smells that sparked corners of his ancestral brain that had lain dormant for decades. He'd once asked Emily if they could get married in a Greek church but she wasn't religious, so refused; they were instead married by a celebrant in the local botanic gardens. And Manolis's son had only set foot in a Greek church a handful of times, usually when his *yiayia* had insisted on going. But at least Emily had given in to Manolis's desire to baptise their son in the church, and also to him not being named Christopher as she'd initially wanted.

The surroundings transported Manolis back to his childhood: Sunday mornings spent wearing tight, uncomfortable clothes when he'd reluctantly accompanied Maria to church, observing when the other parishioners sat and stood, following their lead, and longing for it all to be over so he could go home and play. And yet, in contrast to when he was a child, Manolis now found a strange and meditative calm in the service that he couldn't quite put his finger on. Was it because of the rhythmic chanting? The heady smell of burning incense? The slow pace of village life? Or was it because of Greece itself? He couldn't say, but he felt inclined to go again soon and experience his family's traditions, ideally with young Christos in tow. Manolis figured that he'd never properly lost his religion, although he'd never fully embraced it either.

Manolis stole sideways glances at the other parishioners, the bodies around him radiating heat. Dressed in an ornate gilded robe and stovepipe hat embellished with intricate stitching, Father Petros was a commanding presence. Holding a golden crook, he concluded the service with a series of prayers for Lefty's safe and speedy return. Manolis saw everyone watching attentively except for Sofia, who had her head down, eyes closed, her face frozen in a rictus. She looked like she was asleep. Maybe she was.

With the service over, the churchgoers slowly dispersed. The air outside was no cooler than inside. Kostas and Stavros stood there awkwardly. They lit cigarettes, stared, talked and gossiped. As Sofia ambled by, Stavros looked at her from out of the corner of his eye and spoke with a sneer.

"What's for lunch, Kostas? Does today's menu feature human pie?"

The words were designed to hurt, and they were delivered loudly enough for Sofia to understand, even with her limited hearing.

"How dare you . . ."

She glared at them with the fury of a roused tigress. Standing nearby under the shade of a cherry tree, Manolis wondered whether she might respond with a swing of her handbag. Instead, she hit them with an even more effective weapon: her tongue. Stavros and Kostas swiftly returned fire, with tensions escalating until both camps were arguing over the top of each other. Manolis wanted to intervene and attempt to restore calm, but thought the role of peacemaker would sit better on Father Petros. But the priest was nowhere to be seen, he was still inside the church, packing away the items from the service, changing out of his vestments. In the end, Manolis reluctantly stepped forward.

"Stop it, this is a church!" he implored them.

But it made little difference. The hot-blooded Greeks were now at boiling point, the air filled with allegations and scorn as frustrations simmered over. Sofia was not backing away from her two accusers. Manolis looked across at Roze; she was shaking her head, a look of retreat in her wide eyes, of not wanting to get involved. And Elias had disappeared altogether.

From out of nowhere, a blur of motion rushed past Manolis and pushed Stavros forcefully to the ground. It took him a moment to realise the source of the blow. It was Zain, who now stood above his adversary, panting, and eyeing him with menace. He struck a combative pose straight from the boxing ring, slightly crouched, fists clenched. There was a moment of stunned silence as if all the oxygen had been sucked out of the air. No-one appeared sure of what to do next. Was Zain going to continue his assault and kick Stavros? Was Stavros injured? Would he attempt to fight back? Would Kostas try to stand up for his friend? Should Manolis make a move?

"Argh . . ."

Stavros issued a pained groan that was wheezy and thin. He was injured, which seemed to sober up proceedings. Manolis ran to check that he was alright, no bones broken or organs rearranged, no skin torn or bruised. He helped Stavros to his unsteady feet. Zain took a tentative step forward, as if out of concern, before backing away. He knew he'd gone too far. Placing a protective arm around an emotional Sofia, he walked her home. She was shaking and visibly upset, her eyes wet. Manolis found himself taking pity on her – she was assumed guilty until proven innocent. Still doubled over in pain, Stavros called out to Zain, shouted that he was a barbarian. His words were taken by the wind, blown away like dust.

*   *   *

The parishioners went to the taverna for their traditional post-church roast lunch. Never one to turn down a free meal, Father Petros joined them, and also Elias. Absent were Angelo and Anna, who went home to rest, and Sofia and Zain, for obvious reasons. Stavros sat with a bag of ice on his ribs and a whisky by way of anaesthetic in his hand. His chest and back were tender but he was otherwise fine.

Manolis was uncomfortable. The dead air between the group was no longer the comfort he had once found it to be.

A new lamb that had been roasting to a juicy finish on a slow-turning spit since Saturday night soon repaired the atmosphere. The carcass was brought to the outdoor table by Kostas and Roze. They presented it with ceremony and received a small round of applause. Kostas carved the lamb into perfect slices with a sharp knife, the scent of the fat wafting into the air. Manolis's stomach clenched; he helped himself to salad, creamy slices of cheese, lemony potatoes, bread and *mezethes*, heaping his plate high. The spit reminded Manolis of his father's parties when he was younger. An unfortunate pig or lamb or goat would rotate over hot coals for hours in the backyard as a crowd of men clutching cans of beer stood around watching and carousing. The outer layers would be charred and crispy, while the insides remained succulent and pink. A young Manolis invariably fell asleep in his bedroom listening to a chorus of drunken village songs.

The lake shone with a vital tone of cobalt-blue. At the head of the table, a place was set for Lefty, to acknowledge his absence and invite his return. Manolis watched Father Petros saunter up to Lefty's seat at the table and gently lay a black leather motorcycle cap on the plate. He immediately recognised it as the same hat he'd seen inside Father Petros's house. The priest looked down at the headpiece as if he'd just delivered the last rites.

"Is that Lefty's hat?" Manolis asked.

Father Petros sighed voluminously. "Yes," he said. "He forgot it at the taverna one night. I picked it up and took it home. I hadn't got around to returning it before he vanished. I now bring it to our Sunday luncheon every week." His stomach growled at the sight of the buffet.

It was a touching gesture. Manolis ripped a chunk of white bread with his incisors to hide his disappointment at the death of a good lead.

Conversation around the table quickly centred on Sofia, her pugnacious gardener, and their behaviour at church. Stavros and Kostas maintained that their reactions were further indication of their guilt. They did not consider their own actions to have been at all inflammatory and expressed no regret.

"She's disposed of the meat. It's just a matter of time before Lefty's bones are found on her property," Stavros said, swallowing a pink morsel of lamb.

"Unless she's already ground them up and served him to her pigs," added Kostas. He poured himself some smoky whisky from the thick crystal decanter and took a pull.

"Or used him as fertiliser on her garden," Stavros said. He clinked glasses with his friend.

Elias laughed. "The very same garden that Lefty once destroyed for his amusement. How fitting."

Father Petros stayed quiet, chewing, the topic of conversation perhaps too gruesome even for him, or the food too delicious. Manolis eventually leaned forward.

"I don't think it would be possible to grind human bones," he said. "They're too large and thick. Chicken bones maybe."

"Or rabbit or fish," added Roze.

"But have you seen her collection of hacksaws?" Kostas asked. "They could cut through diamond. She'd use those to break up the bones into more manageable pieces."

"Bone would stand no chance against those saws," Stavros said. "Like a knife through butter."

Father Petros suddenly held up a long and thick lamb bone which he'd been gnawing and sucking clean. It was an evocative image given the topic of conversation.

"People, please. Can we refrain from such discussions while we eat? It is disrespectful to God and this wonderful feast that He has provided us."

The table went quiet; only the sounds of cutlery clinking on crockery, of polite chewing and gentle slurping. The mood was strained. Kostas and Stavros exchanged furtive glances across the table. Elias pushed his plate away and lit a soothing cigarette.

Manolis looked out over the jagged landscape, at the glacial crags and mysterious body of water that was the region's constant backdrop. It held so many secrets within its bleak depths. The history of conflict and the tens of thousands of lost and ragged children had scarred the land and affected generations. Even if residents preferred not to discuss those horrific events, the fallout was plain. Like an amputated limb, the humanitarian disaster continued to haunt this tiny and impoverished region that remained black-eyed and grief-stricken. And soon, the old would die, leaving the area abandoned.

A sense of calm would wash over Manolis whenever he was with his son, once he'd adjusted to Christos's pace and looked at whatever Christos wanted to show him that day, whether it was a book or puzzle or toy. And then, when he returned him to his mother, Manolis always felt a distinct chill in the air from Christos's absence: a loss of energy, of vibrancy, of innocence and youth. Manolis couldn't imagine what that was like tens of thousands of times over and the colossal vacuum it would leave in a community. It would be as if all the warmth disappeared from the sun.

Thinking about Christos made Manolis miss him intensely. He reminded himself that what he was doing was partly for him, so that he could one day bring him to Greece to discover his heritage and learn about his family. But thinking about Christos, sleeping safe and snug in his bed, also made Manolis remember the child he'd killed in that cold, dark basement. He had no home, no sense of security, no support, no chance. It was brutally unfair. Finishing his lunch, wiping his mouth with a paper napkin, Manolis felt the energy drain from his body.

"Kostas, that was delicious," Stavros finally said, laying his knife and fork parallel across his plate. "My compliments to the chef."

"Ah, that would be more for Roze this time," he said.

Roze acknowledged their appreciation and said, "Kostas taught me well." Everyone crossed themselves in unison in thanks for the meal. Manolis did the same, albeit a second later.

Manolis helped Roze clear the table and returned from the kitchen with a tray of baklava for dessert. By then, Kostas had cracked the seal on a box of Cuban cigars and a bottle of aged whisky from his private cellar and was busy pouring solid slugs into lowball glasses. He said it was his birthday, although he actually had three different dates of birth. When he was born, record-keeping was poor, so none of his official records – state records, church records and army records – matched up. Manolis remembered that it had been the same with his dad. It meant that Con had multiple birthday celebrations every year, none of which were ever truly joyous because of the underlying uncertainty.

"Happy birthday anyway," Manolis told Kostas.

Manolis declined the offer of whisky and cigars and sat to eat his baklava. Roze soon returned to the table with cups of hot coffee and cold water and asked if anyone needed anything more. When no-one spoke up, she laid her cheek on her hands.

"It's been a busy morning," she said. "I'm going home for a nap."

Kostas threw back another birthday shot and joked that she was not being paid to rest. Roze fired him a dirty look and kept walking.

"I think I'll stretch my legs," Manolis told the table.

Stavros winked at Manolis as if to communicate that everything was fine. Manolis winked back, and simultaneously felt his skin recoil. The four Greek men downed a shot in Manolis's honour to initiate the inexorable journey into unconsciousness. It seemed part of a hallowed ritual, as if they were worshipping at the feet of an amber god. Manolis thanked Kostas for lunch and left the taverna to the sound of uncontrolled laughter and hacking coughs.

Manolis's feet soon led him to the shores of Great Prespa Lake. Stepping onto the beach, Manolis kicked off his shoes and let his toes sink pleasantly into the warm sand. The sun stirred the surface of the lake into coloured prisms. The syrupy water glugged in the reeds, clotted with marsh plants and plastic bottles and aluminium cans. Ungainly great grebes with black crests and chestnut ruffs trumpeted madly as they bobbed in the water.

The empty landscape made Manolis feel inconsequential, his life minuscule. When cloud hid its far shores, the ancient lake could be mistaken for the sea, allowing Manolis to imagine momentarily that he was looking out at the Mediterranean, holidaying on an island, as he'd intended. Instead, he was stuck in this place of overwhelming solitude and strangeness, trying to locate a walking apparition.

Manolis slumped to the sand. He closed his eyes and filled his ears with the sounds of the lake. Manolis felt as though he was getting further from Lefty, not closer. Part of him wanted to take Con's cherished set of *komboloi* and hurl them into the cold depths of the cavernous lake. It might very well be where Lefty was anyway, his body bloated and slowly decomposing. In which case, and in a roundabout way, Manolis would be fulfilling his late father's wishes that he deliver the heirloom, which was tainted now anyway.

But at least Manolis finally had closure on his aunt. Whatever had happened during that one lamentable Australian summer was now firmly in the past. Constantinos and his sister Calliope were both safe in their cold graves, on different sides of the earth but connected by a common shame. At least Manolis had retrieved the deadly knife from its burial place. He'd wrapped the weapon safely in a towel and stored it in an airtight plastic container under his bed.

"Hey," said a voice from behind.

Manolis spun around. Elias had crept up silently and now loomed over him.

"Oh . . . hi," Manolis said nonchalantly. "Not getting drunk at the taverna?"

"I can't. My liver."

"Ha. Our bodies aren't what they used to be. We're not twenty years old anymore."

"No, we're not," Elias said. "And here's another thing you're not. You're not a labourer. You're a policeman working undercover to investigate Lefty's disappearance, aren't you?"

21

Stunned by Elias's comment, Manolis didn't know what to say. His body went rigid and his face flushed pink as if he'd been slapped. He'd worked undercover before, sometimes for months at a stretch, which was a challenge, the isolation affecting his marriage and mental health. When he closed an undercover investigation, Manolis would have difficulty integrating back into normal life and regular police duty. Occasionally, he even felt the odd pang of guilt at betraying all the drug dealers and crooked businessmen who'd come to trust him. But he'd always accomplished his mission. Manolis had never once been outed.

Manolis immediately wondered who had revealed his true identity to Elias. Roze might have suspected it, but only Stavros knew the truth. But could it really have been his old friend? He had, after all, asked him to take on the case in the first place. But who else could it be? It must have been Stavros, unless Elias had guessed from something that someone in Florina had said. Manolis didn't know many people in the town but they would have known through Stavros that he was coming from Australia and might have spread the word to the Prespes.

Elias's connections through his job as a border guard may also have led him to discover Manolis's true profession in Australia. After all, they were both public servants funded by the taxpayer; they didn't work for private corporations. The enduring financial influence of the *fakelaki* in Greece would have given Elias access to wads of privileged details. If so, that was a second offence: using his dirty smuggling money to source confidential information.

Manolis rose to his feet and eyeballed Elias. A pair of hard eyes stared back, an unlit cigarette dangling precariously from the side of his sneering mouth, his hands on his hips. It was clear he felt he had the advantage over Manolis.

"Policeman, eh?" Manolis said. "That's pretty funny. Who told you that joke?"

"No-one. And it's no joke."

"It's hilarious," Manolis said. "Where did you get that from?"

Elias tucked his cigarette behind his ear. A smug look crept across his face.

"I've been watching you," he said coolly. His breath smelled of scorched spring lamb and whisky.

Why would Elias have been watching him? Was it simply because he worked in law enforcement? Was his mind programmed like Manolis's and always on the lookout for trouble? Maybe it was because Manolis was the village's newest arrival and therefore a person of interest. Or perhaps it was something else altogether.

In Manolis's experience, the guilty were more aware of policemen than the innocent. Innocent people didn't care about law enforcers because they had nothing to hide. But the guilty were always on high alert, looking over their shoulder.

Maybe the wily residents of Glikonero had come to the same conclusion as Elias but hadn't said anything. They'd known all along, and were just humouring the unsuspecting undercover cop.

For a second, Manolis wondered whether to come clean. Could now be the moment to admit his true identity and acquire an ally to help fight what was rapidly becoming a losing battle?

Tossing his head back, Manolis laughed. He needed to lighten the situation.

"Watching me?" he said. "What are you, some kind of sick voyeur?"

"No. I work in border security so it's my job to watch people, to see what they're up to in case it affects my role and the security of our nation. But I also like to think that I'm a responsible citizen who cares for his community."

"What kind of threat would an undercover policeman pose? Surely you should focus on the two illegal immigrants in the village? Robberies are taking place, properties are being vandalised, and a local man is still missing. It sounds to me like another law enforcement official is exactly the kind of person you *want* on your side. Unless, of course, you have something to hide yourself . . ."

Elias smiled wickedly through mustard-yellow teeth and squared his jaw. His bald head showed the hallmarks of a fresh sunburn.

"Nice try," he said. "But frankly, I don't care in the slightest if you're a policeman. I've nothing to hide, I had nothing to do with Lefty's disappearance, or anything else you describe. Search my house if you doubt me."

"I'm not sure what good that would do," said Manolis. "As a labourer, all I might notice is if something needs fixing or painting. If that's what you need help with, I think you'll find my rates pretty reasonable."

Manolis flashed a satisfied grin. Elias chuckled and walked towards the shore. He gazed out across the cold, deep lake, the murky waters filled with fish and fury.

"Of course, I'd be dumb if I expected you to admit it," he said. "No undercover policeman would ever give up his real identity so easily without being shown some proof. And I have none, so don't bother asking. I just wanted you to know that I know who you really are."

Manolis went and stood beside him. He folded his arms across his chest.

"Think whatever you want, I can't stop you from imagining that I'm a policeman or an astronaut or even a brown bear, if that's what you want to believe. In fact, a policeman would be a step up from labouring – better pay, more respect. So, thanks for the compliment. But unfortunately, all I know are building repairs and that's all I've been doing since the day I arrived here in Glikonero."

Elias frowned. "Why don't I believe you?"

Manolis suppressed an impulse to smile. "I don't know. I must be a bad liar."

The men stared silently at the lake a while, gathering their thoughts, the air thick between them. Manolis wondered if Elias was buying what he was selling. The mood remained tense, the two men unwilling to let down their guard. A flock of alarmed blackbirds flew overhead, dark against the sky.

Manolis moistened his lips. A small concession might help convince Elias.

"Of course, I can't lie and say I'm not curious about Lefty's disappearance," he said. "But that's not unexpected, is it? Especially when I'm working on his house all day. I see his things and how he lived. Everyone I've spoken to wants to know what happened to him. It's a mystery, and I love all those mystery shows on TV."

"Me too," Elias said quickly. "It makes my boring job seem a little more interesting."

"I would have thought patrolling an international border defined by a lake would be interesting . . ."

"Trust me, it's not. I have to create my own excitement."

I bet you do, thought Manolis.

"Anyway, being curious about Lefty hardly makes me an undercover policeman," Manolis said. "I'm an amateur sleuth at best. But I think you could say that about the whole village. Everyone wants to be the one who solves the mystery."

"Except Sofia."

Manolis laughed. "Except her. She's enjoying the peace and quiet at the moment, but not so much the extra attention."

Reaching into his pocket, Elias retrieved his lighter and sparked his cigarette within cupped hands. He inhaled deeply, making the tip burn lava-orange.

"Between you and me, I know Sofia is the obvious suspect, but I think that's wrong. As you suggested, I've been watching the village's other new arrivals closely."

"You mean Roze and Zain."

"Yes. I know they're both here in Greece illegally."

"So why don't you do something about it? You're a border guard, aren't you?"

Elias spat a golden orb of mucus into the lake. "I am, but this is more trouble than it's worth, both for me and the residents. Paperwork for me, and it'll only disrupt the village dynamic, annoy Kostas and Sofia. Plus, I need to keep Roze around here. More than anyone else, from what I've seen, she had something to do with Lefty's disappearance."

Manolis rubbed his jaw with concern. Roze's name had been singled out before – Stavros had also been highly suspicious of her. Manolis wasn't sure what to make of these village assessments. Objectively, Roze's status as an illegal immigrant brought her whole character into question. And there was also the outstanding issue of the fake passport found at Lefty's house. But Roze had so far come across as the most helpful resident of all, and her house search had proven the least fruitful. It felt like a local Greek conspiracy against the Albanian migrant, or maybe she was playing everyone for chumps. Manolis also wondered about Zain's history as an illegal immigrant from Syria and how it affected how Sofia was viewed. She was obviously taking advantage of his vulnerability, of his youth and desperation, but there were other reasons to suspect her.

"Really, Roze?" Manolis said, scratching an eyebrow. "I know she's an illegal immigrant, she told me as much herself. But she's always come across as so friendly. How could she be involved? Why would she want to hurt Lefty, what did she stand to gain?"

Elias stroked his chin, choosing his words carefully. He said his suspicion of Roze had nothing to do with her background and all to do with recent history in Glikonero. It had become a running joke within the village community.

"She'll never admit it, but Roze was insanely jealous of Lefty because he had the run of Kostas's taverna and was the unofficial second-in-charge," Elias said. "He was the greeter of tourists, the concierge and entertainer, and she didn't like it."

Manolis tried to work out the connection between being an attention seeker and turning to murder.

"So, she wanted to attract more attention in a one-horse town, and the only way to do that was to eliminate her competition?"

It made Roze sound callow and self-absorbed when she came across as the opposite, as independent and mature and complex.

Elias grinned shiftily. "Not quite," he said. "Being the centre of attention meant that Lefty got way more tips, which are the lifeblood of all hospitality workers. Roze only ever got the scraps. Lefty was a hustler with charisma and half-drunk confidence, and he played on that at every opportunity, be it with a pair of young German tourists or a married couple with kids. He's lived a large life, he has stories and knows how to tell them, he's entertaining. Roze is attractive, but all she really has are her looks. That may work on the men, but it halves her customer base."

Roze had always said that Lefty tipped her handsomely. It could have been a carefully constructed lie, one that played cleverly on the very thing that came between them.

Although it was a world with which he'd never connected, Manolis wondered whether Roze had a social media presence. Did she parade herself across digital screens to her small universe? If Roze had crossed the border illegally, it would not be something she advertised; at least, not under her real name. It was probably the same for Zain.

Unsure what to believe, Manolis decided to flip the script and watch Elias's reaction.

"I can see how money might be an issue to some people," he said. "It never has been to me. But tips can only be so big in a small village taverna."

"Depends on the tourist," Elias said. "We get some rich Russian playboys through here too, you know."

"Be that as it may, you once told me that Lefty owed you a lot of money and that you didn't know if and how you would get it back."

"That's correct ..." Elias seemed suddenly wary, swollen veins appearing in his neck.

"So why does he owe you so much money? You never explained. Was it a big lump sum you gave him, or something he accumulated over time?"

Elias hesitated. Manolis assumed he didn't want to admit to being involved in smuggling and selling black-market goods with Lefty, and especially not to someone he suspected was actually an undercover policeman.

"I made him a loan," he replied. "It was out of my savings. I felt bad for him that he never had any money."

"Who told you he had no money?"

"I thought that was obvious."

"Lefty may have had a bank account somewhere, under a different name. He could have been in a situation to loan you money if you needed it."

"Ha. I doubt it. If he was, he never offered. He only took."

"How much does he owe you?"

Elias shook his bulbous skull. "I'd rather not say, that's personal information. But it was a substantial sum."

"And he never paid any of it back?"

"Not one euro."

Manolis smiled. "Sounds like a pretty good reason to make him disappear, don't you think?"

"Very clever. See, you are a good policeman."

Taking a final drag on his cigarette, Elias flicked the butt into the lake. Manolis watched it float into a clump of reeds clogged with shampoo bottles, pursued by a pair of curious dragonflies.

"Anyway, I'm off home for a nap to sleep off that oily lunch," Elias said. He stroked his moustache with an index finger, making sure it was straight and neat. "See you next time. Don't get into trouble trying to cross the lake."

Manolis watched him disappear back into Glikonero and sat down

213

on the coarse sand to gather his thoughts. He picked up a handful of grains, let them slip through his fingers.

Roze had never struck him as mercenary. But the migrant focus on making money and achieving success was strong. Manolis had seen it in his own parents and many other immigrants who strove for a better life in Australia as shop owners and labourers and cleaners, then as landlords and entrepreneurs. Zain clearly had the same mentality. But it appeared that he had decided to dig or punch his way to success, not make his adversaries disappear. Perhaps Manolis had been too generous in his view of Roze because she was younger, newer to the village, and had shown him the most hospitality. For all Manolis knew, Roze might not even be her real name. Nor might Lefty be Lefty's name.

With the afternoon sun sitting low, Manolis felt its hellish heat intensify on his face. He felt suddenly lethargic, stricken, his limbs strangely heavy like wet cement, his blood sluggish. It had been a tiring, eventful day, and a siesta was a good call on Elias's part. A malaise seemed to hang over the village in the afternoon swelter, a listening quiet descending. With the heavy food playing tricks on his brain, Manolis momentarily considered collapsing where he was and taking a nap on the sand. Remembering Elias's sunburn, he rejected that idea. Reading a chapter of his book and falling asleep in a shaded chair sounded much more appealing.

Achingly, he found his feet and shambled home along deserted roads. But as he came in sight of his front door, his plan to take a nap was forgotten. Lefty's house looked different. The front door was ajar, and a broom lay across the path. Manolis was certain he'd not left it in such a state the day before. He had definitely closed the door.

Stepping lightly to the entrance, Manolis listened for signs of someone inside. Without a firearm, Manolis was at least reassured that he couldn't accidentally shoot them. But what if they had a weapon?

Hearing silence, Manolis entered cautiously. The cottage appeared empty. Manolis checked to see what was missing. Lefty's belongings – useless and otherwise – seemed all to be in their natural state. Manolis sighed with relief. But then, he looked up, remembering what had been hidden in the big empty space above his head.

Grabbing a flashlight, he climbed the ladder and scanned the roof cavity. The metal toolbox that would normally have reflected the light was now gone, and with it the money.

22

Going back into Lefty's cottage, resting on a wooden fruit crate, Manolis thought about what had just happened, and was struck by the timing. In the same way he'd waited for the Sunday morning church service to search the villagers' homes, so too had the thief who'd stolen Lefty's money. It didn't strike Manolis as a coincidence. Had a resident realised that their house had been searched by Manolis and returned the favour? They could very easily have found nothing of interest within the house and decided to search the extremities, as Manolis once had. A toolbox with a hundred thousand euros would have exceeded their wildest dreams. Perhaps Sofia had discovered that a bag of her minced meat had gone missing or Angelo had noticed that something had happened to his passport; after all, Manolis had been careless the day he'd returned it. Or was it simpler than that: the money had been stolen by the only other person who knew of its existence?

The black duffel bag filled with weapons remained in the roof. Either the thief had no need for them or it had been a one-man job. The bag was heavy and needed at least two thieves to move it. But the toolbox was light enough and manoeuvrable enough to be carried by one person.

Manolis cursed. Rubbing his hands anxiously on his thighs, he began to doubt himself. The disappearance of the money on a Sunday morning combined with Elias's accusation made him wonder if he'd been reckless in his investigation.

With Elias's words of warning still ringing in his ears, Manolis suddenly remembered something. It wasn't just Father Petros who had arrived late for the church service that morning – Roze had also been tardy. A full ten minutes after the service had begun. Combined with Father Petros's half-hour delay, it was more than enough time to make away with the toolbox and yet still be present for most of the service to avoid arousing suspicion. Usually, given Father Petros's lack of punctuality, such a brief absence would have gone unnoticed, and probably had been by the rest of the village. But it now meant something to Manolis, and so did Roze's fake passport. In his experience, the simplest answers to investigative questions were likely to be correct.

"Right," he said to the empty room.

He left the cottage. Walking swiftly past sleeping dogs and darting cats and pecking chickens, Manolis's brain worked almost as hard as his feet. What he was about to propose was out of character. But what if Roze denied any wrongdoing? Would Manolis bring up her fake Greek passport as some form of leverage?

Before Manolis had decided his approach, he was knocking on Roze's door. He waited but there was no answer. Imagining her to be asleep, he knocked harder, but was again met with silence.

"Hello? Roze?"

He entered gently so as to not alarm her. But there was no-one to startle. The cabin was empty.

Manolis distinctly remembered her saying she was going home for a nap after a busy morning at the taverna and church. Roze's absence only fuelled Manolis's suspicions of her. If she'd lied about this, what else had she lied about? Her own identity, for a start. Manolis had proof of that.

He went to feel the sheets to see if the bed was warm and recently slept in. It was cold and neat, the bed as narrow as a coffin. Manolis quickly searched Roze's house but found no toolbox. He didn't expect to find it there anyway – any thief worth their salt would have hidden it elsewhere, or buried it for safekeeping.

Could Roze have been involved not only in the theft of the money but also in Lefty's disappearance? Others had said as much. Manolis rubbed his eyes. His experience told him that when one lie was exposed, there were usually others that followed. The fake passport he'd found hidden under Lefty's floor was surely not insignificant . . .

Manolis was soon back outside, searching for her in the village. There was an urgency in his stride now, the ground quickening beneath his feet, adrenaline drilling through his system. At the taverna, Manolis checked whether Roze had returned to work. But she wasn't there either; he found only Kostas, who was outside in a deckchair, snoring his way into an epic hangover after drinking so extravagantly. Father Petros and Stavros had gone. A swarm of feasting blowflies hummed ominously, attracted by the leftover scraps of food.

Manolis stood for a moment, cleared his throat, and waited. But Kostas snored even more loudly, so Manolis clapped his hands together hard. His face plump with alcohol, Kostas half opened his eyes listlessly like a lazy house cat.

"Yes . . . ?" he slurred, tongue thick and slow.

"Is Roze here?"

"No. I don't know. No."

"Where is she?"

Kostas groaned, adjusting his sleeping position to something less uncomfortable.

"How the hell should I know? She got annoyed and left, and there's cleaning up to do . . ."

Realising he would get nothing from him, Manolis left Kostas to drift further into oblivion. He walked on, even faster now.

With every passing minute, with each new location where Roze was not to be found, Manolis's suspicion of her grew. She could have left the area and now be many kilometres away, elsewhere in Greece or even in another country. She had already demonstrated how leaky the international borders were, and she had no qualms about going wherever she pleased.

Manolis returned to the shores of Great Prespa Lake, jogging lightly across the sand, by now a little breathless. The beach was covered with grass and cow manure. Manolis sent pods of loafing pelicans scattering from the water as he passed, their mighty three-metre wings outstretched and flapping in a sudden tumult of panic and activity. When the squawking had subsided, the faint sound of a voice tickled Manolis's ears. He turned and saw Roze walking towards him with an arm outstretched. She was waving and smiling. By the time Manolis reached the wooden jetty, he was fairly panting, hands on knees, glistening with sweat, and in no mood. She was wearing tight sportswear, music in her ears, and stood with a hand on her hip.

"Are you OK?" she asked Manolis, removing her headphones.

"I'm fine. I've been looking for you."

"For me?"

"I thought you said you were going home to nap. Didn't you say you were going home to rest? Where did you go?"

His annoyance was palpable. She took a step back.

"I did go home, and yes, I did try to sleep. But I couldn't in this heat, so I decided to get some fresh air and walk to clear my mind. Is there a problem, do you have an issue with that?"

Her tone was caustic. Manolis ignored it.

"And you were late for church this morning. Why was that?"

"I slept in. I was preparing the roast lamb until late last night and was tired."

"Hmm, OK. When I went home from the taverna after church, I dropped by Lefty's house when I saw the door was open. And you know what else I saw?"

Roze stared back, her face expressionless, unreadable.

"No . . ." she said slowly. "Did you see Lefty, was he back?"

Manolis didn't know if she was being genuine or genuinely sarcastic.

"Of course Lefty wasn't back," he snapped. "He's still missing. Only now, all his money is missing as well. Do you remember that toolbox we found, the bundles of money that were inside? That's all gone now, stolen. And I'm struggling to work out who might have taken it given that only two people knew of its existence and whereabouts – you and me."

Roze stared at Manolis, a line of irritation forming across her forehead. She listened silently as he explained his role as caretaker of Lefty's cottage, and his responsibility for the missing man's belongings.

"That includes items that are gained unlawfully, as well as lawfully. Just because someone else may have acquired something illegally, it doesn't mean you can come in and take it from them. Two wrongs don't make a right."

He finished by saying he would accept return of the money with no further action needed or questions asked. And he wouldn't report her to the Florina police for crossing the border.

Roze waited a moment as his proposal – and allegation – sank in. Manolis folded his arms and waited for her answer, seething. When Roze finally spoke, she chose her words carefully, spitting out each syllable.

"If I understand what you're saying, you're blaming me for the disappearance of Lefty's money, and even suggesting that I stole it. That's all news to me. I'm sorry to hear his money has disappeared, there was a lot there. But no, I didn't take it. And I sure don't appreciate the idea, the *accusation* that I did. I was tired this morning, I slept in. But why should you believe me? Deep down, you're just like everyone else here – quick to point the finger at the shifty Albanian foreigner for whatever goes wrong. So, I guess this is goodbye and good luck finding Lefty and his dirty money."

Roze didn't allow Manolis time to respond. She shoved past him roughly, repositioned the music in her ears, and broke into a run, leaving Manolis with an empty feeling in the pit of his stomach. As he watched her go, his conscience twinged. For a moment, he considered pursuing her but quickly realised there was no way he could keep up.

"Roze, hey wait! Come back! I need to—"

Her headphones blocked his pleas. She ran on, kicking up sand in her wake.

Manolis scratched his jaw. His ash-grey stubble was itchy and rough, in need of a shave. He was certain Roze was lying, but her salty tone had been unequivocal. She hadn't paused or stuttered. Manolis swayed with the biliousness of failure, of helplessness.

But who else could conceivably have taken the money? Could Roze have told anyone else about it? It seemed unlikely but was possible, such was the fuel of gossip that powered a small village. Something so significant and so relevant to Lefty would have been of great interest. Then again, the money's disappearance could somehow have been linked to Lefty's disappearance, with whoever was responsible for the latter deciding now to finish the job by claiming Lefty's assets.

The bag of firearms and ammunition had been left behind. It was worth a fair sum of money on its own and could have been sold for a good price, although it would have required the right connections to the wrong people. It seemed unlikely that the money had been stolen in a random robbery by an opportunist thief – the area was so remote, and someone would surely have seen something had it involved a stranger in broad daylight. But the residents had been at church all morning, and habitually left their doors unlocked. The villagers themselves came into focus. If not Roze, then who? Elias was owed money by Lefty, and so was Kostas. But when would they have found the opportunity? Both men had been at church and the taverna all day, although Roze was very close to Kostas.

The lake spread out before Manolis, boundless and placid, its depths frigid and dark. The surface was mirror smooth. During all his time in the Prespes region, Manolis hadn't found a single map that included the lake territory next door; the bodies of water appeared in blue slices, with only the Greek sections represented. He imagined it was the same in Albania and North Macedonia. Where the national boundary finished, so did the world.

There had once been a time when there had been no borders to separate the people of the region. The lake was a testament to such history. The view from one shore across the water to the surrounding mountains was the same, irrespective of which country you were in. If you stood at the water's edge, the lake's rippling would be the same sound heard on the opposing shore. It underscored the arbitrary nature of the national borders that were once drawn on a map and had become fixed ever since. The fact that the lake was a geographical tripoint highlighted its value – no single country was allowed to own it, the lake had to be shared between three, it transcended borders. When the divisions were established, blood relatives and friends became separated, with only the lake to connect them. The soil was different, it didn't move, but the water remained the same, fluid and flowing. Touching the great lake was like reaching out to a loved one. The water didn't separate people – it linked them.

Staring at the lake, at its unearthly stillness, Manolis contemplated the complexity of human existence and felt dizzy. His mouth was dry, his body dehydrated. Out of the corner of his eye he saw something moving and it snapped him back into the moment. It was a small rowing boat heading north. Manolis put his arm over his eyes to shield them from the glare from the water. He couldn't make out the identity of the occupant.

Was it Zain?

"Hey!" Manolis called, and waved.

The morning's confrontation had raised bile in his throat and had likely done the same for Zain. Manolis bore no ill will towards the boxer, who was simply protecting Sofia. He'd also not forgotten that Zain had saved him from an agonising death in a nest of angry vipers.

Zain was heading to Golem Grad to search for buried treasure again. He needed his ticket out of purgatory. This time, though, he appeared to be rowing faster than usual, as if in a hurry. Manolis called again, louder this time, in case Zain hadn't heard his first attempt. Zain stopped rowing, looked up, stared for a moment, then started to row again at a rate that was even faster and more urgent than before.

"Oh no . . ." Manolis said.

It was only then that he remembered who else had been absent from the morning's church service until he made a last-minute cameo. And the ugly confrontation after the service would have prompted him to seek retribution.

23

His feet clomping across the sand, Manolis dashed for the jetty. Seeing Zain rowing to Golem Grad, he made the snap decision to commandeer a boat and follow him. It would be easier the second time around – the journey was not unknown, he was aware of the reptilian risks at the other end, although he was again wearing his summery open-toed sandals. If Zain had taken the toolbox of money, Manolis didn't just want to catch him red-handed – he needed to.

"For God's sake," Manolis said aloud, putting his hands on his hips. "What are the chances?"

There were no boats at the jetty. Looking north to the island, eyeing the water in between, Manolis considered swimming across. He was a capable swimmer, but the distance was too great and the water too deep. Stavros had said the lake was at its deepest – some fifty metres – at the tripoint where the three countries converged. That was not an insignificant depth of water in which to drown.

Striding along the shore, Manolis searched for another seaworthy vessel. He looked over his shoulder, back towards the village, in case there was something there, perhaps a dinghy or flat-bottomed boat on the land. In the near distance, a circling snake kestrel and flight of raucous jays battled like warplanes in the hot summer air.

In the end, Manolis's salvation came in the form of an old kayak that he found in a clump of reeds. The paddle was several metres away, hidden in another tangle. With their labyrinthine structures, the Prespa reed beds were ideal hiding places for smaller birds: squacco herons, ferruginous ducks and little bitterns. Manolis had never paddled a kayak before but now had little choice other than to try. He'd seen kayakers on TV, how hard could it be? Fortunately, there was also an orange flotation vest.

The kayak was made of plywood and fibreglass and was chipped and discoloured. Manolis capsized the narrow watercraft soon after he got in, and came close to doing so a dozen more times as he made his clumsy way across to the island. The kayak felt decidedly unstable as it rocked back and forth with his shifting weight. Gliding through the water, the professional athletes and experienced adventurers had made it look easy. It didn't help that the kayak lacked a spray deck, which meant it filled with cold lake water, making it even more unwieldy.

The cumbersome kayak cost Manolis valuable time, as he struggled to steer a straight course across the lake. The journey was made longer by Zain's decision to berth on the island's northernmost side. The last time Manolis had followed him, he'd landed on the southern shore, the one nearest to the Greek mainland. Perhaps Zain had intentionally changed his approach to escape prying eyes.

Dripping wet, Manolis finally reached Golem Grad's most distant bank, grateful to be in one undrowned piece. He hurried ashore, dirt and sand sticking to his wet sandals and feet, dodging a few slithering snakes which he hoped were non-venomous. Manolis left his orange flotation vest on the sand; it would do nothing to help his camouflage. The approach to the island from the northern shore was not as steep as from the south. Carrying a toolbox would have been conceivable for one fit person from this side.

Manolis set off for the site of Zain's most recent excavation. There was no guarantee he would be there; he might very well have buried the toolbox elsewhere and be on his way back. But it remained Manolis's best option. Burying the money on Golem Grad would buy Zain time to plan his next move without fear of it being stolen. If the island had protected buried treasure once, it could easily do so again.

Manolis walked swiftly, dodging invisible shapes every few metres and raising his knees high like a prancing horse. His heart pounded, filling his ears with its uneven beat. He pictured himself being punctured on a tasty ankle by a stealthy viper, falling hard and calling for help. Zain might hear and rush to his aid a second time, or he might not, thinking that it served him right; Manolis had been warned and hadn't listened. Either way, Zain wouldn't be carrying antivenom among his tools, and medical help in the form of defibrillators, ventilators and blood transfusions was far away. Manolis's vision would soon flicker and snowstorm from the neurotoxins in his system and his heart would race evermore rapidly. His healthy cells would shrink and collapse, their perforated surfaces erupting in bubbles and boils that sloughed away, leaving only fragmentary mush. His limbs would tingle, and sweat would gush from every pore until eventually everything went black and quiet. A pair of perfectly matched fang marks in his ankle might be the last thing Manolis saw. Finding Manolis's toxin-riddled body, limp and cold, Zain would say a silent prayer and drag it to one of his unsuccessful but convenient excavations, tossing it inside and covering it with earth. He would finish his prospecting for the day and row back to the mainland with a clear conscience – the snakes had sensed a threat and sought to protect themselves; there was nothing he could possibly have done to change the outcome. No-one else would visit the island. Manolis would vanish, just as Lefty had.

Manolis blocked out the ghastly vision and walked faster. He soon heard digging and found Zain in the midst of his usual excavation, shovel in hand, map in pocket. Crouched behind some shrubs, Manolis observed him discreetly.

"I'm too late," he whispered to himself. "He's already buried it."

Manolis went to stand, to approach Zain directly. It was a risky move given the hostilities exchanged at church that morning.

As he adjusted his position, Manolis felt a searing pain in his left foot. He looked down, expecting to find that he'd stood on a sharp twig. But instead he saw a thin tan-coloured snake trying to slither away unnoticed. Inspecting his foot, he saw two small marks.

It took a moment for the dreaded realisation to dawn.

"Argh . . . !"

It was a snakebite. Manolis slumped to the ground, grabbing at his leg as he bent to examine his foot. Then it occurred to him that it was more important he see the snake and identify the source of the bite and venom. It would be needed for medical diagnosis and treatment, if he ever received any.

"*Gamoto*," he mumbled to himself in Greek. "*Oxi oxi*, no no . . ."

Manolis's heart began to flutter, his head pounded and his skin burned as terror took over. His worst nightmare had become reality. He wondered which organ system would shut down first.

Alerted by his panicked scream, Zain appeared, axe in hand. Seeing Manolis grasping his ankle, he knew precisely what had happened.

"Which snake? Where?" he asked swiftly.

Manolis pointed out the assailant. His foot began to sting and throb. Zain raised his axe in preparation for a swift beheading and approached the reptile. But then he lowered it.

"This snake has no venom," he said. "Its eyes are round, not shaped like slits. That is the sign. You have been bitten, yes, and your foot will hurt a while. But it is just holes, you will be fine."

The would-be assassin slithered away and disappeared between some rocks. Manolis felt instant relief at Zain's assessment. He hadn't managed to properly see the snake's eyes for himself, only that the snake lacked a sharp horn on its head, which appeared round and smooth. He didn't know whether to trust Zain when he said it was non-venomous or to go to Florina to be examined by a doctor. The town was at least an hour away, and that was more than enough time for any venom to swarm his blood and course through his body.

"Are you sure?" Manolis asked, an odd sense of dislocation washing over him. He stood and rotated his foot to encourage blood flow. "Are you certain it wasn't poisonous?"

"Yes," Zain said. "I am sure. What are you doing back here? Are you crazy? You did not learn from last time?"

Manolis felt uncomfortable about what he was about to say, particularly since Zain was holding a sharp axe. But he couldn't afford to stutter. He assumed a confident air and put forward his version of reality. His words were met with a long glare, followed by a neutral expression.

"Why would I take your toolbox?" Zain asked. "I already have my own tools."

Manolis crossed his arms. "Stop playing games. You know I don't mean tools."

"Sorry, I do not understand. What else is there in a toolbox? Not tools?"

Unlike Roze, Zain was more deferential, like a child being scolded by a parent for doing something wrong. But, just like her, Zain might have been lying as he protested his innocence. Manolis knew he would have lied and cheated his way out of Syria to Greece. There was no other way. To lie was a necessary survival skill, one that he would have honed like a sixth sense.

"I was home all morning," Zain said. "I was working in Sofia's garden, pulling out weeds and moving heavy rocks, and only left to go to church to walk her home. I am sorry for what happened there with the other men, but she was upset. She is an old lady and I was protecting her like the snakes protect this island."

Manolis walked over to the clearing, inspecting the site for evidence of recent burial. But he found none. There were plenty of holes that gave the area the appearance of a lunar landscape, but none that appeared to have been recently filled in, the dirt still loose and scattered. Manolis wanted to believe that the golden toolbox was the lead that would break the Lefty case wide open, that if he identified the person responsible for the theft of the money, he would somehow be led to whoever was responsible for Lefty's disappearance. Meanwhile, Zain struggled to prove that he hadn't stolen the toolbox.

"If you do not believe me, you can come to my house, I show you I have no toolbox," he said. "This is why I must always borrow tools from the priest."

Zain's bewilderment that a toolbox could be of such value unsettled Manolis. Might he be wrong again?

Just then, Manolis felt a chill crawl up his arms.

"I feel cold," he said. "Are you sure that the snake—"

"No poison," Zain said quickly. "Just bites. You will be OK, I promise."

In an effort to clear his name, Zain leaned against the handle of his shovel and began to recount the events of his morning – a list of the things he had done, mundane errands and gardening and maintenance chores. Manolis sat on the sun-washed grass, listening absently. He was more interested in inspecting his ankle and watching for snakes hidden in the trees or camouflaged on the ground.

"But wait," Zain said suddenly. "Now I do remember something that happened this morning, something different. There was a car near the watermill, a strange car, not from here, it had broken down. I heard loud voices so I went to see if I could help. I saw two men arguing over how to change a flat tyre."

Manolis rubbed his chin with the side of his index finger.

"What men?" he asked. "Had you seen them before? Flat tyre? What kind of car was it?"

Zain looked to the sky as he scanned his memory, his mint-green eyes and high cheekbones catching the afternoon light.

"They were not men I recognised. They were strangers, probably visitors."

"Were they tourists?"

Zain shook his head. "I do not think so."

"What makes you say that?"

"Because of what they were wearing and how they talked. They wore plain clothes, poor clothes, like mine, and they sounded Greek. But they were not men that I knew. Maybe they were from another part of the country."

"How old were they?"

"Not old. But not young."

"And what about their car?"

Zain's expression changed, his face clouding momentarily as if he couldn't think how to convey what he'd seen.

"I have not seen a car like it before. It was old. It was like a car but also not like a car. More like a truck."

"A truck? What colour was it?"

"Red. But what was strange was the wheels. It only had three. The front one had gone flat."

"You mean, it had four wheels and one tyre was flat, so it had three tyres that were fine?"

Zain paused, trying to picture what Manolis had described.

"No, the car had only three wheels. The front one was flat, which left the back two fine. The men changed the flat front tyre after much trouble and argument and drove away at high speed. I did not need to help them."

Manolis tried to visualise the scene, the men and the vehicle. Zain could have been fabricating the story, but Manolis thought they sounded familiar, and soon realised why.

The vehicle sounded like the three-wheeled Styl Kar he'd seen parked outside the *kafenion* in Lefty's former village of Eleftheria, the one heavy with watermelons. It was then that Manolis realised what had happened. Lefty's past had caught up with him; his creditors were seeking to recover what they were owed by taking matters into their own hands. It sounded as if two men from Eleftheria had come to do the financial work of the whole village. The windfall from the toolbox would have exceeded their wildest dreams; there was no need to steal the guns and ammunition as well. Those items would have implicated them in the theft; cash was easier to distribute and harder to trace. Guns and ammunition also had less immediate value and would require connections to translate into funds. The thought that made Manolis's stomach lurch was that it was he who was responsible for unwittingly leading them to Lefty's house. It was he and Stavros who had recently paid them a visit and said where they were from and who they were looking for. Manolis knew it was now up to him to recover what they had taken.

Manolis looked at Zain, his muscles tense, sweat glistening. The area around the bite on Manolis's foot was sore and tender to the touch. The skin was red and angry and beginning to swell in response to the injury.

"OK," Manolis said as he stood gingerly. "I know what to do . . ."

He strode over to Zain and stood in his personal space. The boxing champion didn't flinch. He stood his ground, met Manolis's gaze, and waited for him to finish.

"This is what is going to happen," Manolis continued. "And if you are genuinely telling the truth, then you will help me."

24

The road to Eleftheria was even bumpier in Manolis's Eastern European clunker, and he wasn't driving anywhere near as fast as Stavros had the first time. Manolis was on autopilot. He had no idea how he was going to find Lefty's money. He didn't know where he'd go or what he'd say. He was just a citizen, after all, not a detective on duty; he had no authority, he couldn't flash his badge and make things happen. He would need to be tough yet persuasive with whoever he encountered, and remain calm. The *kafenion* was a starting point, but the money could very well have been distributed by now, stashed under the beds of Lefty's many creditors across Eleftheria. And the worst thought of all that ate away at Manolis was the very real possibility of being wrong for a third time . . .

In the passenger seat, Zain rode beside Manolis in silence. Manolis had explained the situation to him on Golem Grad – the golden toolbox, the nearby village, the outstanding debt – and Zain understood that here was a chance to clear his name. Zain probably felt like he was being taken hostage, Manolis thought, but also that he could handle himself, no matter the adversary. After all, he'd somehow escaped the war zone that was his Syrian homeland, become a boxing champion, and sparred with desert cobras.

Manolis was placing all his trust in the illegal immigrant, who had his own village reputation. He might have made up the story about the broken-down Styl Kar to cover his own tracks. And if he hadn't, it might have been another Styl Kar; Greece was known to still have a few, especially in the impoverished rural areas where modern cars remained a luxury. Manolis was bolstered by Zain's physical presence, but questions remained over his dependability, and how that would manifest during a tense encounter with unhappy locals. Father Petros might have been a better companion; the church admittedly had its own issues with corruption and embezzlement, but surely a man of the cloth would have been more respected in a religious country like Greece and better placed to negotiate calmly over money. Taking a big, strapping foreigner could be inflammatory. But it was too late to change tack now.

The road finally began to smooth. Manolis draped his wrist over the steering wheel, tired and aching from traversing so many strange pitches and tilts. The windows were down but the cabin was still hot and stuffy. Manolis felt a headache ticking away inside his skull and wondered if it was the effect of snake venom. Surely not. Manolis was no toxicologist, but had there been poison in that bite, it would have undoubtedly circulated around his body and killed him by now. Zain had been right. Despite his background, it seemed he was trustworthy after all.

"It's not much further," Manolis said. He could smell the salt from the sea.

Zain nodded.

"I've done some thinking," Manolis went on. "When we get there, here's what I think we should do . . ."

Manolis outlined his strategy. He made it clear that they were not, under any circumstances, going to steal the money back. That would only cause more problems in the long run. Instead, as an experienced negotiator, he planned to speak coolly with the villagers, respect that they had been wronged, acknowledge their sizeable debt, but state that they had taken far too much money by stealing the entire toolbox. The most equitable solution was to come to an agreement that benefited both parties. Zain's role in the negotiation was as window dressing. Any conflict would be settled with words, not actions.

Zain nodded. He understood. "But what will happen if they do not agree?" he asked.

Manolis paused, bit his lip. It was a scenario that burned away at the back of his mind. He refused to entertain it.

"Don't worry, I have a plan for that too," he lied.

When they arrived in Eleftheria, the roads were eerily empty. Manolis's palms were sweating on the wheel. As they pulled up in front of the *kafenion*, Zain positively identified the red Styl Kar as the one he had seen.

Manolis took a second look through the bug-spattered windscreen. "Are you sure?" he asked.

"Yes, I am sure." Zain did not hesitate; he sounded confident.

Manolis was buoyed by the sounds emanating from inside the *kafenion*. It was bouzouki music at ear-splitting volume, punctuated by rounds of applause and cheering in between songs. There was a party underway, probably to celebrate the village's unexpected windfall. Everyone was suddenly a millionaire. Creeping up to a grubby window, Manolis peered inside. He saw a ring of dancers twisting in a jubilant spiral, their arms held high, the dance anarchic and dizzying. People sat at small tables with drinks and plates, while in the corner of the room, proudly displayed on a long table, surrounded by platters of food, was Lefty's toolbox. It was the table's glorious centrepiece.

Manolis smiled with relief. "We're in luck," he breathed. "Are you ready?"

"I am."

"Let's go. Remember to let me do the talking."

"I will."

When Manolis and Zain entered, the music and dancing stopped abruptly. Heads turned in their direction, almost as if their arrival was expected. Manolis prayed that wasn't the case, and that he hadn't walked into a bear trap.

Manolis stepped forward and dropped his arms by his sides in a non-threatening manner. He was only a couple of metres inside the *kafenion*, with Zain two steps behind, blocking the doorway. Manolis explained the situation in a measured tone. He said he was in an unenviable position that required him to take responsibility over Lefty's home and belongings. He nodded at regular intervals towards Lefty's toolbox even though he wasn't even sure if the money was still inside. Above all, Manolis expressed his desire to avoid involving the authorities.

"It's in everybody's interests to work together to find a solution," he said.

His sentiments were met with mutterings and hushed curses. Eventually, the stocky, bald-headed proprietor stepped forward. It was, after all, his castle which the barbarian Manolis had stormed.

"Who in the hell are you to come in here with your foreign thug and try to take what's technically ours?" asked Vangelis. "It is you who is stealing, not us." He turned and spoke to Zain directly. "You people are not welcome here. Not in this *kafenion* nor in this country."

Lukas appeared behind the bar, celebratory beer bottle in his tattooed hand, thick crucifix shining around his neck. He eyeballed Zain coldly.

"You people come over here and don't respect our religion. You defile our churches and icons. Could I go and do the same thing in a mosque? No, I would be executed."

Zain remained expressionless, straight-faced. It was a reaction that Manolis found more disconcerting than if he'd exploded with rage.

"Human beings are human beings no matter where they're from," Manolis said.

"We are human beings too," Vangelis replied. "We are not racists. We just want to live our lives in peace. We never asked for any of this."

Manolis pressed his palms together in a mock prayer, as if appealing to a congregation. "I fully agree with you, but right now, I'm here to talk about Lefty."

"As for him," Vangelis said, "if you truly were Lefty's caretaker, you had the opportunity to repay his debts the last time you were here. But you didn't say a word, you just pretended to take our names and you kept the money quiet. It's not just Lefty we're angry with now."

Lukas stepped out from the bar and stood by his employer's side in staunch solidarity. He sneered through his beard, a thick blue vein pulsing at the centre of his forehead.

"Lefty's probably dead anyway," the barista said ominously. "At least this way something positive comes of it. Isn't that a good thing?"

"If he is dead, he has children who should receive his assets first," Manolis said. He neglected to add that he was yet to locate any sign of a last will and testament. Given Lefty's nature, he doubted if there was such a document.

"Children, pah," scoffed Vangelis. "What about *our* children? What future is there for them in this poor country? What money will we be able to leave them if it gets taken by scam artists and stolen by foreigners?"

"I hear you," Manolis said hastily. Anything involving children touched a nerve. "I know what Lefty did was wrong, I don't deny that. So, I'd like to make it right. This is why I came, to make you a proposition . . ."

He outlined his offer. It was absolutely reasonable that the villagers keep the ten thousand euros that Lefty owed them. But any more was being greedy and was unjustified. It punished a man unfairly.

Vangelis spoke for the crowd. "No deal," he said, folding his hairy forearms across his broad chest. "No way. We want it all. Lefty deserves to be punished for what he did, as a penalty. If we can't take it out on him with sticks and stones, we'll take it out on his bank account."

His threat of village-style retribution was chilling. Vangelis's imposing frame and obese bulk took on a new dimension. Manolis thrust forth his chin, as if to counteract the warning.

"But the punishment needs to fit the crime," he said. "Just as you don't give a man twenty years for a traffic offence, in the same way you don't stone someone to death for having an affair."

"What Lefty did was hardly a parking ticket," Lukas said.

"And it's not our fault there's more money there than Lefty owed us," said Vangelis. "We weren't to know; there might have been less. We rolled the dice and won. Some days you win, some you lose."

"But now that you know there *is* more than you're owed, your thinking should be different," said Manolis.

"No," Lukas said firmly. "This is an eye for an eye, and how we do things around here. He took from us, we take from him. Simple."

"It's hardly an eye for an eye. It's ten eyes for an eye."

"Consider it repayment of interest," Vangelis said with a huge crocodile grin.

"But no interest is that much . . ."

Manolis continued negotiating, trying to get through the impasse. At times, he forgot he was bargaining with people who didn't want to be bargained with, who were dismissive and limited in their arguments. Manolis kept mentioning his desire to avoid involving the authorities but the locals just laughed at the prospect.

"As if the Greek police would do anything," Vangelis said. "The most they would do is turn up, take a cut for themselves or confiscate it, then act like nothing happened."

The *kafenion* howled with amusement, with wild-eyed bravado. Manolis couldn't help but feel he was the butt of his own joke. Deep down, he knew Vangelis was right. It was why he'd avoided calling the authorities in the first place. Anger began to congeal in his throat.

"OK," he said, taking a breath. "I get it. Well, how about I offer you a little more for your trouble by way of a generous interest rate. Would that make us square?"

He proposed a new figure, an increased amount, but it was again rejected out of hand. Despite Manolis's best efforts, the locals were adamant that the money was going nowhere and formed a protective, and symbolic, ring around the toolbox.

"No deal," Lukas said with a scowl. He stepped forward just enough for the light to catch the ink on his arms, and drained his beer.

"If you want even so much as a euro of this money, you're going to have to take it," Vangelis added. He interlocked his hands and cracked his knuckles.

Manolis sighed. "I'm sorry to hear you feel that way," he said. "You don't leave me with much choice."

He hoped his words would sound threatening, but the bouzouki music restarted even louder than before. Manolis looked across at Zain, who stared at him stiffly; he was following instructions, as he had been told to do. Manolis leaned in close so that Zain could hear him over the raucous Greek music.

"I think we should go," he said.

"Really? Why?"

"We need a better plan. This is like a poker game. You've got to know when to hold your cards and when to walk away. I'm not happy to go, and we'll come back. But right now, it's time to walk away."

He turned to leave, prepared for the sound of humiliating laughter to follow him. He expected Zain to do the same. But Zain had other ideas, and without warning lifted up his shirt and pulled out a large handgun from behind his back. He pointed it squarely at Vangelis's heart.

"Please now give us the toolbox," he said calmly. A mischievous light twinkled in his eye.

The music stopped. Lukas dropped his bottle, let it smash into a thousand pieces. Vangelis looked at the weapon, and raised his hands in surrender. The small *kafenion* froze in an impromptu tableau. Manolis stared at Zain as he carried out an armed robbery with Manolis as his unwilling accomplice. A fast sweat broke across his forehead and time seemed to stand still.

"Where did you get that? What the hell are you doing?" Manolis muttered, voice low. He felt relief and dread in equal measure.

Zain rolled his eyes in Manolis's direction but kept the weapon fixed on his target.

"I think we should hold our cards," he said. "So I brought an ace."

"This is crazy, you'll get us killed."

"Please," stammered Vangelis. "Don't shoot anyone. It's only money, dear God. Take it, take all of it."

Zain gestured to the toolbox with a quick flick of his gun barrel. "Go on," he told Manolis. "Take the money." He leaned in and whispered: "Before they realise this is not loaded."

Manolis stepped forward, his left foot pinching as he walked. The sea of stupefied villagers parted to allow him access to the toolbox. They knew they had to do something, but didn't know what. Opening it, Manolis hastily counted what he estimated were ten thousand euros and put them on the table. He added a second pile of approximately the same size as hush money. Manolis closed the toolbox with a light clank and returned to Zain's side.

"I think you'll find you've been more than compensated for both your debt and your trouble," he told the villagers. "It's been a pleasure doing business with you. Sorry for the inconvenience. Enjoy your party, and have a drink on us."

25

Back in Glikonero, Manolis clutched a bouquet of fragrant wild flowers in his right hand. Dodging gold-black bumblebees and butterflies, he'd picked them from a pea-green meadow and was on his way to deliver them to their unsuspecting recipient. Manolis hoped that Roze would see that he was sincere in his apology.

Having wrongly accused Roze of taking Lefty's money, Manolis needed to make amends. And despite his major misgivings over how Zain had handled the return of the toolbox, Manolis was appreciative of his help and gave him a small sum from Lefty's money by way of thanks. With a broad smile, Zain had taken home both his windfall and his unloaded revolver. If he was ever found alive, Lefty would have to be satisfied with what remained of the contents of his toolbox.

Manolis couldn't remember the last time he'd given anyone flowers. It was probably to his ex-wife. He wondered whether he should have given Emily more. No doubt. The gesture might not have saved his marriage but it certainly wouldn't have hurt it like so many other things had.

Knocking firmly on Roze's door, Manolis waited. A strange fluttering sensation hummed away in his ribcage. He could hear her rustling around inside and was glad that she couldn't see him through a peephole or window. If she could, she might not answer. Flinging open the door, Roze saw Manolis give an exaggerated bow and doff an invisible cap. He flashed a smile and quickly held out the bouquet before she could slam the door shut again. She leaned against the door frame, arms folded across her chest, a look of disdain and defiance on her unsmiling face.

Manolis cleared his throat.

"These are for you," he said. "I picked them myself. I'd like to say sorry for accusing you of stealing Lefty's money. I was wrong. I've since tracked down the toolbox and have got it back. I hope you understand why I thought you were the guilty party, and that it was an innocent mistake. I also hope that you can find it in your heart to forgive me for being such an idiot."

Roze watched him closely as he gave his mea culpa, her face cracking into a wry smile as he carefully delivered his pre-prepared lines. Manolis detected a thaw.

"You are very much a big idiot," she grinned, taking the bouquet. She closed her eyes and inhaled its aroma.

"I know I am. Can I make it up to you with dinner?"

She looked up at him, horrified. "Not at the taverna . . ."

"No, definitely *not* at Kostas's taverna. Are you free tonight?"

"As it turns out, it's my night off . . ."

Manolis drove her to Florina. On the way, he recounted the events surrounding the snakebite and the recovery of the money. Roze was both entertained and astonished. She admitted to knowing that Zain was fascinated by weapons and guns but didn't think he had one.

"I suspect he got it from Sofia's house," Manolis said.

"He didn't tell you?"

"No. I'm not sure that Sofia knows about it either. I suspect she doesn't."

"He's a typical young man is Zain. Loves his boxing and games and guns."

"So it seems."

"And it wasn't even loaded . . ."

Manolis laughed. "In one minute, I went from being scared for our lives to being scared for the villagers' lives, then back again. I didn't know what he was capable of."

"How's your foot?"

Manolis rotated his left ankle, heard it click. "It's still a little sore from the bite," he said. "But I'm fine. Zain was correct there too, no poison."

They passed by Stavros's house on the way to dinner. Manolis briefly described what had happened and asked if he could store the toolbox – now fitted with two new combination locks – in Stavros's cellar for safekeeping.

"I knew Lefty had a secret stash hidden somewhere," Stavros said. "I bloody knew it . . ."

"Just keep it quiet," Manolis told him. "We don't want the residents of Eleftheria to return. Although I doubt they will."

In contrast to Kostas's rustic lake taverna, the food at the sleek and modern Florina restaurant offered fine dining, with smaller portions and a selection of boutique European wines. The decor was sustainable wood from top to bottom: tables, wall panels, even the ceiling. The restaurant was owned by a friend of Stavros's who said the food was organic and sourced from the region. The meals were uncomplicated, vibrant and delicious, and would not have been out of place in a big, metropolitan city, though here they cost a fraction of the price. It was Greek food with a modern and creative twist, and Manolis felt right at home.

"It's good to see that Greece isn't just tavernas," Roze said with a smile.

She wore a sleek spaghetti-strap dress and had her hair down, a departure from her usual shorts and tight ponytail. She sat uncharacteristically upright and appeared even more poised and self-assured. Over dinner, Manolis avoided mention of Lefty; he'd taken up enough of their oxygen in recent weeks. Instead, he showed an interest in Roze and made her the centre of attention. After some small talk, she sighed and said she was considering moving on from the Prespes region. It left Manolis surprised and a little disappointed.

"I know there are better places in the world to live and work than poor Greece and even poorer Albania," Roze said. She bit an oily *dolma* in half and hummed her approval.

She asked again about the vast continent of Australia, so far away and so alluring, and the possibility of making it her next move. Manolis was candid, describing everyday life beyond the tourist ideal.

"It's more expensive than you might realise," he said. "Tourists are often shocked. House prices are astronomical, and so is food. The cities are cramped."

"I find that hard to believe. The country is so huge." She sipped her wine.

"The country is big, yes, but much of the land is empty and uninhabited. The climate and landscape are harsh. You've got millions of people crammed into high-rises in just a few cities on the coasts. There are also strict immigration requirements."

"Like everywhere these days . . ."

"It used not to be like that. When my family moved there, the country was desperate for new migrants. We had a big house in the suburbs and an even bigger backyard. But that has changed, which was one reason why we came back to Greece. You would now have a small house and tiny yard, or none at all, which sounds ridiculous in such a massive country."

"What about jobs, work?"

"Getting harder to find, I'm afraid."

Manolis watched Roze's mouth turn down, her brows knitting. She took another slug of wine and pouted. Manolis realised he was painting a grim picture and thought he had better balance the ledger.

"But despite all that, it's a pretty wonderful country. The air's clean, there's plenty of space and quiet, there's beaches and sunshine, and there's also opportunities for those who work hard and are fortunate. Who knows, maybe that's you."

The corners of Roze's mouth turned up a little at the prospect of being a lucky one. She ate a piece of soft bread dipped in warm olive oil to make the feeling last.

"But Greece has its own problems as well," Manolis said. "We have no money, the infrastructure is old, and so many things are inefficient."

"You should see life in Albania," said Roze. "Here is like a paradise."

They paused to bite and chew, to sip and savour. The meals looked like they'd been prepared by an artist. The vegetarian moussaka was perhaps the richest thing Manolis had ever eaten, and yet he couldn't get enough. It sat heavy and oily and luxuriously in his stomach, warming his core. Roze admitted she had an ingrained aversion to eating out, the consequence of a lifetime's frugality under a communist regime.

"I probably shouldn't say this, but Lefty was trying to help me out with a Greek passport," Roze said suddenly. "He was organising one for me through his connections. I knew it was wrong but I couldn't help myself. I just couldn't bear the thought of going back to Albania. Young women who live alone attract nasty gossip and are seen as whores."

Manolis stopped mid-mouthful. He looked at her plainly.

"You remember those passports you found under his floor?" she said. "I want one like those." Her eyes were soft, almost apologetic.

"Oh," Manolis said. "Right . . ."

Roze tousled her hair, which briefly curtained her face. "I guess Lefty hadn't got around to sorting me one yet," she said. "I know that Zain was thinking about asking him for one too so that he could move freely around Europe." She downed her glass of cold white wine.

"Lefty is clearly a man who can pull many strings," Manolis said.

"And to be honest with you, the thought of taking Lefty's money and running off did occur to me," Roze said. "But I couldn't bring myself to abandon the search for him given what happened to my brother. And if Lefty can be found, that would still be my best chance of getting a Greek passport."

Manolis wiped the oil from the sides of his mouth with a crisp white napkin. "Well," he said, "thank you for being so truthful. I hope your passport turns up. I'll take another look when I'm next at Lefty's."

Manolis smiled. Roze did too, at the thought of a better life.

"But what about you, would you ever come to live here in the Prespes permanently?" she asked.

Manolis looked up from his sauce-stained plate. "I wouldn't mind it, but that would make it hard to have regular visits with my son in Thessaloniki."

He talked briefly about the stress of fatherhood, of sleepless nights and screaming tantrums and floor yogurt, then the heartache of being an absent father, his divorce, and rebuilding his life in the years since. The emotions he conveyed were all true, albeit from another hemisphere. Roze came across as genuinely interested; she wanted to learn from Manolis's wisdom and hear more about his life, especially his son. But Manolis was guarded. He didn't want to give away too much personal information and knew that if he started talking about such topics, he might not stop.

"Thessaloniki is a great city," Manolis said. "It has the sea and music and culture and students and life. It is a place for young people."

"Hmm," Roze said. "Maybe. I don't know. Maybe."

Manolis caught flecks of his reflection in her pupils.

The waiter brought their desserts. Manolis had *galaktoboureko*, custard pie coated in syrup, while Roze had *kataifi*, filo rolled and stuffed with walnuts and pistachios. They shared a mouthful of each other's and agreed that the simpler *galaktoboureko* was the standout. A plate of thick Greek yogurt drizzled with preserved *vissino* cherries completed an outstanding meal.

After dinner, Roze suggested they go for a walk down by the Sakoulevas River, which meandered its way through Florina. Manolis agreed, hoping to work off some oily calories and aid his digestion of a luscious yet heavy meal. Roze's ridiculously high stilettos chimed on the uneven pavement as they walked. Having had a little too much wine with dinner, she stumbled on her heels down a steep hill. Manolis grabbed her shoulder to stop her from falling and put his arm around her the rest of the way.

The banks of the Sakoulevas were lined with busy summer cafés and tavernas. The river was next to the old city of Florina, which had been preserved and had a view of the lush mountains in the distance. Manolis and Roze stood on one of the many bridges that criss-crossed the river, listening to its gentle susurration. Besotted couples had attached love padlocks to the bridge and Roze bent over to read them. But then she started swaying and, leaning over the ornate ironwork railings, proceeded to be sick into the river. Manolis held her loose hair back in a makeshift ponytail and helped her to her feet. Roze blamed the rich food for her sudden illness, although Manolis felt fine after eating the same food and suspected the rich wine was more to blame. Draping her arm across his shoulders for support, Roze let Manolis walk her up the hill and back to Stavros's house. He made her drink a big glass of cold water to stave off dehydration and removed her heels. Roze stroked Manolis's hair drowsily as he tucked her into bed in the spare room to sleep it off.

With the summer night still warm and welcoming, Manolis decided to go for a stroll through Florina's tight and winding streets. He thought he might find Stavros out somewhere, to perhaps share the golden warmth of a late-night whisky and chat in a bar. Manolis heard jazz coming out of a tiny *kafenion*; it sounded lonely and sophisticated. Reading the sign, he realised it was Florina's – and Greece's – sole women-only *kafenion* that Stavros had mentioned, and it was packed with patrons. Walking on, Manolis saw young couples kissing under aureoles of apricot lamplight and lanky teenagers playing basketball and trash-talking. One of them wore Manolis's loathed replica football shirt, which made him turn and walk away.

For a brief moment, Manolis thought he had seen Lefty on a street corner – twice – and had to double back to check it was not him. Manolis was seeing Lefty everywhere, which reflected his lack of solid leads and increasing helplessness. He didn't want to admit it, but he was fast giving up hope of finding Lefty. At times, Manolis felt like he was trying to catch a puff of smoke with a fishing net. Perhaps Lefty's creditors from Eleftheria were right to pillage his assets; after all, they weren't helping anyone locked away in a toolbox.

Dawdling past an all-night internet café, Manolis stopped to check his e-mail. It had been some time since he'd connected with the outside world – a conscious decision, a kind of detox. But now, flailing around in an investigative vacuum, Manolis had a powerful need to connect. The café was dark, lit primarily by glowing screens, and filled with young people checking their social media accounts, viewing photos and playing first-person shooter video games. Manolis felt old. He took a seat in the corner and with some embarrassment opened a web browser and his e-mail.

Scanning his hundreds of unread messages, Manolis immediately regretted the decision to reconnect with the electronic world. It threatened the life-affirming link that he'd established with the natural world since arriving in Florina and the Prespes, and felt like a disgusting cigarette in a moment of weakness after he'd worked so hard to quit. The vast majority of messages were spam, but there were a few gems. Manolis read a message from Emily with some new photos of a smiling and happy Christos; they provided spiritual nourishment and scooped his heart from his chest. He caught up on news alerts from Australia, which were generally depressing and isolating. But Sparrow had written a short g'day, which came across like a big, warm smile. Sparrow said he was pretty much a city mouse now but he was feeling good and enjoying his new position and work.

"Sorry I'm not much for writing, boss," he wrote. "But you probably already knew that. Not much happening here. Very quiet. Hope you're having a good break. See ya soon."

He didn't say more. Perhaps that was for the best.

And then Manolis saw a message from Detective Inspector Paul Bloody Porter. It had been sent the previous day and it asked when Manolis was thinking of returning to active duty since he was already late – a full week, in fact, over his approved leave.

"Crap," Manolis muttered to himself.

"Something's come up," his boss had written. "I can't say more over e-mail for security reasons. But I hope you receive this message and that we have you back soon."

It was only then that Manolis realised he'd lost track of how long he'd been away in the remoteness of the Prespes region. The hours, days, weeks had atomised into nothingness. After all, it wasn't as though Glikonero's residents looked at their calendars other than to see what day was Sunday to go to church. Weeks and months didn't seem to matter. Seasons did, for the planting of crops and gathering of firewood. But calendars weren't needed to discern the season.

And now there was an urgency in Manolis. The clock was ticking loudly on the time he had left in Greece to locate Lefty and fulfil his promise to his father.

26

The next morning, having slept fitfully on Stavros's poorly sprung couch, a bleary-eyed Manolis woke up cotton-mouthed. He yawned, stretched and got dressed to go in search of his morning *pita*, which he'd missed since moving to the Prespes. On the way to the bakery, he decided to pay another visit to the Florina police station. He again spoke with Constable Yiannis, who was on the front desk in his usual handsome pose – scrolling vacantly through his phone, smoking a cigarette and sipping a strong Greek coffee.

"Like one?" the constable said, offering his pack. His voice was tired and unsympathetic.

"No thanks."

"What about a coffee? I only just put the *briki* on."

"Yes to the coffee. One sugar, please."

He disappeared into a back room. The walls of the station appeared to sweat in the morning sunshine, stale nicotine, dripping yellow-brown. The ramshackle glory of modern Greek ruins. Manolis felt his empty stomach clench.

The constable returned moments later with an overflowing demi-tasse on a matching saucer.

"Sorry, I overfilled the cup," he said.

"That's fine, thank you," said Manolis. He took a big, hungry sip and scalded his tongue.

"I told you, I only just put the *briki* on. Now, how can I help?"

The police station was quiet. So far as Manolis could tell, there wasn't another soul in the crumbling building.

"I may be wasting my breath, but I was wondering if you'd had any reports concerning Lefteris," Manolis said. He blew on the brown *kaimaki* froth on top of his coffee.

Yiannis shook his head and stared at his phone. "Afraid not," he said. "It's been very quiet."

In view of the police's attitude to Lefty's disappearance, Manolis knew he'd already undertaken a more comprehensive investigation than the entire local force combined.

Defeated, Manolis took a step back and asked about the force's history with invisibles such as Lefty. Constable Yiannis sucked hard on his cigarette, as if drawing strength to deliver grave news.

"There are many such people who go missing in Greece and are never found again," he said. "We have steep mountains, deep seas, frightening myths and some citizens who are best avoided. There are also our neighbours: Turks from the east, Italian mafia from the west, Balkans from the north, African gangs, Russian gangsters and Arabs."

"Quite the combination," Manolis said.

"As police, we're somewhat powerless with people like Lefty. They're low in the pecking order, as you can see. We'd love to help, it is our job after all. But how do you find someone who doesn't want to exist, let alone be found?"

Yiannis gave the slightest of shrugs and blew smoke at the cracked, stained ceiling. Manolis asked if missing invisibles were often found dead. The constable thought for a moment before replying.

"Sometimes, yes. But in my experience, nowhere near as much as ordinary people who go missing. Invisibles tend to stay invisible, in death as in life. They just vanish."

Manolis felt even more beaten now. He drained his coffee, which burned his throat, but he didn't especially care. He thanked Constable Yiannis for his time and hospitality and left the silent station, his feet shuffling on the parquetry tiling. He felt uneasy, as if there was a stone in his shoe. It was the niggling thought that the local police believed Lefty had been murdered but were wholly uninterested in finding the killer.

Paying for another half-hour at the internet café, Manolis booked his return flight to Australia, incurring a hefty rescheduling fee. He then rang his mother to check that she was well and update her on developments, which he spoke about in intentionally vague terms.

"Sorry I didn't call earlier," he said.

"That's OK, *agape mou*," Maria said. "You've been enjoying your holiday. Give Greece a big kiss for me. See you soon, safe travels, *kalo taxithi . . .*"

She sounded weary, her soul heavy, which Manolis put down to it being the middle of the Australian night. But then again, Maria always sounded tired these days and seemed rarely to sleep. Manolis doubted she would ever travel to Greece again. There was no mention of family, Con or otherwise. It was all in the past. Manolis left it there too.

Manolis struggled to remember the last conversation he'd had with Con. He was so exhausted from caring that he'd stopped paying attention. Medical gadgets and vital signs – heart rate, blood pressure, blood sugar readings, oxygen levels – had taken the place of talking. Eyes dulled with chemical agents, the omnipresent stainless-steel kidney dish. There was grief of course when Con died, but there was also a modicum of relief, as if Manolis could finally let out a breath he didn't even realise he'd been holding. Manolis wondered if Con considered admitting his deadly deeds towards the end. He tried not to reflect too deeply on his family. It only led to madness.

Manolis returned via the family bakery with a selection of freshly baked *pita*, his mouth filling with saliva as he walked. He shared them with Stavros and Roze on the balcony. Roze didn't eat; she was still wearing the dress she'd slept in, now lightly crumpled and with one thin strap hanging off her shoulder. She sipped a glass of water assiduously and wore Stavros's big Italian sunglasses to hide her bloodshot eyes and throbbing temples. Manolis announced that his work arrangements had changed and that his time in the region was, regrettably, coming to an end. Stavros was appreciative of all that Manolis had done to help find Lefty and fix up the house in Glikonero. In contrast, Roze appeared downhearted, staring intently at her water glass, nursing her hangover and saying little.

"I'm sad to leave," Manolis said.

And he was. The Prespes region had proven to be a uniquely picturesque location and interesting mix of personalities and wildlife. The natural world had been powerfully therapeutic at a time when Manolis needed to regain his strength. There was a mesmeric quality to the region, a cruel beauty. Its troubled history and volatile neighbours underscored the need for joint conservation efforts to maintain the fragile natural world that humans kept destroying. But Manolis's departure wasn't also without a degree of relief. He'd grown tired of trying to negotiate the tiny lakeside village where grudges ran deep. He'd found labyrinthine feuds, illegal immigrants, dubious Orthodox priests, corrupt border police and women who lived as men, along with stockpiles of guns, knives and cash, eerie lake myths, memories of war and bloodshed, and encounters with deadly bears and snakes, venomous and otherwise. The region had wrapped its sticky tentacles around him, but it existed in a time warp.

Although memorable, the experience left Manolis deflated. He was disappointed to have devoted his entire holiday to it, especially now that he realised he'd been fighting a losing battle from the outset. Whether Lefty had disappeared voluntarily or otherwise, it seemed unlikely he would ever be found.

*   *   *

Manolis decided to savour his remaining time in the Prespes region. He went walking through lush forests and craggy mountains. He listened to the percussive flap of leaves and read his last novel by the lakeside. He helped the villagers with their daily chores and hosted them for simple meals and coffees. He even tried to organise an evening with

Kostas and Stavros in the same room as Sofia in the hope they might reconcile. But once she caught wind of Manolis's true intentions, Sofia didn't show up.

Over morning frappé coffees one day, Manolis and Roze dissected the theories about Lefty's disappearance in case they'd missed an important detail. The iced espresso drinks were served in tall glasses, cool to the touch, and perfectly suited the warmer weather.

"I'm starting to give up," Manolis said. "I've got no firm leads and I'm leaving next week."

Remembering an earlier conversation, Roze proposed they go hiking to scour the land for Lefty.

"It's worth a shot," she said. "Mama always told us kids that you've got to buy a ticket to win the lottery."

Manolis agreed. His dad had also been a committed gambler, preferring to bet on the horses. Manolis was especially keen to search the abandoned hermitages built on the cliffs near Great Prespa Lake. Stavros had pointed them out the day that Manolis had arrived in the Prespes region and, so far, Manolis hadn't found a way to access them.

"Whatever you do, if you see a strange metal object on the ground, don't touch it," Roze said.

"Why's that?" Manolis asked.

"It's an unexploded mine. There are still many of them in the area."

"And they're live?"

"Some are, you can't be sure. Better to be safe than sorry, no?"

Packing food and water into two backpacks, Manolis and Roze headed out one morning, with Roze leading the way in a purple singlet and grey shorts. She was familiar with the terrain and described the journey she'd taken across the border. Many of her young friends had also made the trek, with some moving on to other countries, while others returned to Albania.

"And some have never been heard of again," she added ominously.

Roze said her grandfather had been one of the evacuated children during the Greek civil war.

"So you're saying that your family roots are actually Greek?" Manolis asked.

"Mama has a Greek passport, but I couldn't get one," she said. "It's the reason I wanted to come here, because of my ancestors."

"I would need to go to Turkey to do that . . ." Manolis said.

His grandparents were Orthodox Christian refugees from Turkey who had been forced to flee to Greece during the 1923 Population Exchange. Having endured a long and arduous trek out of Turkey, they'd ensconced themselves in northern Greece. The land there was newly annexed and needed infusing with Greek blood.

"My grandfather never felt safe so close to the borders and wished he was deeper inside Greece, or further south where invasion was less likely. I used to ask my mum why our family hadn't settled on one of the warmer islands in the south instead of here in the cold north. She said the islands were full of mosquitoes and disease a hundred years ago and weren't the holiday paradises they are now."

"I would love one day to visit the Greek islands," Roze said.

"Then you should. You could easily get a job there, working in a taverna or bar or nightclub. You're young, and there are plenty of young people who work there, especially during the summers. You'd get many more tips than here."

"I picture Australia to be like that. The sunshine, the beaches, the ocean, the good times."

She again mentioned her desire to go to the great southern continent and jokingly asked Manolis if he could smuggle her in in his suitcase when he next visited. Manolis noticed her eyes had a certain lustre and that her gaze lingered on him longer than usual. Their conversation had a distinctly flirtatious vibe. When they went out to dinner, he'd attributed it to alcohol, but now wasn't so sure.

There was no denying Roze's physical allure. She was outgoing and intelligent as well as effortlessly attractive. But Manolis held back. First, she was a good deal younger than him. Second, he'd been warned that she was untrustworthy and didn't respect the law. Third, he still wasn't sure of the nature of her relationship with Kostas. And fourth, he would soon be leaving the country. One night stands weren't in Manolis's DNA; as a recent divorcé, he'd been out of the dating game too long. But perhaps this was a way to ease back into it?

They continued walking, an easy quiet surrounding them. Surveying the area, stepping carefully over hazardous ground, they explored deep gorges and secluded ravines searching for signs of human existence – a food wrapper, an empty water bottle, a lost article of clothing. The sky was changing, becoming edged with the haze of a storm. Finally, after climbing up some steep slopes slippery with scree and passing through an echoey cavern, they reached the abandoned hermits' niches that overlooked the greater lake. The ascetic hermitages commemorated the presence of small monastic communities and hermits in the area over many years. So high in the thin mountain air, it was almost as if heaven was in reach, as if God was within earshot. The tiny spaces had preserved wall paintings and stirring rock frescoes that were half a millennium old. They were rich with colourful history and folklore which Roze described as they sat and ate a packed lunch.

"Did you know that the origin of Lake Prespa is actually a love story?" Roze asked.

Manolis swallowed his chunk of dry bread with some effort. "No," he said. "What kind of love story?"

She flicked her head to one side to gaze out over the lake, her ponytail resting lightly on her exposed shoulder.

"Legend has it that there was once a town where the lake now sits, right out there in the middle. Walking through the woods one day, a young prince came across a nymph who was more beautiful than any mortal girl he'd ever seen. The prince immediately fell in love with the nymph and returned to the woods many times to ask for her hand in marriage. He offered her all the riches of his father's kingdom and a place by his side as future queen. But the nymph rejected his advances and said that she could never marry a mortal without dire consequences for the groom and his homeland. Unable to imagine an outcome so awful, and unable to contain his love for the nymph, the prince had the nymph kidnapped and kept her prisoner until she accepted his offer of marriage. When they married, the heavens opened and an enormous downpour of rain ensued. It didn't stop until the entire kingdom was under water and everyone had drowned. The result is the current-day Lake Prespa."

Roze looked back at Manolis with wide, serious eyes. Enthralled by her story, and spellbound by her unflinching, blue-eyed stare, Manolis took a moment to respond.

"So, what you're saying is that that's a mass grave out there in the lake? That there's a whole town of people who drowned there? No wonder it feels so spooky and haunted."

"I think it's a beautiful story. It was true love that created the lake. Don't you think that's beautiful?"

"To some extent. But you said the prince kidnapped the nymph and imprisoned her. I'm not so sure that's really a love story . . ."

"I think you're missing the point. The gesture is deeply romantic. He sacrificed his wealth for love."

Manolis realised that he probably was missing the point, which he attributed to differences in age and culture. Romance didn't come naturally to him.

Elsewhere, they came across faded graffiti sprayed on rock surfaces, fantastical images of skulls and crosses, hearts and swastikas. The graffiti appeared almost as old as the painted frescoes.

"Five different languages," Roze said. "Albanian, Greek, Macedonian, Bulgarian and Serbian."

"What do they say?" Manolis asked.

"Nothing important. Politics, propaganda, rebellion."

They also found reminders of the war: machine-gun dugouts gouged into the hills, stone-walled storerooms, corroded casings. Roze said not to worry, but to Manolis they were sinister. Kicking at a rotten log, Manolis was faced with a fat-tailed scorpion, its tail and curved stinger reared in anger.

"In Greek mythology, a giant scorpion was sent to kill the hunter

Orion, who had said he would kill all the world's animals," Roze said. "Orion and the scorpion both became constellations, and as enemies were placed on opposite sides of the world so that when one rises in the sky the other sets."

They came across some snow-white bones that Manolis briefly thought might be human until Roze said they were probably from a wild goat. Ultimately, and most disappointingly, they found no evidence of any recent human occupation, let alone of Lefty.

By mid-afternoon, Manolis had begun to feel very much like a man in his forties, the expedition having proven more tiring than he'd anticipated. By contrast, Roze still had a rabbity spring in her step. The embodiment of a fit and energetic young woman in her twenties, she seemed to gain strength as the day wore on, while Manolis faded, his feet and calves aching from the steep mountain tracks. Striding ahead, Roze was able to cover far more ground than Manolis, who was deterred by the enormity of the task and the land, although he didn't want to leave any stone unturned.

Eyeing the dipping sun, Manolis called out to Roze.

"It's getting late. Shall we head back before it gets dark?"

Roze didn't reply, perhaps not hearing him, and continued to whistle happily as she walked. They'd not seen another person all day. In the near distance, mercurial clouds were massing, bruised and brooding. A storm was rolling in.

Manolis kept walking but soon lost sight of Roze within some trees. He picked his way carefully over the uneven ground, anxious not to roll an ankle, but he had no choice than to run when he heard the sound of panicked screaming, shrill and desperate.

Could Roze have found a body? Had she finally found Lefty?

27

Darting through a dense thicket of cypress trees, Manolis passed some crows scavenging on the remains of a dead animal. It was an unpleasant discovery, but it wasn't why Roze was screaming. Her cries were louder, so Manolis was closer. But they were also becoming more frantic with each passing second.

Had Roze fallen and broken an arm or leg? She could be bleeding or have a bone sticking out of her skin. Or perhaps she'd stumbled across Lefty's decomposing body. If nothing more, it would bring closure.

Manolis's nostrils flared. There was an acrid smell in the air that slowed his progress. He was running upwind and the stench was filling his lungs like a noxious gas. It was a sharp and tangy smell, distinctly organic.

Stepping out from behind the trees, Manolis discovered at last why Roze was screaming. She was unharmed and had not found Lefty. But she was bent and cowering as a terrifying growl ripped through the air.

Crouching opposite Roze, with its back to a thick cluster of trees on the other side of a grassy clearing, was a monstrous brown bear. It was about ten metres from her, a distance that a fast-moving bear could have covered in seconds. The predator was clearly an adult, fully grown and poised to attack. Manolis couldn't tell if it was male or female, a boar or sow, but it appeared stressed, yawning and clacking its teeth, and pounding its front paws on the ground as it huffed. Its head and ears were pointed up and forward. Manolis didn't know much about wild bears and the frequency of attacks in Greece; most of what he'd read concerned North America. He recalled once hearing that you were more likely to be killed by a bee than a bear, and that brown bears were deadlier than black. Or was it the other way around? It didn't matter. Even Manolis recognised these as ominous warning signs.

"Roze!"

She looked across at Manolis, her eyes enormous and bleached a petrified white. Maybe her whistling had attracted the bear, or she'd had the misfortune to stumble into the bear's territory while it was feeding on an animal carcass. The density of the trees meant that a scavenging bear wouldn't be seen until too late. A bear near a carcass buffet was potential dynamite if it thought another animal was after its food.

"Stay there!" Manolis shouted.

But he'd barely got his words out before the bear charged, bounding on its hefty paws, moving in big leaps. Manolis lurched forward instinctively while Roze let out a cry and braced for impact, throwing up her arms and wrapping them around her head. Her backpack formed a barrier of sorts, but her thin summer clothing offered no protection. And then, a metre away, the bear stopped and reared onto its back feet. The charge turned out to be a bluff, to scare and intimidate. And it had the desired impact: Roze was terrified, too frightened to move.

Manolis considered the options. Running was likely to set the bear off; like dogs, bears chased things that ran, fleeing prey triggering a bear's predatory instinct. And even a sprint champion would find it hard to outrun a bear, which could lumber with deceptive speed.

Playing dead would show that Roze posed no threat. Manolis thought to yell to her to lie flat on her front with her vital organs and head protected. Confrontations between bears usually involved them trying to bite their opponent's face and jaw to disable its most powerful weapon.

Manolis slowly stepped closer until he had formed the third point of an equilateral triangle with Roze and the bear. He didn't want to provoke or hurt it. He knew it was a protected species, and, even if it hadn't been, it was still a living creature. He merely wanted to scare it away so that all three came through the encounter unharmed. And yet, deep down, he knew that if it came to a choice, human life took precedence. Now that they were protected and not hunted, bears had little fear of humans, who they associated with food.

The beast reared up again onto its hind legs and towered over Roze. With its chest puffed out to make it look even more fearsome, it was swaying its head from side to side and sniffing the air intently, trying to work out what kind of animal stood before it. Manolis could feel his heart beating so hard in his throat that he wondered whether the bear could hear it too.

"Hey! Hey! Over here!"

Manolis tried to distract the bear by speaking loudly but calmly and waving his arms above his head to make himself appear bigger. He spoke in purposely low, slow tones. When that failed, Manolis was forced to find a handful of rocks and throw them at the bear's feet and then at its broad body. There was no food left in his backpack; by that late stage of the day, it had all been consumed. The bear acknowledged Manolis's efforts by turning its grand head, locking on to his eyes and growling menacingly. It was a primeval, cautionary stare unlike any that Manolis had experienced from a human criminal. The bear roared and reached its huge paw in the air, slamming it down on a massive log at its feet. It cracked the log in half in a show of strength before whipping its gaze back to Roze and closing in again. The great creature was formidable and demanded respect.

Manolis stayed on his feet to remain as large as possible. Roze should have done the same but she was too scared. Taking another two steps, Manolis tried to lure the bear away, but it continued to take threatening swipes at the air in front of Roze, ropes of saliva dripping from its sharp fangs and mighty jaw. Now down on one knee, she eased her backpack off her shoulders and reached inside, frantically rummaging around. Thrusting an unsteady hand forward, she pointed a double-action revolver at the bear.

Manolis was astonished to find that Roze had brought a firearm on their hiking trip. Pepper spray was what he used to paralyse assailants in the line of duty, and he imagined that a can of bear spray might have been more appropriate. But more extreme weaponry seemed to be the order of the day in the Prespes, no matter who was involved. Seeing the threat, the bear growled again and with its left paw knocked the weapon from Roze's hand before she could pull back. The revolver was sent flying and landed with a clunk not far from where Manolis was standing. The choice was now his. He didn't want to shoot the bear, but for Roze to be killed was unthinkable.

Manolis stepped forward and picked up the revolver. The bear's manner suddenly changed; it thrust its head down and pinned its ears back. The snap of its gums, grit of its teeth and pop of its jaw were even louder now. It woofed and snorted, gurgled and grunted as its lips blew out and its breath emerged in a rush. Methodically swatting the ground with its forepaws, stomping up and down, the bear was clearly agitated and preparing for action. Its next charge would not be a bluff – this one would be for real, and most likely fatal. It was then a case of not just being killed by a bear, but being killed and eaten. And a bear that had killed once had a tendency to do it again, like a human serial killer.

Manolis considered where he might shoot the bear without killing it – its leg was the best option, as with a human assailant. But that might enrage the bear even more, or cause it to bleed to death slowly and painfully. A kill shot to the head, and a quick death, would be the most humane option.

"Shoot it!" screamed Roze. "What the hell are you waiting for?"

Manolis thought back to when he'd seen a bear with Father Petros. Pointing the revolver at the purplish sky, he fired a warning shot. But this bear didn't move. Instead, it growled louder and took another more vicious swipe at Roze.

"Shoot it now!" she implored him. Terror dripped from her words, her limbs quivering like wires.

Manolis lowered the revolver from vertical to horizontal and closed one eye. As he tensed his fingers, he felt a hot flash of panic, transported to the last time he'd struck this deadly pose. Manolis hadn't discharged a firearm since.

Filled with regret, Manolis squeezed the trigger, firing multiple shots in quick succession. He couldn't tell which found their target and which missed. But at least one bullet hit the bear in the side of the head. It let out a booming growl and fell to the ground, landing with a resounding thud. Blood was everywhere, flowing like Texas oil.

Manolis hung his head. His ears echoed from the gunshot. Was it all over? As the ringing cleared and his hearing slowly returned, Manolis made out a low grumbling noise. He approached the bear cautiously and stood over its body. The bear was moaning, its huge head moving. It was mortally wounded but still alive, breathing raggedly. It was not over. Manolis still had work to do.

The bear's body bore scars that spoke of encounters with other bears and wildlife. Its ribs showed through its hide, and there was grass in its teeth. The bear appeared to be sick and starving. Eating Roze might have ensured its survival; given its lack of body fat, hibernation would have been impossible.

Manolis checked the revolver. There was one bullet left in the cylinder.

"I'm sorry, mate," he said aloud, raising the weapon unsteadily. It suddenly weighed a ton in his hand.

The bear was panting, its breathing laboured, eyes glassy. Manolis closed his own eyes, said a silent prayer, and pulled the trigger a final time. As his knees gave out on him, he slumped to the ground, energy leaching from his body.

Roze ran over and collapsed into him, overtaken by relief and emotion. They kissed. Manolis didn't especially want to – he was shaking with shock, not passion – but it was a way to release the tension in them both.

A strange noise interrupted them, a kind of wailing. They unlocked their lips and turned to look. A small brown bear cub walked out from behind the trees, weak and underweight and looking for its mother.

28

The bear cub continued mewing and walked towards them on large but light paws. It was hungry and desperately wanted to find its mother for food and comfort.

The terrible realisation that Manolis had killed a sow dawned on him like an executioner's blow. It was no wonder that the bear had acted so aggressively towards him and Roze – she was driven by maternal instinct. Manolis had seen a similar instinct in his ex-wife, whom he'd jokingly called "mama bear" because of her sometimes aggressively protective mode of parenting. On the one hand, he'd frowned on such an approach since he thought it didn't instil resilience in their young son. On the other, he admired the fact that Emily relished being a mother more than anything else in the world and defended Christos with such ferociousness.

Finding its mother lying on the ground, the cub tried to rouse her by nestling into her side, and it continued its wailing, now more desperate than before. Roze looked away, overcome, and sobbed in Manolis's arms. Manolis felt helpless. He stared at the cub and its dead mother, as if the sight and pain could serve as penance for the harm he'd inflicted.

"It's not our fault," he whispered to Roze. "We weren't to know."

But Manolis knew it definitely was his fault . . . again. His trigger finger was cursed. He reminded himself that he'd had no choice, but it did nothing to alleviate his sense of guilt.

Manolis felt an overwhelming need to come clean to Roze. He wanted to tell her about all the police officers he'd seen kill innocents by accident in the line of duty. He wanted to tell her about the street kid in the city basement whose life he had ended. It was a crushing weight he had carried single-handed throughout his time in Greece, along with Con's murderous legacy. Killing a mother bear was different, but it still hurt like a mortal wound on top of his PTSD. Manolis momentarily thought of Christos and pictured him at Manolis's funeral if he was ever killed on the job. Emily had hated his profession, especially after he became a father. Maria felt the same. They thought Manolis was being selfish in continuing. During his darkest hours, Manolis wondered if they might be right.

"We've got to do something," Roze said.

"Yes," Manolis said, pushing aside his thoughts.

The cub could not have been more than a few months old. Without any food to offer it and only a little water, Roze decided to hold out her hand and let the curious little cub smell her fingers. She hoped that, like a dog, it might sense that she was friendly. It was a little uncertain at first, but the cub did in the end brush up against her hand, enjoying a firm rub and almost purring with pleasure, which drew a tearful smile from her. She picked up the cub and held it close to her chest. Despite having teeth and claws, the furry bundle sat comfortably in the cradle of her arms, feeling the reassuring warmth of her body.

Manolis eyed the western sky with concern. In the evening sun, the earth turned a vibrant umber and the chocolatey mountains became a deep grape-purple. If they didn't make a move, they would find themselves stumbling home in inky blackness. They didn't even have a flashlight. But they couldn't leave the cub to mourn its dead mother and risk dying of starvation or being eaten by another hungry predator.

"It's so cute and helpless. We can't leave it here," Roze said.

"I agree, but what we can do? We can hardly take it home with us, it's a wild animal . . ."

"Sure we can. I can."

"And then what do we do? The bear can't live with you in your small cabin."

Roze looked down adoringly at the playful creature now batting away at her fingers.

"Sure it can," she said dreamily.

"No, it can't. We need to find a veterinarian or an animal shelter that will take it in and offer care. Are there any nearby?"

Roze said there was a bear sanctuary in the ancient Aromanian village of Nymfaio, a two-hour drive to the south-east of the Prespes. Nymfaio's hundred or so residents lived in stone houses, and its cobblestone paths had been rendered smooth by centuries of hooves and feet. The sanctuary was in a beech forest, a natural habitat where the bears could roam, and was part of an environmental protection centre that cared for both bears and wolves too weak to survive in the wild. The sanctuary also took in former circus "dancing bears", captured when young or bred in captivity.

"It's still considered an acceptable form of family entertainment in this part of the world," Roze said with sorrow.

"The sanctuary sounds perfect," Manolis said. "But we won't be able to get there tonight. And there's a second issue . . ."

The carcass of the mother bear was bleeding out and already attracting hungry blowflies. In the distance, a lone wolf howled.

"We can't just leave her here," Manolis said.

The remains would attract nocturnal predators, drawn to the iron-rich blood like sharks in water. Abandoning the body struck Manolis as disrespectful to such a magnificent beast.

Roze refused to look at the sow and continued to entertain the cub by tickling its soft, furry belly.

"We can't carry the mama bear," she said. "She's too heavy."

Manolis stamped the ground with his foot, testing its firmness.

"And we can't bury her," he said. "Even if we had a shovel, we'd break our backs trying."

With the light almost gone, a crescent moon rose in the east. It provided some light, but not enough. The world was soon cast in silhouette, the epic landscape painted a cold blueish-white. Manolis tried and failed to identify in which direction Glikonero lay. The cub yowled in distress. Roze tried to comfort it again but it was clear that food was what it needed. And they would need to find shelter if they didn't want to spend the night in the elements. Manolis reached into his backpack and put on his collared shirt over his T-shirt. It was all he had by way of a second layer. The temperature had dropped in the past hour and a strong wind had whipped up. Sullen clouds, low and ominous, were lancing in the west. As a day's worth of perspiration dried against his skin, Manolis began to feel a chill.

"We need a fire," he said.

A fire would provide not only warmth but also protection from predators coming to feast on the mama bear, and whatever else they could find.

"I don't have a lighter," Roze said. "I've got no matches either."

They hadn't foreseen such a scenario when they left that morning. They hadn't packed enough food and didn't have enough clothes or a tent or any more bullets. They weren't seasoned hikers preparing for a multi-day trek. They hadn't meant to kill a mother bear and orphan her starving cub. They were just trying to locate a frustratingly invisible man and outrun their demons.

Manolis gazed up at the mountains, now carbon-black. They did not look welcoming. He wished that they could return to one of the abandoned hermitages and shelter there for the night, but that was no longer possible. A long lightning bolt fractured the distant sky as a whorl of rainbands rolled over the horizon.

Manolis was no fan of sleeping in the outdoors; spending prolonged periods of time in nature made him uneasy, something he attributed to his Greek DNA, which had triumphed over his Australian upbringing. Manolis's ancestors had toiled to escape from the wilderness, to put a roof over their heads and enjoy indoor plumbing.

"The wilderness is the last refuge of the desperate, not a holiday destination," his father had said.

He cited the *andartiko* rebel guerrilla fighters who had occupied the northern Greek mountains during the war. This was not because of a perceived strategic advantage. Against the military might of Nazi Germany and the Greek army, they had fled to the mountains because they had no other choice.

Manolis now had no choice but to spend the night in the Greek wilderness. He would be guarding a mouth-watering bear carcass and a vulnerable cub, and be surrounded by grey wolves, wild boar, brown bears and whatever supernatural forces dwelled within the hills. The thought made him nauseous with fear.

The cub continued to wail with hunger. Roze fed it a little water from the palm of her hand, which it lapped thirstily.

"We're going to have to hunker down here for the night," Manolis said reluctantly. "And hope for the best."

"I'm more worried about the bear than me," Roze said. "I'll be fine."

Eyeing the dead mother bear, Manolis suggested they move a safe distance away before settling down for the night. As they turned to walk away, the cub became even more vocal and distraught. It could still smell its mother, still believed she was alive. It was a thought that tore at Manolis's heart and made Roze insist they sleep nearby. Manolis was troubled by the likelihood of night-time predators but agreed. He heard his empty stomach grumble and sipped the little water he had left in the faint hope that it might quieten his hunger.

As he lay down under the sparse shelter of a tall cypress tree, Manolis said a silent prayer to an unseen god. He was a man of little faith but at that moment he felt in need of some. Manolis would sleep with one eye open, if he got any sleep at all. And yet, his fatigue was weighing him down, making his limbs heavy. For what it was worth, he clutched the unloaded revolver in his hand. His backpack was his pillow, while Roze lay beside him, their shoulder blades lightly touching. Curling up into the outline and warmth of Roze's body, the cub seemed to find a reluctant peace as Roze sang what sounded like an old Albanian folk lullaby.

The wind picked up again, blowing grains of thick dust into Manolis's eyes and face, and the smell of the decaying sow into Manolis's nose. It reminded him that he was a long way from home. Another flash of lightning lit up the distance, followed by the low, ominous rumble of thunder seconds later before silence returned to the land. The next thing Manolis expected was fat globules of rain splashing on his face and the sound of a starving wolf growling in his ear.

He certainly did not expect to be confronted by a large group of hushed and indistinct figures that appeared in the darkness and encircled Manolis and Roze within the ring of trees, cutting off all avenues of escape.

29

The shadowy forms continued to close in on Manolis, Roze and the bear cub. Their silence was sinister.

Manolis sprang to his feet, which made Roze sit up as well. The cub howled in distress.

"Who are you?" he stammered. "What do you want? Will you help us? We mean you no harm. Can you help us?"

There was no reply. Manolis looked around but couldn't count how many figures there were; their outlines blurred together in the gloom.

His immediate thought was to the disgruntled residents of Eleftheria. Had they caught up with Manolis in the remotest of locations to exact their revenge? They knew the road to Glikonero after all and might have been following them all day, waiting for just the right moment of isolation and desperation. At least the toolbox of money was now stashed safely in Stavros's cellar. But would they believe him? Manolis tried to make out their faces, to determine which figure was the bearded barista and which the bald proprietor, but the light was too dim.

Manolis's second thought was to his unloaded firearm. Should he draw it? The manoeuvre had worked once; could it work again? The villagers hadn't realised it was unloaded when Zain brandished it. Reaching for the revolver, Manolis thrust it forward, pointing it at the nearest advancing shadow. At least now there was no chance of accidentally killing someone.

"Stop right there," Manolis said. "I'm not afraid to use this, to shoot you."

Roze seized Manolis's hand and lowered the weapon.

"Relax," she whispered. "There's nothing to fear. They're just a Romani caravan."

A feathery lemony light was illuminated, a handheld lantern, revealing faces that were lined and weather-beaten and ultimately non-threatening. More people soon emerged, women and children. A white-haired elder puffing on a pipe stepped forward and extended his arm in greeting.

"We heard gunshot," he said. "Are you hurt? What happened?" His accent was coarse and hard to understand.

"We're fine," said Roze.

"But I shot a bear," Manolis admitted swiftly, as if to purge himself of the guilt. "She's dead. We thought she was going to attack us – she was protecting her cub, as it turned out – and we were defending ourselves."

On the elder's word, a crew of young men went and inspected the dead sow. A group of women attended to the cub and offered it food, which the little bear ate heartily. A young child gave Roze a warm blanket.

The men returned and spoke with the elder in a language that Manolis didn't understand. The elder listened, nodded several times, and turned back to Manolis.

"We will bury the bear," he said. "The carcass will only attract predators and threaten human lives."

Multiple shovels set to work, digging into the earth and tossing the soil to one side. Manolis offered to help but was told it was not necessary and was given a chunk of bread to eat.

"What about the cub?" he asked.

The cub was now being fed milk from a baby's bottle by an elderly woman. She wore an apple-red handkerchief over her head.

"We have adopted many orphaned baby animals before, including bear cubs," said the elder. "We can raise this one until it is old enough to be independent and return to the wild. We will see to that, I promise you."

A bundle of dry sticks was collected into a neat pile and lit with a box of safety matches. Faces were soon bathed in the warm orange glow of the campfire. There were men and women of all ages, boys and girls, toddlers and babies. More blankets were handed out, which left Manolis relieved and thankful. He'd never met real-life Romani before and couldn't help but be intrigued. What little he'd heard about these mysterious itinerant communities depicted them as untrustworthy and unwelcoming. They placed curses on people. They stole things. They were closed off from the world, had decided not to be a part of it, to remain untethered and untamed. But that was in stark contrast to the kindness he was now being shown. Through their resourcefulness and intimate knowledge of the land, the Romani had proven to be a highly effective search and rescue party.

Manolis recalled a story that Maria had once told about "gypsies" visiting them when she was a little girl in Florina.

"They would knock on our doors and talk fast to get inside to read our fortunes," Maria said. "Once in, they divided into groups: one would distract the owner with promises of riches while the others tried to steal whatever wasn't nailed down."

But that came from a woman who herself practised divination and claimed she could see the future by studying the browny sludge in the bottom of a coffee cup or by examining the breastbone in a chicken carcass.

Away from the campfire, Roze played with the Romani children and doted on the bear cub. Manolis was handed an enamel bowl of warm soup made from wild grasses and foraged mushrooms. The food was carefully proffered by a young child who showed a clear mental impairment. Manolis thanked him and the child returned to sit by the revered elder's side. The elder kissed the child's forehead in appreciation of his showing hospitality to the stranger.

"We take responsibility for all the earth's children, whether they are our own children or animals in need of care," the elder said proudly. "Whether man or beast, we are all God's children."

Manolis sipped his soup thoughtfully. He sensed that there was something within the elder's statement, that he would have seen a great deal more in his time than he was revealing. Manolis asked what he meant and if he could share more about his history with the region.

"My people have a deep connection to both the land and the lakes," he said. "The lakes were formed when two shepherds came to drink from a spring in the middle of the valley. They fell asleep and forgot to turn off the spring. The valley flooded, and the villages and houses were swallowed up by the water."

It was a different story from the one that Roze had described, but that was the beauty of myths, they came in many flavours. A common feature was the notion of there being a mass grave in the lake. Of many souls having tragically drowned.

"When the water is very calm, you can still see the outline of the houses at the bottom of the lake," the elder added.

"I've not seen the houses," Manolis said. "I'll look closer next time."

"As for the land, my grandparents walked this very soil, and so did my parents," the elder said. "This was when the soil was not Greek, a time when no-one wanted to be here, when the land was empty and barren. But as harsh as our lives as wanderers have sometimes been, we still refuse to live in the village or even to visit."

Manolis paused. "Which village?" he asked. "Do you mean Glikonero?"

"Yes."

"Why is that?"

The elder toked on his pipe and said: "We feel the village is poisoned and haunted by ghosts."

Manolis imagined that all ancient villages were haunted by ghosts to some extent. At times, late at night in his cottage, he'd heard strange noises. He'd gone to investigate the source and found nothing, so dismissed them, but part of him did still wonder. As a cop, he genuinely believed that people who'd been murdered left behind souls that roamed the earth for ever, unable to find peace and rest. He thought about the dead street kid and wondered if his spirit had somehow tracked Manolis down in the remote Prespes region. Manolis hoped so; he wanted to apologise and ask for forgiveness.

"What kind of ghosts?" Manolis asked the elder.

The old man blew out a wreath of silver smoke. Manolis smelled an unfamiliar concoction of herbs, spices, tobacco and something else, perhaps.

"The children," the elder replied. "Our memories cannot forget what happened to the children here. They haunt the land."

"I know about the civil war," Manolis said. "The children who were evacuated against their will."

"No, I do not mean those children. I am talking about others . . ."

The elder went on to explain an even more clandestine practice in the region. It still concerned children, but this practice stemmed from the Greeks' treatment of children with disabilities.

"As Greeks, we are very proud of our strong family values, which is why the child evacuations were so terrible," he said. "But the country still attaches a strange shame to having children born with disabilities in body or mind. These children are seen as signs of weakness, of there being something defective in a family's bloodline in a country where your public face is everything. It was a feeling made worse during a national crisis like the civil war, when your loyalty was questioned. Romani are just like other families, we argue and fight and love. But unlike other families, we do not care what anyone thinks of us, our public face is not important."

He looked adoringly at the child who had given Manolis his soup and was now playing joyfully with a rag doll. The doll had no face. The elder saw Manolis eyeing the doll with curiosity.

"Are you wondering why it has no face?" he asked directly.

"Yes," Manolis said.

"It is because all people are alike in the eyes of God, especially children."

Manolis leaned forward. "So, what happened here after the civil war?" he asked. "Will you please tell me?"

The elder half closed his eyes and again sucked on his pipe. His face was tiger-striped from the campfire.

"In the isolation that followed the civil war, when entire villages had been razed by the Greek army, the Prespes region was cut off from the rest of the country. One village came to be known as the place where Greeks could send their unfortunate children to be looked after, out of public sight. The region was officially closed off, the army had control, but there was still a secret way in and out through the hills. I was young but still remember the route well. Smuggled in late at night, the children were taken in and cared for by the villagers in Glikonero."

"That story is heartbreaking," Manolis said. "What parent could give up their child?"

"Parents who wanted to protect inheritances, who did not want to risk the marriage prospects of their normal children, who did not want to be the subject of gossip," the elder replied. "In some cases, some of the children's mothers did not even know of their existence. When such children were born, the father and hospital told the mother that the baby had tragically died. The baby was then brought here."

Manolis tried to picture a distraught new mother in a hospital bed, sold a lie, soaked in grief, unaware of what had happened, her physical pain compounded with emotional anguish that she would carry for the rest of her life.

"In Greece, such children are branded," the elder said. "People talk about the thousands of child evacuations that happened here, but they still refuse to talk about this. It is our secret shame."

A young woman offered cups of mountain tea in stained enamel mugs. The elder said the tea was made from the dried flowers, leaves and stalk of a native herb. Manolis found the drink earthy and nourishing. The elder sipped his cup earnestly, as if replenishing both his physical and his spiritual strength. A sudden breathlessness came upon him as if he was about to speak of something taboo.

"When this region opened up to the public again, the practice continued due to public demand, but it went underground," he said. "Over the years, the demand got smaller until it died altogether. But we think there is still one house in the village where a group of these children – and perhaps even some adults – remain imprisoned inside a deep basement."

"Really? Is that true?" Manolis said. His forehead was suddenly hot at the mention of a basement.

"We believe so. This is why we see the land and village as poisoned. What has been happening is very wrong and we refuse to set foot there."

Manolis listened carefully, the cogs in his head turning, remembering all he'd seen and heard. As the elder was speaking, a fragmented memory began to blossom in Manolis's mind. Around the time Christos was born, Maria told him a story she'd heard on the Greek news. It concerned a state-run institution where disabled children and adults had been locked up in wooden cages for years at a time. It was allegedly for their own good, to protect them from harm. They slept in small cells furnished with only a single bed, and no personal possessions were allowed. The children had conditions such as autism and Down's syndrome and cerebral palsy and were often heavily sedated. It took a group of university graduates volunteering as helpers to blow the whistle. The staff, of which there were few, insisted there was nothing wrong, and so did the government. The institution's director claimed she had not been paid for more than a year. The vast majority of the children had been abandoned by their families. Maria had told her son the story to prepare him for the realities and responsibilities of new fatherhood and parenting, but all it did was give him sweat-inducing nightmares.

Shaking his head lightly, banishing the memory, Manolis looked across at Roze, now playing a pat-a-cake hand-clapping game with some of the Romani children. More thunder echoed around them. Lit up by flashes of lightning, the horizon burned with an atomic glow. The elder looked to the merciless heavens.

"There's a storm on its way but we should be safe here," he said.

On a whim, Manolis asked if the Romani had recently encountered a lone man on their travels; after all, they were experts at search and rescue. As he described Lefty, the elder's eyes brightened.

"We know him well," he said. "We often see him walking around the hills on his own. He is a friendly man and he always stops to speak to us. The children are especially fond of him and so is he of them."

Manolis's spirits were immediately lifted, a glimmer of hope starting to burn.

"But we have not seen him for some weeks," the elder said. "We wondered where he had gone. Is he a friend of yours?"

Manolis sighed. "He was," he said. "He was a good friend."

30

When the sun rose the next morning, Manolis was miraculously dry and in one uneaten piece. The storm that had threatened had not transpired, and nor had the wild animals hunting for overnight prey. It had been an uncomfortable, interrupted night's sleep filled with unfamiliar noises and chills and grit. But the world now felt fresh and new, the sun bright and the moon pale and receding. Manolis felt a deep gratitude to both the Romani and to Roze. It would be a story to recount to the villagers once they returned to Glikonero, although Manolis felt uneasy at what he'd learned about the village and its dark history.

He had no reason to doubt the Romani elder, who carried himself with a quiet confidence and calm, and had no axe to grind. But Manolis wondered whether he was confusing his dusty old memories and remembering the child evacuations that were such a significant part of the region's history. Manolis had never heard what happened to the disabled Greek children in the horrific state-run institution that his mother had described. He had assumed it was an outlier in a modern European country where children and family were the cornerstone of society.

The electricity that Manolis had felt with Roze also played on his mind. Was it real or merely the product of a stressful situation?

With their water bottles replenished and their bellies full of fried eggs and bread, Manolis and Roze took their leave of the Romani and prepared to hike back to Glikonero. The children were sad to say goodbye to their new playmate, Roze. For her part, she was thankful that the bear cub would be looked after.

"I know you don't want to set foot in Glikonero, but if you do locate Lefty, alive or dead, please let us know somehow," Manolis told the elder.

"We will," he said.

Manolis gave the elder all the cash he had. It was only a small amount, but the elder refused to take it, and seemed almost offended. He eventually gave in when Manolis refused to take no for an answer.

"It would be an insult to me not to be able to thank you for helping us," Manolis said.

"Seeing you safe is our thanks. But thank you and may God protect you."

The landscape soon began to look familiar as they trekked back. It was a direct route to Glikonero, and having a defined destination and not searching for signs of Lefty made the journey go faster. Roze said she hoped Kostas wouldn't sack her for missing a night's work.

"I figure I had a pretty good excuse," she said.

"I'll back up your story," Manolis said.

As they walked, Manolis dodged a pile of fresh donkey droppings full of half-digested rosehips. The source was about a hundred metres to the east and was studying him intently. It brayed loudly to warn the strange humans to keep their distance. Roze pointed out a drift of white asphodels gleaming in the sun.

"The Greeks say this flower carpets the ground in Hades and is a favourite food of the dead."

"I've seen them laid on gravestones in cemeteries," Manolis said.

"We have them in Albania too. I love the name. It would be a beautiful name for a daughter, or even a son."

"Speaking of children, here's a question for you . . ."

Manolis asked if she'd heard any stories about the treatment of disabled children in the Prespes, particularly in the past. Roze wrinkled her forehead in thought.

"Personally, I haven't. But I'm still quite new to the area. Others may know."

"What about in a country like Albania? I imagine kids wouldn't have a lot of institutional support, schools and the like."

Roze scoffed. "Most kids don't even finish high school. I know I barely did. And it's even worse for children with learning difficulties and developmental disorders. The country is broke, which means that kids like that are a burden. Sorry if that sounds awful."

It was a brutally honest reply that painted a grim picture.

"I sometimes feel bad about leaving Albania," she said. "Maybe I should go back, try to find my lost brother. But leaving is the quickest and easiest way to escape poverty."

"So many people leaving won't help the country and its future," Manolis said.

"I know. If everyone leaves, it won't have a future."

There was no flirtation on the return journey. Roze kept saying that she couldn't wait to get home to have a long shower and wash her hair. Manolis was also looking forward to washing off a day's worth of sweat and dirt.

Later that day, Manolis went to the church to see Father Petros. He was fresh from a hot, spine-melting shower and a reinvigorating nap that had included a vivid dream. Walking along the southern shores of Great Prespa Lake, he had come across a man sitting on a wooden fruit box, casually dropping a fishing line into the water. He wore a pair of overalls and black leather motorcycle cap, and of course turned out to be Lefty.

"What took you so long?" Lefty asked flippantly.

Manolis had woken with a start. To Greeks, dreams like that often meant death in some form or other.

On his way to the church, Manolis walked past the lakeside location in his dream just in case it turned out to be a premonition of reality. But all he saw was Dalmatian pelicans feasting in the water, wheeling and diving like warring bombers. At least Lefty had chosen to fish in a plentiful spot.

Manolis lit a long votive candle and planted it in a container of golden sand. Watching the new flame quiver invitingly, he made his cross and dropped some coins into the church donation box. Hearing the cheery jangle of benevolence, the priest appeared, thick Bible in hand.

"Hello, stranger," Father Petros said. "Fancy seeing you here. And thank you for your donation."

"You can buy that island holiday home now," Manolis said.

Father Petros laughed sarcastically. "The Church is wealthy," he said. "The priests are not."

Manolis sat on a hardwood pew and recounted the events of the previous day. He didn't mention that he'd gone searching for Lefty, only that he'd gone out hiking to enjoy the wilderness, then lost his bearings and been unable to find his way home in the fading light.

"It sounds like God was watching over you." Father Petros smiled.

"He must have been, yes."

"I'm glad you are safe. What brings you to the house of the Lord?"

Manolis knew what he wanted to ask. But for some strange, inexplicable reason he found his brain and tongue being sidetracked. Maybe his soul was filled with gratitude that he was alive and healthy, and perhaps divine intervention had played a part in that outcome. Shafts of sunlight filtered through the stained-glass arched windows, slicing the thick molecules of church dust. Father Petros looked at Manolis patiently, his grand head lit by a halo of light from the afternoon sun.

"I killed someone," Manolis said.

The words came out involuntarily, heavy like tungsten.

"Oh . . ." said the priest. "Oh my." His brow furrowed with a combination of surprise and concern.

"It was only recently, a teenager," Manolis went on.

"You'd like to make a confession?" Father Petros asked.

"I think I just have," Manolis said. "Isn't that how it works?"

The priest chuckled warmly. "You've seen too many American movies. It's not like that in the Orthodox religion. Have you ever confessed before?"

"No."

"That's fine. Well, a confession usually takes place before an analogion lectern set up near the iconostasion wall. A Gospel Book and blessing cross are placed on the lectern. The confession is not made to me, but to Christ. I'm just His vessel; my job is to stand as witness and guide."

"Oh . . ."

"Here."

Father Petros fetched a Gospel Book and blessing cross. He positioned Manolis's thumb and first two fingers of his right hand on the feet of Christ on the cross. Manolis bent forward in concentration.

"You can speak now," the priest said. "Christ is listening."

Manolis was uncertain of how, and even whether, to proceed. Would Father Petros report him to the police? In his job, he'd never received any calls from priests; he recalled that there was some religious law or ethical standard that forbade them from disclosing the details of a confession. This law meant that people felt free to confess their sins without fear of retribution.

In the end, Manolis gave a broad outline of what had happened, in a steady, unflinching tone. It might not have been the entire truth, but none of it was a lie.

"I was trying to protect a friend. It was self-defence; our lives were being threatened. The teenager was innocent and in the wrong place at the wrong time. They didn't deserve to die and I didn't deserve to kill them like that and feel so miserably alone ever since."

Father Petros waited to ensure that Manolis had finished. When he nodded solemnly, the priest delivered the prayer of absolution.

"May almighty God have mercy on you, and having forgiven your sins, lead you to eternal life. Amen. May the almighty and merciful Lord grant you indulgence, absolution and remission of your sins. Amen."

"Amen," Manolis repeated in a whisper.

Father Petros beamed. "Well done. That wasn't so bad, was it?"

Manolis sat speechless. Straightening his body, he felt as though a burden had been lifted.

"Now, is there anything else I can help you with?" the priest asked.

"Actually, there is one more thing, Father . . ."

Manolis crossed his legs in a relaxed fashion and relayed what the Romani elder had said about the village.

"What was his name?" Father Petros asked.

Manolis stopped. The elder had never revealed his name. Father Petros tugged at his bushy beard suspiciously.

"I can't say I know these people well," he said. "I've seen them in the hills occasionally, but they've never spoken to me, even when I've approached them and been friendly. They are calm but keep their distance. I can't understand why they're like that but I'm in no position to judge. I know I would like to see them in my church sometime. But no, I can't recall any such awful memories from this village, and I've been here a long, long time. Did they show you any proof or just tell you a story? I suspect the old man may have been remembering the evacuations of children that happened after the civil war."

Manolis scratched his chin. "That thought also occurred to me . . ."

"I imagine the basements he was talking about are the air-raid shelters we have throughout the village. We even have one here at the church. Would you like to see it?"

"Um . . . OK, yes."

Father Petros grinned through his beard. "Follow me."

He led Manolis to the diaconicon, the chamber on the south side of the church where he dressed and prepared for his services. There were wall hangings and altar linens and religious vessels and shelves of books. The spiced smell of burning incense lingered in the hot, humid air.

"This area is usually off limits to the public," Father Petros said. "I imagine that's why they put the shelter here, to keep it hidden from invaders and intruders."

Opening a drawer, he retrieved a flashlight and showed Manolis a small trapdoor in the corner of the room. He led Manolis down a flight of stairs and along a dark and claustrophobic corridor. Manolis felt his anxiety levels rising the further they walked. Reaching a heavy wooden door, the priest swung it open with some effort and flicked a light switch to reveal a long, narrow room that was filled floor to ceiling with blood-red wine bottles.

"I'm the village's unofficial winemaker," he said proudly. "God drinks in mysterious ways."

Manolis eyed the dark, dusty bottles, some of which were unlabelled.

"You'll find bottles in here that are over fifty years old, from the time of the civil war," the priest said. "You can even taste the gunpowder; it's part of the *terroir*, as the French would say. This old shelter makes a perfect wine cellar, the temperature is ideal."

Wooden and metal boxes were stacked high alongside the wine. Each was about the size of a shoebox and had an inscription. "Are those bottles special?" Manolis asked.

Father Petros let out a loud laugh that bounced around the confined space.

"That's not wine," he said. "Those are ossuaries. They contain human skeletal remains. After a body is buried, the bones can be disinterred and placed in a box. I'm talking about several years after burial. We do use wine, though, to wash the bones before storage."

Picking up a bottle, the priest blew the dust off the label. It was marked with a year, but that was all. He reached for a winged corkscrew hanging on a nearby nail on the wall.

"This one's a very good vintage," he said. "For drinking, not washing. Would you like a taste?"

31

Fast running out of days until his departure, Manolis made one final attempt at locating Lefty. Something was gnawing at him that he couldn't let go and that he knew he would regret the second he sat down in his economy class airline seat departing from Thessaloniki. The mere thought of the turbulence made his stomach turn.

Manolis planned to conduct a more thorough search of houses in the area, and this time he would include the abandoned, broken-roofed dwellings that he'd not searched before, and of which there were many. He was no longer looking for clues or assessing suspects – he was looking for underground hiding spaces. It would mean facing his demons, but perhaps it was time. Because they were abandoned, Manolis could search the houses at his convenience and not have to wait for residents to leave. And access was again easy since none of the doors of the abandoned houses were ever locked.

He approached the task with trepidation. Searching abandoned buildings had always made him nervous; he was afraid of what people might have left behind and what might be lurking in the shadows. An occupied residence, even if the occupant was a hardened criminal, was somehow less intimidating. And the prospect of disturbing a congress of ancient ghosts was even more heightened in an abandoned building that was centuries old.

Armed with a flashlight, bolt cutters and protective gloves, Manolis braced himself for the task ahead. He started at the northern end of Glikonero and worked in a southerly direction. The vast number of abandoned houses underscored how the village had once thrived and been well-populated. The houses were some of the most derelict he'd ever seen – a combination of age, economic crises, war and the remoteness of the location, which saw months of freezing snow in winter and blistering heat in the summer. Unexploded military devices briefly occurred to Manolis as he sifted through the rubble and debris, the dirt and mud; the possibility of being blown to kingdom come if he stepped in the wrong place and activated a buried landmine, dusty grenade or wedged bullet.

After several days of searching in the melting heat, Manolis was spent. He'd hefted stones and bricks out of ghost gardens and torn away rusted aluminium sheeting, splintered wooden doors and rotten access panels. He'd located trapdoors and scoured basements and squeezed into crawl spaces and breathed in lungfuls of dust and dirty air. But he'd found nothing suspicious, only Greek grime and garbage and spiders and rats. It had been futile work, again. Lefty was now tormenting Manolis in his dreams as well as in his daily life. No matter what the detective tried, the invisible was always one step ahead. Manolis's only achievement was a marginally improved tolerance of dark spaces. His psychologist would have called it progress, the exposure serving as effective cognitive behavioural therapy for his enduring PTSD.

Manolis's last-ditch attempt at an epiphany before he packed his bags was on the Sunday morning. Twenty-four hours later, he would be boarding his return flight to Australia. With the villagers all at church, he used the brief window of opportunity to again search their houses, paying particular attention to basements and cellars. He found the usual assortment of boilers, water heaters and fuse boxes. In other words, he found nothing.

"That's it," Manolis sighed. "I'm done." He hung his head and laughed to himself in disbelief.

He decided to go to the taverna for a quiet farewell luncheon. Roze had insisted, which was a kind gesture. He would return the favour by leaving her fake Greek passport on her pillow. She would know who had found it.

The last house that Manolis searched belonged to Father Petros. As he went to exit via the back door, he saw again Lefty's motorcycle cap hanging limply on the coat rack. Manolis touched its soft black leather one last time. The hat still smelled foul. Lefty didn't wash it very often, and it showed.

"It's as though he's here in the room with me . . ." Manolis said, and felt a tingle in his fingers. A pack of stray dogs barked loudly outside, which gave him an idea.

Grabbing the cap, he ran outside and offered it to the dogs.

"Here, boys, here," he said. "Smell it, smell the cap. Get a good whiff. Good boys. Recognise the smell? Got it? Now, lead the way . . ."

It was a long shot; these were unqualified mongrels, not trained sniffer dogs.

Expecting food, some form of treat, the scrawny dogs approached en masse, noses first, snuffling the air and cap intensely, tongues protruding. Manolis watched them closely, looking for a flicker in their eyes, a forceful tail wag and a spark of recognition, prepared to follow wherever they led. But the dogs only noticed an empty cap and quickly lost interest, turning to each other to continue their games of tag and wrestle and sniff.

Manolis eyed the sky, the vacant street. It was another dead end. And, almost to his relief, the last.

As the yapping pack of mongrels disappeared down the road, a late-comer rounded the corner and approached Manolis. It was Angelo's loyal companion, Apollo.

"Hey, mate," Manolis said glumly. "Sorry, I've no food."

But Apollo started barking and wouldn't stop. It transported Manolis back to the first day they met, when he feared a vicious attack. Only now Apollo was barking at the motorcycle cap in Manolis's hand and running back around the corner.

"Jesus," Manolis said.

He broke into a jog and then a run, trying to keep up with the swift-legged animal. Apollo had something in his sights. And now Manolis did too. He ran faster.

But it was not what Manolis had hoped. Minutes later, he realised that Apollo had simply run home.

Manolis followed him inside and found Apollo in the living room lying on the large floral-patterned rug. Gasping for breath, Manolis needed to sit down. He fell into an armchair, defeated and deflated, and closed his eyes.

He snapped them back open seconds later when he realised what he was hearing. It was Apollo. He wasn't just lying on the rug. He was sniffing at it, pawing it, and whining frantically.

Manolis jumped to his feet, which startled Apollo. He bolted out the door, barking as he left. Manolis dropped to his hands and knees to inspect the rug and soon noticed a bulge near one edge. Whacking at it, Manolis cursed as he hurt his hand. But then it dawned on him: the lump was fixed to the floor.

"What the hell . . . ?"

Rolling back the rug, Manolis revealed the lump's identity. It was a thick padlock fastened to a large trapdoor.

32

Positioning his bolt cutters, Manolis closed their sharp jaws onto the padlock. It snapped open with a single metallic crack, and he hurled it to one side like a crumpled old can. Lifting up the trapdoor, he saw a single flight of stairs that led down to what appeared to be the village's remaining air-raid shelter. Tossing Lefty's motorcycle cap casually onto his head, Manolis steeled himself and stepped down into the gloom.

It was another soot-black corridor. Manolis switched on his flashlight, which was reassuringly heavy in his hand. With its white beam ploughing through thick cauliflower clouds of dust, he started walking. A strange, sickly odour began to assault his nostrils and gather in his head, making him feel nauseous and a little light-headed. Manolis paused, willing himself not to faint or retch, and to somehow find the strength to keep going amid the doubts and fear and memories and trauma.

"*Ela tora*," he muttered to himself in Greek. "This ends now."

A locked wooden door stood in front of him; the bolt cutters again proved to be effective keys. With his heart beating like a piston, Manolis slowly swung the door open, its rusty hinges squealing in protest. The white beam of the flashlight revealed a small room, the floor strewn with mattresses, blankets and plastic water bottles. But there were also metal buckets and strands of hay, items that would more normally be found inside a barn. Then, as his eyes adjusted to the light and found their focus, Manolis saw that there were four bodies in the room, all adults, lying flat on the mattresses, unmoving.

"Hello . . . ? Hey, are you OK?"

There was no reaction. Were they alive or dead? Manolis could not be sure but he feared the worst. Dear God. Four murders.

He rushed over and tried to rouse them. One of the occupants suddenly looked up and groaned.

"Lefteris?" Manolis stammered. "Lefty, is that you?"

It was no longer a dream. It was Lefty in the grubby, unkempt flesh. It seemed he had been sleeping, or been drugged. He was weak and in desperate need of a shave and a soapy wash. A dirty bandage was wrapped around one leg.

"What's going on here?" Manolis asked. "Lefty, hey, hey . . . Are you OK? How long have you been here? What happened?"

Manolis turned the flashlight on Lefty's face to confirm it was him. Lefty was momentarily blinded by the glare. As his eyes fluttered and adjusted, his first instinct was to reject the strange dark figure. With savage, jerky movements of his arms and shoulders, he pushed back with what little strength he could muster.

"Lefty, hey, stop! It's me, Georgios." Manolis turned the flashlight on himself.

"What, who . . . ? Georgios . . . ? Is it really you?"

Finally recognising Manolis's face, Lefty beamed. But his joy quickly turned to panic as he remembered his surroundings and circumstances.

"Thank the almighty God it's you. When did you get here, what time is it?" Lefty asked.

Manolis reached down and hugged him. A euphoria rushed through his body that made him feel instantly lighter.

"It's the middle of the day, Sunday, and I've been in Glikonero for a while," he said. "What's going on, who are these people, are they OK?"

"Quick, lift me up, my leg . . ."

Manolis rested his flashlight on its side and helped Lefty to stand. His legs were like jelly and he complained of vertigo. He was glassy-eyed and red around his face and neck.

"We have to get out of here right now or we'll be prisoners," Lefty said urgently.

"Prisoners . . . ? How, what happened?"

Lefty hobbled towards the door on rubbery legs. He said he would explain later, but Manolis was mindful of the three other occupants – two men and one woman – and stopped to check on them. Now awake like Lefty, they appeared to be injured. Their arms and legs were strangely contorted and their speech was slurred and incomprehensible. It struck Manolis that these were actually young adults with severe mental disabilities, neglected and uncared for.

"We'll come back for them later but right now we have to go!" Lefty said.

"Why?"

"We have to get out of here before Angelo and Anna return . . ."

Manolis turned to the three prisoners. "I'll be back soon," he said. "I promise you." They continued their agonised moaning as he left the room.

Closing the wooden door, Manolis climbed back up the stairs, shut the trapdoor, and chased after Lefty who was groggily hobbling away as fast as he could. The escapee was muttering to himself, brimming with anger and elation. Deeply traumatised from his experience, he was struggling to think straight. Manolis tried to calm him down and asked again what had happened.

"I need a drink," Lefty said, hands shaking.

Manolis agreed; perhaps alongside a coffee and cigarette.

On the way to the taverna, Lefty kept looking up at the spruce-blue Aegean sky and smiling. Silver tears flowed down his cheeks as he rejoiced in his liberation. Manolis presented Lefty with his beloved black leather cap, which only made him more grateful and emotional. He placed it on his head like a king reclaiming his smelly crown. Roze was already at the taverna preparing Manolis's farewell lunch, and could hardly believe her eyes. She and Lefty hugged, and she poured him a double whisky dose like an angel. He sloshed it down in a single, breath-cutting gulp.

"Hit me," he said. "Another."

Sipping this time, Lefty sat outside in the sunlight, soaking up its welcome warmth and vitamins. As the alcohol took effect, he began to explain the details of his incarceration, never letting go of the whisky glass that sat shakily in his favoured left hand.

"It all began when I got home from the taverna on Saturday night. It had been a long day, I'd had some stressful business to deal with in the afternoon, four Balkan gorillas who tried to rip me off, and had only just made it to work in time. I'd sat down to eat some leftover moussaka that Kostas had given me when I remembered that I'd forgotten to wind Anna's grandfather clock."

It was a regular favour that Lefty performed. Anna liked to hear the sound of the half-hourly chime when she was awake in the night. It soothed her to lie there in bed, hear the ticking and know how many hours there were until dawn. But she didn't want to risk falling off a chair while winding the clock, and break a hip, or worse. Nor did she want Angelo to take that risk. At their age, and with healthcare virtually non-existent in the Prespes region, such a fall was a death sentence.

"I was tired and thought I'd wait until the next day, but that would have meant another night of silence for Anna, which I knew she hated. So I went around to their house. I found it quiet and seemingly empty, so I climbed on a kitchen chair and carefully wound the clock. But as I was finishing, the key slipped from my fingers and fell to the floor. It bounced a few times before disappearing through a gap in the floorboards."

Seeing the rug pulled to one side and the access trapdoor, Lefty went down to retrieve the key, since he was at fault for losing it. As he descended the stairs, he heard echoey barking and thought that Apollo must somehow have got stuck in the cellar. But then he heard voices and came across Angelo and Anna in the underground room. They were caring for three people he'd never seen before, although it was a strange kind of care that involved long-term captivity and isolation from society. It was obvious that these people needed specialist assistance, and that their impairments had likely worsened as a result of the isolation.

"At first, Angelo appealed to me and tried to explain the situation," Lefty said. "You know he's a sworn virgin, right?"

Manolis nodded.

Unable to have children of their own, Angelo and Anna had thrown open their doors to the country's forgotten children during a time of crisis after the Greek civil war. The state was unable to provide adequate support and services, institutionalised children were often abused, and parents felt ashamed and abandoned their duties.

"They said they loved these children as if they were their own and had cared for some their entire lives," Lefty said.

"And our love is returned by the children," Anna had said, her eyes teary. "Please don't let them be taken away."

Lefty took a moment to consider what he'd seen and heard. It was a far from pleasant existence, but he could see that there was a sort of twisted love and care involved.

"Despite being locked up, the three young people didn't look like they were being mistreated or abused," he said. "They were being looked after in an unusual way, which had created this strange co-dependency. I could see the love in everyone's eyes – Angelo and Anna adored being in the role of parents, and the children needed devoted carers. And yet, despite all that, I knew that what was happening was wrong."

Lefty apologised to Anna and Angelo and told them it was clear they had good intentions but that it couldn't go on. Regrettably, he was going to have to alert the Florina police.

As Lefty turned to go, Angelo blocked the doorway. Lefty tried to push past him, but Apollo sensed a threat to his owner and lunged at Lefty. He bit his leg, clamping on and refusing to let go. Lefty slumped to the floor, bleeding, and was helped onto a mattress. Over the course of his incarceration, Anna saw to his wound and treated it daily, although Lefty said it was still sore and possibly infected.

"Almost certainly," Manolis said. "After you visit the police station in Florina, go straight to the hospital for treatment."

Lefty said he would also go and see Stavros since he was no doubt worried about him. Manolis briefly recounted the story of Lefty's toolbox and the ordeal that he and Zain had been through to recover as much money as they could, all of which was now stashed safely in Stavros's cellar. Lefty said he was deeply appreciative of Manolis's efforts to locate him and recover his life's savings.

"Zain's a good kid," Lefty said. "He sides with Satan, but, other than that, he's a good kid."

After such an exchange of information, Manolis felt in need of several whiskies himself, but instead he continued to sip his water and play with his *komboloi*. Reflecting on Lefty's story, he thought that it was just as the Romani had described. Had the other people who'd gone missing in the Prespes region stumbled across the same underground practice as Lefty and met the same fate? A search of the property and the surrounds would confirm that. It was also now clear why Angelo and Anna produced such massive quantities of food in their garden.

The mention of Lefty's toolbox and the recovery mission to Eleftheria also made Manolis recall snowy-haired Odysseas and his vague memories of the Prespes region as being full of sick children. Clearly, the practice had once been as widespread as the Romani elder described.

Manolis shook away such thoughts. The priority was for Lefty to report his ordeal to the police. While that happened, Manolis would place Angelo and Anna under arrest until the cavalry arrived. He would identify himself as an off-duty policeman.

Manolis turned to Roze. "Can I please ask a favour of you? Can you drive Lefty to the police station in Florina? He's in no shape to take himself. I would drive him myself but I think I'll be needed here to see this to its conclusion."

"Of course," she said.

"Great, thank you."

Lefty finished his whisky and he and Roze headed off.

Imprisoning Lefty had been a relatively easy task since he was an invisible. There would have been no paper trail, and people would have thought that he'd vanished of his own accord, as the police believed. If push came to shove, Lefty's captors might even have considered killing him. But Manolis was a different proposition. He was an outsider and had paperwork. He didn't expect much resistance from two such elderly people, particularly when their "children" were vulnerable in their own home. Then again, as a father himself, Manolis knew the strength of the parental bond, which he'd seen again in the protective mama bear. He'd learned from his experiences in the Prespes. He did not intend to approach another potentially tense encounter without some form of insurance.

Leaving the taverna, Manolis headed straight for Lefty's house. He retrieved the large black duffel bag from the roof, armed himself with a handgun and ammunition, then walked swiftly to the church, bracing himself for the confrontation. He felt his adrenaline seep away when he found only Father Petros there, tidying up.

"Nice to see you here again," the priest said.

"Sorry I missed your service today, Father," Manolis said. "I was looking for Angelo and Anna. Do you know where they are?"

"I suspect they went home," Father Petros replied. "They didn't say anything to me but I know they often do that straight after church. To rest."

"Home, eh? Good, thank you."

33

Manolis entered the house cautiously, his firearm at the ready. His flashlight was in his left hand and his heart was in his throat.

It was deathly quiet, the air thick with the stale tang of mould. A ghoulish image flashed through Manolis's mind of five bodies prostrate on the floor, an open bottle of poison on its side, or a warm handgun with an empty chamber. It was effectively a hostage situation, and hostage takers with a personal stake were the most unpredictable. Manolis blocked out the grisly vision and made straight for the living room, where he was met by the sight of the open trapdoor. Someone had returned and seen that Lefty was gone.

With weapon drawn, fingers tense, Manolis walked slowly down the stairs towards the underground room. He kept his back pressed hard against the wall. The benign light that spilled through the trapdoor illuminated the corridor but only for part of the way.

There was no light at the end of the corridor, and no sound either. Manolis's senses were tingling – something felt distinctly awry. The only sound was his heart thumping in his ears. Either somebody was lying in wait in the darkness with a gun aimed squarely at Manolis's head, or there was nobody there at all. What were the odds, should he take the chance? After a few seconds to calm his breathing, Manolis pointed his flashlight in the same direction as his pistol and flicked it on with his thumb. He was acutely aware of the risk he was taking, of killing innocents as well as perpetrators, and of being killed. But he had come too far, both physically and psychologically. There was no turning back now.

The wooden door stood open. Peering inside, barrel first, Manolis scanned the underground room. It was empty. The three occupants were gone from their well-worn mattresses.

"*Theos kai Panagia . . .*"

It was rare that Manolis invoked God and the Holy Virgin. But at that moment, it seemed wholly appropriate.

Manolis let out a slow, long exhalation to rid his lungs of the cancer of disappointment. Inhaling a breath of resilience, he sprinted back upstairs to search the rest of the house, moving swiftly between the rooms. There was no-one there.

His head starting to throb, Manolis ran outside. No longer the hunted, he'd swung into hunter mode. Those people with their infirmities could not have got far. He circled the house, rustling through the dense, lush garden and surrounds, alarming cats, chickens and pigs. But there were no people.

Perhaps someone had helped Angelo and Anna escape, especially if they had raised the alarm and called in reinforcements from a younger, stronger resident. There may have been accessories to the practice; the Romani had said it was once widespread in the region. But even one underground prison basement was too many.

The village appeared suddenly deserted, as if people had sensed there was danger and run for cover. Manolis thought to return to the taverna to recruit backup of his own but was suddenly filled with doubt over who to trust.

Manolis heard a low rumbling sound in the distance, but just as quickly as it had started, it stopped. Manolis froze, listening intently. It was an unfamiliar sound. It came a second time and then a third. It sounded not unlike an old car being started and continually stalling but it wasn't loud or deep enough. The tone suggested a smaller engine. Manolis wondered if it was a Styl Kar and the Eleftheria residents had returned. He'd never heard a working Styl Kar engine and imagined that such an old vehicle might have made a fairly raucous noise. This sounded like something smaller, a motorcycle or even a lawnmower . . .

With a fourth attempt, the unseen engine finally started.

Manolis realised now that the noise was coming from the lake; it was an outboard motor being pull-started, they were escaping via Great Prespa Lake. It was a clever escape route that sought to take advantage of the region's geography, of the close international borders and the potential for asylum in Albania or North Macedonia. And unless there was an agreement in place with those countries, extradition would be difficult, if not impossible, given the tense history between the nations.

It dawned on Manolis that the oceans and seas that surrounded the vast island continent of Australia – his home – precluded such an easy escape. It was no wonder that the British had once sent their convicts there. Today, no fugitive could leave Australia without a commercial airline ticket, passport and multiple security checks – the government had seen to that. The thought that here all it took was a ride in a spluttering two-stroke outboard motor across a small body of water was hard to comprehend.

Rushing down to the shore, Manolis scattered a siege of buff-brown herons that flapped away with croaking dismay, their spidery legs trailing behind. A motorboat was puttering into the distance. Manolis stood up to his knees in the water. If he called out, would that only make them go faster? He couldn't see how many people were on board. It was likely that some had lain down in the bottom of the boat, which appeared to be heading north, not west. Scanning the shoreline, Manolis searched for a motorboat or even a rowing boat in which to give chase. All he could find was the clumsy kayak. Would it be enough to catch something with a motor?

It would not. After some minutes of furious paddling, of getting wet and going nowhere, the distance between Manolis and the motorboat had only grown larger. His pleas for divine intervention in the form of mechanical breakdown or tidal wave or underwater monster had gone unheard. He stopped paddling and pondered his next move. The wind was picking up, making the surface of the lake choppy and the journey even more treacherous.

The weapon had sat in his lap while he was paddling. Manolis took it in his wet hand and thrust it towards North Macedonia. With the motorboat now a shrinking speck on the watery horizon, his chances of hitting anything other than fish were slim. He couldn't see Angelo's and Anna's outlines, and wasn't prepared to risk missing them and hitting one of their innocent "children". Shooting their outboard motor dead and marooning them in the middle of the lake was a better option, but that was again fraught with risk from such a distance and could start a fire. Manolis considered himself a good shot, but he was no crack sniper. He needed Father Petros and his military training.

Manolis contemplated continuing the pursuit on land. There was a chance he could somehow find his way across the border and intercept them on the other side, but there were no paved roads that linked one country to the other. He would need Roze and her illegal border experience, and his hiking boots.

In the end, Manolis lowered his weapon and, seconds later, his head. He was wet, exasperated and ready to go home, to see young Christos and tell him about his failed summer adventure in the wilds of Greece. Christos's big eyes would widen into twin moons when he heard the stories about snakes and bears and buried treasure. Manolis would promise to show him this strange and magical place one day.

Manolis was comforted by the fact that he'd found and rescued Lefty, but he otherwise felt that he'd failed. It was the policeman in him, the bringer of justice. He had watched a perpetrator escape from the law before his very eyes and been helpless to do anything about it. The crafty old villagers had unwittingly thwarted a seasoned undercover cop and avoided arrest. That gnawed a little at his soul. The ancient lake had drawn him in with its cold air of mystery, and had also been his undoing.

Out of frustration at having fallen so agonisingly short, Manolis raised his arm in the air and fired two pressure-releasing bullets into the wide blue yonder. Perhaps the Romani elder would hear the shots and wonder if yet another bear had been killed.

The lake water lapped at Manolis's kayak, the oscillations constant, the rocking rhythmic and gentle. But then the waves picked up and Manolis had to steady himself in his kayak to avoid capsizing. Something was causing a sudden turbulence.

The sound arrived a second later, roaring up behind Manolis. He turned and copped a spray of cold lake water in the face as a dinghy sped towards him, its blue lights flashing.

It was Elias in his border police patrol boat. The air horn blared. Manolis raised his arm and waved.

34

The patrol dinghy chased down the motorboat in a flurry of spray and foam. They had got about halfway across the lake when the interception was made, and were nearer to North Macedonia than to Greece. After a short discussion, Elias escorted the fugitives back to Greek soil, with Manolis paddling in from behind.

As they disembarked onto the sand, Angelo and Anna glared at Manolis with matching looks of surprise. They seemed genuinely shocked to see that it was Manolis, the outsider, waiting there for them.

Manolis identified himself as a policeman, which made Elias smile knowingly and stroke his moustache with satisfaction.

"You're under arrest for false imprisonment and for harming the health of others," he told them. "Elias has authority. Earlier today, I found Lefteris in your basement being held against his will. I found three other individuals as well."

They did not say anything to rebut Manolis's assertion. He identified the three young adults in the motorboat, who were lying in its hull. They were wet and shivering but otherwise appeared unharmed. Apollo watched over them protectively, barking and growling at Manolis, teeth bared.

Manolis needed to keep the perpetrators there until the Florina police arrived, which could be some time, at least an hour. He took Elias to one side to explain the situation, and Elias confirmed that he was on board.

"Whatever you need," he said. "You can count on me."

He was stunned to hear what Manolis had unearthed. When he saw the motorboat crossing the lake, he was merely doing his job – trying to stop it from reaching another country – but he did mention a tragic discovery made by the Greek police a few years earlier of a group of mentally disabled children imprisoned in their rural family homes.

"The first cousins in these families repeatedly intermarried to keep their inheritances secure," he said quietly. "There was no marrying outside the extended family."

"You mean incest?" Manolis asked.

Elias nodded solemnly. "Genetics backfired for those families," he said. "In the end, they had to lock away some of their children so as not to ruin the marriage prospects of the healthy ones. Everything was done to save the family's public face."

Elias cited some other examples of people who had been kept in secret rooms across Europe for one reason or another, some of them stories that Manolis had heard about on the international news.

Manolis turned back to Angelo. "It's clear you were trying to escape by crossing international borders," he said.

Angelo looked down at his feet. "That is not untrue. But we were only trying to save the lives of these special young people and get away from Lefty."

Manolis pulled a face. He didn't understand why they would be trying to escape from Lefty.

"But you imprisoned him," he said. "Isn't that what happened?"

Anna agreed, but said they'd had no choice. "He got us into this mess and he was going to land us in even deeper trouble."

Manolis couldn't follow what was going on and suggested they return to their house to talk further. He had one eye on the three young adults, who seemed distressed, and were moaning and trembling.

They sat in the kitchen while Elias went to inspect the basement. Anna comforted her children and fed them simple food. Manolis noted that they couldn't speak or even acknowledge the presence of new, unfamiliar people.

Angelo tossed Apollo a large lamb bone to keep him quiet. Easing himself into an old armchair, he sipped from a mug of tap water and began to talk about the past. There was nothing more to say about the child evacuations. The focus was now on when he and his sister had taken in and cared for unwanted children from all around the country.

"Those children were unwell," he said. "But they were not so much ill as what we once called 'defective'."

What had become a secret practice was in response to an acute social need and lack of institutional support.

"What else could we do?" Angelo said. "We felt deeply for such children, and it was something – a duty to God – that we were glad to perform because we were unable to become parents ourselves."

Angelo said they had cared for and loved such children, fiercely, for many years. In some cases, this meant caring for some children for the entirety of their natural lives. Others later returned to families who'd had second thoughts, something Anna described as both happy and painfully sad. In yet other instances, where families received support payments from the government, they continued to cash them fraudulently.

"It's the Greek way," Angelo said.

As the years passed, the practice died a natural death. Until the day that Lefty approached them.

"He said he had heard about us, about what we once did," said Angelo.

"He had a young child of his own," Anna said.

Having seen the boy's mother neglect and abuse their son, Lefty took the child away one night, and needed to keep him hidden.

"Our hearts went out to Lefty and his beautiful son," Anna said. "In that situation, we had to help them, and we knew what to do."

Manolis recalled the old photographs of children he'd found hidden at Lefty's house. Lefty had boasted about having fathered four children by four different women from four different countries. Manolis couldn't help but think of his own son and the loving parenting that Emily gave him. Christos was incredibly fortunate. Leaving aside their marital issues, Manolis knew his ex-wife was an excellent mother and he planned to tell her as much when he returned to Australia. He also intended to hug little Christos harder than ever and make sure he knew he was the most important thing in his errant father's life.

At first, things had worked well with Lefty and his son.

"Lefty visited his boy all the time and saw him grow," Angelo said. "Even if the care and conditions were imperfect, and we admit that openly, it was still an improvement on being abused, and far better than electroshock therapy in state-run institutions."

"But then things changed," Anna said, her voice heavy. "Lefty got greedy."

In the course of Lefty's black-market pursuits, he often received strange and nefarious requests. Seizing on a new demand from within Greece's borders and beyond, Lefty identified another opportunity to make money. He was soon bringing more children to Glikonero and asking Angelo and Anna to give them care.

"We were unable to say no," Anna said plaintively, stroking the face of one of her dependants. The young man flashed a crooked but loving smile, his eyes sparkling. "How could we say no?"

Remembering Lefty's stash of money, Manolis now realised why it was so substantial.

But recently, Lefty's son had become sick and died. Angelo claimed his immune system was compromised and his disabilities severe, which came from a premature birth in a poorly equipped Greek hospital. Lefty was distraught, and so were Angelo and Anna. He blamed them for his son's death and told them angrily that he would go to the police.

"He told us that no-one would believe us if we tried to speak out against him," Angelo said. "He pointed out that all the evidence was on our property, and we had been involved in this practice for many years, which is true, we cannot deny that. Lefty had us trapped. Not long after, we had a confrontation, we argued, and Apollo got protective and bit Lefty. Not knowing what else to do, and very scared, we locked him away until we could think of something."

Manolis listened closely but warily. "What proof is there of any of this?" he asked.

There was Lefty's money, but it could have come from a number of illicit sources.

"He has keys to our trapdoor and basement," Anna said. "It allowed him to visit at any time. If you doubt us, go check his house."

Manolis remembered the key ring he had found at Lefty's cottage, which had two large and distinctive keys.

"If you find those keys, you will see they open our locks," Anna said.

That might work but there was something else.

"What did you do with the body of Lefty's son?" Manolis asked.

Angelo and Anna looked at each other for a long time before they responded.

"We are sorry to admit that he is buried just outside the village with all the others we have cared for over the years," Angelo said. "There is a small unmarked burial site in a meadow with flowers." His voice carried sorrow, a spectrum of grief and guilt.

"We never killed anyone," Anna said quickly. "We just looked after them as best we could, which was not easy. Please, please believe us."

"As my sister said, there were happy stories too, positive outcomes," Angelo said. "Like her friend, Calliope. Do you remember, when you came for dinner? You asked about a lady, you thought she was your aunt."

Manolis stopped. He hadn't thought about his aunt since he heard she had died.

"What happened with Calliope?" Manolis asked, trying to hide the urgency in his voice.

"She too brought us a child," Anna said. "Her young son. He was normal but darker skinned. She broke down when she told us that he was illegitimate, misbegotten, and she couldn't possibly raise him. So we did, until adulthood. She visited him from time to time but otherwise kept her distance. He's now living in Florina, working in a *periptero*. We couldn't be prouder."

Manolis asked for the address and location of the kiosk, and the man's name, which Anna was only too happy to provide. It served to verify her story and paint their practice in a better light. Such tiny kiosks were dotted across Florina, indeed all over Greece, although they were becoming scarce as chains of convenience stores moved in. They sold cigarettes, bottled water, soft drinks, newspapers, magazines, ice cream, gum and other confectionery, and were open all day and night.

Just then, the grandfather clock on the wall chimed. Manolis's ears pricked at the sound. He went over to inspect it but couldn't see what he was looking for.

"Where do you wind this clock?" he asked. "Where's the key?"

He was remembering Lefty's excuse for going down into the cellar, that he had dropped the clock's key through a gap in the floorboards.

"Wind it?" Angelo asked. "No, there is no winding involved. That clock runs on batteries."

Alarm bells rang in Manolis's head. As the realisation sank in, his eyes widened. He left the kitchen without a word and raced downstairs to Elias.

"Please come up," Manolis said quickly. "I need you to stay and guard them until the police arrive."

"What's happened, where are you going?" Elias asked.

"To Florina. *Right now.*"

"Why?"

"It's Lefty," Manolis said. "His whole story was fabricated."

Manolis bolted for his car, unable to get enough air into his lungs. Before he sped away, he hurled Con's *komboloi* into the lake's depths in despair and defiance.

Horsepower was not on Manolis's side. He drove out of Glikonero as fast as he could, pushing the sedan to its limit and cursing it for its sluggishness. He blew past rows of grapevines rotting in the late summer heat, blackened with fungus and swarming with fruit flies. Hitting the serpentine mountain road, he drove recklessly, overtaking cars, dodging wildlife and potholes, and smashing his palm into the horn every few minutes. The asphalt was tacky in the heat and felt like a long black road to hell aboard a steel oven. As he was steering and braking and veering, all he could think about was Lefty and his maddening, shapeshifting nature. Anger balled in Manolis's chest, sudden and hard, which made him grip the steering wheel tighter. To have expected Lefty to behave differently – honestly – would have been to deny his true character, his essence. But Manolis was lucky, he had one final chance to make amends. He just needed to get there in time.

Arriving at the police station with a long, screeching skid, Manolis parked his car at a drunken angle. He ran inside, leaving the door half-open. His eyes were gritty from the drive and the emotional aftermath of the morning. He entered just as Constable Yiannis stubbed out one cigarette and ignited another. The cop greeted the panting Manolis with a bored smile and asked what had brought him back so soon.

"Lefty," Manolis demanded. "Where is he?"

Yiannis laughed. "You're joking, right? I haven't seen him. Have you? I thought he was missing."

Manolis didn't wait to hear more.

Dodging stray cats and dogs, he drove through tight streets, passing several *periptera* en route to the local hospital. Manolis had to search through empty corridors for signs of life. A barefoot old man wearing a paper-thin gown and a white wristband staggered past, staring into the middle distance, giving no sign that he had registered Manolis's presence. He finally found a nurse with a clipboard. She was an elderly matron in crisply starched linen who strode with a bung hip. She had dark frizzy hair, unkempt and greasy, and seemed to be in a hurry.

"I'm looking for my friend whose leg is injured," Manolis said. "Here's a photo. Has Lefty been here?"

The nurse took the crumpled photograph and held it close to her bespectacled eyes.

"Yes, this person was here, but they only wanted some painkillers," she said. "They left a short while ago."

The positive identification lifted Manolis's spirits.

"Great, thank you," he said. "Do you know where Lefty was headed?"

"No, she didn't say."

Manolis stopped. He pinched his chin and looked at the nurse.

"I'm sorry," he said. "My friend here is Lefteris, he's a man. You must be thinking of a different patient. Here's the photo again, please look at it closely. Was this the person that you saw, can you remember?"

The nurse examined the photograph a second time.

"Yes, it was definitely this person who was here," she said. "But they are also definitely a woman, not a man."

Manolis looked down at the photo, then back to the nurse. He couldn't believe what he was hearing.

"A woman?" he asked. "How do you know? What makes you so sure?"

The matron didn't seem to appreciate Manolis's doubtful tone. She checked her watch and said briskly:

"What makes me sure is two things. First, we went to school together here in Florina. And second, I delivered her baby many years ago. It was tragic: a baby boy who only just survived the birth and was severely disabled."

Manolis asked for more details but the matron waved him away, studying her clipboard and saying she was busy if Manolis was not in need of medical treatment.

Leaving the hospital, Manolis stared numbly at the photo, shaking his head at the image of the living spectre in his hand. Unless he found Lefty, he knew he would continue to be haunted. It no longer seemed a coincidence that Lefty had lived in the town of Eleftheria. The feminine version of his name – and his true identity – had been there all along.

Outside a nearby coffee house, Manolis found Roze sipping a coffee. He recognised it as the women-only *kafenion*.

"Lefty?" she said. "He brought me here. He said he needed a double shot to perk up and here was the best place. Then he left to go to the police station. He wasn't there?"

Manolis's body stiffened all over. "Are you OK?" he asked.

She nodded blankly and held up her cup. "This really is excellent coffee . . ."

There was only one more place he could go. Manolis arrived at Stavros's house minutes later and searched the rooms methodically, finding them soulless and empty. Running downstairs, multiple steps at a time, nearly tripping, Manolis saw that the cellar door was open and the metal toolbox was missing. Manolis sank to his knees and hung his head in despair. All of a sudden, Stavros appeared in the cellar.

"What are you doing here? What time does your flight leave?" he said.

Manolis rushed outside and stared up at the milk-white cross on the mountain and the verdant hills in the middle distance. Looking back down to the town, he saw a maze of houses and businesses and tiny kiosks. The invisible, who was never truly there, had disappeared again. He had vanished into crisp mountain air.

Acknowledgements

Sincere thanks to Katharina Bielenberg and Paul Engles for incredible publishing; to Robina Pelham Burn for brilliant editing; to Maurits Zwankhuizen, Nigel Palfreman and Matthew Clissold for careful reading and manuscript feedback; to Martin Shaw for being an agent extraordinaire; and to my family for their enduring love, support and belief in my writing.

The region depicted in this book, the remote north-western corner of Greece, is where my family fled as Orthodox Christian refugees from Turkey as part of the monumental 1923 Population Exchange, and where I was born in 1974, in the mountain town of Florina. This is a region not largely seen by outsiders and not on the tourist trail. To this day, my brothers continue to live there in the ancestral home that our paternal grandfather, Vasilios (b. 1890), built with his own hands in 1923 near the centre of Florina. Our grandfather lived in Florina for fifty years until he died in 1973. During every visit to Florina and the Prespes, I've found the region and people to be wholly inspirational, steeped in history and tradition and colour. I know I can't do them full justice here.

At the time of writing this novel, from 2019 to 2022, and since February 2019, the nation directly to the north of Greece, and across the border from Florina, has been known as the Republic of North Macedonia. Before this, the country was known locally and internationally as the former Yugoslav Republic of Macedonia (FYROM), Macedonia, or the Republic of Macedonia. If I have under-represented or misrepresented anyone from the region with the material portrayed in this work of fiction, I apologise. I acknowledge that the region is complex and has understandable sensitivities, which I have tried to accurately capture in the spirit of equity and inclusiveness.